PEN

The Lyre of Orpheus

The son of a journalist, Robertson Davies was born in 1913 in Thamesville, Ontario, and educated at Queen's University and at Oxford. He has had three successive careers: first as an actor with the Old Vic Company in England; then as a publisher of the *Peterborough Examiner*; and most recently as a university professor and the first Master of Massey College at the University of Toronto, from which he retired in 1981. He now holds the title of Master Emeritus.

It is as a fiction writer that Davies has gained international recognition. His work includes three critically-acclaimed trilogies: the Salterton trilogy, composed of *Tempest-Tost*, *Leaven of Malice*, and *A Mixture of Frailties*; the Deptford trilogy of *Fifth Business*, *The Manticore*, and *World of Wonders*; and the Cornish trilogy, *The Rebel Angels*, *What's Bred in the Bone*, and *The Lyre of Orpheus*.

THE
LYRE OF
ORPHEUS

Robertson Davies

Penguin Books

PENGUIN BOOKS
Published by the Penguin Group
Penguin Books Canada Ltd, 2801 John Street, Markham, Ontario L3R 1B4
Penguin Books Ltd, 27 Wrights Lane, London W8 5TZ, England
Viking Penguin Inc., 40 West 23rd Street, New York, New York 10010, USA
Penguin Books Australia Ltd, Ringwood, Victoria, Australia
Penguin Books (NZ) Ltd, 182-190 Wairau Road, Auckland 10, New Zealand

Penguin Books Ltd, Registered Offices: Harmondsworth, Middlesex, England

First published by Macmillan of Canada, a division
of Canada Publishing Corporation, 1988
Published simultaneously in Viking by Penguin Books
in Great Britain and by Viking Penguin in the
United States, 1988

Published in Penguin Books, 1989

1 3 5 7 9 10 8 6 4 2

*Publisher's note: This book is a work of fiction. Names, characters,
places and incidents either are the product of the author's imagination or
are used fictitiously, and any resemblance to actual persons living or dead,
events, or locales is entirely coincidental.*

Manufactured in Canada

Canadian Cataloguing in Publication Data

Davies, Robertson, 1913-
The lyre of Orpheus

ISBN 0-14-011426-2

I. Title.

PS8507.D38L9 1989   C813'.54   C88-094752-7
PR9199.3.D3L9 1989

British Library Cataloguing in Publication Data Available
American Library of Congress Cataloguing in Publication Data Available

*The lyre of Orpheus opens the
door of the underworld*

E. T. A. HOFFMANN

❧ I ❧

Arthur, who had a masterly way with meetings, was gathering this one together for a conclusion.

"Are we agreed that the proposal is crack-brained, absurd, could prove incalculably expensive, and violates every dictate of financial prudence? We have all said in our different ways that nobody in his right mind would want anything to do with it. Considering the principles to which the Cornish Foundation is committed, are these not all excellent reasons why we should accept the proposal, and the extension of it we have been discussing, and go ahead?"

He really has musical flair, thought Darcourt. He treats every meeting symphonically. The theme is announced, developed in major and minor, pulled about, teased, chased up and down dark alleys, and then, when we are getting tired of it, he whips us up into a lively finale and with a few crashing chords brings us to a vote.

There are people who cannot bear to come to an end. Hollier wanted more discussion.

"Even if, by a wild chance, it succeeded, what would be the good of it?" he said.

"You have missed my point," said Arthur.

"I am simply speaking as a responsible member of the Cornish Foundation."

"But my dear Clem, I am urging you to speak as a member of a special sort of foundation with unusual aims. I am asking you to use your imagination, which is not what foundations like to do. I am asking you to take a flyer at an extreme outside chance, with the possibility of unusual gains. You don't have to pretend to be a business man. Be what you are — a daring professor of history."

"I suppose if you put it like that —"

"I do put it like that."

"But I still think my question is a good one. Why should we present the world with another opera? There are lots of operas already, and people busily writing them in every square mile of the civilized world."

"Because this would be a very special opera."

"Why? Because the composer died before he had gone very far with it? Because this girl Schnak-whatever-it-is wants to get a doctorate in music by completing it? I don't see what's special about that."

"That's reducing the whole plan to the obvious."

"That's leaving out the heart of it. That's forgetting our proposal to mount the finished opera and offer it to the public," said Geraint Powell, a theatre man with a career to make, who already looked on himself as the person to get the opera on the stage.

"I think we should bear in mind the very high opinion of Miss Schnakenburg that is expressed by all her supporters. They hint at genius and we are looking for genius, aren't we?" said Darcourt.

"Yes, but do we want to get into show business?" said Hollier.

"Why not?" said Arthur. "Let me say it again: we have set up the Cornish Foundation with money left by a man who was a great connoisseur, who took all kinds of chances, and we have to decide what sort of foundation it is to be. And we've done that. It's a foundation for the promotion of the arts and humane scholarship, and this plan is both art and scholarship. But haven't we agreed that we don't want another foundation that gives money to good, safe projects, and then stands aside, hoping for good, safe results? Caution and non-intervention are the arthritis of patronage. Let's back our choices and stir the pot and raise some hell. We've already made our obeisance to safety; we've established our good, dull credentials by getting Simon here to write a biography of our founder and benefactor —"

"Thank you, Arthur. Oh, many, many thanks. This estimate of my work is more encouragement than I can accept without blushes." Simon Darcourt knew too well that the biographical job was not as easy as Arthur seemed to think, and strongly aware also that he had not so far asked for or received a penny for the work he had done. Simon, like many literary men, was no stranger to feelings of grievance.

"Sorry, Simon, but you know what I mean."

"I know what you think you mean," said Darcourt, "but the book may not be quite such a dud as you imagine."

"I hope not. But what I am getting at is that the book may cost a few thousands, and, without being by any means the richest foundation in the country, we have quite a lot of money to dispose of. I want to do something with a bit of flash."

"It's your money," said Hollier, still determined to be the voice of caution, "and I suppose you can do as you please."

"No, no, no, and again no. It isn't my money; it's Foundation money and we are all directors of the Foundation — you Clem, and you Simon, and you Geraint, and, of course, Maria. I am simply the chairman, first among equals, because we have to have a chairman. Can't I persuade you? Do you really want to be safe and dull? Who votes for safety and dullness? Let's have a show of hands."

There were no votes for safety and dullness. But Hollier

had a sense of having been pushed aside by totally unfair rhetoric. Geraint Powell didn't like meetings and wished this one to be over. Darcourt felt he had been snubbed. Maria knew well how right Hollier was and that the money was really Arthur's money, in spite of all legal fictions. She knew that it most certainly wasn't her money, even though, as Arthur's wife, she might be supposed to have some extra pull. She had not been married very long, and she loved Arthur dearly, but she knew that Arthur could be a great bully when he wanted something, and he wanted passionately to be a vaunting, imaginative, daring patron. He is a bully just as I suppose King Arthur was a bully when he insisted to the Knights of the Round Table that he was no more than the first among equals, she thought.

"Are we agreed, then?" said Arthur. "Simon, would you draw up a resolution? It doesn't have to be in final form; we can tidy it up later. Have you all got drinks? Isn't anybody going to eat anything? Help yourselves from the Platter of Plenty."

The Platter of Plenty was a joke, and, as jokes will, it had become a little too familiar. It was a large silver epergne that stood in the middle of the round table at which they sat. From a central, richly ornamented pedestal it extended curving arms at the end of which were little plates of dried fruits and nuts and sweets. A hideous object, thought Maria, unjustly, for it was a fine thing of its kind. It had been a wedding gift to Arthur and herself from Darcourt and Hollier and she hated it because she knew it must have cost them a great deal more than she supposed they could afford. She hated it because it seemed to her to embody much of what she disliked about her marriage — needless luxury, an assumption of a superiority based on wealth, a sort of grandiose uselessness. Her passionate desire, after making Arthur happy, was to gain a reputation for herself as a scholar, and big money and big scholarship still seemed to her to be irreconcilable. But she was Arthur's wife, and as nobody else took anything from the epergne she took a couple of nuts, for the look of the thing.

As Darcourt worked over the resolution, the directors chatted, not altogether amicably. Arthur was flushed, and Maria was aware that he was speaking rather thickly. It couldn't be that he had drunk too much. He never did that. He had taken a chocolate from the Platter of Plenty, but it seemed to have a bad taste, and he spat it into his handkerchief.

"Will this do?" said Darcourt. " 'It was resolved that the meeting should comply with the request made jointly by the Graduate Department of the Faculty of Music and Miss Hulda Schnakenburg for support to enable Miss Schnakenburg to flesh out and complete the manuscript notes now reposing in the Graduate Library (among the musical MSS left in the bequest of the late Francis Cornish) of an opera left incomplete at his death in 1822 by Ernst Theodor Amadeus Hoffmann, the work to be done in a manner congruous with the operatic conventions of Hoffmann's day and for such an orchestra as he would have known; this to be done as a musicological exercise in partial fulfilment of the requirements for Miss Schnakenburg's attainment of the degree of Doctor of Music. It was further resolved that if the work proved satisfactory the opera should be mounted and presented in public performance under Hoffmann's title of *Arthur of Britain*. This part of the proposal has not yet been communicated to the Faculty of Music or Miss Schnakenburg.' "

"It'll be a nice surprise for them," said Arthur, who took a sip of his drink, and then set it down, as if it were disagreeable.

"A surprise, no doubt," said Darcourt. "Whether a nice surprise is open to doubt. By the way, don't you think we ought to give the work its full title in the minutes?"

"Is there more than *Arthur of Britain*?" said Geraint.

"Yes. In the fashion of his day Hoffmann suggested a double title."

"I know the kind of thing," said Geraint; "*Arthur of Britain, or* — something. What?"

"*Arthur of Britain, or the Magnanimous Cuckold,*" said Darcourt.

"Indeed?" said Arthur. The bitterness in his mouth seemed to be troubling him. "Well, I don't suppose we need to use the full title if we don't need it."

Again he spat into his handkerchief, as unobtrusively as he could. But he need not have troubled, because at the announcement of the full title of the opera nobody was looking at him.

The three other directors of the Foundation were looking at Maria.

(2)

THE DAY AFTER THE MEETING, Simon Darcourt was interrupted, just as he sat down to his day's work, by a telephone call from Maria; Arthur was in hospital with mumps, which the doctors called parotitis. They had not told Maria what Darcourt knew: mumps in the adult male is not trivial, because it causes painful swelling of the testicles, and can do permanent damage. Arthur would be out of commission for some weeks, but he had mumbled to Maria through his swollen jaws that he wanted the work of the Foundation to go on as fast as possible, and she and Darcourt were to take care of it.

How like Arthur! He had in the highest degree the superior business man's ability to delegate responsibility without relinquishing significant power. Darcourt had known him since the death of his friend Francis Cornish; Francis's will had made Darcourt one of his executors, to act beneath the overriding authority of Francis's nephew Arthur, and it had been apparent at once that Arthur was a born leader. Like many leaders he was rough at times, because he never thought about anyone's feelings, but there was nothing personal in it. He was Chairman of the Board of the huge Cornish Trust, and was admired and trusted by people who dealt in big money. But, apart from his business life, he was cultivated in a way not common among bankers; genuinely cultivated, that is to say, and not simply benevolent toward the arts as a corporation duty.

His rapid establishment of the Cornish Foundation, using his Uncle Frank's large fortune to do it, was proof of his intention. Arthur wanted to be a patron on a grand scale, for the fun and adventure. There could be no doubt that the Foundation was his. For the look of the thing he had set up a board to administer it, but whom had he invited to join it? Clement Hollier, because Maria had been his student and had a special affection for him. And what had Hollier proved to be? A great objector, a determined looker-on-the-other-hand whose reputation as a scholar in the realm of medieval history did little to mitigate his gloomy insufficiency as a human being. Geraint Powell was Arthur's own choice, reputedly a rising man in the theatre, with all the exuberance and charm of the breed, who backed up Arthur's most extravagant ideas with his Welsh superficiality. And Maria, Arthur's wife; dear Maria, whom Darcourt had loved, and loved still, perhaps the more poignantly because there was no longer the least danger that he would ever have to play the full role of a lover, but could slave for his lady in a condition of mild romantic dejection.

These were Darcourt's estimates of his colleagues on the Foundation. What did he think about himself?

To the world he knew he was the Reverend Simon Darcourt, a professor of Greek, much respected as a scholar and teacher; he was the Vice-Warden of Ploughwright College, an institution for advanced studies within the university; there were people who thought him a wise and genial companion. But Arthur called him the Abbé Darcourt.

What is an abbé? Was it not a title used for several centuries to describe a clergyman who was really an educated upper servant? Your abbé ate at your table, but had a small room off your palace library where he slaved away as a confidential secretary, intermediary, and fixer. Abbés on the stage or in novels were great fellows for intrigue and amusing the ladies. It is a category of society that has disappeared from the modern world under that name, but the world is still in need of abbés, and Darcourt felt himself to be one of them, but was not pleased that Arthur had put his finger on the matter so plainly.

It is to be presumed that abbés in an earlier day had salaries. Darcourt's canker was that he received no salary from the Foundation, although he was its secretary and, as he put it to himself, worked like a dog on its behalf. Nevertheless, as he received no salary, he felt that his independence was secure. Independent as a hog on ice, he thought, in one of the Old Loyalist Ontario expressions which popped up, unbidden, in his mind when least expected. But if his university work were not to suffer, he had to slave away day and night, and he was a man to whom a certain amount of ease and creative lassitude is a necessity.

Creative lassitude, not to doze and dream but to get matters arranged in his head in the best order. This life of Francis Cornish, for instance; it was enough to drive a man mad. He had accumulated a mass of detail; he had passed an expensive summer in Europe, finding out what he could about Francis Cornish's life in England, where it appeared he had been something-or-other in the Secret Service, about which the Secret Service maintained a blandly closed mouth. Francis had, of course, played an important part in the work of restoring looted works of art to their original owners, in so far as that could be done. But there had been something else, and Darcourt could not find out what it was. Before the Second World War Francis had been up to something in Bavaria which sounded fishier and fishier the more Darcourt dug into it, but the fish could not be hooked. There was a huge hole, amounting to about ten years, in the life of Francis Cornish, and somehow Darcourt had to fill that hole. There was a lead, possibly a valuable one, in New York, but when was he to find time to go there, and who would foot the bill? He was tired of spending what were to him large sums of money to get material for a book that Arthur treated as a matter of small consequence. Darcourt was determined that the book should be as good and as full as it was in his power to make it, but after a year of investigation he felt thoroughly ill-used.

Why did he not simply state his case and say that he had to be paid for his services, and that the writing of the book was costing him more money than he could ever expect to recover from it? Because that was not the light in which he wished to appear to Maria.

He was a fool, he knew, and rather a feeble fool, at that. It is no comfort to a man to think of himself as a feeble fool, secretary to a dummy board of directors, and burdened with an exhausting task.

And now Arthur had mumps, had he? Christian charity required that Darcourt should be properly regretful, but the Old Harry, never totally subdued in him, made him smile as he thought that Arthur's balls were going to swell to the size of grapefruit, and hurt like the devil.

The day's work called imperiously. After he had done some college administration, interviewed a student who had "personal problems" (about a girl, of course), taken a seminar in New Testament Greek, and eaten a sufficient but uninteresting college lunch, Darcourt made his way to the building where the Graduate Faculty of Music existed in what looked, to the rest of the university, like unseemly luxury.

The Dean's office was handsome, in the modern manner. It was on a corner of the building and two walls were entirely of glass, which the architect had meant to give the Dean a refreshing prospect of the park outside, but, as it also gave passing students a splendid view of the Dean at work, or perhaps in creative lassitude, he had found it necessary to curtain the windows with heavy net so that the office was rather dim. It was a large room, and the decanal desk was diminished by the piano and the harpsichord — the Dean was an expert on baroque music — and the engravings of eighteenth-century musicians that hung on the walls.

Dean Wintersen was pleased that money would be forthcoming to support the research work and reasonable living expenses of Miss Hulda Schnakenburg. He became confidential.

"I hope this solves more than one problem," said he. "This girl — I'd better call her Schnak because everybody does and it's what she seems to like — is greatly gifted. The most gifted student, I would say, that we've ever had in my time or in the memory of anybody in the faculty. We get lots of people here who will do very well as performers, and a few of them may go to the top. Schnak is something rarer; she may be a composer of real gift. But the way she is going now could land her in a mess, and perhaps finish her!"

"Eccentricity of genius?" said Darcourt.

"Not if you're thinking of picturesque behaviour and great spillings of soul. There is nothing picturesque about Schnak. She is the squalidest, rudest, most offensive little brat I have ever met as Dean, and I've dealt with some lulus, let me tell you. As for soul, I think she would strike you if you used the word."

"What ails her?"

"I don't know. Whoever does know? Background the essence of mediocrity. Parents utterly commonplace. Father a watch-repairer for one of the big jewellery stores. A dull, grey fellow who seems to have been born with a magnifying-glass in his eye. Mother a sad zero. The only thing that singles them out at all is that they are members of some ultra-conservative Lutheran group, and they never stop saying that they have given the girl a good, Christian upbringing. And what have they brought up? A failed anorexic who never washes her hair or anything else, snarls at her teachers, and habitually bites the hand that feeds her. But she has talent, and we think it is the real, big, enduring thing. Just now she's on the uttermost extreme thrust of all the new movements. The computer stuff and the aleatory stuff is old hat to Schnak."

"Then why does she want to do this work on the Hoffmann notes? That sounds like antiquarian stuff."

"That's what we all want to know. What makes Schnak want to fling herself back more than a hundred and fifty years to complete an unfinished work by a man we generally write off as a gifted amateur? Oh, Hoffmann had a few operas performed in his lifetime, but I'm told they are run-of-the-mill. In music he has a reputation as a critic; he praised Beethoven intelligently when nobody else did. Schumann thought a lot of him, and Berlioz despised him, which was a kind of inverted praise. He inspired a lot of far better talents. A literary man, I suppose one would say."

"Is that a bad thing to be? Mind you, I only know him through that opera — you know, Offenbach's *Les Contes d'Hoffmann*. It's a Frenchified version of three of his stories."

"Odd that it's another unfinished work; Guiraud pulled Offenbach's score together after his death. Not a favourite of mine."

"You're the expert, of course. As a mere happy opera-goer I like it very much, though it's not often intelligently done; there's more in it than meets the eye of most opera directors."

"Well, the puzzle of why Schnak wants to take on this job can only be solved by her. But we on the faculty are pleased, because it fits nicely into musicological research and we'll be able to give her a doctorate for it. She'll need that. With her personality she needs every solid qualification she can get."

"Are you trying to coax her away from her ultra-modernity?"

"No, no; that's fine. But for a doctoral exercise something more readily measurable is better. This may steady her, and make her more human."

Darcourt thought this was the moment to tell the Dean about the Cornish Foundation's plan to present the revived and refreshed opera as a stage piece.

"Oh, my God! Do they really mean that?"

"They do."

"Have they any idea what it might mean? It could be such a flop as operatic history has never known — and that's saying a lot, as you probably know. I know she'll do a good job, but only so far as the material permits. I mean — cosmetic work on the orchestration, and reorganization and pulling-together and general surgery can only go so far. The Foundation, the Hoffmann basis, may not support anything the public could possibly want to see."

"The Foundation has voted to do it. I don't have to tell you that eccentricity isn't confined to artists; patrons can suffer from it too."

"You mean it's a bee in the bonnet."

"I've said nothing. As secretary of the Foundation I am just telling you what they intend. They know the risks, and they are still prepared to put a good deal of money into the project."

"They'll have to. Have they any idea what mounting a full-scale new opera, that nobody knows or has studied, could run to?"

"They're game for it. They leave it to you, of course, to see that Schnak delivers the goods — in so far as there are any goods to deliver."

"They're mad! But don't think I'm quarrelling with any-

body's generosity. If this is what's in the cards, Schnak will
need supervision on the highest level we can manage. A musicologist of great reputation. A composer of some distinction.
A conductor who has wide experience of opera."

"Three supervisors?"

"Just one, if I can get the one I want. But with a lot of
money I think I can coax her."

The Dean did not say who he meant.

(3)

THE WEEK AFTER ARTHUR FELL ILL, Maria could do no work at all.

Ordinarily she had much to keep her busy. Her marriage
had temporarily interrupted her academic career, but she had
once again taken up her thesis on Rabelais, though marriage
made it seem less pressing — she would not say less important
— than before. And she had a great deal to do on behalf of
the Cornish Foundation. Darcourt thought he was over-
worked, but Maria had her own burden. It was she who first
read all the applications for assistance, and it was tedious
work. The applicants seemed to want to do the same few
things — write a book, publish a book, edit a manuscript,
show their paintings, give a concert of music, or simply to
have money to, as they always put it, "buy time" to do any of
these things. Probably many of these requests were worthy,
but they did not fit into Arthur's notion of the Cornish Foundation, and it was Maria who wrote polite personal notes
advising the applicants to look elsewhere. Of course there
were the visionaries, who wanted to dam and dredge the
Thames to discover the foundations of Shakespeare's Globe
Theatre; or who wanted to establish a full-scale *carillon de
Flandres* in every provincial capital in Canada and endow the
post of *carillonneur*; or who wanted to be supported while they
painted a vast series of historical pictures showing that all the

great military commanders had been men of less than average stature; or who yearned to release some dubiously identified wreck from the Arctic ice. These had to be discouraged firmly. Borderline cases, and they were many, she discussed with Darcourt. The few proposals that might appeal to Arthur were sifted from the mass, and circulated to all the members of the Round Table.

The Round Table was a joke Maria did not like. Of course the Foundation met at a circular table which was a handsome antique and had perhaps, two or three centuries ago, served as a rent-table in the workroom of some aristocrat's agent; it was the most convenient table for their purpose in the Cornishes' apartment. Geraint Powell insisted that, as Arthur presided over this table, it had some jokey association with the great British hero. Geraint knew a lot about the Arthurian legend, though Maria suspected that it was coloured by Geraint's lively fancy. It was he who insisted that Arthur's determination that the Foundation should take an unusual and intuitive path was truly Arthurian. He urged his fellow directors to "press into the forest wherever we saw it to be thickest" and would emphasize it by repeating, in what he said was Old French, *là où ils la voient plus expresse*. Maria did not like Geraint's theatrical exuberance. She was in flight from exuberance of another sort, and, like a real academic, she was wary of people outside the academic world — "laymen" they called them — who seemed to know a lot. Knowledge was for professionals of knowledge.

Sometimes Maria wondered if this administrative work was what she had married Arthur to do, but she dismissed the question as foolish. This was what came immediately to hand, and she would do it as what marriage seemed to require of her. Marriage is a game for adult players, and the rules in every marriage are different.

As the wife of a very rich man, she could have become "a society woman" — but what does that mean in a country like

Canada? Social life in the old sense of calls, teas, dinners, weekends, or fancy-dress parties was utterly gone. The woman who has no gainful job devotes herself to good causes. There are plenty of dogsbody jobs associated with art and music which wealthy volunteers are graciously permitted to do by the professionals. There is the great Ladder of Compassion, on which the community arranges a variety of diseases in order of the social prestige they carry. The society woman slaves on behalf of the lame, the halt, and the blind, the cancerous, the paraplegic, those variously handicapped, and, of course, the great new enthusiasm, AIDS. There are also the sociologically pitiable: the battered wives, battered children, and the raped girls, who seem to be more numerous than ever before, or else their plight is more often revealed. The "society woman" shows herself concerned with society's problems, and patiently fights her way up the Ladder of Compassion through a net of committees, convenorships, vice-presidencies, presidencies, past presidencies, and government investigatory bodies. For some there waits, after years of work, a decoration in the Order of Canada. Now and again she and her husband eat an absurdly expensive dinner in the company of their peers, but not for pleasure; no, no, it is to raise money for some worthy cause, or for "research", which has the prestige that belonged, a century ago, to "foreign missions". The possession of wealth brings responsibilities; woe to the wealthy who seek to avoid them. It is all immensely worthy, but it is not much fun.

Maria had an honourable escape from this charitable treadmill. She was a scholar, engaged in research of her own, and thus she justified her seat in the social lifeboat. But with Arthur seriously ill she knew precisely what she had to do: she had to sustain Arthur in every way she could.

She visited Arthur as often and as long as the hospital would permit, chatting to a silent husband. He was very miserable, for the swelling was not only of his jaws; the doctors called it orchitis, and every day Maria lifted his sheets when the nurse was elsewhere, and grieved over the miserable swelling of his testicles, which gave him wretched pain in all the abdominal area. She had never seen him ill before, and his suffering made him dear to her in a new way. When she was not with him she thought about him too much to be able to do any other work.

The world is no respecter of such feelings, and one day she had a visit that troubled her greatly. As she sat in her handsome study — it was the first workroom she had ever had that was entirely her own, and she had made it perhaps a little too fine — her Portuguese housekeeper came to tell her that a man was anxious to speak with her.

"What about?"

"He won't say. He says you know him."

"Who is he, Nina?"

"The night porter. The one who sits in the lobby from five till midnight."

"If it's anything to do with the building, he should talk to Mr. Calder at the Cornish Trust offices."

"He says it's private."

"Damn. Well, show him in."

Maria did not know him when he appeared. Out of his porter's uniform he might have been anybody. He was a small, not very engaging person, with a shrinking air, and Maria disliked him on sight.

"Good of you to see me, Mrs. Cornish."

"I don't think I know your name."

"Wally. I'm Wally the night man."

"Wally what?"

"Crottel. Wally Crottel. The name won't mean anything to you."

"What did you want to see me about?"

"Well, I'll come right to it. You see, it's about m'dad's book."

"Has your father made an application to the Foundation about his book?"

"No. M'dad's dead. You knew him. You know the book. M'dad was John Parlabane."

John Parlabane, who had committed suicide more than a year ago, and had thereby hastened the courtship and marriage of Arthur Cornish. But when Maria looked at Crottel she could see nothing whatever of the stocky frame, the big head, the compelling look of malicious intelligence that had distinguished the late John Parlabane. Maria had known Parlabane far too well for her own comfort. Parlabane the runaway Anglican monk, the police spy, the drug-pusher, and parasite to the most disagreeable man she had ever known. Parlabane, who had intruded himself into her relations with her academic adviser and, as she had once hoped, lover, Clement Hollier. When Parlabane committed suicide, after having murdered his nasty master, Maria had thought she was rid of him forever, forgetting Hollier's repeated warning that nothing is finished until all is finished. Parlabane's book! This called for deep cunning, and Maria was not sure she had cunning of the right kind.

"I never heard that John Parlabane had any children."

"It's not widely known. Because of my ma, you see. For my ma's sake it was kept dark."

"Your mother was a Mrs. Crottel?"

"No, she was a Mrs. Whistlecraft. Wife of Ogden Whistlecraft, the great poet. You'll know the name. He's been dead for quite a while. I must say he was nice to me, considering he was not my real dad. But he didn't want me to have his name, you see. He didn't want any Whistlecrafts hanging around that weren't the genuine article. Not of the true seed, he used to say. So I was raised under my ma's maiden name, which was Crottel. I was supposed to be their nephew. An orphan nephew."

"And you think your father was Parlabane."

"Oh, I know that. My ma leaked it out. Before she passed away she told me Parlabane was the only man she'd ever had a first-class organism with. I hope you'll excuse me mentioning it but that's what she said. She became very liberated, you see, and talked a lot about the organism. Whistlecraft didn't seem to have the knack of the organism. Too much the poet, I guess."

"Yes, I see. But what was it you wanted to talk to me about?"

"The book. M'dad's book. The big important book he wrote that he left in your care when he passed away."

"John Parlabane left a mass of material to me and Professor Hollier. He left it with a letter when he killed himself."

"Yeah, but when he passed away he probably didn't know he had a natural heir. Me, you see."

"I'd better tell you at once, Mr. Crottel, that the typescript John Parlabane left was a very long, somewhat incoherent philosophical work which he had tried to give special interest by including some disguised biographical material. But he had no skill with fiction. Several people who would know about such things read it, or as much of it as they could, and said it was unpublishable."

"Because it was too raw, wasn't that it?"

"I don't think so. It was just incoherent and dull."

"Aw, now, lookit, Mrs. Cornish, m'dad was a very intelligent man. You're not going to tell me anything he wrote was dull."

"That's exactly what I am telling you."

"I heard there was some stuff in it about people high up — government people, some of them — in their youths, that they wouldn't want the public to know about."

"I don't remember anything like that."

"That's what you say. I don't want to be nasty, but maybe this is a cover-up. I heard a lot of publishers wanted it."

"Several publishers saw it, and decided they didn't want it."

"Too hot for them to handle, eh?"

"No. They simply didn't see any way of making a book of it."

"You got letters saying that?"

"Mr. Crottel, you are becoming very pressing. Now listen: the typescript of the book by the man you tell me, without showing me any evidence, was your father was left outright to Professor Hollier and me. And I have the letter that says so. We were to deal with it as we saw fit, and that is what we have done. That's all there is to it."

"I'd like to see that book."

"Impossible."

"Well then, I guess I'll have to take steps."

"What steps?"

"Legal. I've been mixed up with the law, you know, and I know my rights. I'm an heir. Your right may not be as strong as you think."

"Take it to law, then, if you feel you must. But if you hope to get anything out of that book, I can tell you you're in for a disappointment. I don't think we have anything more to say."

"Okay. Be like that if you want. But you'll be hearing from my legal man, Mrs. Cornish."

It looked as if Maria had won. Arthur always said that if someone threatened legal action the thing to do was to tell them to see what it would get them. Such talk, he said, was probably bluff.

But Maria was unhappy. When Simon Darcourt came to see her that evening she greeted him in a familiar phrase:

"Parlabane is back."

It was an echo of what a lot of people had said, with varying degrees of dismay, two years earlier, when John Parlabane, garbed in the robes of a monk, had returned to the university. Many people remembered him and many more were aware of his legend, as a brilliant student of philosophy who had, years ago, left the university under a cloud — the usual cloud, that old, familiar cloud — and had banged about the world making trouble of several ingenious kinds. He turned up at the College of St. John and the Holy Ghost (familiarly "Spook") as a runaway and renegade from the Society of the Sacred Mission, in England, and the Society showed no sign of wanting to get him back. Maria, Darcourt, and Hollier, and many others, hoped that his suicide about a year later — and the suicide note in which he confessed with glee to the murder of Professor Urquhart McVarish (monster of vanity and sexual weirdo) — had closed the chapter of Parlabane. Maria could not help reopening it with this theatrical flourish.

Darcourt was satisfactorily astonished and dismayed. When Maria explained, he looked a good deal better.

"The solution is simple," he said. "Give him the typescript of the book. You don't want it. Let him see what he can do with it."

"Can't be done."

"Why not?"

"I haven't got it."

"What did you do with it?"

"Threw it away."

Now Darcourt was really horrified.

"You *what*?" he roared.

"I thought it was done with. I put it down the garbage chute."

"Maria! And you call yourself a scholar! Haven't you learned rule number one of scholarship: *never, under any circumstances, throw anything away*?"

"What was the use of it?"

"You know the use of it now! You've delivered yourself, bound and gagged, into this man's hands. How can you prove the book was worthless?"

"If he goes to court, you mean? We can call some of those publishers who turned it down. They'll say what it was."

"Oh, yes; I can hear it now. 'Tell me, Mr. Ballantyne, when did you read the book?' 'Mmm? Oh, I don't read books myself. I turned it over to one of my editors.' 'Yes, and did your editor present you with a written report?' 'That wasn't necessary. She took a look and said it was hopeless. Just what I suspected. I took a quick peep into it myself, of course.' 'Very well, Mr. Ballantyne, you may stand down. You see, ladies and gentlemen of the jury, there is no evidence that the book was given serious professional attention. Are masterpieces of what is called *le roman philosophe* to be assessed in this casual way?' — That's the kind of thing, Maria, that you'll hear until every one of your publisher witnesses has trotted in and out of the witness-box. Crottel's lawyer can assert anything he likes about this book — a philosophical masterwork, a sulphurous exposure of sexual corruption in high places — anything at all. He will say that you and Clem Hollier were professionally jealous of Parlabane, and depreciated his talent for the trivial reason that he was a self-confessed murderer. The lawyer will positively sing to the harp about Genêt, the criminal genius, and tie him up in pink string with Parlabane. Maria, you have put your foot in it right up to the hip."

"You're not being very helpful, Simon. What do we do next? — Can't we get rid of Crottel? Fire him, perhaps?"

"Maria, you numbskull! Haven't you understood that under our splendidly comprehensive Charter of Rights it is practically impossible to fire anybody — particularly not if they are making your life a misery? Crottel's lawyers would crucify you. — Look, child, you need the best legal advice, and at once."

"Well, where do we get it?"

"Please don't talk about 'we' as if I were somehow involved in this mess."

"Aren't you my friend?"

"Being your friend is a very taxing experience."

"I see. A fair-weather friend."

"Stop being feminine. Of course I'm with you. But you must let me have my grievance. Do you think I haven't enough trouble with this bloody opera scheme of Arthur's? It's enough to drive me mad! Do you know what?"

"No. What?"

"We've gone ahead much too fast. We've undertaken to back Schnak — I haven't met Schnak but I hear ominous things about her — in putting this sketch for an opera together, and naturally I wanted to see what these Hoffmann papers consist of. It should have been done earlier, but Arthur has rushed ahead. So I had a look. And do you know what?"

"I wish you'd stop asking me if I know what. It's illiterate and unworthy of you, Simon. Oh, don't sulk, sweetie. — Well, what?"

"Only this. There's no libretto. Only a few words to suggest what ought to go with the music. That's what."

"So —?"

"So a libretto has to be found, or else provided. A libretto in the early-nineteenth-century manner. And where is that to come from?"

It seemed to Maria that the time had come to get out the whisky. She and Darcourt rolled and wallowed in their problems till after midnight, and although Maria had only one drink, Simon had several, and she had to push him into a taxi. Fortunately it was after midnight, and the night porter had gone off duty.

(4)

SIMON DARCOURT HAD A BAD NIGHT, and in the morning he had a hangover. He endured something more than the layman's self-reproach. He was drinking too much, no doubt about it. He refused to think of it in the modern sociological term as "a drinking problem"; he told himself that he was becoming a boozer, and of all boozers the clerical boozer was the most contemptible.

Excuses? Yes, plenty of them. Wouldn't the Cornish Foundation drive a saint to the bottle? What a pack of irresponsible blockheads! And headed by Arthur Cornish, who was thought in the financial world to be such a paragon of good judgement. But, provocation or no provocation, he must not become a boozer.

This business of Parlabane's alleged son could be a nuisance. After a queasy breakfast, which he made himself eat because not eating was one of the marks of the boozer, he put through a call to a man who was a private detective, and owed him a favour, for Simon had pushed and pulled his promising son toward a B.A.; the man had connections that were very useful. Then he talked on the telephone to Dean Wintersen, not stressing his worry about the missing libretto, but probing to see what the Dean knew. The Dean was reassuring. Probably the relevant papers had been mislaid or temporarily catalogued under another name, possibly that of the librettist himself, who was thought to be James Robinson Planché. Neither the Dean nor Darcourt knew who Planché was, but they sparred in the accustomed academic manner to find out what the other knew, and worked up a cloud of unknowing which, again in the academic manner, seemed to give them comfort. They arranged a time when Darcourt could meet Miss Hulda Schnakenburg.

When that time came, Darcourt and the Dean cooled their heels in the many-windowed office for twenty minutes.

"You see what I mean," said Wintersen. "Don't think I would put up with this from anyone else. But as I told you, Schnak is special."

Special, it seemed to Darcourt, in a disagreeable way. At last the door opened, and in she came and sat down without waiting to be asked or greeted, saying, "She said you wanna see me."

"Not I, Schnak, but Professor Darcourt. He represents the Cornish Foundation."

Schnak said nothing, but gave Darcourt a look of what might have been malignance. She was not as unusual as he had expected, but certainly she was unusual in a Dean's office. It was not simply that she was sloppy and dirty; lots of girls thought such an appearance obligatory because of their principles, but they were sloppy and dirty in the undergraduate fashion of their time. Schnak's dirt was not a sign of feminine protest, but the real thing. She looked filthy, ill, and slightly crazed. Her dirty hair hung in hanks about a face that was sharp and rodent-like. Her eyes were almost closed in squinting suspicion, and on her face were lines in improbable places, such wrinkles as one does not often see today, even on ancient crones. Her dirty sweater had once been the property of a man, and was ravelled out at the elbows; below she wore dirty jeans, again not the fashionable dirt of rebellious youth, which has a certain coquetry about it; these were really dirty and even disgusting, for there was quite a large yellow stain around the crotch. Her dirty bare feet were thrust into worn-out running shoes without laces. But this very dirty girl was not aggressively dirty, as if she were a *bourgeoise* making some sort of statement; there was nothing striking about her. If it is possible to say so, Schnak was distinguished only by her insignificance; if Darcourt had met her on the street he would probably not have noticed her. But as someone on whom large sums of money were to be risked she struck chill into his heart.

"I suppose the Dean has told you that the Cornish Foundation is giving serious thought to presenting your enlargement of the Hoffmann score as a stage piece, Miss Schnakenburg?" he said.

"Call me Schnak. Yeah. Sounds crazy, but it's their dough." The voice was dry, rebarbative.

"True. But you realize that without your full co-operation it could not be done?"

"Yeah."

"The Foundation could count on that?"

"I guess so."

"They'll want better assurance than a guess. You are still a minor, aren't you?"

"Naw. Nineteen."

"Young for a doctoral candidate. I think I should talk with your parents."

"Fat lot of good that'll be."

"Why?"

"They don't know shit about this stuff."

"Music, you mean? I'm talking about responsibility. We must have some guarantee that you will do what you say. I'd want their agreement."

"Their idea of a musician is a church organist."

"But you think they would agree?"

"How the hell should I know what they'll do? I just know what I'll do. But if it's money they'll probably go for it."

"The Foundation is considering a grant that would pay all your expenses — living, tuition, whatever is necessary. Have you any idea what the amount might be?"

"I can live on nothing. Or I could develop some expensive habits."

"No, Miss Schnakenburg, you couldn't. The money would be carefully supervised. I would probably supervise it myself and anything that looked like the kind of expensive habit you hint at would conclude the agreement at once."

"You told me you had stopped all that nonsense, Schnak," said Wintersen.

"Pretty much. Yeah. I haven't really got the temperament for it."

"I'm glad to hear that," said Darcourt. "Tell me, as a matter of interest, would you pursue this plan — this opera plan — if you did not get the grant?"

"Yeah."

"But I understand that you have been exploring very modern paths in composition. Why this enthusiasm for the early nineteenth century?"

"It kinda grabs me, I guess. All those crazy guys."

"Well then, tell me how you would support yourself if this grant were not forthcoming?"

"Job of some kind. Anything."

Darcourt had had enough of Schnak's indifference. "Would you consider, for instance, playing the piano in a bawdy-house?"

For the first time Schnak showed some sign of animation. She laughed, dustily. "That dates you, prof," she said. "They don't have pianos in bawdy-houses any more. It's all hi-fi and digital, like the girls. You oughta go back and take another look."

Important rule of professorcraft: never show resentment at a student insult — wait and get them later. Darcourt continued, silkily.

"We want you to have freedom to get on with your work, so you needn't worry about jobs. But have you considered all the problems? There doesn't seem to be much of a libretto to go with these scraps of music, for one thing."

"Not my problem. Somebody would have to fix it up. I'm music. Just music."

"Is that enough? I'm no expert on these things, but I would have imagined that the completion of an opera that exists only as sketches and rough plans would call for some dramatic enthusiasm."

"That's what you'd imagine, is it?"

"Yes, that's what I'd imagine. You force me to remind you that nothing has been concluded about this matter. If your parents don't stand behind you, and if you are so indifferent to the money and the encouragement it implies, we're certainly not anxious to force it on you."

Wintersen intervened. "Look, Schnak, don't play the fool. This is a very big chance for you. You want to be a composer, don't you? You told me so."

"Yeah."

"Then get this through your skull: the Cornish Foundation and the Faculty are offering you such a chance, such a springboard toward a career, such a shortcut to important attention, as very great people in the past would have given ten years of life to have. I'm telling you again: don't play the fool."

"Shit."

Darcourt decided the time had come for a strategic loss of temper, a calculated outburst.

"Look here, Schnak," he said, "I won't be talked to in that way. Remember, even Mozart got his arse kicked when he couldn't be civil. Make up your mind. Do you want our help or don't you?"

"Yeah."

"Don't yeah me, young woman. Yeah what?"

"Yeah, I do."

"No. I want the magic word. Come on, Schnak — you must have heard it somewhere in the distant past."

"Please — I guess."

"That's more like it. And keep it that way from now on. You'll be hearing from me."

When Schnak had gone, the Dean was genial. "I enjoyed that," he said. "I've wanted to talk to Schnak like that for months, but you know how cautious we have to be with students nowadays; they're very quick to complain to the Governors that they're being harassed. But money still gives power. Where did you learn your lion-taming technique?"

"As a young parson I was a curate in some very tough

parishes. That girl isn't nearly as tough as she wants us to think. She doesn't eat enough, and what she eats is junk. I suppose she has been on drugs, and I wouldn't be surprised if now she was on the booze. But there's something about her I like. If she's a genius, she's a genius in the great romantic tradition."

"That's what I hope."

"I think Hoffmann would have liked her."

"I'm not very well up on Hoffmann. Not my period."

"Very much in the great romantic tradition. As a writer, he was one of its German inspirers. But there are aspects of the great romantic tradition we can do without, nowadays. Schnak will have to learn that."

"Will she learn it from Hoffmann? Doesn't sound like the teacher I would choose."

"Who would you choose? Have you got the supervisor you want?"

"I'll be talking with her by long-distance tomorrow. I'll be as persuasive as I can and it may take time. I suppose I send the phone bill to you?"

That remark assured Darcourt that the Dean was an old hand at dealing with foundations.

(5)

DARCOURT KNEW THAT, although he had compelled Schnak to say "please", it was no more than a nursery victory. He had made the bad child behave herself for a moment, but that was nothing. He was deeply worried about the whole matter of *Arthur of Britain*.

He grumbled a lot, but he was a faithful friend, and he did not want the Cornish Foundation to fall flat on its face in its first important venture in patronage. News of Arthur's grandiose ambitions were sure to leak out, not from Foundation directors, but from Arthur himself; he would not leak to the press intentionally, but the worst leaks are unintentional. Arthur was riding very high; he was making no secret of his wish to do what other Canadian foundations did not do; he was turning a deaf ear to proven good causes and worthy projects and if he fell, there would be a grand, eight-part chorus of "We told you so" from the right-minded. Arthur was prepared to risk large sums on what were no more than hunches, and that was un-Canadian, and the country that longed for certainties would not forgive him. It made no difference that the money was not public money; in an age when all spending is subjected to ruthless investigation and criticism, any suggestion that large sums were being employed capriciously by a private citizen would inflame the critics who, though not themselves benefactors, knew exactly how benefaction ought to be managed.

Why did Darcourt worry so about Arthur? Because he did not want Maria to be drawn into public rebuke and criticism. He still loved Maria, and remembered with gratitude that she had refused him as a suitor, and offered friendship instead. He still suffered from the lover's idea that the loved one should be, and could be, protected from the vicissitudes of fortune. In a world where everybody gets their lumps, he did not want Maria to get any lumps. If Arthur made a goat of himself, Maria would loyally suppose herself to be a nanny-goat. But what could he do?

A man who is disposed toward the romantic aspect of religion cannot wholly divorce himself from superstition, though he may pretend to hate it. Darcourt wanted reassurance that all was well, or some unmistakable warning that it was not. And where was such a thing to be found? He knew. He wanted to consult Maria's mother, and he knew that Maria would be strongly against any such course, because she was trying to escape from everything her mother represented.

She was not having much success.

Maria thought of herself as a determined scholar, not as a rich man's wife, or a woman of a remarkable beauty which drew all sorts of unscholarly things into her path. She wanted a new mother, the Bounteous Mother, the Alma Mater, the university. Learning and scholarship would surely help her to rise above the fact that she was half Gypsy, and all the Romany inheritance that was abhorrent to her. Her mother was a great stone in her path.

Her mother, as Madame Laoutaro (she had returned to her family name after the death of her husband), practised the respectable profession of a luthier, a doctor of sick violins, violas, cellos, and double basses; her family had a tradition of such work, as her name implied. But she was also in partnership with her brother Yerko, a man of dark skills who saw no reason why he should not palm off instruments that were made of scraps and bits of ruined fiddles, pieced out with portions of his own and his sister's manufacture, on people who accepted them as genuine ancient instruments. Madame Laoutaro and Yerko were not crooks in the ordinary way; it was simply that they had no moral sense at all in such matters. Gypsies through and through, aristocrats of that enduring and despised people, they thought that taking every possible advantage of the *gadjo* world was the normal course of life. The *gadje* wanted to hunt and crush their people; very well, let the *gadje* find out who was cleverest. Madame Laoutaro was a shop-lifter and a fiddle-faker who gloried in her witty impostures, and she supposed that her daughter had taken to education as a means of carrying on the Gypsy battle. Clement Hollier, who was Maria's supervisor in her studies, understood and appreciated Maria's mother pretty well; he thought of her as a wonderful cultural fossil, a hold-over from a medieval world where the dispossessed were cunningly at war with the possessors. But Maria had married a possessor, a priest of the money-morality of Canada, not to despoil him but because she loved him, and Madame Laoutaro could not fully believe it. Small wonder that Maria wanted to get as far as possible from her mother.

Fate — incorrigible joker — saw things differently.

Maria and Arthur had not been married three months before Madame Laoutaro's house burned down, and she and Yerko were homeless. The house, so respectably situated in the Rosedale area of Toronto, looked every bit as blamelessly respectable as it had done in the days of Madame Laoutaro's blamelessly respectable and well-doing Polish *gadjo* husband, the late Tadeusz Theotoky. But no sooner had Tadeusz died, rich and well-regarded, than Madame (having noisily mourned a man she had loved as deeply as Maria loved Arthur) reverted to her maiden name, and her Gypsy ways, which were the only ways she really knew, and she and Yerko despoiled the house. They cut it up into a squalor of mean apartments in which a variety of hopeless people, chiefly old women, were able to dwell, paying much more than the apartments were worth, but trusting to the protective power of their landlady. One such old woman, Miss Gretser, a virgin of ninety-two (though she gave out that she was a mere eighty-eight), fell asleep with a cigarette in her fingers and it was not much more than an hour before Miss Gretser was a cinder, and Madame Laoutaro, luthier, and her ingenious brother Yerko were homeless. Madame declared, with much outcry, that they were also penniless.

They were certainly not penniless. As soon as the fire broke out Madame and Yerko hurried to their cellar workshops, pulled two cement blocks out of a wall, and rushed to the back garden, where they threw a leather bag of money into an ornamental pool. Then they returned to the front of the house for much enjoyable despair, hair-tearing, and noisy grief. When the last ember was quenched, and the excitement was over, they rescued the bag, hurried to Maria's splendid penthouse, and set to work to pin sodden currency in bills of large denomination to all the upholstery and curtains, to dry it out. They insisted on sleeping on the floor of the handsome drawing-room till every bill was dried, ironed, and counted; they were suspicious of Nina, the Portuguese housekeeper, who made no secret of the fact that she looked on the Laoutaros as riff-raff. Which, of course, from a Portuguese Catholic point of view, they were.

Oh no, not in the least penniless. In addition to the funds in the bag, the late Tadeusz had left a lot of money behind him, tied up in a trust fund, which provided them with an ample income. There was also the matter of insurance. To Yerko and Madame Laoutaro, insurance was a form of wager; you bet with the insurance company that your house would not burn down, and if it did you were deemed the winner, and cleaned up handsomely. Unfortunately, however, when the Laoutaros converted the handsome mansion into a crowded lodging-house, they did not reinsure it as a commercial venture; they continued to pay the lower rate applicable to a dwelling. The insurance company, pernickety about such matters, threatened suit for fraud. Arthur was displeased, but Yerko managed to persuade him to allow the Gypsies to deal with the matter in their own way. Would a great financial company harass and oppress two poor Gypsies, ignorant of the complexities of business? Surely not! The Laoutaros were happily confident that they would get big money out of the insurance. But to the Gypsy mind all invisible money is fairy money and a fire is an immediate disaster. Where were these two homeless victims to go?

Madame's proposal that they might stay for an indefinite time in the penthouse, which was, she pointed out, big enough for a whole tribe of Gypsies, was immediately ruled out of the question by Maria. Yerko had a plan, which was that they should rent an ancient stable behind a shop a Gypsy friend of his kept on Queen Street East. A little work would make it habitable, and the luthier business and his coppersmith's forge would be handsomely accommodated.

This might have been acceptable if Madame had not had a bright idea which would, she said, repair their ruined fortunes. A lot of women, not nearly so gifted as herself, were advertising themselves as palm-readers, clairvoyants, and purveyors of personal counsel. A few of them openly promised restoration of lost sexual power, and reports were that business was brisk. As Madame said with scorn, these women were crooks, but if people appeared with money in their hands and positively demanded to be cheated, who was she to spit in the face of Providence?

Darcourt asked her if she would really prostitute her considerable gift as a psychic for money. Her response was positive.

"Never!" she said. "Never would I use my real gift in such trashy work! I would just give them the sort of thing they would get from some low sideshow mitt-camp. It would just be a hobby. I have my pride and my ethics, like anyone else."

This notion put a sharp spur into Arthur. As the chairman of the board of an important trust company, he could not have it known that his mother-in-law was running a mitt-joint in a depressed part of the city. Arthur had not liked the coroner's remarks in the inquest on Miss Gretser. The coroner had been rough about the lack of proper safety precautions in a house which he described, all outer appearances to the contrary, as a slum. Had Madame Laoutaro no advisers to keep her straight in such matters? Arthur had not been at the inquest, but he felt the gimlet eye of the coroner in his luxurious office in the Cornish Tower. Therefore Arthur declared that he would find a place for the refugees to repose themselves. To Maria's horror he offered them accommodation in the basement of the very apartment house in which she and Arthur lived, where he could keep his eye on them.

Hollier tactlessly pointed out to her the almost mythical beauty of the scheme. She, at the very top of the splendid building, exposed to sun and air: her roots, the matrix of her being, ever present in the lowest depths of the same building. The root and the flower, beautifully exemplified. Maria could snarl, and she snarled at Hollier when he said that.

She became accustomed to it. The Laoutaros never came up to the penthouse, not because they were forbidden, but because they did not like it; the air was thin, the food was unwholesome, they would be expected to sit on chairs at all times, the conversation was boring, and Yerko's pungent farting was reprehended. It was no place for people with any real zest for life.

When Darcourt next visited Maria he talked of Schnak but his mind was on Madame Laoutaro. He was a favourite with that lady, who respected him as a priest, though of a somewhat eccentric kind. She sensed the superstition in the heart of the holy man, and it established a kinship. The matter of a visit to the sibyl had to be approached with tact.

"I've been boning up on Hoffmann," said Maria. "It's time somebody on the Foundation knew what kind of world we are getting ourselves into."

"Have you been reading the famous *Tales*?"

"A few. I didn't read his music criticism because I don't know anything about the technical side of music. I've found out a little about his life, and obviously this opera, *Arthur of Britain*, was what he was working on when he was dying. He had lucid fits when he would call for pen and paper and do something, though his wife, who seems to have been rather a simple woman, didn't say what it was. He was only forty-six. Rotten life, knocking about from pillar to post because Napoleon was making things so difficult for people like him; not as a musician or an author, of course, but as a lawyer, which is what he was when he had the chance. He drank, not habitually but on toots. He had two miserable love affairs, of which the marriage was not one. And he never made it as a composer, which was what he wanted more than anything."

"Sounds like the complete Romantic."

"Not quite. Don't forget his being a lawyer. He was much respected as a judge, when Napoleon allowed it. I think that's what gives his writing its wonderful quality; it's so matter-of-fact and then — bang! You're right out of this world. I'm trying to get a wild autobiographical novel he wrote in which half is the work of a nasty Philistine tom-cat, who jeers at everything Hoffmann held dear."

"A real tom-cat, or a human tom-cat?"

"A real one. Name of Kater Murr."

"Ah well — you read German. I don't. But what about the music?"

"It doesn't get very good marks, because musicians don't like dabblers, and literary men don't like people who cross boundaries — especially musical boundaries. If you're a writer, you're a writer, and if you're a composer, you're a composer — and no scabbing."

"But lots of composers have been splendid writers."

"Yes — but in their letters."

"Let's hope the music was better than its reputation, or Schnak is in the soup, and so are we."

"My hunch is that the poor man was just hitting his stride when he died. Maybe it'll be wonderful."

"Maria, you're taking sides. Already you're an advocate for Hoffmann."

"Why not? I don't think of him as Hoffmann any more. His name was Ernst Theodor Amadeus (he took the name of Amadeus because he worshipped Mozart) Hoffmann. E. T. A. H. I think of him as ETAH. Makes a good pet-name."

"ETAH. Yes, not bad."

"So. Have you found out anything about Crottel?"

"Not yet. But my spies are everywhere."

"Hurry them up. He gives me funny looks when I come in at night."

"A security man has to give funny looks. What kind of look does he give Yerko?"

"Yerko has his own entrance, through the professional part of the building. He and Mamusia have a special key."

This seemed the moment to propose a visit to the Laoutaros. Maria hummed and hawed.

"I know I sound like a miserable daughter, but I don't want to encourage too much coming and going."

"Has there been any coming? No? Then just for this once, Maria, might we do a little going? I terribly want to get your mother's slant on this business."

So, after a little more demur, they sank down as far into the building as the elevator would carry them, into the basement where the owners of the condominiums had their garage space.

" 'The lyre of Orpheus opens the door of the underworld'," said Maria, softly.

"What's that?" said Darcourt.

"A quotation from ETAH," said Maria.

"So? I wonder if it does. We're none of us musicians, on the Foundation. Are we headed toward the underworld? Maybe your mother can say."

"You can depend on her to say something, relevant or not," said Maria.

"That's unkind. You know your mother is a very deft hand with the cards."

They walked to the farthest end of the basement, in the rather sinister light that seems appropriate to parking areas, went round an unobtrusive corner, and tapped at a faceless metal door. This gave access to an unused space where the architect had meant to put a sauna and exercise room, but in the end that idea had been abandoned.

Tapping was useless. After some banging, the door was opened a very little way on a chain, and Yerko's voice, in its deepest bass register, was heard to say: "If it's a professional visit please use the entrance on the floor above. I will meet you."

"It's not professional, it's friendly," said Darcourt. "It's me, Yerko — Simon Darcourt."

The door opened wide. Yerko, in a purple shirt and corduroy trousers that had once been a rich crimson, clasped Darcourt in a bear's embrace. He was a huge and impressive man with a face as big as one of his own fiddles, and a Gypsy's mane of inky hair.

"Priest Simon! My very dear friend! Come in, come in, come in! Sister, it's Priest Simon. And your daughter," he added in a markedly less welcoming tone.

Only the Laoutaros could have turned a derelict space, enclosed in concrete and in the highest degree impersonal and comfortless, into a version of Aladdin's cave, part workshop and part chaotic dwelling, stinking of glue, fumes from the forge, the reek of two racoon skins that were drying on the wall, the wonderful scent of precious old wood, and food kept too long without refrigeration. Some of the concrete walls were bare, covered with calculations done in chalk and corrected by erasures of spit, and here and there hung rugs of Oriental designs. Hovering over a pan of burning charcoal, the fumes from which escaped through a stovepipe that ran to one of the windows just below the ceiling, was Maria's mother, the *phuri dai* herself, stirring something smelly in a pan.

"You are in time for supper," she said. "Maria, get two more bowls. They are in the *abort*. I've been making *rindza* and *pixtia*. Wonderful against this flu that everybody has. Well, my daughter, you have been a long time coming, but you are welcome."

It was wonderful to Darcourt to see how the beautiful

Maria was diminished in the presence of her mother. Filial respect works in many ways, and Maria was suddenly a Gypsy daughter, disguised in some fine contemporary clothes, though she immediately kicked off her shoes.

The Gypsies are not great kissers, but Maria kissed her mother, and Darcourt kissed her sooty hand, which he knew she liked, because it recalled her youthful days as an admired Gypsy musician in Vienna.

They all ate bowls of *rindza* and *pixtia*, which was tripe seethed in pig's-foot jelly, and not as bad as it sounds. Darcourt showed great appetite, as was expected; those who consult oracles must not be choosy. The dish was followed by something heavy and cheesy called *saviako*. Darcourt thanked God for a strong shot of Yerko's home-made plum brandy, which was stupefying to the palate, but burned a hole through the heavy mixture in the stomach.

The god of hospitality having been adequately appeased, there followed at least half an hour of general conversation. When consulting an oracle, there should be no haste. At last it was possible to get to Darcourt's questions.

He told Mamusia — for that was what Maria called her — about the Cornish Foundation, of which she had some slight and inaccurate knowledge.

"Yes, yes; it is the Platter of Plenty," she said.

"The Platter of Plenty is just a joke," said Maria.

"It doesn't sound like a joke," said Mamusia.

"Yes, it is a joke," said Darcourt. "It is that big silver epergne that Maria puts on the table when we meet. It is filled with snacks — olives and anchovies, and pickled oysters, and sweets and little biscuits, and things like that. Calling it the Platter of Plenty is a joke by one of our directors. He's a Welshman, and he says it reminds him of a Welsh legend about a chieftain who had a magic platter on his table from which his guests could ask for and receive anything they desired."

"I know that story from other lands. But it's a good name. Isn't that what your Foundation is? A heaping platter from which anybody can get anything he wants?"

"We hadn't really thought of that."

"This Welshman must have a good head on him. You are guardians of plenty, aren't you? It's simple."

Darcourt thought it might be a little too simple, when he thought of what the Platter of Plenty was offering to Schnak. He explained as well as he could, in terms he thought Mamusia would understand, about the uncompleted opera, and Schnak, and his misgivings. He made the easy mistake of being too simple with someone who, although not educated in the ordinary sense, was highly intelligent and intuitive. Maria did not speak; in her mother's presence she was silent unless spoken to. Mamusia's glance moved constantly between her daughter's face and Darcourt's and in her own terms she understood them better than they knew.

"So — you want to know what is going to happen and you think I can tell you. Don't you feel shame, Father Darcourt? You are not a real Catholic, but you are some kind of priest. Isn't there something in the Bible that tells you to keep away from people like me?"

"In several places we are warned against them that have familiar spirits, and wizards that peep and mutter. But we live in a fallen world, Madame. Last time I visited my bishop he was very busy over Church investments, and he could not see me because he was deep in discussion with an investment counsel, who was peeping and muttering about the bond market. If there is any risk to my soul in consulting you, I take it upon me gladly."

So the Tarot cards were brought out, in their fine tortoiseshell box, and Mamusia shuffled them deftly. Carefully, too, for they were a fine old pack and somewhat limp with age.

"The nine-card deal, I think," said she.

At her bidding Darcourt cut the deck, which had been

reduced to the picture cards; he began by setting aside four cards, face down; then he put the top card in the middle of the table. It was the Empress, ruler of worldly fortune and a strong card to stand at the heart of the prediction. The next card he drew went to the left of the Empress, and it was Force, the handsome lady who is subduing a lion by tearing open its jaws, apparently without any special effort on her part. Above the Empress went the Lover, and Mamusia's quick eye saw a change in Maria's face. Next card, placed on the right of the Empress, was the Female Pope, the Great Mother. Last card, to go below the Empress, made Darcourt wince, for it was the Death card, the dreadful skeleton which is scything up human bodies. He hated the Death card, and hesitated.

"Down it goes," said Mamusia. "Don't worry about it until you see what it means. Turn up your oracle cards."

These were the four that had been set aside, and they were the Tower of Destruction, at the top, the card of Judgement, next in order, the Hermit, and last of all, the Fool.

"How do you like it?" said Mamusia.

"I don't like it."

"Don't be afraid because there are some dark cards. Look at the Empress, who can get you men out of any mess you can make. This is a very womanly hand of cards you have found, and lucky for you, because men are awful bunglers. Look at Strength, or Force, or whatever you want to call her; is she just brute force, like a man's? Never! She is irresistible force and she does not get it from being a man, let me tell you. And this High Priestess — this Female Pope. Who do you suppose she is? It's a fine spread."

"I can never see that Death card without shuddering."

"Pooh! Everybody shudders at the Death card, because they don't think what it means. But you — a priest! Doesn't Death mean transfiguration, change, turning the whole spread into something else — and you tell us into something better?

And look at your oracle cards. The Tower — well probably somebody will take a tumble; it would be queer if they didn't considering what you tell me about your Foundation. And Judgement. Who escapes it? But look at the Hermit — the man who lives alone — that sounds like you, Priest Simon. And most powerful of all — the Fool! What's the Fool's number in the pack?"

"The Fool has no number."

"Of course not! The Fool is zero! And what is zero? Power, no? Put zero to any number and in a wink you increase its power by ten. He is the wise joker who makes everything else in the hand conditional, and he is in the place of greatest power. The Empress and the Fool govern the spread, and with the Tower of Destruction in the first place among the oracles that probably means that there will be a lot of — what's the word — is it higgledy-piggledy? Lots of upsets and turn-arounds —"

"Topsy-turveydom," said Maria.

"Is that the word?"

"Topsy-turveydom seems all too likely," said Darcourt.

"Don't fear it! Love it! Give it the big kiss! That's the way to deal with destiny. You *gadje* are always afraid of something."

"I didn't ask you about my own fate, Madame, but about this venture of the Foundation's. They are my friends and I am worried on their behalf."

"No use worrying on anybody else's behalf. They must take care of themselves."

"Are you going to explain the spread?"

"Why? It looks clear enough. Topsy-turveydom. I like that word."

"Would you consider associating the Empress, the guardian woman, with Maria?"

Mamusia went into one of her infrequent fits of laughter; not the cackling of a witch, but a deep, gutty ho-hoing.

Darcourt had been mistaken if he expected her to relate her daughter to any figure of power.

"If I try to explain, I will just confuse you, because I am not at all sure myself. Your Fool-zero could be your Round Table, or that Fool-zero my son-in-law; I love him pretty well, I suppose, but he can be a Fool-zero as much as anybody else, when he gets too high and mighty. And that Great Mother, that High Priestess, could be your Platter of Plenty who can dish it out — but can she take it? I don't know. It could be somebody else, somebody new in your world."

"Couldn't Arthur be the Lover?" said Maria and was vexed to find herself blushing.

"You want him to be that, but the card is in the wrong place. Life is full of lovers, for people whose minds are set on love."

Darcourt was disappointed and worried. He had seen Mamusia discourse on a spread of cards many times, and never had she been so reluctant to speak about what she saw, what she felt, what her intuition suggested. It was not common for her to ask somebody else to lay out the cards; did that mean something special? He began to wish he had not asked Maria to bring him to the Gypsy camp in the bottom of her apartment house, but as he had done so he wanted something from the oracle that was positive, even if in small measure. He talked, he coaxed, and at last Mamusia relented a little.

"You must have something, eh? Something to lean on? It's reasonable, I suppose. Three things come to me that I would be very careful about, if I had dealt this hand for myself. The first is, be careful how you give money to this child."

"To Schnak, you mean?"

"Awful name. Yes, to Schnak. You tell me she has great talent as a musician. I know a lot about musicians; I'm one myself. I used to be greatly admired in Vienna, before I married Maria's father. I sang and played the fiddle and the cimbalom and danced my way into hundreds of hearts. Rich men gave me jewels. Poor men gave me what they couldn't afford. I could tell you —"

"Hold your gab!" said Yerko, who had been busy with the plum brandy. "Priest Simon doesn't want to hear you blow your horn."

"Yes, yes, Mamusia," said Maria, "we all know how wonderful you used to be before you became even more wonderful as you are now. You could break hearts still, if you wanted to be cruel. But you don't, dear little mother. You don't."

"No. You have embraced your fate as a *phuri dai*," said Darcourt, "and become a very wise woman and a great help to us all."

The flattery worked. Mamusia liked to be thought a wonderful old woman, although she could not have been far over sixty.

"Yes, I was wonderful. Perhaps I am even more wonderful now. I'm not ashamed to speak the truth about myself. But this Schnak — keep her short. You people on Foundations ruin a lot of artists. They need to work. They thrive on hunger and destruction. So keep this child from going on the streets, but don't drown her talent with money. Keep her short. Be careful the Platter of Plenty doesn't become the instrument of destruction."

"And the second thing?"

"Not clear at all, but it looks as if some old people, dead people, were going to say something important. Funny-looking people."

"And the third?"

"I don't know if I should say."

"Please, Madame."

"These things have nothing to do with the cards. They are just things that come to me. This third one comes very, very strong; it came when you were shivering over the Death card.

I don't think I should say. Perhaps it was something just for me, not for you."

"I beg you," said Darcourt. He knew when the seeress wanted to be coaxed.

"All right. Here it is. You are wakening the little man."

Mamusia had a strong sense of the dramatic, and it was plain that this was the end of the session. So, after protestations of gratitude, and astonishment, and enlargement — there could never be too much unction for Mamusia — Darcourt and Maria returned to the penthouse and whisky, of which the abbé drank more than he intended, though less than he wanted.

Whatever Mamusia might say, he hated the Death card and it soured his feeling toward the whole of the prediction. He knew how stupid that was. If the prediction had been all positive he would have accepted it happily, at the same time retaining in another part of his mind a patronizing feeling toward the Tarot and all Gypsy vaticination. To put full trust in a sunny future would be un-Canadian, as well as unworthy of a Christian priest. But now, when he had been shown fear by the cards, that other part of his mind told him he was a fool to play King Saul, and resort to wizards who peep and mutter. Christian priest that he was, he deserved to suffer for his folly, and suffer he did.

The three random predictions he liked even less. He did not believe that artists should be kept short of money. Fat cats hunt better than lean. Don't they? Does anyone know? Poverty was not good for anybody. Was it? As for utterances by funny-looking people, he felt no response at all.

But — Wakening the little man? What little man?

The little man he knew best was his own penis, for that was what his mother had called it. Always keep the little man very clean, dear. Later he had heard it called the old man, by friends of his days as a theological student, for to those jokers it meant the Old Man, or Old Adam, whom the Redeemed Man was bidden to cast out. As a bachelor whose sexual experience, for a man of his age, had been sporadic and slight, he suffered frequent reminders from the little man that there was a side of his nature that was not being given enough attention.

His physical desire for Maria had never been overwhelming, but it was a fretting element in his life. When they met she kissed him, and he rather wished she wouldn't because it aroused inadmissible longings. But had they not agreed, when he had proposed marriage to her, that they should be friends? It had possessed deep meaning for him then, and their friendship was one of the fostering things in his life, but he was aware that there was a farcical side to it. *We are just good friends*. Wasn't that what people said when they were denying insinuations of a love affair in the press? Oh, intolerable torment! Oh, frying lust — yet not a lust that would drive him to shoot Arthur and carry Maria away to a love-nest in the East. Oh, farce of priesthood, which demanded so much that was unnatural, but failed to give the strength to banish worldly desires! Oh, misery of being the Reverend Professor Simon Darcourt, Vice-Warden of Ploughwright College, professor of Greek, a Fellow of the Royal Society, who was, in the most pressing areas of his life, a poor fish!

You are wakening the little man. Maria's mother saw through him like a pane of glass. It was ignominious. Oh, the unlit lamp and the ungirt loin! Oh hell!

(6)

ETAH IN LIMBO

YOU ARE WAKENING THE LITTLE MAN — *as if the Little Man had ever been asleep! No, no, this Little Man has been wide awake in Limbo, for* ever since I died I have been aware of people reading what I wrote about music, and now and then seeing **Undine**, my best completed opera, on the stage, and never forgetting my tales of wonder where, the critics say, the fantastic meets the everyday. The Little Man has certainly not been gnawing his nails because of earthly neglect.

Mine was a life of better than merely respectable achievement, but I died with one thing left undone that should have been done. That was the completion of my opera **Arthur of Britain**, in which it would have been plain to the stupidest that my apprenticeship as a composer was finished, and that I had written a masterwork. Yes, a masterwork at least as good as, and perhaps better than, the best of my dear friend Weber. But it was not to be; I had barely laid the keel of that work before I was cut down, laid out, polished off, not suddenly, but at some wretched length. It was my own doing, I admit it freely. I was unwise in my life. I emptied my purse too readily, playing the great gentleman with my health and talents. So I was cut off untimely, and that is why I find myself now in Limbo, in that part of it reserved for those artists and musicians and writers who never fully realized themselves, never quite came to the boil, so to speak. Limbo: not the worst of hereafters, for it is free of the chains of space and time, and permits its denizens a great deal of versatility and, shall I say it, some posthumous influence?

Still, not to be too delicate about it, Limbo is a bore. Should I complain? My fate is not the worst. There are artists and writers and scholars here who have had two thousand years of neglect, and would be grateful if some candidate for a Doctor of Philosophy degree would stumble on their work and seize it with joy, as material that nobody has hitherto pawed over and exhausted. The dullest thesis — and that is saying much — may be enough to release an artist from Limbo and allow him to go — we don't really know where, but we hope for the best, because to people like ourselves, used to a creative life, boredom is punishment enough. When we were good children of the Church, some of us, we heard about sinners who roast on beds of coals, or stand naked in Siberian hurricanes. But we were not sinners. Just artists who, for one reason or another, never finished our work on earth and so must wait until we are redeemed, or at least justified, by some measure of human *understanding. Heavenly understanding, it appears, is what brings us to Limbo; we never really did our best and that is a sin of a special kind, though not, as I say, the worst.*

Can this be my great chance? Is this extraordinary waif Schnak to be my deliverer? I must not build my hopes too high. I did that when, however long ago it was, that curious French-German-Jew Jacques Offenbach took some of my stories as the basis for his last piece, **Les Contes d'Hoffmann** *(thank you, Jacques, for giving my name such prominence), but it proved not to be the sort of work that gets a man out of Limbo. Tuneful, mind you, and reasonably skilled in orchestration (thank God he controlled his impulse to use the bass drum too much), but Offenbach had spent too much time writing* opéra bouffe *to be happy with the real thing. And he had too much French humour, which can be fatal to music. I always keep my own sense of humour, which is German and therefore deeper than his, in check when I am composing. After a man has died he understands what a betrayer of great things humour can be, when it is not in the Shakespearean or Rabelaisian mode. I am glad to see that this child Schnak has no sense of humour whatever, though she is pretty well stocked with scorn and derision, which pass for humour with stupid people.*

Is this my great chance? I must do everything I can to help. I shall stand at Schnak's shoulder and push her in the right direction, so far as I can. So all those crazy guys grab her, do they? Crazy guys like Weber, and Schumann, I suppose. What about that magnificently sane guy Mozart, whose name I took as an act of homage? Is Schnak biting off more than she can chew? Schnak is going to need luck, or she will simply make a mess of my hastily scribbled intentions. I must be Schnak's Luck. Her greatest luck would be not to find that terrible libretto, in which that ass Planché was in a fair way to make a mess of **Arthur** *when I died. Same trouble as Offenbach; too much sense of humour — English this time — too much experience of what would "go" in the theatre — meaning what "went" last time and which the public was beginning to be tired of. Again, I thank God that Schnak knows nothing about the theatre and has no sense of humour. If it is possible to keep her from those two plagues I shall be at hand to do it.*

Did I really die in order to save my opera from Planché's dreadful libretto? Even now I cannot tell. There are limits to what one can know about one's former life, even in Limbo.

Why did the old woman, the seeress, tell that well-meaning fellow Darcourt, and her lovely but uncomprehending daughter, that they were wakening the little man, as if that were something that should not be done? I am very happy to be awakened in this way. Luckily Darcourt thinks she meant his pizzle, egotistical jackass that he is. But does the old woman know something I cannot know, placed as I am? Is it likely?

By God, I am thoroughly awake, and I shall not rest until I have seen this thing through to the end. Then, if my luck enables me to be Schnak's Luck, I may have a chance to sleep eternally, my work accomplished.

II

As a group of Schnak's professors assembled in the auditorium of the Faculty of Music to see the film *After Infinity*, Simon Darcourt heard a good deal more about Hulda Schnakenburg than he had known before, and it surprised him. Her bad manners toward the Dean had no relation to the work she did for her instructors; they admitted, with reluctance, that it was of unusual quality. Were her exercises grubby, asked Darcourt, remembering the letter she had sent to the Cornish Foundation. No indeed; they were notably clean, clear, and almost — they hated to use the word — elegant in their musical calligraphy. As a student of harmony, counterpoint, and analysis she was exemplary, and her flights into electronic music, environmental music, and any sort of noise that could be evoked from any unusual source were admitted to be innovative, when they could be distinguished from mere racket.

It was even agreed that she had a sense of humour, though not a pleasant one. She caused a sensation with a serenade she had composed for four tenors whose larynxes had been constricted to the point of strangulation with adhesive tape; there had been some cautious approval from professors who had not noticed that its performance took place on April 1. Her manners were admitted to be dreadful, but instruction in manners was not part of the Faculty's job. Nevertheless, it was agreed that Schnak went rather too far. As one professor, who had some recollection of the music-hall of an earlier day, sang in Darcourt's ear,

> *It ain't exactly what she sez —*
> *It's the nasty way she sez it!*

She had qualified beyond question for her Master of Music, and her reputation as a brat and a nuisance had nothing to do with the matter — apart from making her disliked and even feared by some members of the Faculty.

Predictably Schnak had not chosen to appear at Convocation, properly gowned and dressed to receive her degree at the hands of the Chancellor. She rejected all such ceremonial, or suggestion of a *rite de passage*, with her favourite term of disapproval. Shit. But she had set to work immediately on preparations for her doctorate, and when autumn came, and she presented herself at the seminars in Romantic Themes in Nineteenth-Century Opera, Traditional Compositional Techniques, and History of Performance Practice, she had already done more reading than most of the other students would do during the year to come, and she threw herself into the obligatory work on Composition and Theory Research with what would have looked like enthusiasm in someone else, but seemed more like angry zealotry in Schnak.

As well as heavy involvement in her university work, she had found time to write the music for *After Infinity*, and the auditorium was filled with students of drama, of film; and of any manifestation of the *avant-garde*. An admired student genius had written the scenario and directed the film; great things were expected. There was to be no dialogue, in order that the immediacy of the early silent film might be recaptured and any taint of merely literary values avoided. There would, however, be music, for Chaplin had given his blessing to music as an accompaniment to film, particularly when he wrote the music himself. The student genius could not write music, but he discerned a fellow genius in Schnak, and she had provided music. She had rejected the idea of using a synthesizer, and had composed her score for a piano that had been doctored with pieces of parchment fastened over the strings, assisted by a Swanee whistle ingeniously played under a metal tub, and that simplest of instruments, a comb covered with tissue paper. The effect was of a vaguely melodious but unfocussed buzzing, punctuated by shrieks, and everyone agreed that it had added much to the general effect.

The film-maker was scornful of what he called "linear" quality in a script, so his film bounded along in unconnected sections, leaving the spectators to make out as best they could what was going on. It was not too difficult. Humanity was facing the ultimate predicament; a nuclear leak had rendered all mankind, male and female, sterile. What was to become of the race? Could a woman be found, almost at the point of bearing a child, whose child would have escaped the curse of sterility? If that child could be brought to birth, how should it be nourished? Its mother's breasts would obviously — well, obviously to the film-maker — be dry, or a source of poison. Might a man, in case of dire global need, suckle a child? This question enabled several sequences to be shown in which male friends of the film-maker — the cast had all worked on a voluntary and friendly basis — strained with selfless zeal to produce milk from their flat and unlikely paps, and one or two of them actually did so, the milk being simulated very cleverly with shaving cream. But it was discovered — during one of the portions of the story that had not been thought worth filming — that one fertile female had escaped the nuclear curse. She appeared as a simple child of twelve (the daughter of the film-maker's landlady) who must take upon her the task of continuing the race, if a male could only be found still able to impregnate her. The search for a fertile male was indicated by shots of vast emptinesses; long resonant corridors up and down which there was much coming and going by unseen searchers, whose footsteps Schnak had simulated with two halves of a coconut shell. There were scenes of the anguish of a Very Wise Man (played by the film-maker's great and good friend, who chose unaccountably to do it in a Prince Albert coat and a flowing tie) who, in the culminating scene, had to explain to the twelve-year-old what Sex was, and what would be required of her. The child's face, filled with a wonderment that could also have been puzzled vacuity, was photographed from unusual angles, and she emerged as an Infans Dolorosa, a Nubile Saviour, and, of course, as a Transporting Symbol. The film was greeted in the main with solemn wonderment, though there were a few coarse souls who sniggered when the child knelt before the startlingly white bare feet of the Very Wise Man emerging from the bottom of his formal trousers, and seemed to adore them. In the great tradition of student despair the fate of mankind was left undecided at the end, which Schnak marked by three descending *glissandi* on the Swanee whistle.

Subtle campus critics professed to detect a hint of irony in the music, but the majority, while admitting that it might be so, felt that it added a dimension to a brilliant film which would, if everybody had their rights, command a variety of international awards.

When, a few days later, the Faculty met to discuss thesis topics, they were astonished that Schnak proposed to complete her work on *Arthur of Britain* within one university year. She had done her year of courses for her doctorate and nothing stood in the way except the unusually short time she had allotted to her thesis-composition. A thesis of operatic length and complexity? They demurred.

"I am through with trying to control or advise Schnak," said Dean Wintersen. "If it kills her or drives her mad, let it be so. I hope to hand over my supervision of work to a distinguished visitor."

Of course there was curiosity about the distinguished visitor, but the Dean said it was too early to talk of what was not yet assured. As always, the Faculty wished to show its academic scruple by doubt and debate.

"This thesis exercise," said a professor of musicological research; "who can say what it may involve? I am not at all impressed by this passion to complete what fate has ordained should be incomplete."

"Ah, but you must admit that it has been done, and well done," said another musicologist, who did not like the first speaker. "Look at Janet Johnson's excellent reconstruction of Rossini's *Journey to Rheims*. And what about Deryck Cooke's completion of Mahler's Tenth? What this girl wants to do is a forward, not a backward, step. She wants to display for us a Hoffmann who has never been heard before."

"I have heard one of Hoffmann's operas in Germany, which I think is something nobody else present can say, and I do not leap with joy at the prospect of another. These early-nineteenth-century operas are mostly very thin stuff."

"Ah, but that's the fault of the libretti," said his enemy, who had indeed never heard a note by Hoffmann but who had a nice private specialization in libretti where nobody could challenge him. "What is the libretto for this one like?"

The question was directed to the Dean, and it gave him a chance to display those qualities which mark a dean off from ordinary professors. He did not, in fact, know anything about the Hoffmann libretto and he would not pretend that he did; if his listeners chose to think on the grounds of what he said that he had seen the libretto, the assumption was wholly their own.

"A certain amount of work will have to be undertaken before that question could be satisfactorily answered," he said. "Of course we shall have to make sure that all that side of the work is properly handled. We are not literary experts. We shall have to arrange a committee for Schnak that includes somebody from Comparative Literature."

This was greeted with groans.

"Yes, I know," said the Dean. "But you must admit that they are very thorough. I had thought of asking Professor Penelope Raven to act. Would that be agreeable?"

There were other matters to be decided, and it was nearing the time when professors feel the need of a pre-dinner drink, so they said it was agreeable.

(2)

PROFESSOR RAVEN was not pleased to be asked to join a committee supervising a thesis in the Faculty of Music; she would be the only non-musician, and she knew that the odd man out in such an academic group was expected to be modest and keep out of what didn't concern him, while lending scope and respectability to everything that was done. This looked like a job involving a great deal of work and very little satisfaction. She thought differently when she had lunched at the Faculty Club with her old friend Simon Darcourt, and had drunk her full share of a bottle of wine.

"I didn't know you were in on this, Simon," she said. "That makes a difference, of course."

"I'm not in it academically, but I'll have a good deal to say about what goes on," said Simon. Then he told Penny in extreme confidence — knowing that she was as leaky as a sieve — about the Cornish Foundation, its support for Schnak, and its determination to present *Arthur of Britain* on the stage. He also told her that any research in which she was involved on the libretto would, of course, be generously rewarded by the Foundation. That made a great deal of difference.

"The problem seems to be that the libretto is very scrappy," he explained.

"How much have you got?" she asked.

"I've taken a quick look, and to be frank there's virtually

nothing," he said. "What the chances are of digging anything up, I couldn't even guess. It isn't going to be easy, Penny."

"With my flair for research, and the money you've got your hands on, much may be achieved," said Penny, looking owlish. "I've taken a look, you know, and it was a quick look, like yours, and there's really nothing but a few notations in German, written by Hoffmann himself, because he had written quite a lot of music he wanted to use. I assumed that somebody must have some really solid stuff I hadn't seen. I gather there was some sort of dispute, amounting almost to a row, between Hoffmann and the English librettist."

"Who was — ?"

"None other than the redoubtable James Robinson Planché."

"Yes, the Dean did mention that name. What was redoubtable about him?"

"Very popular nineteenth-century playwright and librettist. Just about forgotten, now. Though everybody uses a phrase of his: 'It would have made a cat laugh', he says in one of his innumerable works. I suppose the opera world knows him, if it knows him at all, as the man who wrote the libretto for the unfortunate Weber's *Oberon*, one of the resounding flopperoos of operatic history. Music splendid. Libretto — well, Schnak has a word for it."

"Shit?"

"Of the most rejectable and excrementitious order."

"Then why — ?"

"I can't tell you why, and if you didn't have all that lovely money to throw around I might never find out. But I can, and I will."

"How?"

"The Cornish Foundation — I see it all now in a vision — is going to pay my expenses to go abroad and find out."

"Where will you look?"

"Now Simon, you know the research game better than

that. *Where* is for me to know, and for you and Schnak and the Cornish Foundation to find out when and if I get it. But if it's to be gotten, I'm the girl to get it."

With that Simon had to be content. He liked Penny. She must have been nearer forty than thirty, but she had charm, and spirit, and in a favourite Rabelaisian phrase of his, she was "a jolly pug and well-mouthed wench". And beneath all that, she had the steely core of the woman who has scrambled up the academic ladder to a full professorship, so Simon knew that it was useless to press her further.

After lunch, in order to avoid going back to his rooms in Ploughwright, where he would have to face the heap of type-script of his life of the late Francis Cornish — the biography with that disastrous, abysmal gap in the very heart of it — he went to the Club library. He looked with distaste at the table on which were displayed a selection of the less obscure among the innumerable academic quarterlies, dismal publications in which scholars paraded pieces of research that meant all the world to them, but which their colleagues in general found supremely resistible. He ought to look over those that touched on his own subject, he knew, but outside it was spring, and he could not force himself to his scholar's task. So he strayed to another table, where unscholarly magazines lay, and picked up *Vogue*. He never read it, but he had hopes, inspired by the wine he had drunk and the cheering companionship of Penny Raven, that it might contain some pictures of women with very few clothes on, or perhaps none at all. He sat down to read.

He did not read. He looked at the advertisements instead. There were young women displayed there, in various stages of undress, but in the fashion of the time they looked so angry, so crazed, so furious, that they gave him little comfort, aroused no pleasing fantasy. Their hair stood on end or was wildly tangled. Their eyes glared or were pinched in squints that hinted at lunacy. But then he came to a picture so sharply contrasted with its neighbours that he looked at it for several minutes, and as he looked something in the back of his mind stirred, moved, was aroused, until he could hardly believe what he saw.

It was not a photograph, but a drawing of the head of a girl, in silver-point, touched here and there with white and red chalk; it was delicately executed but not weak, without any modern flash or challenge. Indeed, it was drawn in the manner, and also in the feeling, of a time at least four centuries before the present. The head was aristocratic, not haughty but modestly confident; the eyes were innocent but not simple-minded; the line of the cheek had neither the pudding-faced nor the lantern-jawed look of the models whose photographs appeared in the other advertisements. It was a face that challenged the viewer, particularly if he were a man, by its self-possession. This is what I am: what are you? it seemed to say. It was by far the most arresting picture in the magazine.

Beneath were a few lines in a clear, beautiful type, but again it was not attenuated or falsely elegant. Darcourt, who knew something about types, recognized it as a modern version of the type-face reputedly based upon the handwriting of a poet, churchman, bibliophile, scholar, humanist, and, in some respects, rascal, Cardinal Pietro Bembo. The message was brief and clear:

> *Your make-up is not a matter of current fashion. It is the realization of what you are, of that period of history to which your individual style of beauty pertains. What Old Master might have painted you, and seen you truly? We can help you to discover that, and to learn to apply the only cosmetics made to realize the Old Master quality in you. We do not seek the most customers, only the best, and our services and our products are not cheap. That is why they are obtainable only at a few selected shops from our*

own maquilleuses. *What Master are you? We can help
you to achieve the distinction that is yours alone.*

The advertisement was signed, in an elegant Italic hand,
"Amalie", and below were half a dozen addresses of suppliers.

Glancing around to be sure that nobody saw him doing
what was academically unspeakable, Darcourt carefully tore
the page out of the magazine and hurried back to his rooms,
to write a most important letter.

(3)

THE MEETING between the Cornish Foundation and Schnak's
parents took place late in May, in the drawing-room of the
penthouse. It had better be done, everyone agreed, though
nobody expected anything to come of it. Two months had
gone by since the decision to support Schnak in her work to
revive and re-flesh and re-clothe Hoffmann's notes for *Arthur
of Britain*, and the meeting should have taken place earlier, had
Arthur not been too much under the weather to do anything.
Now, at the end of May, he was mending, but pale and subject
to sudden loss of energy.

Arthur and Maria were supported by Darcourt only, for
Hollier said he had nothing to contribute to such a meeting,
and Geraint Powell was too busy with the forthcoming Festival season in Stratford for anything else to claim his attention.
The Schnakenburgs had been asked to come at half past eight
and they were prompt.

Schnak's parents were not the nonentities Dean Wintersen's description had led Darcourt to expect. Elias Schnakenburg was not very tall, but he was very thin, which made
him look tall; he wore a decent grey suit and a dark tie; his
grey hair was receding. His expression was solemn and had a
distinction Darcourt had not expected; this watch-repair man

was a master craftsman and nobody's servant. His wife was as grey and thin as he; she wore a felt hat that was much too heavy for May weather, and grey cotton gloves.

Arthur explained what the Foundation had in mind, making it clear that they were prepared to back a young woman who was said to have great promise, and whose project appealed to the imagination. They expected that a good deal of money would be spent, and without in any way holding the Schnakenburgs responsible for the outcome, they felt that Hulda's parents should be aware of what was being done.

"If you don't hold us responsible, Mr. Cornish, just what do you expect of us?" said the father.

"Your goodwill, really. Your assent to the project. We don't want to appear to be doing anything over your head."

"Do you think our assent, or our doubts, would make any difference to Hulda?"

"We don't know. Presumably she would like to have your encouragement."

"No. It would mean nothing to her either way."

"You regard her as an entirely free agent, then?"

"How could we do that? She is our daughter and we have not given up our feeling that we are responsible for her, nor have we stopped loving her very dearly. We think we are her natural protectors, whatever the law may say about it. Her natural protectors until she marries. We have not rejected her. We are made to feel that she has rejected us." A slight German accent but carefully phrased English.

Mrs. Schnakenburg began to weep silently. Maria hastened to give her a glass of water — why add water to tears? she thought as she did so — and Darcourt decided that he might suitably intervene.

"Dean Wintersen has told us that the feeling between your daughter and yourselves is strained. And you see, of course, that we cannot interfere in that. But we must behave

in a proper way, without being parties to any personal disagreement."

"Very business-like and proper of you, of course, but it
isn't a matter of business. We feel that we have lost our child
— our only child — and this arrangement that you intend so
kindly can only make that worse."

"Your daughter is still very young. The breach may not
last long. And of course I can assure you that anything Mr.
and Mrs. Cornish can do, or I can do, to put things right will
be done."

"Very kind. Very well meant. But you are not the people
to do much about it. Hulda has found other advisers. Not of
your sort. Not at all."

"Would it help to tell us about it?" said Maria. She had
seated herself by Mrs. Schnakenburg and was holding her
hand. The mother did not speak, but her husband, after some
sighing, continued.

"We blame ourselves. We want you to understand that. I
guess we were too strict, though we didn't mean it. We are
very firm, you see, in our religion. We are very strict Lu-
therans. That was how Hulda was brought up. We never let
her run wild, as so many kids do these days. I blame myself.
Her mother was always kind. I wasn't as understanding as I
should have been when she wanted to go to the university."

"Did you oppose that?" said Darcourt.

"Not entirely. Mind you, I didn't see what good it could
do. I wanted her to do a business course, find a job, be happy,
find a good man, get married — kids. You know."

"You didn't see her musical gift?"

"Oh, yes. That was clear from when she was little. But she
could have done that, too. We paid for lessons until they got
too expensive. We're not rich, you know. We thought she
might give her music to the church. Lead a choir and play the
organ. There's always a place for that. But can you build a
whole life on it? We didn't think so."

"You don't think of music as a profession? The Dean says she has possibilities as a composer."

"Well — I know. He told me that, too. But is that the kind of life you want your daughter — your only daughter — to get into? Do you hear much good of it? What kind of people? Undesirables, many of them, from what you hear. Of course the Dean seems to be a good man. But he's a teacher, eh? Something solid. I tried to put my foot down, but it looks like the time for parents putting their feet down has gone."

This was a familiar story to Darcourt. "So you have a rebellious daughter, is that it? But don't all children rebel? They must —"

"Why must they?" said Schnakenburg, and for the first time there was a note of combat in his voice.

"To find themselves. Love can be rather stifling, don't you agree?"

"Is the love of God stifling? Not to a truly Christian spirit."

"I meant the love of parents. Even the kindest, most well-meaning parents."

"The love of parents is the love of God manifesting itself in the life of their child. We prayed with her. We called on God to give her a contrite heart."

"Yes. And what happened?"

After a silence: "I can't tell you. I wouldn't repeat the things she said. I don't know where she picked up such language. Or — yes, I do know; you hear it everywhere nowadays. But I would have thought a girl brought up as she was would have deafened her ears to such filth."

"And she left home?"

"Walked out in what she stood up in, after a few months I wouldn't go through again for any money. Have any of you people any children?"

Shaking of heads.

"Then you can't know what Mother and I went through.

We never hear from her. But of course we hear about her, because I make inquiries. She's done well in the university, I grant you. But what has the cost been? We see her, sometimes, when we take care she doesn't see us, and my heart is sore to see her. — I'm afraid she's fallen."

"What do you mean by that?"

"Well — what would I mean? I'm afraid she's living an immoral life. Where else would she get money?"

"Students do get jobs, you know. They do earn money, quite legitimately. I know scores of students who finance their own studies doing jobs that only a young, strong person could do, and keep up a program of studies at the same time. They are a very honourable group, Mr. Schnakenburg."

"You've seen her. Who would give her a job, looking the way she does?"

"She's as thin as a rake," said Mrs. Schnakenburg. It was her only contribution to the conversation.

"Do you really hate the idea of us giving her this chance?" said Maria.

"To be frank with you, Mrs. Cornish — yes, we do. But what can we say? She's not a minor, according to law. We're poor people and you're rich people. You have no children, so you can't know the pain of children. I hope for your sake it will always be so. You have ideas about all this music and art and other stuff that we don't have and don't want. We can't fight you. The world would say we were standing in Hulda's way. But the world doesn't come first with us. There's other things to be thought of. We're beaten. Don't think we don't know it."

"We certainly don't want you to think that you are beaten or that we have beaten you," said Arthur. "I wish you would try to see things a little more our way. We sincerely want to give your daughter the chance her talents entitle her to."

"I know you mean kindly. When I say we're beaten I guess I mean we're beaten for the present. But we've given Hulda something too, you know. We've given her the source of all real strength. And we pray — we pray every night, for as much as an hour, sometimes — that she will come back to that before it's too late. God's mercy is infinite, but if you kick Him in the face enough, He can be pretty stern. We'll bring our girl back to God if prayer can do it."

"You don't despair, then," said Maria.

"Certainly not. Despair is one of the worst sins. It questions God's intentions and His power. We don't despair. But we are human, and weak. We can't help being hurt."

That was that. After a few more exchanges in which Schnakenburg yielded nothing, while remaining perfectly polite, the couple left.

There was heavy silence in the room. Arthur and Maria seemed greatly put down, but Darcourt was in good spirits. He went to the bar-cupboard in the corner and set to work to make the drinks they had not thought it polite to have while the Schnakenburgs, obviously dry types, were present. As he poured, he sang under his breath:

> "Tell me the old, old story
>   Of unseen things above,
>   Of Jesus and His glory
>   Of Jesus and His love."

"Simon, don't be facetious," said Maria.

"I'm only trying to cheer you up. Why are you so down in the mouth?"

"Those two have made me feel absolutely rotten," said Arthur. "The unfeeling, fancy-pants rich man, childless and obsessed with vanities, steals away the jewel of their lives."

"She stole herself away long before you heard of her," said Darcourt.

"You know what I mean. The overbearingness of the rich and privileged."

"Arthur, you are not well. You are open to subtle psychological attack. And that's what you've had. That man Schna-kenburg knows every trick in the book to make people feel rotten who don't share his attitude toward life. It's an under-dog's revenge. You are not supposed to kick the underdog, but it's perfectly okay for the underdog to bite you. One of the insoluble injustices of society. Pay no heed. Just go right on as before."

"I'm surprised at you, Simon. That man was talking from the depths of a profound religious feeling. We don't share it, but we must in decency respect it."

"Look, Arthur. I'm the expert on religion here. Don't bother your head about it."

"You are a High Church ritualist, and you despise their simplicity. I didn't think you were such a snob, Simon." Maria spoke angrily.

"In your heart you are still a superstitious Gypsy girl, and when anybody talks about God you go all of a doodah. I don't despise anybody's simplicity. But I know when a pretence of simplicity is a clever play for power."

"What power has that man?" said Arthur.

"Obviously the power to make you feel rotten," said Dar-court.

"You're unjust, Simon," said Maria; "he talked with such certainty and trust about God. It made me feel like a frivolous ninny."

"Look, children — listen to old Abbé Darcourt and stop hating yourselves. I've listened to hundreds of people like that. They have certainty and depth of belief but they buy it at the price of a joyless, know-nothing attitude toward life. All they ask of God is a kind of spiritual Minimum Wage and in return they are ready to give up the sweets of life — which God also made, let me remind you. I call believers like that the Friends of the Minimum. God, who is an incorrigible joker, has landed them with a daughter who wants to join the Friends of the Maximum, and you can help her. Her parents' faith is like a little candle, burning in the night; your Cornish Foundation is, let's say for the sake of modesty, a forty-watt bulb which may light her to a better life. Don't switch off the forty-watt bulb because the candle looks so pitiably weak. Schnak is in a mess. Indeed, Schnak looks like a mess, and is an odious little creature. But the only path for Schnak is forward, not backward toward a good job, a nice husband like Daddy, and kids born in the same chains. Father Schnakenburg is very tough. You've got to be tough, too."

"I didn't know you were a stoic, Simon," said Arthur.

"I'm not a stoic. I'm that very unfashionable thing, an optimist. Give Schnak her chance."

"Of course we will. We must, now. We're committed to it. But I don't like feeling that I'm trampling on the weak."

"Oh, Arthur! You sentimental mutt! Can't you see that being trampled on is victuals and drink to Schnakenburg? In the great electoral contest of life he is running for martyr, and you are helping him. He has his depth and certainty of belief. Where's yours? You are running for the satisfaction of being a great patron. That's a reasonable cause for certainty and belief. What ails you?"

"I suppose it's money," said Maria.

"Of course it is! You people both have the guilt that our society demands of the rich. Don't give in to it! Show 'em that money can do fine things."

"By God, I believe you really are an optimist," said Arthur.

"Well, that's a start. Join me in my optimism and in time you may believe a few other things that I believe, which I never mention to you, because one thing I have learned in my work as a priest is that preaching to the poor is easy work compared with preaching to the rich. They have so much guilt, and they are so bloody pig-headed."

"We're not pig-headed! We are the ones who feel for the Schnakenburgs. You, the Abbé Darcourt, are sneering at them and urging us to sneer. You Anglican! You ritualist! You pompous professorial poop! You disgust me!"

"That is not argument. That is vulgar abuse, for which I will not even stoop to forgive you. I've played a part in the sort of scene we have just gone through more times than you can imagine. The jealousy of the humble parents for the gifted child! Old, stale goods, to me. The hitting below the belt because somebody has a bigger bank account than you, and must therefore be a moral inferior! The favourite weapon of the self-righteous poor. The use of a mean form of religion to gain a status denied to the unbeliever: they tell you the Old, Old Story, and expect you to cave in. And you do. Real religion, my friends, is evolutionary and revolutionary and that's what your Cornish Foundation had better be or it will be nothing."

"You could have been a popular preacher, Simon," said Maria.

"I've never fancied that sort of work; it inflates the ego and can lead to ruin."

"You've made me feel rather better. I don't know about Arthur."

"You're a good friend, Simon," said Arthur. "I'm sorry I was nasty to you. I withdraw pompous and even poop. But you are professorial. Let's forget the Schnakenburgs, in so far as we can. Are you making any headway with that book about Uncle Frank?"

"At last I think I am. I think I may be on to something."

"Good. We want to see the book published, you know. I joke about it, but you understand. We trust you, Simon."

"Thanks. I'm going ahead. By the way, you won't see me for a week or so. I'm going hunting."

"You can't. It's out of season."

"Not for what I'm hunting. The season has just begun."

Darcourt finished his drink, and departed, singing as he left the room,

> *"Tell me the old, old story,*
>   *Tell me the old, old story,*
>   *Tell me the old, old story*
>   *Of Jesus and His love."*

But the tone of his voice was ironic.

"A really good friend, the old Abbé," said Arthur.

"I love him."

"Platonically, I hope."

"Of course. Can you doubt it?"

"In love I can doubt anything. I never take you for granted."

"You could, you know."

"By the way, you never told me what Mamusia told Simon while I was in hospital."

"Just that we'll all get our lumps, really."

"I think I've had my lumps for a while. My mumps-lumps. But I'm coming round, at last. I think I'll sleep in your bed tonight."

"Arthur — I'd love that. But is it wise?"

"Darcourt's doctrine of optimism. Let's give it a go."

And they did.

(4)

THE ROOM IN THE APARTMENT on Park Avenue was splendid beyond anything Darcourt had ever experienced. It was the work of a brilliant decorator — so brilliant that he had been able to make a room of modest size in a New York apartment building seem authentically to be a room in a great house, perhaps a minor palace, in Europe. The grisaille panelling had certainly come from a palace but had been adjusted, pieced out, and trimmed so that it gave no hint that it had ever been anywhere else. The furniture was elegant, but comfortable in a way palace furniture never is, and enough of it was modern to allow people to sit on it without the uneasiness demanded by a valuable antique. There were pictures on the walls the decorator had not chosen, for they spoke of a coherent and personal taste, and some were rather ugly; but the decorator had hung them to greatest advantage. There were tables loaded with bibelots and bijouteries — what the decorator called "classy junk" — but it was classy junk that belonged to the owner of the room. Photographs in sepia colouring stood on a *bonheur du jour*; they were in frames decorated with coats of arms and crests that obviously belonged to the people whose likenesses were fading inside them. A beautiful but not foolish desk marked the room as a place of business. An elegantly uniformed maidservant had seated Darcourt, saying that the Princess would be with him in a few minutes.

She came in very quietly. A lady who might be in her fifties, but who looked much younger; a lady of great, but not professional, beauty; by far the most elegant lady Darcourt had ever encountered.

"I hope you have not been waiting long, Professor Darcourt. I was detained by a tedious telephone call." The voice gentle, and hinting at merriment. The accent of someone who spoke English perfectly, as though instructed by an English governess, but with a hint of some underlying cradle tongue. French, perhaps? German? Darcourt could not tell.

"It is good of you to come to see me. Your letter was very interesting. You wanted to ask about the drawing?"

"If I may, Princess. It is Princess, isn't it? The drawing caught my eye in a magazine. As of course it was intended to."

"I am so glad to hear you say that. Of course it was meant to attract attention. You wouldn't believe the trouble I had persuading the advertising people that it would do so. They are so very conventional, don't you think? Oh, who is going to look at such an old-fashioned picture? they said. Everybody whose eye is wearied by the gaudy, pushy girls in the other advertisements, I said. But that is the way things are being done this year, they said. But what I am advertising is not just of this year, I said. It is meant to be more lasting. It is meant to appeal to people whose lives are not just fixed in this year, I said. I couldn't persuade them. I had to insist."

"And now they admit that you were right?"

"And now they are convinced it was their idea all the time. You do not know advertising men, Professor."

"No, but I know people. I can quite believe what you tell me. Of course they have recognized the subject?"

"The head of a girl, early-seventeenth-century style? Yes, they know that."

"They have not recognized the girl?"

"How would they?"

"By using the eyes in their heads. I knew the girl as soon as you came into this room, Princess."

"Did you, indeed? You have a very keen eye. Possibly she was an ancestress of mine. The drawing is a family possession."

"May I come directly to the point, Princess? I have seen preparatory studies for that drawing."

"Have you really? Where, may I ask?"

"Among the possessions of a friend of mine, who was a gifted artist — particularly gifted in assuming the styles of earlier ages. He made countless drawings, copies from collections of such things; others from life, I should imagine, from the notations he made on the studies. There are five studies for the head which resulted in the picture you own, and which you have made public in your advertisements."

"Where are these drawings at present?"

"In the National Gallery of Canada. My friend left them all his drawings and pictures."

"Has anybody but yourself observed this astonishing resemblance?"

"Not yet. You know how galleries are. They have masses

of things they have not catalogued. I saw the drawings when I was preparing my friend's things for transfer to the Gallery. I was his executor in such matters. It could be years before those particular studies are given any careful scrutiny."

"What was the name of this artist?"

"Francis Cornish."

The Princess, who had seemed amused during all their conversation, burst into laughter.

"*Le beau ténébreux!*"

"I beg your pardon?"

"That was what my governess and I called him. He taught me trigonometry. He was so handsome and solemn and proper, and I was longing for him to throw down his pencil and seize me in his strong arms and rain kisses on my burning lips and cry Fly with me! I shall take you to my ruined castle in the mountains and there we shall love, and love, and love until the stars bend down to marvel at us! I was fifteen at the time. *Le beau ténébreux!* What became of him?"

"He died about two years ago. As I say, I was one of his executors."

"Had he some profession?"

"He was a collector and connoisseur. He was very rich."

"So he had retired?"

"No indeed; he was quite active as a connoisseur."

"I meant from his work."

"His work?"

"I see you did not know of his work."

"To what work do you refer? He had studied painting, I know."

The Princess went off into another peal of laughter.

"I don't think I understand you, Princess."

"Forgive me. I was just thinking about *le beau ténébreux* and his studies in painting. But that was not his real work, you know."

Darcourt glowed with delight; here it was, at last! What

had Francis Cornish been up to during those years of which he had no record? The Princess knew. Now was the time to spill the beans.

"I am hopeful that you are going to tell me what his real work was. Because I have undertaken to write a life of my old friend, and there is a long period from about 1937 until 1945, when he became active with the commission that was sorting out all that mass of pictures and sculptures that had gone astray during the war, about which information was very scant. Anything that you can tell me about that time in his life would be most helpful. This portrait of yourself, for instance; it suggests that you knew him on terms that go a little beyond being a tutor in trigonometry."

"You think so?"

"I know a little about pictures. That drawing was made with unmistakable affection for the subject."

"Oh, Professor Darcourt! I am afraid you are a dreadful flatterer!"

So I am, thought Darcourt, and I hope it works with this vain woman. But the vain woman was going on.

"Nevertheless, I think it is ungallant of you to suggest that I can remember 1937 at all, not to speak of studying trigonometry at that time. I had hoped that my looks did not betray so much."

Damn, thought Darcourt; she must be in her middle sixties; I've put my foot in it. Never was good at figures.

"I assure you, Princess, that nothing of the sort entered my head."

"You are still too young yourself, Professor, to know what time means to women. We take refuge in many helpful things. My line of cosmetics, for instance."

"Ah, yes: I wish you every success."

"How can you say that, when you mean to expose my very special mark of excellence, my seventeenth-century drawing, as a fake? And yet I suppose you must do it, if your book about *le beau ténébreux* is to be honest and complete."

"It cannot be honest and complete unless you will tell me what you know about Francis Cornish during those years for which I have no records. And I assure you I never thought of saying anything about your drawing."

"If you don't, somebody else will. It could be ruinous. The cosmetic business is quite sufficiently ambiguous, without any associations of art faking creeping in."

"No, no; I would never mention it."

"So long as these preliminary sketches are in your National Gallery collection, there is very great danger."

"That is unfortunate, of course."

"Professor Darcourt" — the Princess was flirting with him — "if you had known what you know now, about my drawing and the use I am making of it, would you have sent those five sketches to your National Gallery?"

"If I had thought that you held the key to the most interesting part of Francis Cornish's life, I doubt very much if I would have done so."

"And now they are utterly irretrievable?"

"You see how it is. They are government property. They belong to the Canadian nation."

"Do you suppose the Canadian nation is ever going to attach much importance to them? Can you see queues of Indians and Eskimos, and Newfoundland fishermen, and wheat-growers, standing patiently in line to look at those drawings?"

"I am afraid I do not follow you."

"If I had those drawings in my own hands, I could tell you things about Francis Cornish that would be the making of your book. They would inspire and refresh my memory."

"And if you do not get them into your own hands, Princess?"

"No deal, Professor Darcourt."

(5)

THE CORNISH FOUNDATION was assembled in full palaver. The five members sat at the Round Table, upon which was the Platter of Plenty, heaped high with the fruits of late August. Dusty purple grapes hung from the various bowls of the wondrous epergne; for once, thought Maria, the damned thing looks beautiful even to my eye.

People who live in beautiful surroundings grow accustomed to them, and even indifferent to them. Neither Maria nor the other four members of the Cornish Foundation gave much attention to the room in which they sat at the Round Table. It was a very high room, and had what the architect had called a "cathedral roof" which, in the fading light of day, seemed higher and duskier than it was; below it was a row of small clerestory windows through which the green-blue sky and the first stars could be seen; on the walls below hung Arthur's fine pictures, which were his own choosing, for the late Francis Cornish, who had enough good pictures to outfit a small museum, had left him none. There was a piano, but there was so much space that it did not dominate, as pianos sometimes do. Indeed, there was not much furniture in the room. Arthur liked space, and Maria gloried in uncluttered space, having been brought up in the more than cluttered house of her parents, even before Mamusia had reverted to Gypsydom, and established the midden in the basement beneath all this beauty. The foul rag-and-bone shop of the heart was what Darcourt had once called the Gypsy camp, and Maria had been angry with him, because it was so true.

The Foundation sat at the Round Table in candlelight, assisted by some discreet lighting under a cornice. A stranger coming suddenly into the room would have been struck and perhaps awed by its look of wealth and privilege and the elegant quietness which is one of the avails of wealth and privilege. Such a stranger was Professor Penelope Raven; she was impressed, and determined not to show it.

Expectation was high, and even Hollier had returned early from one of his expeditions to Transylvania, where he rooted for what he called cultural fossils. How handsome he is, thought Maria, and how unfairly his good looks lend weight to whatever he says; Simon isn't in the least handsome, but he does far more for the Foundation than Hollier. Arthur is handsome, but not in the distinguished mode of Hollier; yet Arthur can set wheels to turning and kettles to boiling in a way quite out of Hollier's range. I suppose I am as beautiful, for a woman, as Hollier is for a man, and I know just how little beauty adds up to, when things have to be done.

About the fifth member of the Foundation, Geraint Powell, Maria thought nothing at all. She did not like Powell, or the challenging way Powell looked at her; he was handsome in an actorly style — lots of wavy dark hair, rocking-horse nostrils, a large mobile mouth — and like many good actors he was better not examined at too close range. If the Cornish Foundation should ever be presented on the stage, thought Maria, Geraint Powell would be cast for the role of Clement Hollier; his overstated good looks would carry to the back of the theatre, as Hollier's fine good looks would not.

They were all present, and eager, because Professor Penelope Raven had returned triumphant from her search abroad for the libretto to *Arthur of Britain*, and was on hand to tell what she had found.

"I've got it," she said; "and, as this kind of research goes, it wasn't too hard to find. It's always like *The Hunting of the Snark*, you know; at the very last moment your Snark may turn out to be a Boojum. I guessed it would be in the British Museum library, among the theatre stuff, but as I expect you know, finding things there — if they are as obscure as this — depends a lot on research skill, and a nose for oddities, and sheer baldheaded luck. Of course I traipsed through the opera archives and libraries in Bamberg, Dresden, Leipzig, and Berlin — and I didn't find a thing. Not a sausage. Lots of stuff about Hoffmann but nothing about this opera. I had to be thorough or I would have been wasting your money. But I had a hunch that London was where it would be."

"Because of this man Planché," said Arthur.

"No. Not Planché. I was on the track of Charles Kemble. Now I'm going to have to lecture you a bit, I'm afraid. Kemble was a member of the famous theatrical family; you'll all have heard of Mrs. Siddons, who was his sister and the greatest actress of her time; you've seen Reynolds' picture of her as the Tragic Muse. Charles Kemble was manager and lessee of Covent Garden Theatre from 1817 till 1823, and in spite of a lot of marvellous successes, he was always in trouble about money. Not his fault, really. It was the theatre economics of the time. The owners of the theatre demanded an immense yearly rental, and even a successful manager was often in hot water.

"Charles adored opera. He was always encouraging composers to write new ones. He was really an awfully nice man, and he encouraged anybody who had talent. He had his eye on our man, James Robinson Planché, because Planché could deliver the goods; he was a first-rate theatre man, and working with him meant success. Kemble had heard about Hoffmann — all the Kembles were awfully well educated, which wasn't at all the usual thing among theatre people then — and I suppose he read German, or had seen something of Hoffmann's in Germany. He persuaded Hoffmann to write him an opera, and insisted that Planché, who was still under thirty and obviously started on a successful career, should provide the libretto.

"So — the work was begun, and there was some correspondence between Planché and Hoffmann, which is lost, I fear; poor old Hoffmann was in bad health, and died before

anything much came of it. And Hoffmann and Planché fought
like cat and dog in the very polite epistolary fashion of the
time, so I imagine Planché was relieved when the whole affair
came to nothing. As it turned out he wrote a little thing to
replace it, called *Maid Marian*, with music by a clever hack
called Bishop.

"The story, so far as I could dig it up, was in Charles
Kemble's papers in the B.M. Want to hear it?"

"Yes, we certainly do," said Arthur. "But first, can you
reassure us that there actually is a libretto, of some sort, for
this opera?"

"Oh there is. Yes indeed there is, and I have transcripts of
it right here. But I think it would all come clearer if I read
you some of the exchange between Planché and Kemble."

"Fire away," said Arthur.

"This is the first letter to Kemble that I found.

My dear Kemble:

I have exchanged letters with Herr Hoffmann, and it
would appear that we are working at cross purposes, as he
has only a very imperfect notion of the English theatre as
it pertains to opera. But I am confident that we shall
arrive at an agreement when I have explained the facts of
the situation to him. We correspond, by the way, in
French, and I may say that his command of that language
may be at the root of certain of our differences, for he is
far from perfect.

As you know, I like to work quickly, and having much
on my hands at the moment I wrote to Hoffmann as soon
as I heard from you that he would prepare the music for a
piece for the approaching Covent Garden season. I outlined a plan I have had in my mind for some time for a
fairy piece which might as well be attached to King
Arthur as to any other popular hero. In brief, it is this:
King Arthur and his companions, wearying of the plea-

sures of the chase, hit upon the capital notion of establishing a Round Table with a view to raising the level of chivalry in England, which has been the source of some complaint from Queen Guenevere. (Opportunity here for a duet of a comic nature between Arthur and his Queen, who thinks herself ill-used.) Arthur knows how to deal with that, so he calls upon his enchanter, Merlin, to transfer his Court *tous sans exception* to the Kingdom of the Grand Turk, to see how ladies are treated *there*, and Merlin calls upon the Fairy Court, led by King Oberon and Queen Titania, to effect this change. But the fairy rulers are at odds, as are Arthur and Guenevere, and refuse their office. (Opportunity for a fairy ballet, which is agreed by everyone at present to be a sure card, and very pretty.) Merlin seeks assistance from Pigwiggen, the only one of Arthur's knights who is also a fairy, and they unite their enchantments to move the British Court to Turkestan. Lively end to Act One.

Turkestan is the scene of the second act, and provides opportunities which I am sure the excellent Mr. Grieve will seize upon for scenic display of a lavish and very striking order. We involve the Grand Turk, who lays siege to Queen Guenevere, arousing the jealousy of Arthur. (Great opportunity here for mischief by Pigwiggen.) To Arthur's dismay his principal Knight, Sir Lancelot, falls in love with the Queen, and he and Arthur quarrel and nothing will settle their difference but a duel. More business for Pigwiggen, who knows that Elaine, the Lily Maid, loves Lancelot and he has encouraged her. Must get Elaine onstage in Act One. The Grand Turk will have no duelling in his kingdom and, by an opportune stroke of chance, Oberon and Titania appear, having resolved their dispute, and transport the whole Round Table back to Britain. I thought of a scene here in which the Fairy Court, all carrying tapers, lead the English away from Turkestan, climbing a mountain in darkness. (You are aware that Covent Garden has such a mountain among its scenes in store, which was used in *Barbarossa* three seasons ago, and could be easily refurbished to repeat the great effect it made then.) Strong conclusion to Act Two.

Act Three is again in Britain, and the duel between Arthur and Lancelot is in preparation, but first we present a Grand Parade of the Seven Champions — all played by ladies, of course — with plenty of amusing valour for St. Denis of France and St. Iago of Spain; it might be stylish if St. Anthony of Italy sang in Italian, Denis in French, and Iago in Spanish. Follow this with comical songs in characteristic dialect for St. Patrick of Ireland and St. David of Wales and St. Andrew of Scotland, with perhaps a mock combat between the three British Champions which is resolved by St. George of England, who subdues all three. Under the stewardship of St. George — a parade of Heralds at this point and a great show of heraldry, which looks splendid and costs little — Arthur and Lancelot prepare to fight — real horses, don't you think? Horses never fail with an English audience — which is halted by the appearance of Elaine, the Lily Maid of Astolat, who enters floating down a river in a skiff, apparently dead, a scroll in her hand proclaiming her to be a *petite amie* of Lancelot's whom he has jilted. Accused by Guenevere, Lancelot admits his guilt, and Elaine leaps from her bier and claims him for her own. Reconciliation of Arthur and Guenevere, assisted by Merlin and Pigwiggen, and St. George declares the triumph of chivalry and the Round Table. Grand patriotic conclusion.

I do not need to explain to you, my dear Sir, who know the resources of your theatre so well, that I have prepared this plan with singers in mind who are at once available, with the exception of Madame Catalani, who is willing to come out of retirement, and could be tempted with the role of Guenevere if opportunities for her splendid *coloratura* were plentifully supplied, which presents no difficulty. If Hoffmann proved not up to it our friend Bishop could write something in his usual florid style. Otherwise, who but Braham for Arthur, Duruset for Lancelot, Miss Cause for Elaine, Keeley as Merlin (his voice is gone but I conceive of Merlin as a minor comic figure), Madame Vestris as Pigwiggen — with a costume which would give ample play for her magnificent limbs? Wrench would do very well as Oberon as he can dance, as can Miss Paton, who would be sufficiently *petite*, despite her growing *embonpoint*, for Titania. I see Augustus Burroughs as a fine St. George. Neat, do you not agree?

Now there, I should certainly think, we have a splendid opera fitted, and chances innumerable for the fantasy and *grotesquerie* which you assure me are Herr Hoffmann's *spécialités de la maison*. But no. Oh, no!

Our German friend replies with many compliments in very stiff French — honoured to be collaborating with me, conscious of the *éclat* deriving from association with Covent Garden, etc. etc. — and then he goes on to read me a truly German lecture about opera. As he sees it, the day of the sort of opera I propose — he actually spoke of it as 'a delightful Christmas piece for children'! — is over, and something musically more ambitious is at hand. There are not to be single numbers, or songs, for the characters, with dialogue to link them together, but a continuous flow of music, the *arias* being joined by *recitativo stromentato* — so that, in effect, the orchestra never gets any rest at all, but saws and blows away all evening! And the music should be dramatic, rather than occasions for vocal display by specially gifted singers — 'performers on that seriously overrated instrument, the human neck' he calls them (and what would Madame Cat make of *that*, if she heard it?) — and every character should have a musical 'motto', by which he means a phrase or instrumental flourish that signifies that character alone, and can be presented in different ways according to the spirit of the action. He declares this would make a very striking effect and signal a new mode of opera composition! As it certainly would, and empty the theatre, I am sure!

Very well. Music is his business, I suppose, though I am myself not wholly ignorant of that science, as I have shown before this. But when he laughs at my notion for the dramatic part of the piece, I think I have some cause to speak plainly. He wants to go right back to the original Arthurian tales, and dramatize them 'seriously' he says, and not in a spirit of *'un bal travesti'* — I suppose that is a hit at my Seven Champions being represented by ladies, which I am certain would go down well, as ladies in armour are, I may say, the rage at present — partly because of legs, of course, but what of that? Spangled tights for each Champion, in the colours of the nation represented, would create a very fine effect, and give pleasure to that part of the audience which is not intensely musical. The opera house is not, and never has been, a nunnery. He speaks of the *'ambience Celtique'* of the Arthurian legend, not understanding, apparently, that the Arthurian tales have long been — by conquest, I suppose — the property of England, and therefore of her national opera house.

But do not discompose yourself, my dear friend. I am writing a reply that will explain some things to Herr Hoffmann which he clearly does not know, and we shall proceed very amicably, I am confident, once I have done so.

I have the honour to subscribe myself,

> Yours very sincerely,
> JAMES ROBINSON PLANCHÉ."

April 18, 1822

"My God," said Arthur; "I foresee trouble."

"Don't worry," said Geraint. "This is all familiar stuff to me. Theatre people go on like that all the time. It's what's called the creative ferment from which all great art emerges. At least that's what it's called when you are being nice about it. There's more, I suppose?"

"Lots more," said Penny. "Wait till you hear Letter Number Two.

My dear Kemble:

When I had conquered my understandable chagrin — for I make it a principle never to speak or write in anger — I wrote again to our friend Hoffmann, in what the Bard calls a 'condoling' manner, repeating my principal points and supporting them with some passages of verse which I put forward as the sort of thing we might use in the opera. For instance, I proposed a Hunting Chorus as a beginning. Something spirited, and with plenty of brass in the orchestration, along these lines:

> We all went out a-hunting
> The break of day before,
> In hopes to stop the grunting
> Of a most enormous boar!
>
> But he made it soon appear
> We'd got the wrong pig by the ear,
> Till our Fairy Knight
> To our delight
> In his spare rib poked a spear!

— this to be followed by a thigh-slapping song for Pigwiggen (Madame Vestris, did I say?) about the hunting of the boar (with some *double entendre* on 'boar' and 'bore') and the Huntsmen to sing the chorus again.

I want the fairy element to be very strong, and Pigwiggen's power to be deft and quick, like Puck's, in contrast to the heavier comic magic of Merlin. Perhaps a song here? Pigwiggen should appeal to both the ladies and the gentlemen in the audience — to the former as a charming boy, and to the latter as a charming girl in boy's dress — a trick the Bard knew so well. I suggested to Herr H. that Pigwiggen's song might be along these lines:

> *The Fairy laughs at the wisest man*
> *There's none can do as the Fairy can;*
> *Never knew a pretty girl in my life*
> *But wished she was a Fairy's wife."*

"That could get a very bad laugh in a modern opera," said Darcourt. "I don't mean to interrupt, Penny, but nowadays all fairy business has to be handled very carefully."

"Just you wait, my boy," said Penny, and went on with the letter.

The love scenes between Lancelot and Guenevere provide the chief romantic interest in the opera, and I sketched out a duet for Hoffmann to think about. I am not a composer — though no stranger to music, as I have said — but I think this might bring out something really fine in a man who *is* a composer, as we have reason to believe Hoffmann is. Lancelot sings under Guenevere's window:

> *The moon is up, the stars shine bright*
> *   O'er the silent sea;*
> *And my lady love, beneath their light*
> *   Has waited long for me.*
> *O, sweet the song and the lute may sound*
> *   To the lover's listening ear:*
> *But wilder and faster his pulse will bound*
> *   At the voice of his lady dear.*
>
> *Then come with me where the stars shine bright*
> *   O'er the silent sea:*

> *O, my lady love, beneath their light*
> *I wait alone for thee."*

"I wonder if I might trouble you for a drop more whisky?" said Hollier to Arthur in an undertone.

"Indeed you may. Much more of this and I shall want a very big one myself," said Arthur, and circulated the decanter. Darcourt and Powell seemed to need it, as well.

"I must say a word for Planché," said Penny; "no libretto reads well. But listen to what Guenevere replies, from her balcony window:

> *A latent feeling wakes*
> *Within my breast*
> *Some strange regard that breaks*
> *Its wonted rest.*
> *Let me resist, in heart,*
> *However weak*
> *What love with so much art*
> *Can speak.*

And then I suppose he means to follow with a love scene in prose, Lancelot mooning under Guenevere's window."

"Oh, not mooning, I hope," said Powell. "First fairy knights, and then mooning ladies. You'll have the show closed by the police."

"No coarse jibes, if you please," said Penny. "Not all the love songs are so sentimental. Listen to what the Grand Turk sings, when the Round Table party arrives in his court. He is immediately smitten by Guenevere and here he goes:

> *Though I've pondered on Peris and Houris,*
> *The stars of Arabian Nights,*
> *This fair Pagan more beautiful sure is*
> *Than any such false Harem Lights;*
> *No gazelle! no gazelle! no gazelle!*
> *Has such eyes as of me took the measure!*

She's a belle! she's a belle! she's a belle!
I could ring with the greatest of pleasure!"

"Penny, are you offering this seriously?" said Maria.

"Planché was certainly offering it seriously — and confidently. He knew his market. I assure you this is in the real early-nineteenth-century vein, and people loved just this sort of thing. It was the Regency, you know, or as near as makes no difference. They whistled and sang and barrel-organed and played *Grand Paraphrases de Concert* of stuff like this on their lovely varnished pianofortes," said Penny. "It was a time when they used to do Mozart with a lot of his music cut out, and jolly new bits by Bishop interpolated. It was before opera went all serious and sacred and had to be listened to in a holy hush. They just thought it was fun, and they treated it rough."

"What was Hoffmann's response to this muck?" said Hollier.

"Oh, muck's a bit strong, don't you think?" said Penny.

"It's so God-damned jocose," said Arthur.

"He seems to be patronizing the past, which I can't bear," said Maria. "He treats Arthur and his knights as if they had no dignity whatever."

"Oh, very true. Very true," said Penny. "But do we do any better, with our *Camelots* and *Monty Pythons* and such? Pretending your great-great-infinitely-great-grandfather was a fool has always appealed to the theatrical mind. Sometimes I think there ought to be a Charter of Rights for the Dead. But you're quite right; it *is* jocose. Listen to this, for Elaine to sing to Lancelot when he gives her the mitt:

On some fine summer morning
If I must hope give o'er,
You'll find, I give you warning,
My death laid at your door.
And if at your bedside leering

> Some night a ghost you spy,
> Don't be surprised at hearing
> 'Tis I, 'tis I, 'tis I!"

"She sounds very like Miss Bailey — unfortunate Miss Bailey," said Arthur.

"What about the grand patriotic conclusion?" said Darcourt.

"Let's see — where is it? Yes:

> From cottage and hall
> To drive sorrow away,
> Which in both may befall
> On some bright happy day
> Reign again over me, reign again over thee,
> The good king we shall see!
> Oh! long live the king!"

"That doesn't even make sense," said Hollier.

"It's patriotism — doesn't have to," said Penny.

"But is this what Hoffmann set to music?" said Hollier.

"No, he didn't. There is a final letter which seems to put an end to the whole business. Listen:

My dear Kemble:

I wish I had better news for you from our friend Hoffmann. As you know, I sent him some sketches for several songs for the Arthur piece, with the usual librettist's assurances that I would alter them in any way he felt necessary, to fit music he had composed. And of course that I would write additional verses for theatrical situations we agreed on, and when everything else was finished, I would pull it all together with passages of dialogue. But as you see he keeps nagging away at his *idée fixe*. I felt that any differences there were between us were a matter of language; I do not know how well he understands English. However, he has chosen to reply to me in English, and I enclose his letter —

Honoured Sir:

In order that I may make myself as plain as possible I am writing this in German, to be translated by my esteemed friend and colleague Schauspieldirektor Ludwig Devrient, into English, of which I have myself only the most imperfect knowledge. Not so imperfect, however, that I cannot seize the spirit of your beautiful verses, and declare them to be utterly unsuited to the opera I have in mind.

It has been my happiness during my life to see great changes in music, and many musicians have been so generous as to say that I have been not unhelpful in bringing such changes about. For as you doubtless do not know, I have written a great deal of musical criticism and have been happy in the commendation of the eminent Beethoven, to say nothing of the friendship of Schumann and Weber. It was Beethoven's regret that he had at last completed his *Fidelio* as an opera with spoken dialogue — a *Singspiel* as we call it. Since the completion of my last opera, *Undine*, of which Weber was so generous as to speak in the highest terms, I have thought much about the nature of opera, and now — when I assure you time is running out with me, for reasons I shall not elaborate here — I greatly wish either to write the opera of my dreams, or to write no opera at all. And, distinguished Sir, though I am sorry to speak so bluntly, your proposed libretto is no opera at all, for any purpose known to me.

When I speak of the opera of my dreams, it is no forced elegance of words, I assure you, but the expression of what I believe music to be, and to be capable of expressing. For is not music a language? And of what is it the language? Is it not the language of the dream world, the world beyond thought, beyond the languages of Mankind? Music strives to speak to Mankind in the only possible language of this unseen world. In your letters you stress again and again the necessity to reach an audience, to achieve a success. But what kind of success? I am now at a point in my life — an ending, I fear — when such success has no charms for me. I have not long to speak and I can only be content to speak truth.

I beg you to be so good as to reconsider. Let us not prepare another *Singspiel*, full of drolleries and elfin persons, but an opera in the manner of the future, with music throughout, the arias being linked by dialogue sung to an orchestral accompaniment and not simply to the few notes from the harpsichord, to keep the singer in tune. And, O my very dear Sir, let us be serious about *la Matière de Bretagne* and not present King Arthur as a Jack Pudding.

No, I see the drama as springing from King Arthur's recognition of the noble love of Lancelot for Guenevere, and the great pain with which he accepts that love. You have all that anyone could need in your English romance *Le Morte d'Arthur*. Draw upon that, I beg you. Let us have that great love, and also the sorrow with which Lancelot knows that he is betraying his friend and king, and Lancelot's madness born of remorse. Let us make an opera about three people of the highest nobility, and let us make Arthur's forgiveness and understanding love for his Queen and his friend the culminating point of the action. The title I propose is *Arthur of Britain, or The Magnanimous Cuckold*. Whether that has the right ring in English I cannot tell, but you will know.

But let us, I entreat you, explore the miraculous that dwells in the depths of the mind. Let the lyre of Orpheus open the door of the underworld of feeling.

With every protestation of respect and regard I am, Honoured Sir,

May 1, 1822   E. T. A. HOFFMANN

Post Scriptum: I enclose a quantity of rough notes I have prepared for the sort of opera I so greatly desire, hoping that they will convey to you a measure of the feeling of which I speak — a feeling, to use a word now coming much into fashion, that is profound in its Romanticism.

Now, there, my dear Kemble, what do you make of that? What do I make of that? It all sounds to me like Germans who have been smoking their long pipes and sitting up late over their thick, black beer. Of course I know what he is talking about. It is Melodrama, or verses spoken or chanted to music, and it is quite useless for the purposes of opera as we know it at Covent Garden.

But I kept my temper. Never be out of temper with a musician is a good principle, as you know from your frequent altercations with the explosive Bishop, in which you have always prevailed by your splendid Phlegm. I wrote again, trying to coax Hoffmann to see things from my point of view, which is not to push forward the frontiers of music, I assure you, or plunge into the murky world of dreams. Humour, I assured him, is what the English most value, and whatever is to be said to them must be said humorously or not at all, if music is in question. (I except, of course, Oratorio, which is a wholly different matter.) Indeed, I tried upon him a rather neat little thing I dashed off, proposing it as the song which establishes the character of the Fairy Pigwiggen (Madame Vestris):

> *King Oberon rules in Fairyland,*
> *Titania by his side;*

But who is their Prime Minister,
Their counsellor and guide?
'Tis I, the gay Pigwiggen, who
Keeps hold upon the helm
When their spitting and spatting
Their dogging and catting
Threatens the Fairy Realm.

Who, think you, rules in Fairyland?
Not these who hold the sceptre!
Nay, devil a bit
Not Nob and Tit,
But I, their gay preceptor!
Pigwiggen, the merry minikin
Is Nob and Tit's preceptor!

Now, I think I may say, not in vanity but as a man who has won his place in the theatre with several pieces, all markedly successful, that this is rather neat. Do you agree?

Several weeks have elapsed, and I have had no word from our German friend. But time wears on, and I shall stir him up again, as genially as I know how.

Yours, etc.

June 20, 1822   J. R. PLANCHÉ

There is a notation on this letter in Kemble's hand, which says: 'News reaches me of Hoffmann's death at Berlin, on 25 June. Inform Planché at once, and suggest an immediate council to decide on a new piece and a new composer — Bishop? — as it must be ready for Christmas.'"

There was heavy silence among the Cornish Foundation, as Penny helped herself to a bunch of grapes from the Platter of Plenty.

It was Hollier who spoke first. "What do you suppose poor dying Hoffmann made of Nob and Tit?"

"A modern audience would certainly see it as jocose indecency. Language has taken some queer turns since Planché's time," said Darcourt.

"Queer's the word," said Arthur.

"Don't be too sure about a modern audience," said Powell, who seemed to be the least depressed of the group. "You recall that song in *A Chorus Line*? Rather a lot about Ass and Tit, sung by a girl with magnificent limbs? The audience couldn't get enough of it."

"I have to agree about the changes of language," said Penny. "I have spared you Planché's notes for dialogue, which he sent to Kemble. He wanted Pigwiggen to talk a lot about her Knockers."

"Her *what*?" said Arthur, aghast.

"Her Knockers. She meant some underground spirits who worked in the mines of Britain, and were called Knockers."

"Is there something ambiguous about Knockers?" said Hollier. "I'm sorry. I'm not very well up on the latest indecencies."

"Knockers nowadays means breasts," said Powell. "Door knockers, you know, which show up so prominently on the front. 'She has a great pair of knockers,' people say. Probably better known in England than here."

"Ah yes. I wondered if it were a misreading for Knackers," said Hollier. "Meaning the testicles. Perhaps the Magnanimous Cuckold would be the person to talk about those."

"For God's sake try to be serious," said Arthur. "We are in very deep trouble. Doesn't anybody understand that? Are we seriously going to spend a great amount of Uncle Frank's benefaction to stage an opera that is all about Knackers and Knockers and Nobs and Tits and gay fairies? Is my hair going white, Maria? I distinctly feel a withering of my scalp."

"As a student of Rabelais, all this sniggering, half-hearted indecency makes me throw up," said Maria.

Penny spat out a mouthful of grape seeds, not very elegantly, on her plate. "Well — you have the music, you know. Or plans and sketches for it."

"But is it any good?" said Maria. "If it is on the Planché level, we're through. Absolutely through, as Arthur says. Was Hoffmann any good? Does anybody know?"

"I'm not a judge," said Penny. "But I think he wasn't half bad. Mind you, music's not my thing. But when I was in London the BBC broadcast Hoffmann's *Undine* in a program called Early Romantic Operas, and of course I listened. Indeed, I took it on tape, and I have it here, if you're interested. Have you got the right sort of machine?"

It was Maria who took the tapes and put them in the hi-fi equipment that was concealed in a cupboard near the Round Table. Darcourt made sure that everybody had a drink, and the Cornish Foundation, in the lowest spirits it had known since its establishment, composed itself to listen. Nobody wore an expression of hope, but Powell was the least depressed. He was a theatre man, and was accustomed to abysses in the creative process.

It was Arthur who first was jolted into new life by the music.

"Listen, listen, listen! He's using voices in the Overture! Where have you heard that before?"

"They're the voices of the lover and the Water Sprite, calling to Undine," said Penny.

"If he goes on like that, maybe we're not in too much trouble," said Arthur. He was a musical enthusiast, a bad amateur pianist, and it was his regret that his Uncle Francis had not left him his enviable collection of musical manuscripts. He would then have had the uncompleted opera safe in his own hands.

"This is accomplished stuff," said Maria.

As indeed it was. The Cornish Foundation, according to individual musical sensitivity, roused themselves. Darcourt knew what he was hearing; he had first become acquainted with Francis Cornish because of a shared enthusiasm for music. Powell declared music to be one of the elements in which he lived; it was his desire to extend his experience as a director of opera that had made him urge the Foundation to consider putting *Arthur of Britain* on the stage. Hollier was the tin-eared one, and he knew it, but he had a feeling for drama and, though now and then he dozed, *Undine* was unquestionably dramatic. By the end of the first act they were all in a happier frame of mind, and demanded drinks as cheer, rather than as pain-killers.

Undine is not a short opera, but they showed no weariness, and heard it to the end. It was then almost four o'clock in the morning and they had been at the Round Table for nine hours, but except for Hollier they were alert and happy.

"If that's Hoffmann as a composer, it looks as if we were right on the pig's back," said Arthur. "I hope I'm not carried away by relief, but I think it's splendid."

"He truly does use the lyre of Orpheus to open the underworld of feeling," said Maria. "He used that phrase often. He must have loved it."

"Did you hear how he uses the wood-winds? Not just doubling the strings, as even the best Italians were apt to do when this was written, but declaring another kind of feeling. Oh, those magical deep wood-winds! This is Romanticism, right enough," said Powell.

"New Romanticism," said Maria. "You catch Mozartian echoes — no, not echoes, but loving recollections — and some Beethovenian beef in the big moments. And God be praised he doesn't wallop the timpani whenever he wants intensity. I think it's great! Oh, Arthur —" and she kissed her husband with relief and joy.

"I'm glad we heard his letter to Planché first," said Darcourt. "You know what he's getting at, and what he hoped to achieve in *Arthur*. Not music just to support stage action, but to be action in itself. What a shame he never got his chance to go ahead!"

"Well, yes; I don't want to pour cold water," said Hollier, "but as the least musical among you, I can't forget that we haven't a libretto. Assuming, as I am sure you do, that the Planché stuff is totally unusable. No libretto, and is there enough music to make an opera. Does anybody know?"

"I've been to the library for a look," said Arthur, "and there's quite a wad of music, though I can't judge what shape it's in. There are scribbles in German on some of the manuscript which seem to suggest action, or places where action would come. I can't read that old German script well enough to say much about it."

"But no words?"

"I didn't see any words, though I could be mistaken."

"Do you think we can really turn Schnak loose on this? Does she know German? I suppose she may have picked up some from her parents. Not poetic German, certainly. Nothing Romantic about the senior Schnaks," said Darcourt.

"I don't want to nag, but without a libretto, where are we?" said Hollier.

Powell was impatient. "Surely with all the brains there are around this table we can put together a libretto?"

"Poetry?" said Darcourt.

"Libretto poetry," said Powell. "I've read dozens of 'em, and the poetic heights are not enough to make you dizzy. Come on! Faint heart never made fair libretto."

"I'm afraid I'm rather the fifth wheel of the coach so far as music is concerned," said Hollier. "But the *Matière de Bretagne* is right in my line, and I have a pretty clear recollection of Malory. Anything I know is at your service. I can fake a late-medieval line as well as most people, I suppose."

"So there we are," said Powell. "Right on the pig's back, as Arthur so Celtically puts it."

"Oh, don't be hasty," said Hollier. "This will take some time to establish, even when we've decided which of the Arthurian paths we are going to follow. There are many, you know — the Celtic, the French, the German, and of course Malory. And what attitude do we take to Arthur? Is he a sun-god embodied in legend by a people half-Christianized? Or is he simply the *dux bellorum*, the leader of his British people against the invading Saxons? Or do we choose the refinement of Marie de France and Chrétien de Troyes? Or do we assume that Geoffrey of Monmouth really knew what he was talking about, however improbable that may seem? We can dismiss any notion of a Tennysonian Arthur: he was wholly good and noble and a post-Freudian audience wouldn't swallow him. It could take months of the most careful consideration before we decide how we are going to *see* Arthur."

"We're going to see him as the hero of an early-nine-teenth-century opera, and no nonsense about it," said Geraint Powell. "We haven't a moment to lose. I've made it clear, I think, that the Stratford Festival will allow us to mount ten or twelve performances of *Arthur* during its next season and I've persuaded them to slot it as late as possible. Late August — just a year from now. We've got to get cracking."

"But surely that's absurd," said Hollier. "Will the libretto be ready, not to speak of the music? And then I suppose the theatrical people will have to have a little time to get it up —"

"The theatrical people will have to be got under contract not later than next month," said Geraint. "My God, have you no idea how opera singers work? The best are all contracted three years ahead. A thing on this scale won't need the biggest stars, even if we could get them, but intelligent singers of the next rank won't be easy to find, especially for an unknown work. They'll have to shoehorn this piece into very tight schedules. And there's the designer, and all the carpentry and painting work, and the costumes — I'd better stop, I'm frightening myself!"

"But the libretto!" said Hollier.

"The libretto is going to have to hustle its stumps. Whoever is responsible for it must get to work at once, and be quick. The words have to be fitted to whatever music exists, remember, and that is tricky work. We can't fart around forever with sun-gods and Chrétien de Troyes."

"If that is your attitude, I think I had better withdraw at once. I have no desire to be associated with a botch," said Hollier, and took another very big whisky from the decanter.

"No, no, Clem, we'll need you," said Maria, who still cherished a tenderness for the man who had — it seemed so long ago now — taken her maidenhead, almost absent-mindedly. Not that, as a girl of her time, she had possessed anything so archaic as a maidenhead, but the word was suitable to the paleo-psychological spirit of Clement Hollier.

"I have a certain reputation as a scholar to protect. I am sorry to insist on that, but it is a fact."

"Of course we'll need you, Clem," said Penny Raven. "But in an advisory capacity, I think. Better leave the actual writing to old battered hacks like me and Simon."

"As you please," said Hollier, with drunken dignity. "I admit without regret that I have no theatrical experience."

"Theatrical experience is precisely what we're going to need, and lots of it," said Powell. "If I'm to see this thing through, I shall have to crack the whip, and I hope nobody will take offence. There are a lot of elements to be pulled together if we're going to have a show at all."

"As a member of the academic committee that is supposed to be midwife to this effort, I have to remind you that there is an element you've left out, that will have a big say in whatever is done," said Penny.

"Meaning?"

"Schnak's special supervisor. The very big gun who is coming to the university to be composer-in-residence for a year, for this express purpose," said Penny.

"Wintersen keeps hinting about that," said Darcourt; "but he's never mentioned a name. Do you know who it is, Penny?"

"Yes, I do. It's just been finally settled. No one less than Dr. Gunilla Dahl-Soot."

"Golly! What a name!" said Darcourt.

"Yes, and what a lady!" said Penny.

"New to me," said Arthur.

"Shame on you, Arthur. She's acknowledged to be the successor to Nadia Boulanger, as a Muse and fosterer of talent, and general wonder-worker. Schnak is a very, very lucky child. But Gunilla is also said to be a terror, so Schnak had better look out or we shall see some fur flying."

"From what point of the compass does this avatar appear?" asked Arthur.

"From Stockholm. Doesn't the name tip you off?"

"We are greatly privileged to have her, I suppose?"

"Can't say. Is she a Snark or a Boojum? Only time will tell."

(6)

ETAH IN LIMBO

I LIKE THAT MAN POWELL. He has the real professional spirit. My God, when I think what it was like for me, getting operas on the stage in Bamberg, and even in Berlin, and sometimes wondering where I would find enough musicians to make up the orchestra we needed! And what musicians some of them were! Tailors by day, and clarinetists by night! And the singers! The chorus were the worst. I remember some of them sneaking offstage when there was no work for them to do and sneaking back in three minutes, wiping their mouths with the back of a hand!

And wearing their underpants beneath their tights, so that the courtiers of Count Whoever-it-was looked as if they had just stumbled in from the wastes of Lapland. Things are much better now. Sometimes I can intrude myself into a performance of something by Wagner — Wagner who wrote so very kindly of me and admitted my influence in his splendid use of the leitmotif *— and, so far as a shade can weep, I weep with pleasure to see how clean all the singers are! Every man seems to have been shaved the very day of the performance. Every woman, even though fat, is not more than five months pregnant. Many of them can act, and they do, even if not well. No doubt about it, opera has come a very long way since my days in Bamberg.*

*To say nothing of money! The artists who appear in my **Arthur** will be able to go to the treasury every Friday night with confidence that a full week's salary will be forthcoming. How well I remember the promises, and the broken promises, of opera finance in my time. Of course, as director — and that meant conductor and sometimes scene-painter as well — I usually had my money, but it was wretchedly little money. These modern theatre people don't know they're alive, and when I consider their good fortune I sometimes forget that I am dead. As dead, that's to say, as anybody in Limbo is.*

*At last I begin to pluck up hope. I may not be in Limbo forever. If Geraint Powell puts my **Arthur** on the stage, and even five people stay till the end, I may win my freedom from this stoppage in my spiritual voyage, this* mors interruptus *(to give it a classical ring).*

My own fault, of course. If I died untimely, I must admit that I died by my own hand, though not as surely as if I had used the rope or the knife. Mine was death by the bottle, and by — well, enough about that. Death by Romanticism, let us call it.

But by the Almighty's great mercy, an existence in Limbo is not all tears of regret. We may laugh. And how I laughed when that woman professor — that is something new since my time, when a learned woman might be a bas bleu *but would never have thought of intruding herself into a university — when that woman professor, I say, read those letters from Planché to Kemble.*

They were new to me. I remember his letters, and the high spirits and assurance they gave off like a perfume. He was so certain that I, who had not written an opera in some time — seven years, was it — would welcome his jaunty assistance. But these letters, in which he reported our exchanges to Kemble, were quite new, and brought back all that trouble in a new and funny light. Poor Planché, industrious Huguenot, with his determination to do his best for Madame Vestris and her magnificent limbs. Poor Planché, with his certainty that an opera audience could not be persuaded to sit still while anything important was being played, or sung. Of course his notion of opera was bad Rossini, or Mozart defaced by that self-loving brigand Bishop. His Covent Garden was a theatre where nobody listened unless one of the Great Necks was shrieking or trumpeting; where people took baskets of cold grouse and champagne to their boxes and stuffed themselves during the music; where those of the right age — between fourteen and ninety — flirted and nodded, and sent billets doux from box to box, wrapped around little bags of sweets; where the soprano, if the applause was sufficiently insistent, would pause in the opera to sing some popular air; after my death it was often "Home, Sweet Home", which was Bishop's monumental contribution to the art of music; where a soprano's jewels — the real thing, achieved by lying complaisantly under the bellies of rich, old fumbling noblemen — were of as much interest as her voice; as the Great Neck declined, the Grande Poitrine became the object of interest, and the bigger it was the more diamonds it would accommodate. Service medals, jealous rivals called them.

In Germany — even in Bamberg — we knew a little better than that, and we were at work to beget Romanticism, and bring it to birth.

I wept — Oh yes, we can weep here, and often do — to hear my **Undine** *again, done better than I ever heard it in my lifetime. How good orchestral playing is now; hardly a tailor to be heard in the music the bas bleu conjured out of her astonishing musical machine.* **Undine** *was my last completed attempt to draw opera forward from the eighteenth century into the nineteenth. Not in the least rejecting Gluck and Mozart, but following them in our attempt to coax something more out of the unknown of man's mind into his consciousness. So we turned from their formal comedies and tragedies toward myth and legend, to release us from* the chains of classicism. **Undine** — yes, my wonderful tale of the water nymph who marries a mortal, and at last claims him for her underwater kingdom; what does it not say of the need for modern man to explore the deep waters that lie beneath his own surface? I could do it better now, I know, but I did it pretty well then. Weber — my generous, gentle friend Weber — praised the skill with which I had matched music to subject in a beautiful melodic conception. What praise from such a source!

Now, at long last, **Arthur** may come to something. No libretto, they say. Only the wind-eggs that Planché blew about so confidently. Where will they turn? Again, I put my faith in Powell. I think he knows more about the myth of Arthur than any of the others, especially the professors. Dare I hope that my music, so far as I was able to sketch it in, will set the tone for the work? Of course. It must.

I wish I understood everything they say. What does the bas bleu mean about a Snark or a Boojum? It sounds like some great conflict in the works of Wagner. Oh, this tedious waiting! I suppose this is the punishment, the torture, of Limbo.

III

SIMON DARCOURT sat in his study at Ploughwright College planning his crime. A crime it undoubtedly was, for he meant to rob first the University Library, and then the National Gallery of Canada. Princess Amalie had left him in no doubt; the price of the information she had about the late Francis Cornish was possession of the preliminary studies for the drawing which she was now using to sell her new line of cosmetics. She offered that drawing to the public as coming from the hand of an Old Master — though no particular Old Master was mentioned. But the delicacy of line, the complete command of the silver-point technique, and above all the evocation of untouched but not unaware virginal beauty, spoke in unmistakable terms of an Old Master hand.

Photographs of Princess Amalie had, for some years, appeared in the gossip portions of the fashionable magazines in which she advertised, and it was clear to anybody that this finely preserved aristocrat, perhaps in her fifties, was of the same family as the virgin child in the advertising picture. Of the same family, though obviously many generations separated them. Oh, the magic of aristocracy! Oh, the romance of family descent! How beauty passed, like a blessing, through four centuries! Aristocracy cannot, of course, be bought over the counter, but something of its magic might be imparted by

Princess Amalie's lotions and unguents and pigments. Ladies and, it was known, quite a few gentlemen hastened to put down their names for appointments with the Princess's skilled *maquilleuses* who would (it took a whole day) discover precisely which Old Master (the range was large and came down as near to the present time as John Singer Sargent) had dwelt upon their special type of beauty and had employed colours to preserve it for the ages — colours which only Princess Amalie could duplicate in cosmetics. It was very expensive, but certainly it was worth it thus to associate oneself with the great world of art, and the great world that the greatest artists had chosen to paint. To be seen as an Old Master type; was not that worth big money? "Selling like hot cakes" was the coarse term the advertising geniuses used to describe the success of the campaign. Don't wear the look of the latest fashion. Look like the Old Master subject you are, in your deepest soul, and at your exquisite best!

Obviously, if it leaked out that the Old Master drawing of Princess Amalie's ancestor was from the hand of a Canadian who had known her as a girl, millions of dollars would go straight down the drain. Or so it seemed to the advertising world. If some Nosy Parker, rummaging in the stacks of drawings preserved in the National Gallery of Canada, were to turn up preliminary drawings for the superb imposture, from the hand of the Canadian faker and scoundrel — he could be nothing less — the Princess, again in the idiom of the advertising world, would have egg all over her beautiful face. Or so it seemed to Princess Amalie, who was as sensitive as the world expects an aristocrat to be.

The Princess wanted those preliminary sketches, and the price she offered was information which, she hinted, would be the making of Simon Darcourt's life of the late Francis Cornish, connoisseur and benefactor of his country.

Darcourt yearned for that information with the feverish lust of a biographer. Without the slightest evidence that the

Princess could tell him anything important, he was convinced that she would do so, and was ready to dare greatly to find out what she knew. Surely — he felt it in his bones — it would fill in the great hole right in the middle of his book.

Much of the book was completed, in so far as a book can be completed when important information is still missing. He had written the concluding chapters, describing Francis's later years when he had returned to Canada, and played a role as a benefactor of artists, a connoisseur of international reputation, and a generous giver to the collection of contemporary and earlier paintings in the National Gallery. Indeed, he had left the Gallery all his portfolios of drawings, many of which were by undoubted early masters, and among which those preliminary sketches of Princess Amalie lay concealed. But a book about a collector and benefactor, however well written, is not necessarily a gripping story, and readers of biographies like their meat rare.

He had finished the early part of the book, about Francis's childhood and early years, and considering how little real information he had, it was a brilliant piece of work. Darcourt did not permit himself the use of the word "brilliant", for he was a modest man, but he knew it was well done, and that he had made bricks of substantial value with the wrong kind of straw. It was his good fortune that the late Francis Cornish was a man who never threw away or destroyed anything, and among his personal possessions — those which now were in the keeping of the University Library — were several albums of photographs taken by Francis's grandfather, the old Senator and founder of the family wealth. Old Hamish had been a keen amateur of photography and had made countless records of the streets, the houses, the workmen, and the more important citizens of Blairlogie, the Ottawa Valley town in which Francis had spent his early years. Every picture was carefully identified in the Senator's neat Victorian handwriting and there they were — the grandmother, the beautiful mother and the distinguished but oddly wooden father, the aunt, the family doctor, the priests, even Victoria Cameron, the Senator's cook, and Bella-Mae, Francis's nurse. There were many pictures of Francis himself, a slight, dark, watchful boy, already showing the handsome, clouded face that had caused Princess Amalie to call the adult Francis *le beau ténébreux*. On the evidence of these photographs, which the Senator liked to call his Sun Pictures, Simon Darcourt had raised a convincing structure of Francis's childhood. It was as good as much research, aided by Darcourt's lively but controlled imagination, could make it.

As biography goes, it was excellent, for biography has to rely heavily on some evidence but a great deal on speculation, unless there are diaries and family papers to provide firmer ground. But biography at its best is a form of fiction. The personality and sympathies of the biographer cannot be sifted out of what is written. Darcourt had no diaries. He had a handful of school reports from Francis's Blairlogie schools, and from Colborne College, where he had gone at a later date; there were some lists and records of grades from the university days. Of what was personal there was little, but Darcourt had done wonders with what he had.

Nevertheless, the book lacked a heart, to make it live. Did Princess Amalie have anything of that heart, however rheumatic or slow, that would give life to his book, and fill out the story of those years when, so far as he knew, Francis had messed about in Europe as an art student? Darcourt sometimes came near to desperation. A receipted bill from a bawdy-house would have filled him with gladness. Now, here was a chance, and a pretty good chance, to find information that would bridge that horrible gap between the aspiring young Canadian who had apparently gone into hiding after Oxford, and had emerged in 1945, when he was part of the commission that inspected pictures and works of art that had gone astray during the war, and were to be returned whenever possible to their original owners. The price of that information was crime. No other name for it — crime.

Darcourt did not hesitate from moral scruple. He was a clergyman, of course, though he lived as a professor of Greek; he still wore his Roman collar from time to time, but it had long ceased to be a fetter on his spirit. He now regarded himself as a biographer, and the scruples of a biographer are peculiar to the trade. Any hesitation he felt was not about how could he bring himself to steal, but how could he steal without being found out? "Prof Nabbed In NatGal Heist" — he could see the headlines in the gloating press. The exposure of a trial would be horrible. Of course he would not go to prison. Only tax-evaders go to prison nowadays. But he would be fined, and doubtless compelled to report monthly to a parole officer as to how he was getting on with his new job, teaching Latin for Berlitz.

How was it to be done? Sherlock Holmes, he recalled, sometimes solved crimes by thinking himself into the criminal mind, and thus discovering method, if not motive. But so far as he could adventure into the criminal mind, no solution to his problem occurred. Whenever he tried it, all that came up on the computer screen of his imagination was a picture of himself, wearing a black eye-mask, dressed in a turtleneck sweater and a slouch cap, emerging from the National Gallery carrying over his shoulder a large sack plainly marked SWAG. This was farce, and what he needed was a strong injection of elegant comedy.

Did he see himself then as a fictional figure, Darcourt the Clerical Cracksman? Beneath the sober dress of the cleric and the modest dignity of a professor of classics lurks the keen mind that plots thefts that baffle the keenest among the police — was that his character? Would that it might be so, but those smart crooks in fiction lived in a world where thought possessed absolute power, and careful plans never went wrong. Darcourt was well aware that he did not live in any such world. To begin with, he had discovered, now that he was well into middle age, that he did not know how to think. Of course he could pursue a logical path when he had to, but in his personal affairs his mental processes were a muddle, and he arrived at important conclusions by default, or by some leap that had no resemblance to thought, or logic, or any of the characteristics of the first-rate fictional criminal mind. He made his real decisions as a gifted cook makes soup: he threw into a pot anything likely that lay to hand, added seasonings and glasses of wine, and messed about until something delicious emerged. There was no recipe and the result could be foreseen only in the vaguest terms. Could one plan a crime like that?

To change the metaphor — he was always changing metaphors and trying not to mix them ludicrously — he ran off in the viewing-chamber of his mind scraps of film in which he saw himself doing various things in various ways until at last he found a plan of action. How was he to accomplish his crime?

It must be a twofold criminal job. To the best of his recollection, there were five drawings that were studies for the finished portrait of the Princess Amalie as a girl, in the large bundle of Francis Cornish's Old Master portfolios, and those were what he had to abstract and take to New York. He knew that the portfolios had not been carefully examined, and certainly not catalogued, in the storage room where they lay at the National Gallery in Ottawa. But uncatalogued as they were, those drawings had probably been seen in what he hoped was a cursory inspection, and they would be missed. But would they be remembered in any detail? They had probably been numbered. Indeed, he had submitted a loose catalogue himself when, as Francis Cornish's executor, he had sent that mass of material to Ottawa. "Pencil sketch of a girl's head" — that sort of thing. Oh, if only the hasty, determined Arthur had not been so insistent that his uncle's pictures and books and manuscripts and other valuable miscellany should be cleared out of his huge apartment and storehouse in Toronto in the shortest possible time! But Arthur had so insisted, and pinching pictures from a large public gallery was tricky work.

However — and a very big and hopeful "however" it was — a great mass of Francis Cornish's personal papers had been sent to the University Library, and among those papers were pictures that seemed to Darcourt, when he bundled them up, to be of personal rather than artistic merit. Some were pictures that belonged to the Oxford period of Francis's life, when he had been drawing from models as well as making copies of Old Master drawings in the Ashmolean Museum. Darcourt had assumed, without asking anybody for an opinion, that the National Gallery would not want such stuff, accomplished though much of it was. Could he make a switch? Could he sneak a few pictures from the Library and put them in the Gallery portfolios, and would anyone be the wiser? That seemed to be the solution to his problem, and all that remained was to decide how he might manage it.

The morning after the Round Table had met to hear Penny Raven read what existed of Planché's libretto for *Arthur of Britain*, Darcourt was sitting in his dressing-gown gazing at his interior movie-show when he heard a spluttering, snorting, farting uproar in the street outside his study window, and he knew that it could only be the noise that Geraint Powell's little red sports car made when it was brought to a halt. In a very short time there was a banging on his door that was certainly Powell, who brought a Shakespearean *brio* to quite modest daily tasks.

"Have you slept?" he said, as he pushed into the study, threw a heap of papers out of an armchair, and flung himself into it. The chair — a good one, which had cost Darcourt a lot of money in the shop of an antique pirate — creaked ominously as the actor lolled in it, one leg thrown over a delicate arm. There was about Powell a stagy largeness, and whatever he said was said with an actor's precision of speech in an unusually resonant voice, from which the Welsh intonation had not wholly disappeared.

Darcourt said that no, he had not slept very much, as he had not come home until almost five in the morning. He had found the conversation, and hearing *Undine*, exciting and his rest had been scant. He knew, of course, that Powell wanted to tell him about his own rest, as now he did.

"I didn't sleep a wink," he said. "Not a wink. I have been turning this business over and over in my head and what I see before us is a gigantic obstacle race. Consider: we have no libretto, an unknown amount of music, no singers, no designs, no time reserved with all the artificers and carpenters and machinists we shall need — nothing but high hopes and a theatre. If this opera is not to be the most God-Almighty ballocks in the history of the art, we shall have to work day and night from now until it is on the stage, and at the mercy of those rapists and child-abusers, the critics. You think I exaggerate? Ha ha" — his laugh would have filled a large theatre, and it made the windows in Darcourt's study ring — "From the depths of no trivial experience I assure you that I do not exaggerate. And upon whom are we depending, you and I? Eh? Upon whom are we depending? Upon Arthur, the best of fellows but innocent as the babe unborn in all of this world we are entering with our hands tied behind our backs. Arthur is armed only with a fine managerial spirit and barrels of money. Who next? This kid whom I have never met who is to come up with an opera score, and her supervisor — the woman with the grotesque name, who is probably some constipated pedant who will take an eternity to get anything done. There's Penny, of course, but she's an outsider and I don't know how far to trust her. Of the scholarly Professor Hollier I forbear to speak; his obvious inability to distinguish between his arse and his elbow — speaking theatrically —

rules him out as anything but a pest, easily dealt with. What a gang!"

"You say nothing of Maria," said Darcourt.

"I could speak cantos of rhapsodic verse about Maria. She is the blood of my heart. But of what use is she in such a situation as this? Eh? Of what conceivable use?"

"She is the strongest possible influence with Arthur."

"You are right, of course. But that is secondary. Why did she not stop Arthur when he decided to embark on this rashest of rash enterprises?"

"Well — why didn't you? Why didn't I? We were swept away. Don't underestimate the power of Arthur's enthusiasm."

"Once again, you are right. But then you are so often right. And that is why I am talking to you now. You are the only member of the Round Table who seems to have enough wits to come in out of the rain. Excepting myself, naturally."

Darcourt's heart sank. This sort of flattery usually meant that some time-consuming task that nobody else would undertake was going to be dumped on his desk. Powell went on.

"You are the man in the Cornish Foundation who gets things done. Arthur gets ideas. He shoots them off like rockets. The rest of us are hypnotized. But if anything really happens, you are the man who makes it happen, and you can patiently persuade Arthur to listen to common sense. You know what you are, boy? They call that thing the Round Table, and if it's the Round Table who are you? Eh? No one but Myrddin Wyllt, the great king's counsellor. Merlin, that's who you are. You've seen it, of course. How could you miss it?"

Darcourt had not seen it. He wanted Powell to develop this idea, so flattering to himself, so he pretended ignorance.

"Merlin was a magician, wasn't he?"

"He looked like a magician to those other morlocks at the

Round Table because he could do something besides fight and play Chase the Grail. In every great legend there are a lot of heroes and one really intelligent man. Our Arthur's a hero; people admire him and eat out of his hand. I suppose Hollier is a hero in his own way. I'm a hero, fatally flawed by intelligence. But you are no hero. You're Merlin, and I want you to work with me to get this wild scheme into some sort of workable order."

"Geraint —"

"Call me Geraint *bach*. It signifies friendship, understanding, complicity."

"Bach? You mean as in Johann Sebastian Bach?"

"Old Johann Sebastian was born a German, but in spirit he was a Welshman. The word is a diminutive. It's as if you were calling me Geraint, my darling, or Geraint, my pretty one. Welsh is a great language for intimacies and endearments. I'll call you Sim *bach*. It will signify our nearness in spirit."

Darcourt had never been aware of any special nearness of spirit between himself and Powell, but Powell was leaning forward in his chair, his lustrous eyes gleaming, and complicity coming out of him like heat out of a stove. Well, here goes, Simon thought. He could always retreat if the intimacy became outrageous.

"So what is it you want, Geraint *bach*?"

Powell spoke in a hiss. "I want a *dramatis personae*, a cast of characters, and I want it right away."

"Well, I don't suppose that presents insuperable problems. Even Planché had to agree that an opera about Arthur has to have Arthur somewhere in the cast. And if you have Arthur, you must have Queen Guenevere, and a few knights of the Round Table. And Merlin, I presume. You can certainly count on the opera including those, whatever turn it may take."

"Aha! You grasp it at once! I knew you would. You are a golden man, Sim *bach*. And you see what that means? We must have the Operatic Four. Soprano — Guenevere, of course, though I dislike that Frenchified version of the name. I always think of her as Gwenhwyfar. Much finer, you agree? But too difficult for the thick-tongued English-speakers. Now — who's your contralto? There has to be one, you know."

"Oh, dear. Let's see? Hm. Morgan Le Fay, do you think?"

"Of course! Arthur's wicked sister. A contralto, obviously. All wicked women in opera must have those rich, enchanting low notes. Now — who's my tenor?"

"Surely Arthur himself?"

"No. Arthur must have authority. A baritone, I think. A fine, velvety bass-baritone. Make him both a tenor *and* a cuckold and you lose all sympathy, and Arthur must compel sympathy. But we need an even deeper bass for quartets as well as the plot."

"That must be Modred, who destroys Arthur."

"Precisely."

"But no tenor? Can you have an opera without a tenor?"

"Of course. The public expects a tenor. Must be Lancelot, the seducer. Tenors are great seducers."

"All right. That gives you the four you want. Five, as a matter of fact."

"So — there we are. We'll want another woman for Elaine, the Lily Maid. Better be a nice mezzo — good for pathos but not deep enough for villainy. And a few tenors and basses for the Knights of the Round Table, but they are really just Chorus, and not hard to find."

"You make it all sound simple."

"Not simple at all, Sim *bach*. I must get on the phone at once and see who I can round up for these parts. I told them so last night. Singers aren't picked up at the last minute. They're worse than hockey-players; you have to get them under contract, or at least under written agreement, as far ahead as you can do it."

"But won't the musical people — Schnak and this woman

with the strange name — want some say? I know, and you know, that we have no libretto. How can you hire singers when you have no story and no music?"

"Must be done. Can't wait. And anyhow, we have the skeleton of a libretto."

"We have? Since when?"

"Since last night when I lay tossing in my bed, pulling it together. We have a story. You can't bugger about with the story of Arthur. I have a skeleton of the plot. All it needs is some words and music. And that's where you come in, old Merlin. You must hustle 'em up and get it on paper as soon as dammit."

"Powell — sorry, Geraint *bach* — have you told anybody but me?"

"Not yet. But we're to meet the great lady, the genius, the Muse, the shepherdess of Schnak, at dinner on Saturday night. Didn't anybody tell you? Well, they will. And then I'll tell her what the plot of *Arthur of Britain* is to be and you and Pretty Penny must start feeding her words as fast as you can go."

"How simple you make it sound."

"Aha — irony! I love your irony, Sim *bach*. It is what first drew me to you, boy. Well, I'm more happy than I can say that you agree, and I'll go at once and get on the phone. It's going to cost a fortune in phone bills. I send them to you, I suppose."

Geraint seized both Darcourt's hands and wrung them. Then he drew the astonished Simon to his breast and gave him a Shakespearean hug, during which he brushed a cheek against Simon's, exhaling a lot of last night's whisky, as though in an ecstasy of relief, and dashed out the door. Surprisingly soon afterward he was heard in the street, roaring abuse at some engineering students who had gathered to snoop under the hood of his car, and with snorts and hootings he was gone.

Greatly depleted in spirit, Darcourt sat down to think about his crime. Was it a crime? The law would certainly think so. The University would undoubtedly think so, for to rob the Library would create a general coldness toward himself, though criminality might not be quite enough to justify the revocation of his professorship. A tenured professor could commit the Sin Against the Holy Ghost and get away with it, if he could find the right lawyer. Still, in decency he would have to resign. Robbing the National Gallery was something else. That was crime, real crime.

Nevertheless, the law was not everything. There was a thing called natural justice, though Darcourt was not certain where it resided. Had he not been one of the late Francis Cornish's executors, chosen by Francis Cornish himself presumably because he was expected to use his judgement in doing what the dead man would wish? And would not the dead man want the best possible story of his life written by the friend and biographer best qualified to tell it?

Well — would he? Francis Cornish had been a very odd man, and there were many corners of his character into which Darcourt had never probed or wished to probe.

That was beside the point. Francis Cornish was dead, and Darcourt was alive. A Charter of Rights for the Dead might appeal to Penny Raven, but no true biographer wants to hear about it. Darcourt had in full measure the vanity of the author, and he wanted to write the best book he could, and a good book was a better thing for his dead friend than any pallid record of scanty fact. Crime it must be, and let the consequences be as they would. The book came before everything.

As Darcourt thought in this vein, allowing all sorts of visions of crime, and Francis Cornish, and Princess Amalie, and a scene in a law court in which Darcourt defended his action to a robed judge, in whose intelligent eyes understanding could be read, he was conscious that other images were popping into view on that mental movie-show, and they were related to what Geraint Powell had said about the opera and the necessary figures to make it a reality.

There had been slight mention of Merlin. Why not? Was Merlin so trivial a figure that the plot could be managed without him? Or could the role be played by any hack, any singer recruited from a church choir at the last moment? He would have something to say about that when Geraint unfolded his opera plot at dinner on Saturday night.

Darcourt had long known that he was a man fated to do much of the world's work when other people took the credit for it, but he was not without self-esteem.

No Merlin? Was that how Geraint *bach* saw the story of Arthur? Not if he, Simon Darcourt, was to play the role of Merlin in private life. He'd show 'em!

But for the moment, crime must be given his best energies.

(2)

NO TIME LIKE THE PRESENT. Darcourt made a phone call to the librarian in charge of special collections, an old friend. A man whom he would not, for the world, deceive, except when his book was at stake.

"Archie? Simon here. Look — I've run into a little matter in connection with my book. My life of Francis Cornish, you know. I want to verify something about his Oxford life. Would there be any objection to my taking a look among the papers we sent to you?"

No objection whatever. Come when you please. This afternoon? Certainly. Would you like to use my office? No, no need to disturb you. I'll just look at them in the storage, or wherever they are.

That was the worry. Where were they? Would he have to

look at them in a room with a lot of sub-librarians and other snoops hanging around? Not likely, but not impossible. With luck he might be able to use one of those little cubicles near a window, in which some favoured graduate students were occasionally allowed to spread their papers about.

Into the Library with a light step. Nod to right and left with the assurance of a well-known, greatly trusted member of faculty. Stop at Archie's room and pass the time of day. Listen to Archie's groans about the lack of funds for cataloguing. The Cornish stuff he would find just as he had bundled it up for the Library. But have no fear; it would be properly catalogued as soon as funds could be found. Might the Cornish Foundation be interested in funding that project? Darcourt assured Archie that he thought the Cornish Foundation would certainly be interested, and he would put the matter before them himself. Oh, by the way, would Archie like him to leave his briefcase in the office? Yes, yes, he knew that he was not a likely suspect — ha ha — but one should not expect other people to observe rules that one did not observe oneself. To which Archie agreed, and with each man somewhat sanctimoniously respecting the other's high principle, the briefcase was left in a chair.

Thus, cloaked in righteousness, Darcourt went into the large room, filled with steel racks, in which the Cornish papers, among many others, were stored. A young woman who was working at the slow task of cataloguing showed him where they were, and whispered — why whispered? there was nobody else in the room, but it was a place that seemed to call for whispering — that there was a nice quiet spot at the back of the room, with a big table where he could spread out the papers he wished to examine. He knew that this was not regular, that he should declare what he wanted even though it might be difficult to find; but after all, it was he who had brought the papers to the Library in the first place, and he was a generous member of the Friends of the Library, and he should be shown all possible courtesy. Nothing like a good reputation when you are about to commit a crime.

The crime took no time at all. Darcourt knew precisely which of the big bundles he was looking for, and in a moment he had opened it, and found the group of drawings he wanted.

They were drawings Francis Cornish had done in his Oxford days, and most of them were copies of minor Old Masters he had made when learning the technique which had been one of his chief sources of pride. By the most laborious and greatly talented practice, he had found the way to draw with the costly silver pencil on the carefully prepared paper. As works of art, the drawings were of little interest. Fine student work, no more.

There were some, however, which were in the old silver-point technique, but differently labelled — for Francis had labelled every copy of an Old Master with great care, naming the master, or that prodigiously productive artist *Ignotus*, and the date upon which the copy had been made. But several were labelled more simply: "Ismay, November 14, 1935", or some date reaching into the spring of 1936.

Several of them were heads, or half-lengths, of a girl not precisely beautiful, but of a distinguished cast of feature. Others were of the same girl, nude, lying on a sofa, or leaning on a mantelpiece. There was something about them that made it abundantly clear that they had been drawn by a loving hand. The curves of neck and shoulder, waist and breasts, hips, thighs and calves, were rendered with an exquisite care that set them apart from the work of an art student faced with a good model. Nor had the technique the Old Master remoteness: it spoke of desire, here and now. But the face of Ismay did not speak of love. In a few of the drawings it was petulant, but in most it wore a look of amusement, as though the model felt something like pity, and a measure of superiority, toward the artist. In these there was nothing of the accomplished deadness of the Old Master copies. They were alive, and they were the work of a man who had ceased to be a student.

Who was Ismay? She was Mrs. Francis Cornish, one of the many figures in his biography about whom Darcourt could discover nothing. Or very little. The daughter of Roderick and Prudence Glasson of St. Columb Hall, in Cornwall; a girl who had left Oxford (Lady Margaret Hall) without a degree after a single year; a girl who had married Francis Cornish in St. Columb's Church on September 17, 1936; a girl who thenceforward seemed to have no existence, so far as documents or other evidence was concerned. A girl whom Darcourt had come upon by accident, and identified by research, for Francis had never spoken of her.

The biographer had done his scholarly best. He had written to Sir Roderick Glasson at the Foreign Office in London, asking for details about his sister, and had received a cold reply saying that so far as Sir Roderick knew, his sister Ismay had died in the Blitz, in a northern city, probably Manchester, and that nothing was known of her, as it was impossible to identify many bodies found in that destruction, and many had never been recovered.

So this was Francis Cornish's wife as she appeared before their marriage. A girl born to fascinate, and doubtless to be loved by a man of romantic disposition. But what had happened to Ismay? She was part of the gap in the middle of Francis Cornish's life that tormented Darcourt and made his task as a biographer a nagging burden.

Darcourt could not stop long to admire. He did not want the friendly sub-librarian to approach him with offers of help, or a cup of coffee. Which to take? The heads, obviously. The nudes were too compelling to escape notice even by a hasty examiner. Darcourt, who had a weakness for female beauty that was not wholly rooted in the feelings of an amateur connoisseur, would greatly have liked to take one of them for himself, but that would be dangerous. The Clerical Cracksman must show self-denial and austerity in what he was doing. Only the heads.

So, with a rapidity that he had practised that morning as he dressed, he took off his jacket and his waistcoat — he was in clerical garb and the waistcoat was one of those broad black expanses of ribbed silk that Anglicans call an M.B. waistcoat, meaning Mark of the Beast because of its High Church and Romanist implications — and lowered his trousers. From under his shirt at the back he took a transparent plastic envelope measuring eighteen inches by twelve, slipped the drawings into it, and shoved it under his shirt again. Up with the trousers, on with the M.B., which had a convenient back strap that held the envelope firmly in place, on with the jacket, and all was completed.

"Thank you very much," he said to the sub-librarian; "I've bundled everything up ready to go back on the shelf." And he smiled in answer to her smile as he left the room.

"Many thanks, Archie," he called to his friend, as he picked up his briefcase.

"Not at all, Simon. Any time."

Out of the Library, step as light as ever, went the Clerical Cracksman, half of his crime completed. But not wholly completed. He must not go tearing back to his rooms at Ploughwright, like a guilty thing, to hide away his swag. No; he went to the Faculty Club, seated himself in the reading-room, and called for a beer. There was only one other member in the reading-room, and that member was to be his alibi, if one should be needed. The person who had seen him come there on his way back from the Library, as innocent as a new-laid egg.

The other member also had a beer, for it was a warm day. He lifted his glass to Darcourt.

"Cheers," said he.

"Here's to crime," said the Clerical Cracksman, and the other member, a simple soul, sniggered at such a jest from a clergyman.

(3)

"I LOOK UPON YOU as a daring group, a party of adventurers of extraordinary courage, set upon great risk. Perhaps the word for you is doom-eager," said Dr. Gunilla Dahl-Soot, as the Cornish Foundation sat down to dinner at the Round Table.

"That's a fine Scandinavian word, but surely rather negative, Doctor?" said Arthur, at whose right hand the guest of honour was seated.

"No, not in the least. It is realistic. You must know that never has any opera or play about King Arthur succeeded with the public, or with the world of art. Never. Not one."

"Didn't Purcell write a pretty good opera about Arthur?" said Maria.

"Purcell? No. It is not an opera. I would call it almost a *Posse mit Gesang*, a sort of vaudeville or fairy-piece. It has some interesting pages, but it has not travelled," said the Doctor, with immovable gloomy conviction.

"Perhaps we shall succeed where others have failed," said Arthur.

"Ah, I admire your courage. That is in part what has brought me here. But courage alone is not enough. Certainly not if you follow Purcell. His *Arthur* is too full of talk. All the action is in speech, not in music. The music is mere decoration. That is not opera. An opera is not talk. Indeed, there should be no talk. Music throughout."

"Well, isn't that very much under your control?" said Arthur.

"It may be so. Only time will tell," said the Doctor and drained her glass of wine at a draught. She had had her full share of the martinis before dinner; she had three at least but appeared to be thirsty still.

"Let's not begin the evening in a spirit of defeat," said Maria. "I've prepared a very special dinner. It's an Arthurian dinner. You are going to get what Arthur's court might have eaten — making necessary allowances."

"Thank God for necessary allowances," said Hollier. "I doubt if I could get through a sixth-century meal. What are we having?"

"What a question! Don't you trust me?" said Maria. "You are beginning with poached salmon, and I'm sure Arthur had excellent salmon."

"Yes, but. this Hochheimer — do you call that Arthurian?" said the Doctor. "I thought King Arthur drank beer."

"You forget that Arthur was a Cambro-Briton, with five centuries of Roman civilization behind him," said Maria. "I'll bet he drank very good wine, and took enormous care about having it transported to Camelot."

"It may be," said the Doctor, draining another large glass. "This is a good wine." She spoke as if uncertain about what might follow.

Dr. Gunilla Dahl-Soot was not an easy guest. She seemed to bring an atmosphere of deep autumn into the penthouse, though it was still no more than early September. The dinner party felt uneasily that it might decline into a hard winter if the Doctor did not cheer up.

The Round Table had not known what to expect, and nobody had foreseen anything in the least like the Doctor. It was not that she was eccentric in any of the ways that might be expected in an academic who was also a distinguished musician. She was beautifully dressed, her figure was a marvel of slim elegance, and her face was undeniably handsome. What made her strange was that she seemed to have stepped out of a past age. She wore a finely designed version of male dress; her jacket was in appearance a man's tight-waisted blue frock coat, and her tapering green velvet trousers descended toward elegant patent leather boots; she wore a very high, soft collar bound with a flowing cravat, and on her hands were a number of big, masculine rings. Her thick, straight brown hair was parted in the middle and hung to her shoulders, framing a long, distinguished, deeply melancholy face. She's got herself up as Franz Liszt before he put on his abbé's cassock, thought Darcourt. Does she get her clothes from a theatrical costumer? But odd as she is, she's dead right for *what* she is. Who is she modelled on? George Sand? No, she's much too elegant. Darcourt, who was interested in women's clothes, and what went under them, was prepared to be fascinated by the Doctor, but her first ventures in conversation made it clear that the fascination might be a depressing experience.

"I'm glad you like our wine," said Arthur. "Let Simon fill your glass. Do you like Canada? That's a silly question, of course, but you must forgive me; we always ask visitors if they like Canada as soon as they step off the plane. Don't answer."

"But I will answer," said the Doctor. "I like what I have seen. It is not strange at all. It is like Sweden. Why not? We are geographical near neighbours. I look out of my window and what do I see? Fir trees. Maple trees already turning to red. Big outcroppings of bare rock. It is not like New York. I have been in New York. It is not like Princeton, where I have also been. It has the smell. It smells like a northern land. Do you have terrible winters?"

"They can be difficult," said Arthur.

"Ah," said the Doctor, smiling for the first time. "Difficult winters make very great people, and great music. I do not, generally speaking, like the music of lands that are too far south. I will have another glass of the Hochheimer, if I may."

This woman must have a hollow leg, thought Darcourt. A

boozer? Surely not, with that ascetic appearance. Let's tank her up and see what happens. As an old friend of the family he had made the martinis, and his was the task of serving the wine at dinner; he went to the sideboard and opened another bottle of the Hochheimer and handed it to Arthur.

"Let us hope that you can charm some fine northern music out of the fragments of Hoffmann's score," said Arthur.

"Let us hope. Yes, hope is the thing upon which we shall build," said the Doctor, and down went the Hochheimer — not at a gulp, for the Doctor was too elegant to gulp — but without a pause.

"I hope you don't think it rude of us to speak of the opera so soon," said Maria. "It is so much on our minds, you see."

"One should always speak of what is uppermost in one's mind," said the Doctor. "I want to talk about this opera, and it is uppermost in my mind."

"You've looked at the music?" said Arthur.

"Yes. It is sketches and indications of the orchestration, and themes that Hoffmann wanted used to suggest important things in the plot. He seems somewhat to have anticipated Wagner, but his themes are prettier. But it is not an opera. Not yet. This student was too enthusiastic when she told you it was an opera. It is very pretty music, but not foolish. Some of it could be Weber. Some could be Schumann. I like all that. I love those wonderful failed operas by Schumann and Schubert."

"I hope you don't see this as another failed opera."

"Who can say?"

"But you aren't going to set to work with failure as your goal?" said Maria.

"Much may be learned from failure. Of course that is the theme of the opera, so far as I can see. *The Magnificent Cookold*, he called it. Am I right to think a cookold is a deceived husband?"

"You are. The word is pronounced cuckold, by the way."

"As I said. Cookold. — Ah, thank you. This Hochheimer is really very good. — But, now — a cookold; why is it a man? Why not a woman?"

"You are just as right to say cookold as cuckold," said Professor Hollier, who had also been getting into the Hochheimer with quiet determination. "That was a Middle English form. The French was, and still is, *cocu*. Because of the notorious goings-on of that bird." He bowed to Dr. Dahl-Soot over his raised glass.

"Ah, you are a man who knows language? Very good. Then why is it masculine? A person deceived in marriage. Are not women also deceived in marriage? Again and again and again? So why no word for that, eh?"

"I do not know how you would form a feminine from cuckold. Cuckoldess? Clumsy. Or how about she-cuckold?"

"Not good," said the Doctor.

"Does it matter? It is Arthur who is the cuckold in the Arthurian legends," said Penny Raven.

"So it is. This Arthur was a fool," said the Doctor.

"Oh, come on! I won't have that," said Maria. "He was a noble man, bent on lifting the whole moral tone of his kingdom."

"But still a cookold. He did not pay enough attention to his wife. So she gave him a big pair of horns."

"Perhaps there is no feminine of cuckold because the female of the species does not grow horns, however much she is deceived," said Hollier, solemnly.

"She knows a better trick than that," said the Doctor. "She gives him the ambiguous baby, eh? He looks in the cradle and he says, What the hell; this is a funny-looking baby. By God, I am a cookold."

"But in the Arthurian legends there is no child of the adultery of Guenevere and Lancelot. So he could not have exclaimed what you have just exclaimed, madam."

"Not madam. I prefer to be called Doctor. Unless after a long time we get on close terms; then perhaps you will call me Nilla."

"Not Gunny?" said Powell.

"I despise Gunny. But this Arthur — this stupid king — he does not need a baby to tell him. His wife and his very good friend tell him straight out. We have been in the bed while you have been lifting the moral tone. It could be a comedy. It could be by Ibsen. He was often funny like that."

Maria thought the time had come to change the direction of the conversation at the Round Table. "My next course is truly Arthurian. Roast pork, and with apple sauce. Very popular dish at Camelot, I am certain."

"Pork? No, never pork! It must be roast boar," said the Doctor.

"My butcher didn't have a good roasting boar," said Maria, perhaps a little too sharply; "you will have to put up with very good roast pork."

"I am glad it isn't roast boar," said Hollier. "I have often eaten roast boar in my travels, and I don't like it. A heavy, dense flesh and a great provoker of midnight melancholy. In me, anyhow."

"You have not had good roast boar," said the Doctor. "Good roast boar is excellent eating. I do not find it provokes to melancholy."

"How would you know?" said Penny Raven.

"I do not understand you, Professor Raven."

"You seem to be melancholy without any roast boar," said Penny, who had not been neglecting the Hochheimer. "You are depressing us about our opera, and you are disparaging Maria's wonderful roast pork."

"If I depress you, I am sorry, but the fault may not be mine. I am not a merry person. I take a serious attitude toward life. I am not a self-deceiver."

"Nor am I," said Penny. "I am enjoying Maria's fine Arthurian feast. She is Arthur's lady and I declare her to be a splendid *hlafdiga*."

"A fine what?" said the Doctor.

"A fine *hlafdiga*. It is the Old English word from which our word 'lady' is derived, and it means the person who gives the food. A very honourable title. I drink to our *hlafdiga*."

"No, no, Penny, I must protest," said Hollier. "A *hlafdiga* does not mean a lady. That is an exploded etymology. The *hlafdiga* was the dough-kneader, not the loaf-giver as you ignorantly suppose. You are muddling up the Mercian with the Northumbrian word."

"Oh, bugger you, Clem," said Penny. "The modern word 'lady' comes from *hlafdiga*; the *hlafdiga* was the loaf-giver and down through *leofdi* and thus down to *lefdi* and so to 'lady'. Don't try to teach me to suck eggs, or *aegru* if you want it in Old English. The *hlafdiga* was the wife of the *hlaford* — the lord, you pretentious ass — and thus his lady."

"Abuse is not argument, Professor Raven," said Hollier, with tipsy dignity. "The *hlafdiga* could be quite a lowly person —"

"Possibly even of Gypsy origins," said Maria, with a good deal of heat.

"For Christ's sake, are we going to get any pork?" said Powell. "Or are we going to get into an etymological wrangle while everything goes cold? I hereby declare that Maria is a lady in every sense of the word, and I want something to eat."

"There are no ladies now, thank God," said Dr. Dahl-Soot, holding out her glass. "We are all on equal footing, distinguished only by talent. Genius is the only true aristocracy. Is that a red wine you are pouring, Professor Darcourt? What is it? Let me see the bottle."

"It is an excellent Burgundy," said Darcourt.

"Good. You may pour."

"Of course he may pour," said Powell. "What do you think this is? A restaurant? That's the wine there is and that's the wine you are going to get, so shut up."

Dr. Dahl-Soot drew herself up in her chair. "Monsieur, vous êtes une personne grossière."

"You bet your sweet ass I am, Gunny, so you mind your manners and be a good girl."

There was a pause, during which Darcourt hovered over the Doctor's wineglass. Unexpectedly she burst into loud laughter.

"I think I like you, Powell," she said. "You may call me Nilla. But only you." She cast an excluding eye over the rest of the table. Then she raised her glass of Burgundy toward Powell, smiled with an elegant sweetness, and drained it to the bottom.

"More," she said, thrusting it at Darcourt, who now was attending to Penny Raven.

"You wait your turn, Nilla," said Powell.

"You are teaching me manners?" said the Doctor. "Which manners? In my country the guest of honour is allowed certain freedoms. But I see how it is. You think you are a lion-tamer and probably a lady-killer. Let me tell you that I am a lion who has eaten many tamers, and you shall not kill me because I am not a lady."

"Funny thing. That had just begun to pop into my mind," said Penny Raven. "But if you are not a lady, how do you describe yourself?"

"Not long ago we spoke of the aristocracy of genius," said the Doctor, whose glass Darcourt had hastened to fill, out of turn.

"Now Penny, no fighting," said Maria. "It isn't the custom for the lady to propose toasts, but as Arthur is busy carving this authentically Celtic piglet, I shall claim the privilege of a *hlafdiga* and propose the health of Dr. Gunilla Dahl-Soot; I declare her to be not less than a countess in the aristocracy of genius. May we enjoy the proof of her genius."

The health was drunk, with enthusiasm by all but Penny Raven, who muttered something into her glass. The Doctor rose to her feet.

"My dear new friends," she said; "you do me honour and I shall not fail you. Have I teased you just a little bit? Perhaps I have. It is my way. I am a great joker, you should know. There often lurks behind my words some *double entendre* which you may not understand, perhaps until much later. Perhaps even in the night, you wake up laughing. Ah, the Doctor, you say. She is deep, deep, deep. You have drunk to my health. I shall drink back at you. You, reverend sir, with the wine — may I have something in my glass? Ah, thank you. — Though I am not sure about wine at this Arthurian feast. I am not sure that our *hlafdiga* is right in saying that Arthur had wine at his court. Surely it was that stuff they made with fermented honey — "

"Mead," said Hollier. "You mean mead."

"Just so. Mead. I have drunk it. And it is nasty, sweet, awful stuff, let me tell you. I casted up my stomach — "

"Not surprising, the way you go at it," said Penny, with a smile which did not entirely rob her remark of offence.

"I can drink anybody here under the table," said the Doctor, with grave belligerence. "Man, woman, or dog, I can drink him under the table. But I want no nasty words here. I want to drink to you all. Though as I say, I cannot believe that King Arthur had wine — "

"I've just thought of it," said Hollier. "The Welsh did have wine in the ancient days. You remember the old cry — *Gwin o eur* — Wine from the gold! Not only did they have wine, but they drank it from golden vessels. Not out of cow-horns, like a road company doing the banquet in *Macbeth*. *Gwin o eur!*"

"Clem, you're drunk!" said Penny. "And that's a very dubious, ill-founded quotation."

"And your Welsh is terrible!" said Powell.

"Is that so? If this were not a friendly gathering I'd let you have one right on the nose for that, Powell."

"Would you, boy?" said Powell. "I dare you."

"Yes. Right on the snot-box," said Hollier. He half rose, as if to fight, but Penny pulled him back into his chair. "The Welsh are a despicable people," he said in a murmur.

"That's right. Real scum. Like Gypsies," said Powell, winking at his hostess.

"Am I, or am I not, making a speech?" said the Doctor. "Am I returning thanks for this splendid dinner, so exquisitely chosen and so elegantly served under the lustrous eye of our *hlafdiga*?" She bowed deeply toward Maria. "Yes, I am. So I bid all you rowdies and learned hoggleboes keep silence, until I am finished. I love this country; it is, like my own land, a socialist monarchy and thus unites the best of the past and the present; I love my hosts, they are true patrons of art. I love you all; you are comrades in a great adventure, a Quest for something a man longed for but did not achieve. I drain my glass to you." And she did so, and sat down, rather heavily.

It must have been the martinis, thought Darcourt. They all drank martinis before dinner as if they never expected to see drink again. The Doctor certainly had three, because I gave them to her myself. Now, following her speech of thanks and her toast to Maria, the Doctor was silent, and ate a large helping of roast pork and applesauce and a variety of vegetables — probably not Arthurian but nobody questioned them — in a mood that could only be called morose. The other guests murmured, more or less politely, to one another.

The Canadians — Arthur, Hollier, Penny Raven, and Darcourt — were abashed by what the Doctor had said; they closed up at any imputation of high motives, of splendid intention, of association with what might be great, and therefore dangerous. They were not wholly of the grey majority of their people; they lived in a larger world than that, but they wore the greyness as a protective outer garment. They did not murmur the national prayer: "O God, grant me mediocrity and comfort; protect me from the radiance of Thy light." Nevertheless, they knew how difficult and disquieting too bold a spirit might be. They settled to their plates, and made small talk.

In the hearts of the two who were not Canadians, Maria and Powell, the Doctor's toast struck fire. Powell was possessed by ambition, but not the ambition that puts the reward and the success before the excellence of the achievement. He meant to use his colleagues, and the Cornish Foundation, for his own purposes, but he thought the purposes good, and would provide ample reward and acclaim for anyone associated with them. He would ply the whip, and drive everyone to the last inch of their abilities, in order to get what he wanted. He knew he was dealing with a group who were primarily academics, and that the horses must amble before they could be made to gallop. But he would have his way, and in the Doctor he sensed an ally.

As for Maria, she felt, for the first time since her marriage, a stirring of real adventure. Oh, it was wonderful to be Mrs. Arthur Cornish, and to share the thoughts and ambitions of a man of fine — yes, noble, she would say noble — spirit. There was nothing she could want in a man that she did not find in Arthur. And yet — was it the northern nature, or the Canadian greyness — there was just the least hint of chill about her marriage. They loved. They trusted. Their sexual life was a warm manifestation of love and trust. But, if only for a moment, there might be some hint of the improbable, of a relaxation of control. Maybe this opera would bring that. It was risky. It was a long time since she had sniffed the sharp, acrid smell of risk. Not since the time of Parlabane, over a year ago. Who would have thought of regretting Parlabane?

And yet — he had brought something rare and pungent into her life.

What her place might be in this opera adventure she did not know. She was not a musician, though she was musical. She would not be allowed to work on the libretto; Penny and Simon had that marked off for themselves. Was she to do no more than write cheques, as an official of the Cornish Foundation? Money, as a host of grant-seekers assured her, was seminal. But it was not true seed of her seed.

Darcourt was eating and wool-gathering at the same time, a frequent trick of his. I wonder what we should look like, he thought, if a mischievous genie were to pass over this table and strike us all naked? The result would be better than at most tables. Maria would be a stunning beauty, clothed or naked. Hollier was absurdly handsome for a professor (but why? Must a professor always be a broomstick or a tub?) and without his clothes would reveal, in middle age, a Michelangelesque symmetry, agreeable to his splendid head. Arthur would be sturdy; passable but not astonishing. Powell would be less than he seemed in his clothes; like many an actor he was slight, almost thin, and his head was the best part of him. As for Penny Raven — well, there were the remains of a fine woman about Penny, but to Darcourt's probing eye the breasts were a little languid, and there was a hint of a rubber tire around the waist. The sedentary life of the scholar was running Penny down, and her jolly face was sagging a little at the chops.

As for the Doctor — well, he was reminded of a remark he had heard a student make about another student, a girl: "I'd as soon go to bed with a bicycle." The Doctor, under the fine, Chopinesque get-up, might have the wiriness, the chill, the impracticable resistance of a bicycle to a sexual approach, but she was probably interesting. Any breasts? One cannot get beneath the coat. Any hips? The skirts of the coat concealed them, whatever they might be. But an elegantly formed waist. Long, elegant feet and hands. The Doctor might be very interesting. Not that he was the man who would find out.

As for himself, Professor the Reverend Simon Darcourt, he had to admit that he did not peel well. He had been a fatty from his mother's womb and now the stretch-marks on his belly were the wound stripes of countless lost battles against overweight.

The table is almost silent, he thought; an angel must be passing. But not the stark-striking genie. The servant removed his plate and he got up to attend to the next service of wine. It was to be champagne. Who would be the first to protest that whatever wine Arthur of Britain may have served at the Round Table, it was certainly not champagne? Nobody. They accepted it with murmurs of pleasure.

Maria allowed the next course to be served without comment. It was a pretty confection of eggs and cream stiffened with something elusive.

"What is this?" asked the Doctor.

"Nobody can say that it isn't a genuinely Arthurian dish," said Maria. "Its name is washbrew."

The company was reduced to silence. Nobody liked to ask what washbrew might be, but when they heard the name their minds misgave them.

Maria said nothing for a minute or two, then she relieved their apprehension.

"It can't hurt you," she said. "It is just very fine oatmeal, with a few things to give it a nice taste. Geraint's Welsh ancestors called it flummery."

"Buttermilk and flummery say the bells of Montgomery," sang Powell, to the tune of "Oranges and Lemons".

"The flavour," said Penny. "Elusive. Delicious! Reminds me somehow of childhood."

"That is the hartshorn," said Maria. "Very Arthurian. You were probably given hartshorn candy for sore throats."

"But not just hartshorn," said Hollier. "There is another flavour, and I think it's brandy."

"I am certain Arthur had brandy," said Maria. "and if anybody contradicts me I shall send it back to the kitchen and get you some raw turnips to chew, and that will be authentically Early Britain, and I hope it will satisfy all you purists. The champagne should help you to worry down a few turnips."

"Please don't be annoyed, dear," said Arthur. "I'm sure nobody means to be disagreeable."

"I am not so sure, and I'm sick and tired of having my dinner tested for archaeological accuracy. If my intuition tells me something is Arthurian, it's thereby Arthurian, including champagne, and that's that!"

"Of course," said the Doctor, and her tone was as smooth as the cream they were eating. "We are all being intolerable, and I demand that everyone stop it at once. We have insulted our *hlafdiga*, and we should be ashamed. I am ashamed. Are you ashamed, Professor Raven?"

"Eh?" said Penny, startled. "Yes, I suppose I am. Anything served at Arthur's Round Table is thereby Arthurian, isn't it?"

"That is what I like about you Canadians," said the Doctor; "you are so ready to admit fault. It is a fine, if dangerous, national characteristic. You are all ashamed. And I am ashamed, too."

"But I don't want anybody to feel ashamed," said Maria. "Just happy. I do wish you could be happy and not nag and quarrel all the time."

"Of course, my dear," said Hollier. "We are ungrateful beasts, and this is a delightful dinner." He leaned across Penny Raven to pat Maria's hand, but he misjudged his distance and got his sleeve in Penny's flummery. "Oh, hell," he said.

"About this opera," said Arthur. "I suppose we ought to give it some thought?"

"I've given it many hours of thought," said Powell. "The first thing we must have is a story. And I have a story."

"Have you so?" said the Doctor. "You have not seen the music, and you have not talked to me, but you have a story. I suppose we are to be permitted to hear the story, so that we little people may set to work on it?"

Powell drew himself up in his chair, and swept the table with the smile with which he could melt fifteen hundred people in a theatre.

"But of course," said he. "And you must not suppose that I wish to impose my story on anyone, and least of all on the musicians. That is not the way we librettists work. We know our place in the hierarchy of operatic artists. When I say I have a story, I mean only that I have a basis on which we may begin discussions of what this opera is to be about."

How well he manages us, thought Darcourt. He uses at least three levels of language. There is his Rough Demotic, in which he tells the Doctor to bet her pretty little ass on something, and another form of that is the speech in which he calls me "Sim *bach*", and "boy", and reverses his sentence structure in what I suppose is a translation from his cradle Welsh; and there is his Standard English, in which he addresses the world of strangers, about whom he cares little; and there is his Enriched Literary Speech, finely pronounced and begemmed with quotations from Shakespeare and the more familiar poets, and soaring at need into a form of rhapsodic, bardic chant. It's a pleasure to be bamboozled by such a man. What lustre he gives to the language that most of us treat as a common drudge. What is he going to give us now? The Enriched, I suppose.

"The story of Arthur," said Powell, "is impossible to gather into a single coherent tale. It comes to us in an elegant French form, and a sturdy, darkly coloured German form, and in Sir Thomas Malory's form, which is the richest and most enchanting of all. But behind all of these forms lies the great Celtic legend, whence all the elegance and strength and enchantment take their life, and in the brief story I offer you for this opera you may be sure I have not forgotten it. But if we are to have an opera that will hold an audience, we must above all have a strong narrative that can carry the weight of music. Music can give life and feeling to an opera, but it cannot tell a tale."

"By God, you are right," said the Doctor. Then she turned to Darcourt. "Champagne," she hissed.

"Yes! *Gwin o eur!*" said Hollier.

"Now — listen. You will agree, I hope, that there can be no tale of Arthur that leaves out Caliburn, the great magic sword; I do not like the later form Excalibur. But — economy! We cannot go back to the beginning of his life to tell about how he came by Caliburn. So I propose a device that was put in my head by Hoffmann himself. You remember how in the overture to *Undine* he strikes the right note at once by using the voices of the lover and the water-god, calling the name of the heroine? I propose that almost as soon as the overture to *Arthur of Britain* begins, we raise the curtain on a vision scene — you do it behind a scrim which makes everything misty — and we see the Magic Mere, and Arthur and Merlin on its shore. At a gesture from Merlin the great sword arises from the water, gripped in the hand of an unseen spirit, and Arthur seizes it. But as he is overcome with the grandeur of the moment, there arises from the Mere a vision of Guenevere — the name means White Ghost, as you surely know — presenting the scabbard of Caliburn; Merlin bids Arthur accept the scabbard and makes Arthur understand — don't worry, I'll show 'em how to do it — that the scabbard is even more important than the sword, because when the sword is in its scabbard there is peace, and peace must be his gift to his people. But as Arthur turns away, the visionary Guenevere shows by a gesture that the scabbard is herself, and that unless he knows her value and her might, the sword will avail him nothing. You follow me?"

"I follow you," said the Doctor. "The sword is manhood and the scabbard is womanhood, and unless they are united there can be no peace, no splendour through the arts of peace."

"You've got it!" said Powell. "And the scabbard is also Guenevere, and already Arthur is losing Guenevere because he trusts in the sword alone."

"The *symbolismus* is very good," said the Doctor. "Aha, the sword is also Arthur's thing — you know, his male thing — what do you call it — ?"

"His penis," said Penny.

"Not much of a word. Latin — means his tail. How can it be a tail when it is in front? Have you no better word in English?"

"Not in decent use," said Darcourt.

"Oh — decent use! I spit on decent use! And the scabbard is the Queen's thing — what is your indecent word for that?"

Nobody quite liked to reply, but Penny whispered in the Doctor's ear. "Middle English," she added, to give it a scholarly gloss.

"Oho, *that* word!" said the Doctor. "We know it well in Sweden. That's a better word than that silly tail-word. I see that this will be a very rich opera. More champagne, if you please. Perhaps the best thing would be to put a bottle here beside me."

"Do I understand that you are telling the spectators even before the opera begins that there can be peace in the land only if there is sexual unity between the King and Queen?" said Hollier.

"Not at all," said Powell. "This Prologue tells that the greatness of the land depends on the uniting of masculine and feminine powers, and that the sword alone cannot bring the nobility of spirit Arthur seeks. Don't worry. I can get it across with some very nice lighting. There will be no raunchy shoving the sword in and out of the scabbard to please the people who think that sex is just something that happens in bed."

"More to that game than four bare legs in a blanket," said Penny, nodding sagely.

"Exactly. It is a union of two opposite but complementary sensibilities. Maybe that is what the Grail means. I leave that to the librettists, if they think it useful."

"The wine in the gold," said Maria.

"I never thought of the Grail like that," said Penny. "Interesting idea."

"Even the blind pig sometimes finds an acorn," said Powell, bowing toward her. "Now, to get into the opera proper.

"Act One begins with Arthur's evil sister, Morgan Le Fay (who is an enchantress and thus understandably a contralto), trying to worm secrets out of Merlin: who shall be Arthur's heir? Merlin squirms a bit, but he can't resist a fellow magician, and he confides that it must be someone born in the month of May, unless Arthur should have a child of his own. Morgan Le Fay is exultant, for her son Modred was born in May, and as the King's nephew he is the nearest heir. Merlin warns her not to be too sure, for Arthur loves Guenevere greatly, and a child is very likely. Not if Arthur risks his life in war, says the contralto.

"Then we have an assembly of the Knights of the Round Table: Arthur gives them their charge — they are to disperse and seek the Holy Grail, which will bring lasting peace and greatness to Britain. The Knights accept their duty, and are sent their different ways. But when Lancelot presents himself the King refuses to give him a direction; he must remain behind to govern because the King is eager to go on the Quest himself, bearing the great Caliburn; he draws it and sings of his overmastering ambition. Guenevere pleads with Arthur to let Lancelot go on the Quest, for she fears that the guilty love she and Lancelot have for each other may bring shame to the kingdom. But Arthur is resolute, and as he is being armoured for his Quest — very spectacular that will be — Morgan Le Fay steals the scabbard and Arthur, in his exalted state, refuses to wait until it is found, and goes on the Quest, declaring that bravery and strength, symbolized by the naked sword, will suffice. Everybody buggers off in search of the Grail, and Guenevere is filled with dread, and Morgan Le Fay is exultant. End of the Act."

"What about Modred?" said Maria. "We haven't heard anything of him yet."

"He's one of the Knights, and he doubts the Grail," said Powell. "He can scowl and sneer in the background."

"Strong stuff, but is it nineteenth-century?" said Hollier. "A bit too psychological, perhaps?"

"No," said the Doctor. "Nineteenth-century need not mean simple-minded. Look at Weber's *Der Freischutz*. The nineteenth century had psychology too. We didn't invent it."

"Very well," said Hollier. "Go on, Powell."

"Act Two is where we get into really big operatic stuff. Begins with a scene of the Queen's Maying; she and her ladies are in the forest, gathering the May blossoms. I think she should ride a horse. A horse is always a sure card in opera. Suggests that no expense has been spared. If the horse has been given an enema an hour before curtain time, and there are enough people to lead it, even a coloratura soprano should be able to stick on its back long enough for a very pretty effect. In the forest she meets Lancelot, and they sing of their passion — after the horse and the maidens have gone, of course. But Morgan Le Fay is eavesdropping, disguised as a hag, an old witch of the forest. She cannot contain herself. She bursts upon the couple and denounces them as traitors to the King; they protest their innocence and devotion to

Arthur. When the witch has gone, Merlin appears, and warns the lovers of the evil that lurks in the May blossoms, and the danger of the month of May. But they do not understand him."

"Stupid, like all characters in opera," said Hollier.

"Enchanted, like all people in love," said the Doctor. "Characters in opera are really just like ordinary people, you know, except that they show us their souls."

"If a witch and a sorcerer warned me about something, I think I would have enough wits to heed them," said Hollier.

"Probably. That is why there has never been an opera about a professor," said the Doctor.

"That is only Scene One of the Act," said Powell. "Now we have a quick change — I know how to do it — to a Tower up the river above Camelot, where Guenevere and Lancelot have gone and consummated their love. They are in ecstasy, but in the river below the Tower there appears a Black Barge guided by Morgan Le Fay, and bearing Elaine, the Lily Maid of Astolat, who accuses Lancelot of being false to her, and says that she carries his child. Guenevere is horror-struck, when Lancelot confesses that it is indeed true, but that he lay with Elaine when he was under a spell, and that he suspects the spell was cast upon him by Morgan Le Fay, who can get in a lot of very effective mockery in the ensuing quartet. But Guenevere is desolate and when the barge sweeps on, down the river to Camelot, her reproaches drive Lancelot mad. Now of course in Malory he is mad for years, and dashes about the forest banging into trees and getting into all sorts of injurious mischief, but we have no time for that, so he rages for a while. This could be quite a novelty; a Mad Scene (à la *Lucia*) for a tenor. Lancelot proposes to Guenevere that he should kill himself, as expiation for his faithlessness, even though it was not precisely his fault. No, says Guenevere; there shall be no needless killing, and she herself puts his sword back into its scabbard. As the scene concludes, a messenger arrives in hot haste, with news that there has been a great battle, and that Arthur has been killed. His body is being brought back to Camelot for burial. End of scene."

"Nobody can say that this opera lacks for incident," said Maria.

"Operas devour incident," said the Doctor. "Nobody wants to listen to people going into musical ecstasies about love for two hours and a half. Go on, Powell. What next? You have killed Arthur. That is bad. The character who gives the name to the opera should not peg out until the end. Look at *Lucia di Lammermoor*; the last act is tedious. No Lucia. You'll have to arrange something different."

"No I won't," said Powell. "The next and final Act is in the Great Hall of Arthur's palace in Camelot, and Arthur returns triumphant, though wounded. He tells of the battle in which he has been engaged, and how a Knight in black armour appeared who challenged him to single combat. But when he seemed to be overcome, and fell from his horse, he drew his shield before him just as the Black Knight was about to give him the *coup de grâce* — "

"The what?" said Hollier.

Penny flew at him. "The *coup de grâce*, Clem. You know: the knockout. Do pay attention. You keep nodding off."

"I do nothing of the sort."

"Yes you do. Sit up straight and listen."

"As I was saying," said Powell, "the Black Knight was about to give Arthur the *coup de grâce* when he saw on the shield the painting of Our Lady, whereupon he turned and fled, and Arthur, though wounded, was spared. Arthur sings in praise of Our Lady, who saved him at need. The Eternal Feminine, you see."

"*Das Ewig-Weibliche*," said the Doctor. "That ought to teach the masculine idiot. Go on."

"Everybody is immensely chuffed that Arthur has returned. But Arthur is uneasy. He knows he has an inveterate enemy. And this is where several Knights appear, bringing in Modred, the Black Knight, and Arthur is stricken that his nephew and the child of his dear sister should have sought his life. Modred mocks him as an idealistic fool, who holds honour greater than power, and displays the scabbard of Caliburn, without which he says honour is powerless, and the sword must settle everything. He challenges the wounded King to fight, and though Guenevere, who has seized the scabbard, begs him to sheathe Caliburn, the King will not hear of it. He and Modred fight, and once again the King is wounded. As he lies dying, Guenevere and Lancelot confess their guilty love. Now — this is the culmination of the whole affair — Arthur shows himself greatly magnanimous, and declares that the greatest love is summed up in Charity, and not in sexual fidelity alone; his love for both Guenevere and Lancelot is greater than the wound they have given him. He dies, and at once the scene changes to the Magic Mere, where we see Arthur floating out into the mists in a barge, attended only by Merlin, who sheathes Caliburn for the last time and casts it back into the water from which it first came, as Arthur nears the Isle of Sleep. Curtain."

There was applause from Darcourt and Maria. But Hollier was not content. "You drop too many people along the way," he said. "What happens to Elaine? What about her baby? We know that baby was Galahad, the Pure Knight who saw the Grail. You can't just dump all that after Act Two."

"Oh yes I can," said Powell. "This is an opera, not a Ring Cycle. We've got to get the curtain down around eleven."

"You've said nothing about Modred being the incestuous child of Arthur and Morgan Le Fay."

"No time for incest," said Powell. "The plot is complicated enough as it stands. Incest would just mess things up."

"I will have no part of any opera that includes a baby," said the Doctor. "Horses are bad enough on the stage, but children are hell."

"People will feel cheated," said Hollier. "Anybody who knows Malory will know that it was Sir Bedevere, not Merlin, who threw Caliburn back into the water. And it was three Queens who bore Arthur away. It's all so untrue to the original."

"Let 'em write to the papers," said Powell. "Let the musicologists paw it over for the next twenty years. We must have a coherent plot and we must wind it up before the stagehands go on overtime. How many people in an opera audience will know Malory, do you suppose?"

"I have always said the theatre was a coarse art," said Hollier, with tipsy dignity.

"That is why it is a live art," said the Doctor. "That is why it has vitality. Out of the ragbag about Arthur we have to find a straight story, and Powell has done so. For myself, I am very well pleased with his *schema* for the opera. I drink to you, Powell. You are what I call a real pro."

"Thank you, Nilla," said Powell. "I can't think of a compliment that would please me better."

"What's a real pro?" whispered Hollier to Penny.

"Somebody who really knows his job."

"Somebody who doesn't know Malory, it seems to me."

"I like it tremendously," said Arthur; "and I am glad you agree, Doctor. Whatever you say, Clem, it's miles ahead of that rubbish about Nob and Tit we were listening to when Penny discovered Planché's stuff. At last I feel as if a huge weight had been lifted from my shoulders. I was terribly worried."

"Your worries have only begun, boy," said Powell. "But we'll meet 'em as they come. Won't we, Nilla *fach*?"

"Powell, you go beyond what is decent," said the Doctor. "How dare you speak to me in that way!"

"You misunderstand. The word is a Welsh endearment."

"You are gross. Do not attempt to explain."

"*Fach* is the feminine of *bach*. I say 'Sim, *bach*' and it is as if I said dear old Sim."

"I want nothing to do with old dears," said the Doctor, who was again becoming belligerent. "I am a free spirit, not the scabbard of any man's sword. My world is a world of infinite choice."

"I'll bet," said Penny.

"You will oblige me by confining yourself to the libretto, which is your business, Professor Raven," said the Doctor. "Have you comprehended the *symbolismus*? This will be wonderfully modern. The true union of man and woman to save and enlarge mankind."

"But how can it be wonderfully modern if it is true to Hoffmann and the early nineteenth century?" said Hollier. "You forget that we are to restore and complete a work of art from a day long past."

"Professor Hollier, you are wonderfully obtuse, as only a very learned man can be, and I forgive you. But for the love of Almighty God, and for Our Lady whom Arthur bore on his shield, I beg you to shut up and leave the artists' work to the artists, and stop all this scholarly bleating. Real art is all one, and speaks of the great things of life, whenever it is created. Get that through your great, thick, brilliantly furnished head and shut up, shut up, *shut up*." The Doctor was roaring, in a rich contralto that might have done very well for Morgan Le Fay.

"All right," said Hollier. "I am not insulted. I am above the ravings of a drunken termagant. Go ahead, the whole pack of you, and make asses of yourselves. I withdraw."

"You mean you withdraw till next time you feel like sticking your oar in," said Penny. "I know you, Clem."

"Please. Please!" Now it was Darcourt who was shouting. "This is unbecoming an assembly of scholars and artists, and I won't listen to any more. You know what the Doctor is saying, don't you? It's been said since — well, at least since Ovid. He says somewhere — in the *Metamorphoses*, I think — that the great truths of life are the wax, and all we can do is to stamp it with different forms. But the wax is the same forever —"

"I have it," said Maria. "He says that nothing keeps its own form, but Nature who is the great renewer is always making up new forms from old forms. Nothing perishes in the whole universe — it just varies and renews its form —"

"And that's the truth that underlies all myth," shouted Darcourt, waving at her to be quiet. "If we are true to the great myth, we can give it what form we choose. The myth — the wax — does not change."

The Doctor, who had been busy lighting a large black cigar she drew from a silver case, said to Powell: "I am beginning to see my way. The scene where Arthur forgives the lovers will be in A minor, and we shall dodge back and forth in and out of A minor right until the end when the magician sees Arthur sailing off to his Island of Sleep. That's how we'll do it."

"Of course that's how we'll do it, Nilla," said Powell. "A minor comes right up out of the wax, hot and strong. And don't fuss about the opera being true to the nineteenth century. It will be artistically true, but you mustn't expect it to be literally true because — well, because a literal fidelity to the nineteenth century would be false. Do you see?"

"Yes. I see very well," said Arthur.

"Arthur, you are a darling," said Maria. "You see better than any of us."

"Well — I see many difficulties," said Hollier.

"I see the wax, and I am sure you two pros see the form, and I'm very happy about it," said Darcourt.

"God bless you, Sim *bach*," said Powell. "You are a good old Merlin, that's what you are, boy."

"This Merlin — this magician — is more important in the

story you have told, Powell, than I had expected," said the Doctor. "In opera terms, I should say he is Fifth Business, and the singer will have to be chosen with great care. What voice, do you think? We have a bass villain, and a baritone hero and a tenor lover, and a contralto villainess and a coloratura heroine and a mezzo simpleton — that deceived girl, what's her name, Elaine. What for Merlin? What would you say to a *haute contre* — you know, one of those high, unearthly voices?"

"A counter-tenor, you mean? What could be better? Makes him unlike any of the others."

"Yes, and very useful in ensembles. Those male altos are like trumpets, only strange —"

"The horns of elfland faintly blowing," said Powell.

"You seem to be pleased with the libretto just as Geraint has outlined it," said Arthur.

"Oh, it will need some small changes here and there as we work," said the Doctor. "But it is a fine *schema*; coherent and simple for people who can't follow a difficult plot, but with plenty of meaning underneath. An opera has to have a foundation; something big, like unhappy love, or vengeance, or some point of honour. Because people like that, you know. There they sit, all those stockbrokers and rich surgeons and insurance men, and they look so solemn and quiet as if nothing would rouse them. But underneath they are raging with unhappy love, or vengeance, or some point of honour or ambition — all connected with their professional lives. They go to *La Bohème* or *La Traviata* and they remember some early affair that might have been squalid if you weren't living it yourself; or they see *Rigoletto* and think how the chairman humiliated them at the last board meeting; or they see *Macbeth* and think how they would like to murder the chairman and get his job. Only they don't think it; very deep down they feel it, and boil it, and suffer it in the primitive underworld of their souls. You wouldn't get them to admit anything, not if you begged.

Opera speaks to the heart as no other art does, because it is essentially simple."

"And what do you see as the deep foundation of this one?" said Arthur.

"It's a beauty," said Powell. "Victory plucked from defeat. If we can bring it off, it will wring the heart. Arthur has failed in the Quest, lost his wife, lost his crown, lost life itself. But because of his nobility and greatness of spirit when he forgives Guenevere and Lancelot, he is seen to be the greatest man of all. He is Christ-like; apparently a loser, but, in truth, the greatest victor of them all."

"You'll want a first-rate actor," said Maria.

"Yes. And I have my eye on one, but I won't tell you until I've got his name on a contract."

"It's the alchemical theme," said Maria. "Gold refined from dross."

"Do you know," said Hollier, "I believe you're right. You have always been my best student, Maria. But if you get that out of an authentic nineteenth-century stage piece, you'll be alchemists indeed."

"We are alchemists," said the Doctor. "It's our job. But now I must go home. I must be fresh tomorrow to go over all this Hoffmann stuff again with what we have been talking about fresh in my mind. I must do that before I talk with this little Schnakenburg, whoever she is. And so I shall say good-night."

Upright as a grenadier and without a stumble, the Doctor circled the room, shaking hands with everyone.

"Let me call you a taxi," said Darcourt.

"No indeed. The walk will refresh me. It cannot be more than two miles, and the night is very fresh."

Saying which, the Doctor seized Maria in her arms and gave her a lingering kiss. "Do not worry, little one," she said. "Your dinner was very good. Not authentic, of course, but

better than the real thing. Like our opera." And away she
went.

"My God," said Penny, when the Doctor had gone, "did
you see what that woman drank? And not once — not once in
six hours — did she go to the loo. Is she human?"

"Very human," said Maria, wiping her mouth with a
handkerchief. "She stuck her tongue almost down my
throat."

"She didn't kiss me, you observe," said Penny. "Not that I
care. Raunchy old lesbian lush. You watch yourself, Maria.
She has her eye on you."

"That cigar! I'll taste it for a week!" said Maria, and
picking up her glass of champagne she gargled noisily, and
spat into an empty coffee cup. "I never thought of myself as
attractive in that way."

"You're attractive in so many ways," said Penny, tearfully. "It isn't fair."

"When you sink into self-pity," said Hollier, "it's time for
me to go home."

"I'll drive you, Clem," said Penny. "I have a large, forgiving soul, even if you are a rotten old bastard."

"Thank you, Professor Raven," said Hollier; "I would
prefer not to be driven by you. Last time you drove me home
we were spoken to by a policeman because of your driving."

"He was just being officious."

"And when we arrived outside my house you honked your
horn derisively to waken my mother. No, Penny, no. I won't
drive with you when you've got your paws in the sauce."

"Paws in the sauce! I like that! Who was falling asleep
while Geraint was talking? You bloody old woman, Clem!"

"In this age of female liberation, I do not understand why
'old woman' is still considered an insult." And with careful
dignity Hollier took his leave, closely followed by Penny, who
was squealing incoherent abuse.

"She'll drive him, of course," said Darcourt. "Clem is as tight as the bark to a tree. He can never resist a free ride. I'll give them a minute, then I'll go too."

"Oh, Simon, when do I see you again?" said Maria. "I've got something to tell you. Crottel wants to come again and nag about Parlabane's miserable book."

"I'll be here when you need me," said Simon, and went.

"What do you make of the Doctor, Geraint?" said Arthur to the lingering guest.

" 'Oh, she doth teach the torches to burn bright!' " said Powell. "I'm mad for Old Sooty. We shall get on like a house afire — literally like a house afire."

"She won't yield to your charm," said Maria.

"Exactly. That's why we'll work well together. I despise easy women." And, kissing Maria on the cheek, he went.

Maria and Arthur looked around their large room. The candles on the Round Table were guttering. In the middle stood the Platter of Plenty, from which no guests had taken anything, whether from sixth-century scruple or not it was impossible to guess. Like all dinner tables, after prolonged dinners, it was a melancholy sight.

"Don't worry, my darling," said Arthur. "It was a wonderful dinner, and a great success, really. But I never really understand your university friends. Why do they quarrel so?"

"It doesn't mean anything," said Maria. "It's just that they can't bear anybody else to have an advantage, even for a moment. That woman stirred them up."

"She's a disturber, no doubt about it."

"A good disturber, would you say?"

"As she said herself, we must hope," said Arthur, and led his wife off to bed. Or rather, to their separate beds, for Arthur was still not fully himself.

(4)

ETAH IN LIMBO

OLD SOOTY! Does Powell really understand Dr. Gunilla Dahl-Soot if he can speak of her thus? Yet I believe it is meant to be affectionate, and is just his theatrical way; theatre people have little reverence — except when they look in the mirror.

The Doctor fills me with hope. Here is someone I can understand. She knows the lyre of Orpheus when she hears it, and does not fear to follow where it may lead.

I love the Doctor. Not as a man loves a woman, but as an artist loves a friend. She reminds me gloriously of my dearest friend on earth, Ludwig Devrient. A very fine actor, and the most sympathetic and dearest of men.

What great nights we had together, in Lutter's tavern, just across the square from the house in which I lived. And why was I not in my house? Why was I not at the domestic hearth with my dear, faithful, long-suffering wife Michalina?

I think it was because Michalina loved me too much. Dear girl, when I was writing my tales of horror and grotesquerie, and my nerves were red-hot and I thought my mind might lose itself forever in the dangerous underworld from which my stories came, she would sit by my side, and keep my glass filled, and sometimes hold my hand when I began to tremble — for I did tremble when the ideas came too fast and were too frightening — and I swear it was she who kept me from madness. And how did I reward her? Certainly not with blows and harsh words and the brutality of a ruffian, as so many husbands do. When I was a judge, I heard awful tales of domestic tyranny. A man may be the most respectable of bourgeois to his acquaintances, but a brute and a devil at home. Not I. I loved Michalina, I respected her, I gave her whatever my earnings, which were not trifling, could command. But I was always conscious that I pitied her, and I pitied her because she was so devoted to me, never questioned me, treated me as a master rather than a lover.

Not that it could have been otherwise. Too soon after my marriage I *took a pupil, Julia Marc, and I loved her with all my heart and soul; all the entrancing women in my stories are portraits of Julia Marc.*

It was her voice. I was teaching her to sing, but there was little enough to teach, for she had such a gift and such a voice as comes rarely in anyone's experience. Oh, I could refine her taste, and show her how to phrase her music, but as I sat at the harpsichord I was lost in a dream of love, and would have made a fool of myself, or perhaps a Byronic demon lover of myself, if she had given me any encouragement. She was sixteen, and she knew I loved her, though not how profoundly, because she was too young, and the devotion of such a man as I was seemed to her to be in the natural order of things. Very young girls think themselves made to be loved, and they may even be kind to their lovers, but they do not really understand them, and I think her secret dream was of some young officer, wondrous in a uniform, with a maddening moustache, who would turn her bowels to water with his valour and his aristocratic ways. So what was the music-master, a little man, with a strange, sharp face, who made her tune her scales until she sang with a melting purity and never strayed from the key? A nice old fellow, nearly twenty years older than herself, and at thirty-six already with some grey hairs in the parenthetic side-whiskers that framed his rat-like face. But I loved her until I thought I might die of it, and Michalina knew, and never spoke a jealous word or a reproach.

So what came of that? When she was seventeen, Julia's hard-headed, Philistine mother arranged a good marriage for her to one Groe-pel, who was nearly sixty, but rich. I suppose she could imagine no finer future for her daughter than to be a rich widow. What the good woman did not know was that Groepel was a drunkard of terrible assiduity. Not a roaring, heroic drinker, or a romantic melancholy drinker, but a deter-mined fuddler. I still cannot permit myself to think what her life with Groepel may have been like. Perhaps he beat her, but it is more likely that he was coarse and sullen and abusive and never knew a single thing of any importance about what my Julia was or might be. Whatever, the marriage had to be dissolved after a few years, and it was the mercy of God that it was not in my courtroom that the process was examined and the dissolution approved by law. By that time the wonderful voice was gone, and there was nothing left of my Julia but a pitiable woman of substantial means bewailing her misfortunes to her cronies over innumerable cups of coffee and rich unwholesome little cakes. It was the lovely girl of sixteen I treasured in my heart, and now I see that she was in great part my own creation. For Julia, too, was a Philistine in her heart and nothing I could do as her teacher could touch that.

What is a Philistine? Oh, some of them are very nice people. They are the salt of the earth, but not its pepper. A Philistine is someone who is content to live in a wholly unexplored world. My dear, dear faithful Michalina was a Philistine, I believe, for she never attempted to explore any world but that of her husband, and because E.T.A. Hoffmann could not love her with the fervour of his love for Julia, that was not enough.

Was this a tragedy? Oh, no, no, no my dear cultivated friends. We know what a tragedy is, don't we? Tragedy is about heroic figures, who make their sufferings known to the world and demand that the world stand in awe of their sufferings. Not a little lawyer, who wants to be a great composer and is in reality rather an unusual writer, and his devoted Polish wife. There can be no tragedy about such ordinary people. Their lives at best are melodrama, in which the harsh realities are interspersed with scenes of comedy or even farce. They do not live under the pewter sky of tragedy. For them there are breaks in the clouds.

Such a break in the sky, such a burst of fine weather, was my friendship with Ludwig Devrient. A man most decidedly not a Philistine, but one of a great theatre family, himself a great actor, a man of such magnetism and personal beauty as might even have satisfied the girlish dreams of Julia Marc. Between us there was friendship and sympathy that perfectly suited us both, for we were both what it was then becoming fashionable to call Romantics. We did explore the world, so far as we could. And, I am sorry to say, our compass in our explorations was the bottle. The champagne bottle. In those days it was not a prohibitively expensive wine, but a wine we could apply ourselves to in seriousness and abundance. In Lutter's tavern, night after night we did so, and a group of friends would gather to hear us talk and range over that world of which the Philistines wish to know nothing.

When I died, at forty-six, of a complication of ailments of which *champagne was not the least, Devrient did something that made him the mockery of those who could not understand, and won him the respect of some who could. After my funeral he went to Lutter's and made himself gloriously drunk. He was not a roaring drunk or a silly drunk or a stumbling drunk, but a man who had gone over entirely into that other world that the Philistines do not wish to explore or even to allow on the neat chart of their universe. He put two bottles of champagne into his pockets, and walked to the graveyard, and there he seated himself on my grave; and all the cool night of June 25, 1822, he talked to me in his best manner. Some of the wine he drank and some he spilled on the clay. Though I could not answer him, it was surely our best night together, and helped me kindly through the first loneliness of death.*

In this woman I see Devrient, or something of him, once again. That was why, when the party was over, I walked at her side through the autumn streets of a strange but not unkindly city, until we came to her house, and there I sat by her bedside the whole night through. Did I speak to her in her dreams? Those who understand such things better than I must answer that question, but that was my hope. In Dr. Gunilla I recognized another Romantic, and though many aspire to that condition, it is a gift of birth, and we are few.

IV

M R. MERVYN GWILT was thoroughly enjoying himself. This, he thought, was what the practice of the law should be — fine surroundings, a captive audience of distinguished people, and he, Mervyn Gwilt, advising them, for their own good, from his rich understanding of the law and human nature.

Mr. Mervyn Gwilt was every inch a lawyer. Indeed, the expression is inadequate, for there were not many inches to Mr. Gwilt, and there was an awful lot of lawyer in him. He could not have been anything else. He habitually wore a wing collar, suggesting that only a few minutes before he had whipped off his gown and bands and was attempting to reduce his courtroom demeanour and vocabulary to the needs of common life. He always wore a dark three-piece suit, lest he be summoned to court in a hurry. He particularly liked Latin; the priests of Rome might have abandoned that language as a cloak for their mystery, but not Mervyn Gwilt. It was, he explained, so pithy, so exact, so wholly legal in its underlying philosophy and its sound, that it could not be beaten as an instrument for subduing an opponent, or a client. The law had not, up to the present, shown much favour to Mr. Gwilt, but he was ready, should such favour suddenly declare itself.

"At the outset," he said, smiling around the table, "I want to make it amply clear that my client's wish in pursuing this matter carries no taint *ad crumenam* (that's to say he isn't looking for money) but is actuated solely by an inborn respect for the *ius naturale* (meaning what's right and proper)."

He smiled at Maria; at Hollier; at Darcourt. He even smiled at the large man with the big black moustache who had been introduced simply as Mr. Carver. Finally he smiled, with special radiance, at his client Wally Crottel, who was sitting at his side.

"That's right," said Wally. "Don't think I'm just in this for what I can get."

"Let me handle it, Wally," said Mr. Gwilt. "Let's put it all on the table and look at it *ante litem motam* (by which I mean before we think of any court action). Now look: Mr. Crottel's father, the late John Parlabane, left at his death the manuscript of a novel, the title of which was *Be Not Another*. Am I right?"

Maria, Hollier, and Darcourt nodded.

"He left it to Miss Maria Magdalena Theotoky, now Mrs. Arthur Cornish, and to Professor Clement Hollier, as his literary executors. Right?"

"Not precisely," said Hollier. "He left it with an appeal that we should get it published. The term literary executors was not used."

"That remains to be seen," said Mr. Gwilt. "It might well have been implied. So far my client and I have not had a chance to examine that letter. I think this is the time for us to have it on the table. Right?"

"Out of the question," said Hollier. "It was a letter of the most intimate character, and the bit about the novel was only a small part of it. Whatever Parlabane wanted made public he sent in other letters to the newspapers."

Mr. Gwilt made stagy business of hunting in his briefcase for some newspaper clippings. "Those were the portions that spoke of his unhappy determination to take his life because of the neglect his great novel had met with."

"They were also the portions that described his elaborate and disgusting murder of Professor Urquhart McVarish," said Hollier.

"That is not relevant to the matter in hand," said Mr. Gwilt, rebuking this crude reference.

"Of course it is," said Hollier. "He knew the murder would get a lot of publicity, and draw attention to his book. He said so. 'The book a man murdered to have published' was the way he suggested it should be advertised. Or words of that sort."

"Let us not be diverted by irrelevancies," said Mr. Gwilt, primly.

"Maybe he was off his nut and didn't know what he was saying," said Wally Crottel.

"Wally! Leave this to me," said Mr. Gwilt, and kicked Wally sharply under the table. "Until we have indisputable evidence to the contrary, we assume that the late Mr. Parlabane knew precisely what he was saying, and doing."

"He was Brother John Parlabane, I believe, even though he had gone over the wall and parted from the Order of the Sacred Mission. Let's not forget he was a monk," said Maria.

"In these times many men find that they are not fully attuned to the religious life," said Mr. Gwilt. "The exact status of Mr. Parlabane at the time of his unhappy death — *felo de se*, and which of us dares point the finger — is not our business here. What concerns us is that he was my client's father. And my client's status as his heir is what we are talking about now."

"But how do we know Wally was his son?" said Maria. As a woman she wanted to get to the point, and was restless under Mr. Gwilt's ceremonious approach.

"Because that's what my late mum always told me," said Wally. " 'Parlabane was your dad, sure as guns; he was the only guy ever gave me a real organism.' That's what my mum always said."

"Please! Please! May I be allowed to conduct this investigation?" said Mr. Gwilt. "My client was brought up as the child of the late Ogden Whistlecraft, whose name is a word of magic in the annals of Canadian poetry, and his wife, the late Elsie Whistlecraft, my client's undisputed mother. That there had been a liaison of a passionate character — let's just call it an *ad hoc* thing, maybe two or three occasions — between Mrs. Whistlecraft and the late John Parlabane, we do not propose to deny. Why should we? Who dares to point the finger? What kind of woman marries a poet? A woman of deep passions and rich feminine sympathies, obviously. Her pity extended to this family friend, likewise a man of profound literary temperament. Pity! Pity, my friends! And compassion for a lonely, great, questing genius. That was what explained it."

"No. It was the organism," said Wally, stoutly.

"Orgasm, Wally! For God's sake how many times do I have to tell you? Orgasm!" Mr. Gwilt's speech was a hiss.

"She always said organism," said Wally, mulishly. "I know what my mum said. And don't think I blame her. She was my mum and I stand by her, and I'm not ashamed. You said something about that, Merv; you said it was, like, Latin, *De mortos* or something. 'Don't crap on your folks' you said it meant."

"All right! All right, Wally! Just leave it to me."

"Yeah, Merv, but I want to explain about my mum. And Whistlecraft — he didn't like me to call him Dad, but he was nice about the whole thing. He never really talked to me about it, but I know he didn't hold it against my mum. Not much. There was something he said once, in poetry —

> Don't be ashamed
> When the offensive ardour blows the charge

— as the fellow says."

"What fellow was that?" said Darcourt, speaking for the first time.

"The fellow in Shakespeare."

"Oh — that fellow! I thought it might have been something Whistlecraft wrote himself."

"No. Shakespeare. Whistlecraft was prepared to overlook the whole thing. He understood life, even if he wasn't much of a hand at the organism."

"Wally — I call your attention to the fact that there is a lady present."

"Don't mind me," said Maria; "I suppose I am what used to be called a woman of the world."

"And a fine Rabelaisian scholar," said Hollier, smiling at her.

"Aha! Rabelaisian scholar? Old-time Frenchman? Dead?" said Mr. Gwilt.

"The truly great are never dead," said Maria, and suddenly remembered that she was quoting her mother.

"Very well, then. Let us continue on a rather freer line," said Mr. Gwilt. "I don't have to remind you university people of the great changes that have taken place in public opinion, and one might almost say in public morals, in recent years. The distinction has virtually vanished, in the newspapers and also in modern fiction — though I haven't much time for fiction — between what we may define as the O.K. and the Raw. Discretion of language — where is it? Obscenity — where is it? On stage and screen we live in the Age of the Full Frontal. Since the *Ulysses* case and the *Lady Chatterley* case the law has had to take unwilling cognizance of all this. If you are a student of Rabelais, Mrs. Cornish — not that I've read his stuff, but he has a certain reputation, you know, even among those who haven't read him — we must assume that you are thoroughly broken to the Raw. But I digress. So let us get back to our real interest. We admit that the late Mrs. Whistlecraft's life was in some degree flawed —"

"But not Raw," said Maria. "Nowadays we call it liberated."

"Exactly, Mrs. Cornish. I see you have an almost masculine mind. So let us proceed. My client is John Parlabane's son —"

"Proof," said Mr. Carver. "We'll want proof."

"Excuse me, my friend," said Mr. Gwilt. "I don't understand your position in this matter. I have assumed that you are in some way an *amicus curiae* — a friend of the court — but if you are going to advise and interfere I want to know why, and who you are."

"Name's George Carver. I was with the RCMP until I retired. I do a little private investigation work now, so as not to be bored."

"I see. And have you been investigating this matter?"

"I wouldn't say that. I might, if it came to anything."

"But you don't regard this meeting as anything?"

"Not so far. You haven't proved anything."

"But you think you know something relevant."

"I know that Wally Crottel got his job as a security man in this building by saying, among other things, that he had seen some service with the RCMP. He hasn't. Failed entry. Education insufficient."

"That may have been indiscreet but it has nothing to do with the matter in hand. Now listen: I said at the beginning that my client and I are relying on the *ius naturale* — on natural justice, what's right and proper, what decent people everywhere know to be right. I say it is his right to benefit from anything that accrues from the publication of his father's novel, *Be Not Another*, because he is John Parlabane's rightful heir. And I say that Professor Clement Hollier and Mrs. Arthur Cornish have suppressed that book for personal reasons, and all we ask is some recognition of my client's right, or we shall be forced to resort to law, and insist on recompense, after publication of the book."

"How would you do that?" said Darcourt. "Nobody can be forced to publish a book."

"That's as may appear," said Mr. Gwilt.

"Well, it will appear that nobody wants to publish it," said Maria. "When all the scandal blew up, a great many publishers asked to see the book, and they turned it down."

"Aha. Too Raw for them, eh?" said Mr. Gwilt.

"No. Too dull for them," said Maria.

"The book was chiefly an exposition of John Parlabane's philosophy," said Darcourt. "And as such it was derivative and tediously repetitious. He had interspersed his long philosophical passages with some autobiographical stuff that he thought was fiction, but I assure you it wasn't. Stiff as a board."

"Autobiographical?" said Mr. Gwilt. "And he may have included portraits of living persons that would have caused a fine stink. Political people? Big people in the world of business? And that was why the publishers wouldn't touch it?"

"Publishers, too, have a fine sense of the O.K. and the Raw, and of that lively area where the two kiss and commingle," said Maria. "As my dear François Rabelais puts it: *Quaestio subtilissima, utrum chimaera in vacuo bombinans possit commedere secundas intentiones*. I make no apologies for the Latin, as you are such a dab hand with that language."

"Aha," said Mr. Gwilt, imparting a wealth of legal subtlety into the exclamation, though his eyes flickered with incomprehension. "And precisely how do you apply that fine legal maxim to the matter in hand?"

"Translated very roughly," said Maria, "it might be taken to suggest that you are standing on a banana skin."

"Though we would not dream of disparaging your admirable *argumentum ad excrementum taurorum*," said Hollier.

"What's he say?" said Wally to his legal adviser.

"Say's it's all bullshit. Well, we don't have to take that kind of thing from people just because they have money and position. Our legal system guarantees a fair deal for everybody. And my client has not had a fair deal. If the book had been published, he would have a right to a share, if not all, of the payment proceeding from that publication. You have not proceeded to publication and we want to know why. That's what we're doing here. So I think I'd better be more direct than I've been up to now. Where's this manuscript?"

"I don't know that you have a right to ask that," said Hollier.

"A court would have that right. You say publishers refused it?"

"To be scrupulously exact," said Maria, "one publisher said he might take it if he could put a ghost on it and make whatever could be made of the story, leaving out all Parlabane's philosophy and moralizing. He said it would have to be made sensational — a real murderer's confession. But that would have been utterly false to what Parlabane wanted, and we refused."

"I put it to you that the novel was Raw, and brought in recognizable portraits of living people, and you are protecting them."

"No, no; so far as I remember the novel — what I read of it — it wasn't Raw. Not for modern tastes," said Hollier. "There were references to homosexual encounters, but Parlabane was so allusive and indirect — as compared to his description of how he murdered poor old Urky McVarish — that it came out as rather mild stuff. Not so much Raw as half-baked. He was not an experienced writer of fiction. The publisher Mrs. Cornish has spoken of wanted to make it really Raw, and we would not degrade our old associate Parlabane in that way. What's Raw and what isn't is really a matter of taste; the taste may be pungent, but it shouldn't be nasty. We didn't at all trust the taste of that publisher."

"Do you tell me you haven't *read* the novel?" said Mr. Gwilt, with stagy incredulity.

"It was unreadable. Even a professor, who is professionally obliged to read a great deal of tedious stuff, couldn't get through it. Outraged nature overcame me at about page four hundred, and the last two hundred and fifty pages remain unread, so far as I am concerned."

"That's how it was," said Maria. "I couldn't read it either."

"Nor I," said Darcourt. "And I assure you I tried my very best."

"Aha!" said Mr. Gwilt. It was a verbal pounce. "You admit ignorance of this book, considered by its author to be one of the greatest works of fiction in the realm of the philosophical novel to be produced in history, and yet you have had the mind-boggling gall to suppress it —"

"Nobody would take it," said Darcourt.

"Please! I'm speaking! And I'm speaking now, not as a man of the law, but as a human soul peering into an abyss of snotty intellectual infamy! Now see here — if you don't produce that manuscript for our examination and the opinion of the experts we shall put to work on it, you face legal action which will make you smart, let me tell you!"

"No alternative of any kind?" said Maria. She and the two professors seemed calm under the threat of exposure and ignominy.

"My client and I don't want a stink, any more than you do. I know it may seem strange for me, as a lawyer, to advise against going to court. I suggest that a composition might be made."

"A pay-off, you mean?" said Hollier.

"Not a legal term. I say a composition in the sum of, let's say, a million dollars."

Hollier and Darcourt, both of whom had experience of publishing books, laughed aloud.

"You flatter me," said Hollier. "Do you know what professors are paid?"

"You are not alone in this," said Mr. Gwilt, smiling. "I

don't suppose Mrs. Cornish would have much trouble over a million."

"Oh, not a bit," said Maria. "I fling such sums to the needy, at church doors."

"Let us keep this serious," said Mr. Gwilt. "A million's the word."

"On what grounds?"

"I have already spoken of the *ius naturale*," said Mr. Gwilt. "Common justice and decency. Let me recap: my client is the son of John Parlabane, and at the time of his death the late Mr. Parlabane did not know of the existence of that son. That's the nub of it. If Mr. Parlabane had known, at the time he made that will, would he have overlooked the claim of his own child?"

"As I remember Mr. Parlabane he might have done anything at all," said Darcourt.

"Well, the law wouldn't allow it, if he tried to cut out his natural heir. This isn't the eighteenth century, you know."

"I think it's time I put in my two cents' worth," said Mr. Carver, who had been as still as a very large cat during all that had been said. He now looked like a very wide-awake cat. "You can't prove your client is the son of John Parlabane."

"Oh, can't I, indeed?"

"No, you can't. I've made a few inquiries, and I have at least three witnesses, and I could probably find more, who had a crack at the late Mrs. Whistlecraft in her high and palmy days. If you'll pardon a bit of the Raw, one of my informants said she was known as Pay As You Enter, and poor old Whistlecraft was laughed at as a notorious cuckold, though a decent guy and quite a poet. Who's the father? Nobody knows."

"Oh yes they do," said Wally Crottel. "What about the organism? Eh? How about that? None of these guys you mention ever gave her the organism. She said so herself; she was always a very open woman. And without the organism how do you account for a child? Eh? Without the organism, no dice."

"I don't know what you've been reading, Mr. Crottel," said Mr. Carver, "but you're away off base. Take my wife, for instance; four fine kids, one of them just last week called to the bar (a lawyer like yourself, Mr. Gwilt), and she never had one of those things in her life. Told me so herself. And a very happy woman, adored by her family. You ought to see what goes on in our house on Mother's Day! This organism, as you call it, may be all very well, but it's not the real goods. So bang goes your organism. So far as it's evidence, that's to say."

"Well, anyways, that's what my mum always said," said Wally, loyal even in defeat.

Mr. Gwilt seemed to be groping in his mind, perhaps for a useful scrap of Latin. He decided to do what he could with an old one.

"The *ius naturale*," he said. "Natural justice. Are you going to fly in the face of that?"

"Yes, when it's demanded at the point of a gun, and it's an empty gun. That would be my advice," said Mr. Carver, a pussy who had not yet retracted his claws.

"Come on, Merv," said Wally. "Time to go."

"I haven't finished yet," said his lawyer. "I want to get to the bottom of why that will is withheld."

"Not a will," said Hollier; "a personal letter."

"The nearest thing to a will the late John Parlabane ever made. And why are these people refusing to produce the *corpus delicti*, by which I hasten to say I do not mean the body of the late John Parlabane, as it is commonly misunderstood, but the material object relating to the crime. I mean the manuscript of the novel about which all this dispute has arisen."

"Because there's no reason to produce it," said Mr. Carver.

"Oh, there isn't, eh? We'll see about that?"

Mr. Carver was a pussycat again, his claws well in. He used an expression perhaps unexpected in a former member of the Royal Canadian Mounted Police, and a working private eye.

"Fiddlesticks!" he said.

With a great display of indignation, and inaudible mutterings, Mr. Mervyn Gwilt rose slowly, like a man who goes, only to return with renewed strength, and, followed by his disgruntled client, left the apartment. He gave vent to his feelings by slamming the door.

"Thank God we're rid of them," said Maria.

"Rid of Gwilt, maybe. I wouldn't be sure you're rid of Wally Crottel," said Mr. Carver, rising. "I know a few things about Wally. Fellows like that can be very nasty. You'd better keep your eye peeled, Mrs. Cornish."

"Why me? Why not Professor Hollier?"

"Psychology. You're a woman, and a rich woman. People like Wally are very jealous. There's not much to be got out of the professor, if you'll excuse me for saying so, but a rich woman is an awful temptation to a fellow like Wally. I just mention it."

"Thanks, George. You've been wonderful," said Darcourt. "You'll send me your statement, won't you?"

"Itemized and in full," said Mr. Carver. "But I must say it's been a pleasure. I never liked that guy Gwilt."

Mr. Carver declined the offer of a drink, and moved out of the apartment on pussycat feet.

"Where did you find that wonderful man?" said Maria.

"I was able to do something for his oldest boy when he was a student. Taught him a little Latin — just enough," said Darcourt. "George is my key to the underworld. Everybody ought to have one."

"If that's that, then I'll be going," said Hollier. "Some work I want to finish. But if I may say so, Maria my dear, you really oughtn't to throw anything away; as a scholar you ought to know that. Throw things away and what is there for the scholars of the future? It's simple trade-unionism. Throw things away and what becomes of research?"

And he went.

"Do you have to go right away, Simon?" said Maria. "There are one or two things — Would you like a drink?"

An unnecessary question, thought Simon. In his state of authorial anxiety about his book he was always ready for a drink. He would have to watch that. A drunken priest. A drunken professor. Oh, shame!

"I will make you a drink if you want one," he said. "It seems to me you drink a great deal more than you did when you were a student."

"I need more than when I was a student. And I have inherited my Uncle Yerko's head. I'm a long way from being a serious drinker, Simon. I'll never be in the class with Dr. Gunilla Dahl-Soot."

"The Doctor is heroic in her application to the bottle. But somehow I don't think she has what Americans call a Drinking Problem. She likes it and she holds a lot. Simple."

"You won't join me?"

"I'm afraid I'm drinking too much, and I haven't got the splendid head of you and the Doctor. I'll just have some bubbly water."

"Are things getting to be too much for you, Simon?"

"This opera is worrying me, in a way that is quite absurd, because it's really none of my business. If you and Arthur want to spend hundreds of thousands on it, the money is yours. You're doing it for Powell, of course?"

"No, not of course, though it must look like that. He has certainly rushed us into the whole thing. I mean, we simply thought we would put up some money so that Schnak could do a job on the Hoffmann manuscripts, in so far as they exist. But Powell suggested that the opera might be presented, and was so full of enthusiasm and Welsh rhetoric that he infected Arthur, and you remember how Arthur went overboard about the whole idea. So here we are, up to our necks in something we don't understand."

"I suppose Powell understands it."

"Yes, but the mixture of Arthur's idealism and Powell's opportunism doesn't please me at all. The person who is going to come out on top of the heap, if the thing isn't a horrible failure, is Geraint Powell. I suppose Schnak might benefit, though how I can't pretend to see; but Powell, as the force behind the whole affair, is bound to get a lot of attention, which is what he wants."

"Why are you willing that Schnak should benefit, and so hostile to Powell?"

"He's using Arthur, and consequently he's using me. He's a climber. He's been a pretty successful actor, but he understands the limitations of that, so he wants to be a director. Because he's really very good at music, he wants to be a director of opera, and on the highest level. There's nothing wrong with any of that. He talks as if Arthur rushed everybody into this affair, but it's the other way around. He's the whirlwind. I feel he really looks on Arthur and me simply as a ladder toward his own success."

"Maria, you'd better get things straight in your head about what a patron is. I know a lot about patronage because I've seen it in the university. Either you exploit, or you are exploited. Either you demand the biggest slice of the pie for yourself, and get a gallery, or a theatre, or whatever it may be, named after you, and insist that people put up your portrait in the foyer, and toady to you, and listen to whatever you have to say with bated breath, or else you are simply the moneybags. And when you're dealing with artists of any kind you are dealing with the people who have the most gall and the most outrageous self-esteem in the world. So you've got to be tough, and insist on being first in everything, or you've got to do it for the love of the art. Don't complain about being used. Got to be magnanimous, in fact. Magnanimity, I needn't remind you, is as rare as it is splendid."

"I'm perfectly willing to be magnanimous, but I'm jealous for Arthur — Simon, I hate, and detest, and loathe and abhor the alternative title of this God-damned opera: *The Magnanimous Cuckold*. I feel that Arthur is being screwed."

"Cuckolds aren't screwed; they are deceived."

"That's what I mean."

"Arthur is most at fault, if that's what's happening to him."

"Simon, I wouldn't say this to anybody in the world but you. You understand what I mean when I say that Arthur has a truly noble nature. But noble isn't a word that's used any more. Elitist, I suppose. But there's no other word for Arthur. He's generous and open in a way that is marvellous. But it also exposes him to terrible abuse."

"He's very fond of Powell. He asked him to be best man at your wedding, as I needn't remind you."

"Yes, and I'd never heard of Powell till he turned up then, all elegance and eloquence — full of piss and vinegar like a barber's cat, to use the old expression."

"You're getting heated, and your heat makes me thirsty. I will have that drink, after all."

"Do. I want your best advice, Simon. I'm worried, and I don't know why I'm worried."

"Yes you do. You think Arthur is too fond of Powell. Isn't that it?"

"Not in the way you mean."

"Tell me what I mean."

"I think you mean some homosexual thing. Not a bit of that in Arthur."

"Maria, for a very brilliant woman you are surprisingly

naive. If you think homosexuality means no more than rough stuff in Turkish baths, and what Hamlet calls a pair of reechy kisses and paddling in necks with damned fingers in some seedy motel bedroom, you are right off your trolley. As you say, and as I believe, Arthur has a noble nature, and that isn't his style at all. Nor, to be just, do I think it's Powell's. But an obsessive admiration for a man who has qualities he envies, and for whom he is ready to give great gifts and take great risks, without grudging — that's homosexuality too, when the wind is right. Nobility isn't cautious, you know. Arthur is really Arthurian: he seeks something extraordinary — a Quest, a great adventure — and Powell seems to offer it and is, therefore, irresistible."

"Powell is a self-seeking bastard."

"And just possibly a great man — or a great artist, which is by no means the same thing. Like Richard Wagner, another self-seeking bastard. Remember how he exploited and horn-swoggled poor King Ludwig?"

"Ludwig was a crazy weakling."

"And his craziness has endowed us all with some magnifi-cent opera. Not to speak of that totally insane fairy-tale castle of Neuschwanstein, which cost the people of Bavaria what was literally a king's ransom, and has recovered them the money a dozen times over, simply as a tourist sight."

"You're appealing to a piece of dead history, and a messy scandal, which has nothing to do with what we're talking about."

"History is never dead, because it keeps on repeating itself, though never in quite the same words or on quite the same scale. Remember what we said the other night at that Arthurian dinner, about the wax and the stamp? The wax of human experience is always the same. It is we who put our own stamp on it. These shared obsessions between patron and artist are as old as the hills, and I don't think you are going to be able to change that. Have you talked to Arthur?"

"You don't know Arthur. When I bring it up he just tells me to be patient, and that omelettes aren't made without breaking eggs, and all that sort of calm, uncomprehending thing."

"Have you told him he's in love with Powell?"

"Simon! What do you think I am?"

"I think you're a jealous woman, among other things."

"Jealous of Powell? I hate Powell!"

"Oh, Maria, haven't you learned anything in your university years?"

"Meaning what?"

"Meaning that hatred is notoriously near to love, and both are obsessions. Passions when they are pushed too far sometimes flop over into their opposites."

"What I feel about Arthur isn't going to flop over into its opposite."

"Bravely said. And what is it you feel about Arthur?"

"Doesn't it show? Devotion."

"An expensive devotion. As devotion always is, of course."

"A devotion that has enlarged my life more than I can say."

"A devotion that seems to have cost you what meant most to you in the world before you married."

"So?"

"Yes, so. How much work have you done on your edition of that unpublished Rabelais manuscript that was found in Francis Cornish's papers? I remember your raptures when it was turned up — thanks to that monster Parlabane — and how Hollier said it would make your reputation as a scholar. Well — that's something like eighteen months ago. How's it getting on? Arthur gave it to you as a wedding present, as I recall. Now *there's* something significant: bridegroom gives bride a gift that will demand the best of her energies and understanding. Something that might mean more to her than her marriage. That would almost certainly mean reputation and scholarly fame of a special kind. A dangerous gift, certainly, but Arthur risked it. So what have you been doing?"

"I've been getting used to living with a man, and running this house, which is the exact opposite of the Gypsy *tsera* where I lived with my mother and uncle, and all the hair-raising crookedness of the *bomari* and the *wursitorea* that hung over that awful place. I only go there when you insist on it, Simon —"

"Don't forget it was Arthur who settled what was left of all that Gypsy mess in the basement of this very building where you are playing the fine lady, Maria."

"Don't be so disgusting, Simon! I'm not playing the fine lady — My God, you sound like my mother! — I'm trying to work my way finally and utterly into modern civilization, and put all that past behind me."

"It sounds as if modern civilization, which is largely rooted in Arthur, so far as you are concerned, had cut you off from what was best in you. I don't mean the Gypsy connection; forget that for the moment; but from what made you a scholar. From what drew you to Rabelais — the great humane spirit and the great humour that saves us in a rough world. I remember when you first got that manuscript; you wouldn't have called Professor M. A. Screech your uncle, and he's a mitred abbot among you Rabelaisians, I understand. And now — well, now —"

"I have by degrees dwindled into a wife?"

"You still have a nice touch with a quotation. That's something saved out of the wreck."

"I won't be called a wreck, Simon."

"All right. And I don't knock wives. But surely a woman of your qualities can be both scholar and wife? And the one all the better for the other?"

"Arthur takes a lot of looking after."

"Well — don't let him eat you. That's what I'm saying. Why do you look after him so much? He seemed to be getting on pretty well before he married you."

"He had needs that weren't being gratified."

"Aha."

"Don't say 'Aha!' like Mervyn Gwilt! You think I mean sex."

"Well — don't you?"

"Now you are the one who is being naive. Celibate priest that you are."

"And whose fault is that, may I ask? I gave you your chance to enlighten me."

"No use crying over spilt milk."

"I don't recall that we spilled any milk."

"You know perfectly well it wouldn't have done. You'd have been a worse husband than Arthur."

"Aha! Now I can say it — Aha!"

"I'm tired and you're bullying me."

"That's what women always say when they are getting the worst of things. Now come on, Maria: I'm your old friend, old tutor, old suitor. What's wrong between you and Arthur?"

"Nothing's *wrong*."

"Then perhaps too much is right."

"Perhaps. It's not that I'm panting for continual excitement and passion and all that kid stuff. But the stew could do with a little more salt."

"How about the organism?"

"In that department I suppose I rank somewhere between Mrs. Carver and the Roman candle Elsie Whistlecraft. It takes two to make an organism, you know. — We'd better stop using that word as a joke, or we'll use it seriously, and disgrace ourselves in the eyes of all right-thinking people."

"It isn't a word I find coming up much in conversation,

but I suppose you're right. — So you find marriage quieter than you expected?"

"I don't know what I expected."

"Maybe you expected to see more of Arthur. Where is he now?"

"In Montreal. Comes back tomorrow. He's always dashing off on business. The Cornish Trust is very big business, you know."

"Well — I wish I had some good advice to give you, Maria, but I haven't. Every marriage is different and you have to find your own solutions. Apart from saying that I think you ought to get back to work, and have some business of your own — scholarly business — I haven't a thing to suggest."

"You don't have to give advice, Simon. I'm grateful to you for listening. We've had a real, proper *divano*. That's what Gypsies call it — a *divano*."

"A lovely word."

"Sorry if I've been a bore."

"You could never be a bore, Maria. Not yet. But unless you recover your fine Rabelaisian spirit it just might happen, and that would be dreadful."

"Fair's fair. Bore me with your own problems."

"I've said what they were. Or I've said what I feel about the opera. And of course there's the book. It never stops nagging."

"Aha!"

"Now who's being Mervyn Gwilt?"

"I am. I have something for you. Something about Uncle Frank that I bet you didn't know. Wait a minute."

Maria went to her study, and Darcourt seized the opportunity to — no, not to pour himself another drink, but to refresh the drink he had. With a generous hand.

Maria returned with a letter. "Read this, and rejoice," she said.

It was a letter in a square envelope, of the sort English people use for personal correspondence. A substantial letter, making quite a wad of paper, each sheet bearing the heading West Country Pony Club, and covered with that large, bold handwriting characteristic of people who write little, and squander their paper in a way that immediately sets the scholar on his guard. The letter itself was wholly in accord with its appearance. It said:

Dear cousin Arthur:

Yes, it's cousin, right enough, because you are the nephew of my father, the late Francis Cornish, and so we are from the same stable, if I may speak professionally. I should have written to you months ago but — pressure of business, and all that, and I'm sure you know what pressure of business means. But I only got wind of you last spring, when a Canadian colleague asked if I knew you, and it seems you are quite a nob in your own country. Of course I knew there were Canadians hanging somewhere on the family tree, because my grandfather — he was a Francis Cornish too — and the father of your uncle, who was my father — Oh dear, this is getting very mixed-up! Anyhow he married a Canadian, but we never knew him, because he was in some very hush-hush stuff which I don't pretend to understand. My father, too. The family were always very close-mouthed about him for a variety of reasons, and one of them was that he was very hush-hush too. But anyhoo (as they say) he was my father and as far as he went a very good father, because he looked after me very generously, so far as money goes, but I never saw him after I was too small to really know him, if you understand me. He married his cousin Ismay Glasson — rather a dark horse, I understand — and I was brought up on the family place — not Chegwidden Hall, but at St. Columb's because my grandmother was his cousin Prudence and that was where she lived with granddaddy, who was Roderick Glasson. Oh, crumbs, what have I said! Of course she *lived* with him because she was his wife — nothing in the least funny *there*, I assure you! St. Columb's had to be sold up, in the end, and the poor old place is a battery-hen place now, but I managed to buy the dower-house and it is from there that I run my little stable and am rather the High Mucky Muck of the West Country Pony Club, as you see from this paper. The only paper I have, I'm afraid, because I'm up to my ample hips in the pony biz, and it's a handful — you'd never believe! But to come to the point, I'm coming to Canada in November, because I'm to be a judge at your Royal Winter Fair in the pony division — jumping and all that — and I understand you have some wonderfully keen kiddies showing and I can't wait to see them! And I'd love to see you! So may I give you a tinkle when I can get away from pony business, and perhaps we could tear a herring together and exchange family news! I don't suppose you've ever heard of me, unless somebody mentioned Little Charlie — that's me! And not so little now, let me say! So here's hoping to see you, and tons of family affection, though sight unseen!

Love —

CHARLOTTE CORNISH

"Did you know Uncle Frank had a child?" said Maria.

"I knew there was somebody called Charlotte Cornish to whom he left a quarterly allowance for life, because Arthur told me so," said Darcourt. "But I didn't know she was a daughter. Could have been any sort of old relation. The parish register recorded the marriage of Francis and his cousin Ismay Glasson, but there was no word of a child. Fool that I was, when I was snooping around in Cornwall I discovered that Francis had been married to Ismay Glasson, but when I made inquiries about her everybody shut up and knew nothing. And nobody said a word about Little Charlie or the Pony Club. Just shows that I am not much of a detective. Of course, all the Glassons had vanished, and when I got in touch with Sir Roderick in London he couldn't have been less forthcoming, and was too busy to see me. Well, well! Little Charlie is certainly no great letter-writer, is she?"

"But she's a reality. She must have heard something about Uncle Frank, even if she can't remember him. So you may have struck gold for the book, Simon."

"I'm too cautious to expect any such thing. This letter puffs and blows and giggles a bit, doesn't it? But it's a ray of light in the very dark centre of Francis Cornish's life."

"So we've both got something — not much, but something — out of the *divano*, Simon."

(2)

WHEN DARCOURT HAD GONE, Maria went to bed, leaving a note for Arthur, saying that he was to wake her when he came in from the airport. This was something she always did, and a request that Arthur always ignored — part of his extraordinary consideration, and his refusal to understand that she wanted to be wakened, wanted to see him, wanted to talk with him.

She did not read herself to sleep. Maria was not a reader-in-bed. Instead she set her mind to work on something that would bring sleep at last. Something substantial, some old friendly theme, but not so demanding as to keep her awake.

What should it be tonight? Darcourt had told her not to subdue her Rabelaisian nature; not to starve the full Rabelaisian humour that had been hers when she first met Arthur; not to dwindle into a wife, lest she cease to be a real wife. A good, sleepy theme might be the Seven Laughters of God. Of the angers, the vengeances, the punishments, the manifold Bellyaches of God the modern world seemed to know enough, even when it was most eager to banish God from all serious consideration. Let's have the Laughters.

The idea of the Seven Laughters was such an odd one, in the light of modern religion. Gnostic, and of course heretical. Christianity could not countenance a merry God. That God should have rejoiced, and taken delight in what he was making, and that the whole Universe sprang from delight — how foreign to a world obsessed by solemnity, which so quickly became despair. What were the Seven Laughters?

The first was the Laughter from which came light, as Genesis says. Then the Laughter of the Firmament, which our world has just begun to explore — to put a technological toe into space, and to invent bugaboos about spaceships, and Little People with antennae growing out of their heads, who might be spying on us unseen, and a sense of our inferiority in the face of immensity. Not much laughter there for us, whatever it may be for God.

What was the Third Laughter? Mind, wasn't it? Now *there* was a God one could really love, a God who laughed Mind into being just as soon as he had a place for it. Mind, the old thinkers said, was Hermes, and Hermes was a very good conception of Mind, because he was so various, so multitudinous, so many-shaped, certainly so ambiguous, but if you took him the right way, such a cheerful creation — so inventive and vigorous. Then what?

The Fourth Laughter was called Generation, which wasn't just sex, but growth and multiplicity. Nevertheless, sex was certainly a part of it if not the whole, and how God must have laughed when he confronted astonished Hermes with that pretty kettle of fish! And how Hermes, after his first astonishment, must have seized upon it as the splendid joke it was — though God and Hermes would certainly have known that many people would never see the joke. Would, indeed, spoil the joke. So, to cope with the people who could not understand jokes, God laughed again and Fate, or Destiny, came into being. The wax, in fact, upon which Darcourt insisted we all set our seal, without always knowing what the seal was.

God, rolling about on His Throne, knew Destiny would never work unless it had a frame, so — probably choking on the Joe Miller of the thing — laughed Time into being, so that Destiny would function serially, permitting people who never saw jokes to haggle about the nature of Time forever.

Last Laughter of all, when God, probably prompted by Hermes, had seen that He was perhaps being a little hard on the creatures who would inhabit the Creation, was Psyche — the Soul, the Laughter that would give creation, and mankind above all, a chance to come to terms with all God's merriment. Not to master it, and certainly not to understand it fully, but to find a way to partake of some part of it. Poor old Psyche! Poor old Soul! How our world was determined to thwart her at every turn, and speak of her — when it did speak of her — as a gloomy, gaseous maiden who did not, most of the time, know her spiritual arse from her metaphysical elbow! Never for a moment seeing her as the Consort, the true mate, of Hermes.

Well, there they were, and the effort of dredging them up from memory, where Maria had filed them some time ago, had made her sleepy. Not so sleepy, however, that she did not understand afresh what Darcourt meant when he urged her not to starve the Rabelaisian nature in herself. There were her Hermes and her Psyche, and with them she must live in truest amity, or she would cease to be Maria and her marriage would go to ruin.

She must not forget that Rabelais had known and delighted in the Arthurian stories, and had drawn upon their spirit even as he parodied them. Surely she would love her own Arthur better if she did not take him quite so seriously. Magnanimous? Of course. But a virtue in excess may slither into a weakness.

She slept. When Arthur returned, about one o'clock, he smiled affectionately at her note, and went to another bedroom, so as not to waken her.

(3)

"DO YOU WANT ME to cut your grass?"

A simple question, surely? Yet as Hulda Schnakenburg uttered it to Dr. Gunilla Dahl-Soot it was total surrender; it was Henry IV standing barefoot in the snow at Canossa; it was an act of vassalage.

Schnak had been working with the Doctor for two weeks, and this was the end of their sixth session together. The work had not begun promisingly. What the Doctor saw in Schnak was "a woman of the people", not a peasant but an urban roughneck, and she had spoken to her very much from on high. In the Doctor, Schnak thought she had met yet another tedious instructor, perhaps greatly skilled but not greatly talented, and as snotty as they come. If she had been surly and mocking with Dean Wintersen, she was rude and ugly with the Doctor, who had countered with icy courtesy. But in a short time they had begun to respect one another.

Schnak always made it her business to find out what her instructors had achieved, and what that amounted to in most cases was a respectable body of unexceptional music, fashionably but cautiously experimental, that had been performed a few times and had won fashionable, cautious approval; rarely had it travelled far beyond the borders of Canada. It was music, surely enough, but in Schnak's expression it did not grab her. She wanted something more interesting than that. In the published work of Dr. Gunilla Dahl-Soot she found something that grabbed her, something she did not feel she could rival, an unmistakable, individual voice. Not that the Doctor was one of the world's great composers, by any means. Critics tended to describe her work as "notable". However, these were the best critics. She had been one of the better pupils of Nadia Boulanger, and had first attracted attention with a String Quartet, in which the idiom of an original voice had been discerned — a voice not that of her great teacher; Schnak had read the score with a reserve that began as derision, but that had to be abandoned, for this was unquestionably music marked by a fine clarity of thought, expressed through conventional techniques used in a wholly independent manner. It was not a long work; indeed, as music goes, it was terse, rigorous, strictly argued. But in the later Violin Sonata there was a quality even Schnak could not deride, and which she knew she would not rival; to speak of wit in music is uncritically vague, but there was no other word for it. Every succeeding work showed the same distinction of mind: a Suite for clarinet and strings, a Second String Quartet, a Symphony on a small scale (as compared with the block-busters, demanding more than a hundred players, following on the nineteenth-century masters), a body of songs that were real songs and not merely measured utterance undertaken in rivalry with an argumentative piano, and last of all a Requiem for Benjamin Britten which knocked the breath out of Schnak, and made her aware beyond a doubt that she had met her master. The Requiem was not witty, but deeply felt and poignant; these were qualities Schnak knew she lacked in herself, but which, she discovered to her amazement, she desired intensely. This was the real goods, she admitted.

Every article about the Doctor in the reference books, however, emphasized that it was as a teacher that she was most influential. She had studied with Nadia Boulanger; the musical historians said that she came nearest to imparting the spirit of her great mentor. Nobody said she was as good as Nadia Boulanger, or different; it is a firm critical principle that nobody living is quite as good as somebody dead.

A teacher, then? A teacher whom Schnak could truly respect? She had not quite known that that was what she wanted more than anything else in the world, and she came to such self-knowledge with mulish resistance. Now, at the end of her sixth session, she offered to cut the Doctor's grass. Schnak had met her master.

The grass badly wanted cutting. The Doctor had never, in her life, been a householder, but the School of Music had established her in a pleasant little house, on a street very near the University, which belonged to a professor who had gone on a year's sabbatical, taking his wife and children with him. It was a domestic little house, and the furniture, without being in ruins, spoke of a family life that included small children. It had bookshelves in every room, in which books, chiefly of a philosophical nature, were ranged tightly, with other books laid sidewise on whatever space there was above them. Small hands had marked the walls; philosophical bottoms had made deep nests in every chair. There was no complete set of any sort of china, and the cutlery was odds and ends of stainless steel which had managed, somehow, to acquire stains. The pictures were of philosophers — not a notably decorative class of men — and photographs of conferences where the professor and his wife had been snapped with colleagues from many lands. Whatever branch of philosophy the professor taught, it was clearly not aesthetics. When the Doctor had been introduced to the house she had sighed, removed most of the pictures, and set upon the mantelpiece her great treasure, without which she never left her Paris flat for long; it was a small, exquisite bronze by Barbara Hepworth. Beyond that, she felt, there was nothing to be done.

But the grass! When she arrived, the lawn had the battlefield look of a children's playground, and in no time at all the grass had grown long and rank. What was to be done? The Doctor did not know, and did not really care, but she could not ignore the fact that the little lawns on either side were neatly trimmed. The Doctor had never before lived in a place where grass obtruded itself, or if it did, men came from somewhere and trimmed it. As the grass grew, she began to feel like La Belle au Bois Dormant, overgrown and shut in by uncontrollable herbage. As well as the problem of the grass there was a wasps' nest over the front door, and the windows were muddy from the rains and dusty winds of the Canadian autumn. The Doctor had no gift for domesticity.

And here, in Hulda Schnakenburg, was somebody who seemed to know what to do about grass!

Schnak went to the back premises where there was, of course, a lawn-mower in a shed. It was not a good lawn-mower, for the professor was not far above the Doctor in his understanding of bourgeois domesticity, but it worked after a fashion, tearing up whatever grass its ancient jaws could not chew, and with this antique Schnak set to work to chop the lawn, if not positively to trim it. She worked with the devotion of the willing slave, and after the lawn had been harried into submission she raked up the cuttings, and cut it again. She gathered the harvest and put it in a plastic bag, which went into the garbage can, which the Doctor regarded with disgust and used as little as she could; it was her custom to pack the leavings from her scant meals into paper bags, which she later, by stealth and in darkness, threw over a nearby fence into the back lawn of a professor of theology.

When at last Schnak was finished, the Doctor was standing at the front door.

"Thank you, my dear," she said. "And now, your bath is ready."

Bath? Schnak did not take baths. Now and then, under pressure from some outraged companion, she took a shower at the Women's Union, careful not to get her hair wet. She had a horror of colds.

"You are hot and tired," said the Doctor. "Look — you sweat. You will take cold. Come with me."

The bath was such as Schnak had never seen before. The professor's bathroom was not Neronian in its luxury, but it had everything that was needed, and the Doctor had banished all the smelly sponges, the balding brushes, and the celluloid ducks and rubber animals of the previous regime. The tub was contemporaneous with the house itself and was a large, old-fashioned affair with brass taps, and claw feet; it was full of hot water, bubbling fragrantly with the bath-oils the Doctor used upon herself, for she was a voluptuous bather.

What puzzled Schnak was that the Doctor seemed determined to remain in the bathroom with her, and gestured to her to take off her clothes. This was strange indeed, for in the Schnakenburg household baths were secret ceremonies, hinting of medical indecency, like enemas, and the bather always bolted the door against intruders. Schnak had stripped in front of somebody else before, because the three boys with whom she had undergone some sort of crude sexual experience were all great on what they called "skin", but since childhood she had never stripped in front of a woman, and she felt shame. The Doctor knew it, and laughing a little, but with fastidious fingers, she pulled off Schnak's filthy sweater, and nodded to her to kick off her degraded loafers and her stained jeans. So, very shortly, Schnak stood naked on the bathmat, and the Doctor looked at her consideringly.

"My God, you are a dirty child," she said. "No wonder you smell so bad. Get into the water."

Would marvels never cease? Schnak discovered that she was not to bathe, but to be bathed. The Doctor had somewhere found a large apron which she wore over her clothes, and kneeling beside the tub she gave Schnak such a bath as she had never had in twelve years, at which time she had been instructed by her mother to bathe herself. What soaping, what rubbing, what scouring of the feet in a this-little-piggy-went-to-market detail they had not known since childhood! It took a long time and the beautiful water was slick and grimy when at last the Doctor pulled out the plug and let it all drain away.

"Out with you," said the Doctor, standing with a large towel in her hands. She rubbed and scuffled Schnak's unaccustomedly clean body in a businesslike fashion that admitted of no assistance, and included intimacies that astonished Schnak, for they were not the rough maulings of her three engineering students. And while this was going on the Doctor was drawing another tubful of water.

"In you get again," said she. "Now we do the hair."

Schnak obediently stepped back into the tub, wondering greatly, but aware that out of her sight there was some very rapid undressing, and in no time the Doctor had slipped into the tub behind her, enclosing Schnak's thin body between her long elegant legs. Much dowsing of the dirty head; much shampooing with deliciously scented oil; much rinsing and at last a rough but playful drying.

"And now," said the Doctor, laughing, "you are a pretty clean girl. How does it feel?"

Lying back in the tub herself, she drew Schnak backward against her own body, and, slipping her arms around her, caressed Schnak's astonished nipples with soapy hands.

Schnak could not have said how it felt. Words were not her means of expression, or she might have said that it was paradisal. But it did float into her mind that all the books of reference concluded their pieces about the Doctor by saying that she was unmarried. Well, well, well.

Later they ceremoniously burned Schnak's discarded clothes. The Doctor wanted to do it in the fireplace, but Schnak tested the chimney by burning some paper in the grate, and the immediate belching of smoke bore out her suspicion that there was a bird's nest in the chimney. The Doctor was much impressed by this show of domestic wisdom. They burned the clothes in the back yard, after dark, and even danced a few steps around the bonfire.

Because Schnak had no clothes, she could not go home, nor did she wish to do so. She and the Doctor retired to bed, and there they drank rum mixed with rich milk, and Schnak lay in the Doctor's arms and told her the story of her life, as she understood it, in a version that would greatly have astonished and angered her parents.

"An old story," said the Doctor. "The gifted child; the Philistine parents. Loveless religion: craving for a larger life. Do you know what a Philistine is, child?"

"Somebody in the Bible?"

"Yes, but now the people who are against the things that you and I love — art, and the freedom without which art cannot exist. Have you been reading Hoffmann, as I told you?"

"Some of the stories."

"Hoffmann's life was a long fight with the Philistines. Poor devil! You have not read *Kater Murr* yet?"

"No."

"Not an easy book, but you cannot understand Hoffmann without it. It is the biography of the great musician Kreisler."

"I didn't know he was as old as that."

"Not Fritz Kreisler, stupid! A character invented by Hoffmann. One of his many *alter egos*. The great musician and composer Kapellmeister Johannes Kreisler, the romantic genius whom nobody understands and who has to put up with insults and slights from all the Philistine crew of the society in which he lives. His life has been written by a friend, and left on the desk; the tom-cat Murr finds it and writes his own life on the back of the sheets. So off goes the copy to the printer, who stupidly prints the whole thing as a unity, Kreisler and Kater Murr all mixed up in one book. But Kater Murr is a deeply Philistine cat; he embodies in himself everything that Kreisler hates and that is hostile to Kreisler. Kater Murr sums up his philosophy of life: '*Gibt es einen behaglicheren Zustand, als wenn man mit sich selbst ganz zufrieden ist?*' You understand German?"

"No."

"You should. Without German, very poor music. The tom-cat says: 'Is there a cosier condition than being thoroughly satisfied with oneself?' That is the philosophy of the Philistine."

"A cosy condition; like having a good job as a typist."

"If that is all you want, and you cannot see beyond it. Of course not all typists are like that, or there would be no audiences at concerts."

"I want more than a cosy condition."

"And you shall have it. But you will find cosy places, too. This is one of them."

Kisses. Caresses of such skill and variety as Schnak would never have thought possible. Ninety seconds of ecstasy, and then deep peace, in which Schnak fell asleep.

The Doctor did not sleep for several hours. She was thinking of Johannes Kreisler, and herself.

(4)

THE WINE WAS VERY GOOD. Beyond that, Simon Darcourt would not have dared to speak, for he did not consider himself knowledgeable about wines. But he knew a good wine when he drank it, and this was undoubtedly very good. The bottles, as Prince Max had called to his attention, bore conservative, rather spidery engraving that declared them to be reserved for the owners of the vineyard. Nothing there of the flamboyant labels, with carousing peasants or Old Master pictures of fruit, cheese, and dead animals that marked commonplace wines. But at the top of these otherwise reticent labels was an elaborate achievement of arms and underneath it a motto: *Du sollst sterben ehe ich sterbe*.

Thou shalt perish ere I perish, thought Darcourt. Did it refer to the owners of the display of arms, or to the wine in the bottles? Must be the aristocrats; nobody would claim that a wine would outlive anyone who might be drinking it. Suppose a very young person — sixteen, let us say — were given a glass at the family table; suppose some child of a wine-drinking home were given a little, mixed with water, so that it would not feel left out at a family feast. Was it asserted that sixty years later the wine would still be in first-rate condition? Not likely. Wines like that were sold by the greatest auctioneers, not by popular wine merchants. So the boast, or assertion, or threat — it could be all or any of those — must apply to the people whose blazon of nobility this was.

There those people were, sitting at the table with him. Prince Max, who must be well into his seventies, was as straight, as slim, and as elegant as when he had been a dashing young German officer. Only his spectacles, which he somehow managed to make distinguished, and the thinness of his yellowish-white hair, so carefully brilliantined and brushed straight back from his knobby brow, gave any sign of how old he might be. His gaiety, his exuberance, and his unquenchable flow of anecdote and chatter could have belonged to a man half his age.

As for the Princess Amalie, she was as beautiful, as well-preserved, and as becomingly dressed as when Darcourt had first seen her when, during the past summer, she had made it so tactfully clear that if he wanted to know certain facts about the late Francis Cornish he must somehow provide her with the preliminary studies, from the hand of that same Francis Cornish, that had resulted in the Old Master drawing she used so lavishly, yet with such splendid understatement, in her advertisements. And that was what he had done.

The Clerical Cracksman, as he now thought of himself, had been just as adroit and just as lucky at the National Gallery as he had been at the University Library. The same approach to the curator of drawings, who was a friend and would not think of doubting Simon; the same casual, but swift, examination of the drawings in a special portfolio; a quick substitution of the drawings he had pinched from the Library, and which he carried tucked under the back strap of his M.B. waistcoat, for those that were the price of the Princess's confidence; the same cheerful greeting to his friend as he left the archives of the Gallery. The Gallery had not yet got around to putting those beastly little marks on the drawings that set off alarms when one passed certain snoopy ray machines; indeed, it looked as if nobody had looked into the portfolio since first it had come to the Gallery over a year before. It was a very neat job, thought Simon, if he said so himself, and he had been lucky in the day he chose for his robbery, because it was a day when the Pope was visiting Ottawa, and everybody who might have been snooping about was in a distant field, watching the charismatic Pontiff celebrate an outdoor mass, and utter instructions and adjurations for their future conduct to the people of Canada.

Was he dead to shame, Simon had asked himself? Was he now a contented, successful criminal, unhampered by his clerical vows? He did not attempt a philosophical answer; he was wholly in the grip of the biographer's covetous, unappeasable spirit. He was on to a good thing, and nothing should stand in his way. He would chance losing his soul, if only he could write a really good book. A deathbed repentance would probably square things with God. Meanwhile, this was Life.

"My wife is quite delighted with what you have brought," said Prince Max. "You are sure it is complete — every preliminary study?"

"To the best of my knowledge," said Simon. "I went

through all Francis Cornish's drawings, his own and all the Old Masters he had copied, and I saw nothing related to the portrait of the Princess except the studies I have put in your keeping."

"Admirable," said the Prince. "I shall not say we do not know how to thank you, because we do. Amalie shall tell you all she knows about *le beau ténébreux*. And so shall I, though I did not know him so well as she. I only met him once, at Düsterstein. He made an immediate favourable impression. Handsome; modest, even witty, when wine had overcome his reticence. But you must continue, my dear. Meanwhile, another glass of wine?"

"Francis Cornish was everything Max says, and a great deal more," said the Princess. She drank little; a great professional beauty and a razor-sharp woman of business cannot afford to be a soaker. "He came into my life just as I was emerging from girlhood, and was beginning to be seriously interested in men. Seriously, I say; every girl notices men and dreams about them from the time she begins to walk. But he came to my family home just when I was beginning to think about lovers."

"It is strange to think of the Francis I knew as greatly attractive," said Simon. "He became rather an oddity as time went on."

"But I am sure it must have been a ruined beauty you saw as oddity," said the Princess. "Men do not notice such things, unless their romantic interest is in other men. Surely you have photographs?"

"He hated being photographed," said Simon.

"Then I can surprise you. I have many photographs, that I took myself. A girl's snapshots, of course, but revealing. I have one that I used to keep under my pillow until my governess discovered it and forbade it. I told her she was jealous and she laughed, but it was a laugh that told me I had hit the mark. Very handsome, and he had a nice deep voice. Not quite American; there was a Scottish burr in it that melted my soul."

"I am already jealous," said the Prince.

"Oh Max, don't be silly. You know what girls are."

"I knew what you were, my darling. But I knew what I was, too. So at the time I was not jealous."

"Odious vanity!" said the Princess. "Anyhow, we all have our early loves whom we keep in the back of our minds all our lives. I am sure you know what I mean, Professor."

"There was a girl with ringlets, when I was nine," said Darcourt, taking a sip of his wine. "I know what you mean. But please go on about Francis."

"He had everything a very young girl could love. He even had a rather untrustworthy heart. He had to keep watch on it, and report to his doctor in London."

The Prince laughed. "The heart was as useful to him as his skill with the brush," he said.

"And I am sure the dicky heart was as real as the skill."

"Of course. But we know what those reports to his doctor were, don't we?"

"You knew," said the Princess. "But I did not know, not then. You knew a lot of things I did not know."

"You are going to explain, I hope?" said Darcourt. "Bad heart. I knew something of that. Of course it was the heart that killed him at last. But was it something else?"

"I knew about the bad heart at the other end — the London end," said the Prince. "Francis sent accounts of his heart to his doctor, who passed them on at once to the right people at the Ministry of Information, because they were a code. Francis was watching the trains that passed by Düster-stein two or three times a week, carrying poor souls to a nearby internment camp — a labour camp or something of the sort. Anyhow, one of those infamous camps from which very few people escaped alive."

"Are you telling me Francis was a spy?"

"Of course he was a spy," said the Prince. "Didn't you know? His father was a well-known spy, and I suppose he introduced the boy to the family trade."

"But *le beau ténébreux* wasn't a very good spy," said the Princess. "Lots of spies aren't, you know. I don't suppose he was a very important spy. He came to Düsterstein as an assistant to that old rogue Tancred Saraceni, who was restoring the family pictures, and if Saraceni wasn't a spy he was certainly one of the great busybodies of his time. He was on to Francis at once. And so was my grandmother."

"Nobody put anything over on the old Gräfin," said the Prince. "She was up to every dodge."

"Sorry," said Darcourt. "You've lost me completely. What was Düsterstein, and who was the old Gräfin, and what is all this spy business? I'm completely in the dark."

"Then we shall be able to pay for those drawings in full," said the Prince.

"You have the key to the missing years in Francis's life. I knew he had been in Europe for some time as a student of painting, and that he had worked with the great Saraceni, but nothing beyond that."

"Düsterstein was Amalie's family home. She lived there with her grandmother, who was the old Gräfin."

"I was an orphan," said the Princess. "Not a pitiable orphan, or a Dickensian orphan, but just an orphan, and I was brought up at Düsterstein by my grandmother, and a governess. It was as dull as could be, till old Saraceni came to work on the family collection of pictures, and not long afterward *le beau* turned up to help him. Exciting, under the circumstances."

"And he was a spy?"

"Certainly he was a spy. So was my governess, Ruth Nibsmith. Germany was full of spies during the years of the Reich. With so many spies everywhere it is astonishing that Britain made such a goat of herself as the war approached."

"He was spying on a nearby internment camp?"

"He never went near it. Nobody could do that, and certainly not a Canadian in a little sports car. No; he just counted the number of freight cars in each train that chugged along the track not far from our house. I used to watch him. It was funny, really. There I was, in my window in a tower — sounds romantic, doesn't it — watching Francis count — you could almost hear him — as he stood at his window, invisible, as he thought, in the darkness of night. And there in the garden below, behind some bushes, was my governess, spying on Francis. I used to watch them both, almost helpless with laughter. And I suspect that my grandmother was watching too, from a room next to her business office. She was a very big farmer, you know."

"The thing about spies," said the Prince, "is that unless they are of the small number of very good ones, you can almost smell them. They have balloons coming out of their heads, like people in the comic strips, with 'I'm a snoop' written in them. One doesn't pay too much attention to them, because most of them are harmless. But if a strange, handsome young man turns up in your castle, to help a crook like Saraceni, with every credential including a bad heart, who sends regular letters to a Harley Street address — he's probably a spy."

"But Francis was a genuine assistant to Saraceni?" said Darcourt. "There was no deception about that."

"Saraceni was the soul of deception. Not, mind you, that I think he was dishonest in a trivial or purely self-seeking way. He had an artistic passion for illusion, far beyond fakery. He thought of it as playing tricks with Time. He was a very great restorer; you know that. And when he was working on a painting of value, like the pieces in the Düsterstein collection, he worked faithfully in the spirit and the mode of the artist who had made the picture. He turned back the clock. But he could take a piece of very indifferent painting, and skilfully make something fifth-rate look second-rate. That is art of a very special kind — knowing just how far to go."

"One of the best things of that kind to come from Saraceni's studio was, in fact, the work of Francis Cornish," said the Princess. "*Drollig Hansel* — you remember it, Max?"

"No, no; that was no patched-up thing. That was an original. The queerest little panel you ever saw, of a dwarf jester. Extraordinary little face; you felt it saw everything."

"It frightened me," said the Princess. "Of course I should not have seen it at all. But you know what children are. Saraceni used to lock up his studio every evening, and probably thought that all his secrets were safe. But I used to take my grandmother's key from her desk every now and then, and have a look. That dwarf seemed to me to speak of all the tragedy of human life — imprisonment in an ugly body, deformity that put him beyond the understanding of other people, the yearning for vengeance and the yearning for love. So much of the horrible pathos of life, on a panel eight inches by ten."

"Where is that picture now?" said Darcourt.

"I have no idea," said the Prince. "I believe it was in Hermann Goering's collection for a time, but I have heard nothing of it since. Unless it was destroyed — and I can't imagine anybody destroying it — it will certainly turn up some day."

"You speak as if Francis had really been a great painter," said Darcourt.

"Yes," said the Prince. "Shall we have coffee now?"

For coffee the three went into a large drawing-room. Darcourt had not been there before; his earlier talks with the Princess had been in a room she used for business, but it was so elegant that only a coarse soul would have thought of questioning any proposal of a business nature that was made there. Haggling, one presumed, was done elsewhere. But haggling there must have been, for Max and Amalie plainly conducted their businesses on a large and highly competitive level. The drawing-room seemed to occupy the whole of one side of the splendid penthouse in which they dwelt.

Darcourt was beginning to be an expert on rich people's penthouses. The Cornishes' penthouse in Toronto was wonderful because it was very modern, and some of its walls were composed entirely of glass, commanding a sweeping view over much of the city, and beyond it so that — enthusiasts insisted — on a fine day it was possible to see the mist rising from Niagara Falls in the farthest distance. But its modernity paradoxically gave it a somewhat timeless air, for it had no obtrusive architectural features, and took its character from the furnishings, many of which were in the seventeenth-century manner that appealed to Arthur and which Maria did not challenge. But Max and Amalie had chosen to give their dwelling a strong eighteenth-century character. That was why the picture that dominated the room was so surprising.

It was a triptych that hung against the damask covering of the south wall. Its subject was not immediately apparent, for it was filled — filled but not crowded — with figures dressed in the manner of the earliest sixteenth century; figures in ceremonial dress, figures in ceremonial armour, and some figures in the robes that artists have for so long used to clothe characters from biblical history. But a rather longer inspection told Darcourt that he was looking at a representation — a most unusual representation — of *The Marriage at Cana*. It was not until the Princess spoke that he became aware that he was gaping at it.

"You are admiring our treasure," she said. "Do sit here where you can see it."

Darcourt took his coffee, and sat by her. "A magnificent picture," he said. "And most unusual in terms of its subject. The figure of Christ is relegated to an inferior position, and He might almost be said to be looking in wonder at the bridegroom. May I ask if it is known who the artist was?"

"The picture is one of five or six we thought of selling a few years ago," said Prince Max. "It would have been a wrench, but we needed money badly, as I was at that time extending my wine business to North America, and you can imagine how much money that would take. The Düsterstein collection, of which we had managed to salvage some of the best pieces after the ruin and spoliation of the war, came to our rescue. We sold all but this one. Great American galleries were eager to get them. Indeed, for a time it looked as if this one might go to the National Gallery of Canada, but the deal fell through. Some trouble about finance. We had the money we needed from the other sales, so we decided to keep it."

"But you do not know who painted it?"

"Oh, yes. We know. Indeed, it was a Canadian art historian who went as far as possible into the whole question of the picture, and attached to it the name of The Alchemical Master. Because he found elements in it that suggested a knowledge of alchemy."

"The historian's name was Aylwin Ross, wasn't it?" said Darcourt.

"That was the man," said the Prince. "A very personable fellow. He helped us a great deal in placing our other pictures. You can dig up what he wrote about *The Marriage at Cana* in the files of art journals. Nobody has challenged his opinion, so far as I know. So the picture will probably always be attributed to The Alchemical Master — unless we discover who he was. But here is our other guest."

The other guest was, like the Prince, a marvel of personal preservation. Close inspection suggested that he was well over seventy, but his step was light, his figure trim, and his teeth, though of a surprising brilliance, appeared to be his own.

"Let me introduce Professor Darcourt," said the Princess, thereby making it clear that the newcomer was, at least in her estimation, someone who outranked Darcourt. "He comes from Canada, and he has brought me the things we discussed earlier — so that is that. Professor, this is Mr. Addison Thresher. You recognize him, of course."

Darcourt did not recognize him, but the name rang a faint bell — a tinkle — somewhere in his mind. Ah, yes; one of the Grand Panjandrums of the art world, a man who advised museums, established authenticities, and struck down deceptions with a personal Sword of Truth.

"Addison has helped us so much about pictures," said the Princess. "And we asked him to drop in this evening because he is someone else who knew Francis Cornish. Professor Darcourt is writing a life of Cornish," she said to the man with the wonderful teeth. "You have often spoken about Cornish."

"Yes, indeed. I was present when Cornish leapt in a single bound from the status of a pupil of Tancred Saraceni into a place as a great detector of fraud. I saw him skewer Jean-Paul Letztpfennig. Nailed him to the cross, you might say. Exposed him as the painter of a fraudulent Van Eyck. It was a matter of an indiscreet monkey, that Letztpfennig had allowed into a picture where no such monkey could have entered by the hand of Van Eyck. The shrewdest, most elegant destruction of a fraud I have ever witnessed. But he never built on it as everybody expected him to do. Not much was heard of him afterward except as a member of that commission that attempted to restore works of art to their owners after the war."

"Yes, I know about that," said Darcourt. "It is the hidden days, the Düsterstein days I suppose I may call them now, that have puzzled me. What was he like then? Can you tell me?"

"I saw him at the great scene at The Hague," said Thresher, "and, of course, I was with him on the Commission that had the job of restoring lost or looted art after the war, but we had very little direct contact then. He was impressive, as you know better than I do. Tall, quiet in manner, but with a quality that I suppose could be called Byronic. A whiff of brimstone."

"Exactly as I remember him," said the Princess. "A whiff of brimstone. Irresistible. And Byronic."

"He ended as a shambling eccentric," said Darcourt. "Agreeable, when you knew him. But a long way from *le beau ténébreux*."

"Wouldn't you have expected that?" said Thresher. "What would Byron have been like if he had lived to be an old man? A fat, bald Tory with fearful indigestion. Probably an embittered woman-hater. These romantic heroes are lucky if they die early. They are not built for long wear."

Although the conversation continued throughout an evening that Darcourt ended by leaving sharp at eleven o'clock, he heard nothing more of significance about Francis Cornish. The talk touched on Cornish again and again, then veered away to some matter of concern to the art world, about which Thresher had an endless fund of hints and stories that might have been illuminating if Darcourt had been better informed than he was about the great sales, the great exposures, and the stupefying prices.

His evening, however, had not been quite so limited in its information as it might have seemed. Max and Amalie did their best to requite him for the drawings he had placed in their hands before dinner. They played fair in that, and when he left, the Princess gave him all her photographs of her adolescent love. But all evening his eyes turned again and again toward *The Marriage at Cana*, and when he caught his plane the next morning he was on fire to continue some research which would, he greatly hoped, tell him something about Francis Cornish that would make his book much more than a respectable, respectful biography.

(5)

WAS ARTHUR PLEASED that such an important meeting of the Cornish Foundation should be taking place somewhere other than at the Round Table? That instead of the nuts and fruits and sweets from the Platter of Plenty they were refreshing themselves from a slapdash smorgasbord Dr. Gunilla Dahl-Soot and Schnak had whipped up with a few biscuits and tins of smoked fish? That a potent aquavit was being drunk — drunk rather too freely by Hollier — with beer chasers?

No, Arthur was not pleased, but his self-control was so great that nobody would have known it, and indeed he was not fully aware of it himself, except as a generalized discomfort. He felt that control of the opera project had been taken out of his hands without any obvious snatching, and he was now an adviser only, rather than in his accustomed place as Chairman of the Board.

They had come to listen to music. There was a piano in his splendid penthouse, and if a piano was needed to learn what Hoffmann's music was like, and what Schnak had been able to make of it, why had the Doctor somewhat imperiously demanded that they come here? Schnak was playing now.

She was a competent pianist, for a composer. That is to say, she could play anything at sight but she could not play anything really well. She could play from an orchestral score, giving what she called "a notion" of what was written there, piecing out what she could not play with her ten fingers by hoots, whistles, and shouts of "Brass!" or "Woodwind choir!". When she wished to indicate that a melody was for a singer, she sang in a distressing voice, and as there were no words she took refuge in Yah-yah-yah.

As astonishing as Schnak's noise was her altered appearance. Clean, to begin with. Dressed in some new clothes that looked as if they might have been chosen by the Doctor, for they were severe and might have had style if Schnak had worn

them better. No longer haggard, but puffily plump, like someone who has been eating too much after a long abstinence.
Her hair was now a respectable colour, an undistinguished
brown, and flew about in uncontrolled wisps. She looked
happy, and deeply engaged in what she was doing. A Schnak
transformed.

Will I get a bill for those new clothes, or will the Doctor
have the tact to conceal them among her own expenses,
thought Darcourt. Reasonable enough. So many odd bills
were reaching his desk that he began to feel like a Universal
Provider. But it all made sense, in a way.

No member of the Round Table was a trained musician,
but all were intelligent listeners — concert-goers and buyers
of recordings — and they thought that what they heard was
good. Melodious, certainly, and passionate. There seemed to
be lots of it, and it was being presented in chunks of unde-
veloped, non-continuous sound. When at last Schnak ceased
to play, the Doctor spoke.

"That is what we have, you see. That is what Hulda must
develop and stitch together, and occasionally amplify with
stuff that is akin to Hoffmann without being genuine Hoffmann. He left quite a lot of notes in prose, indicating what he
had in mind. But it is a long way from being an opera. What
we must have now is a detailed libretto, with action and
words. Words that fit these melodies. At this moment we have
not even a final list of the characters in the piece. Of course
we know what the orchestration will be — the sort of thirty-
two-piece group that Hoffmann would have been able to use
in an opera theatre of his own. Strings, woods, a few brasses,
and kettle-drums — only two, for he would not have had
sophisticated modern timpani. So — what have the literary
people been doing?"

"We have a scheme for the libretto. That's to say, I have a
scheme, pretty much like the one I outlined a few weeks
ago," said Powell. "As for characters, there are the seven

leading roles: Arthur, Guenevere, Lancelot, Modred, Morgan Le Fay, Elaine, and Merlin."

"And Chorus?" said the Doctor.

"For the men you have the Knights of the Round Table, and there must be twelve, to make up thirteen with Arthur. Linking it with Christ and the Disciples."

"Oh, that's very dubious," said Hollier. "That's nineteenth-century romanticism and utterly discredited now. Arthur had over a hundred Knights."

"Well, he certainly isn't going to have them in this opera," said Powell. "As well as Lancelot and Modred he can have Sir Kay, the seneschal, Gawaine and Bedevere who are the good guys, and Gareth Beaumains, who can be a pretty boy if we can find one. Then we want Lucas, the butler, and Ulphius, the chamberlain. For funnies we can have Dynadan, who was a wit and lampoonist and can be a high-comedy figure, and Dagonet the Fool, who can be a jackass now and then to keep things lively. And the two blacks, of course."

"Blacks?" said Arthur. "Why blacks in sixth-century Britain?"

"Because if you have an opera nowadays without a black or two, you're in hot water," said Powell. "Luckily we can use Sir Pellinore and Sir Palomides, who are both Saracens, so that takes care of that."

"But Saracens were not black," said Hollier.

"They will be in this show," said Powell. "I want no trouble."

"It will be incredible," said Hollier.

"No it won't. Not when I get it on the stage," said Powell. "Nothing is incredible in opera. Now, as for women —"

"But wait," said Hollier. "Are you sending this whole thing up? Making it into a comedy?"

"Not at all," said the Doctor. "I see what Powell means. Opera presents mythic truth, even when it is about nineteenth-century whores with golden hearts. And mythic truth sets you free to do a lot of very practical things. Wha⁺ about women?"

"A woman for every Knight," said Powell. "They don't need names or characters. Except for the Lady Clarissant, who must be Number Two to Guenevere and carry her fan, or catch her when she faints, or whatever may be necessary. Basically, Clarissant is Chorus, though she will have to have a few more bucks because she plays a named character. So there you are. Twenty-nine in all; and a few extras for heralds and trumpeters, and of course understudies, and you'll get out with less than forty, and never more than thirty-four on stage at one time. We can't get any more on that stage in Stratford if it is to look like anything but the subway at rush-hour."

"How expensive is it likely to be?" said Darcourt.

"Expense is not our first consideration," said Arthur. "This is an adventure, you remember."

"A Quest. A real Arthurian Quest," said Maria. "A Quest in search of something lost in the past. Let's not be cheap."

Was Maria being ironic, Darcourt asked himself. Since their talk — their *divano* — he had sensed something in Maria that was not new, but a return to the Maria he had known before she became Mrs. Arthur Cornish, and seemed to dwindle. Maria was returning to her former stature.

"I'm glad you feel like that," said Powell. "The more I think about this opera the more expensive it becomes. As Maria says, the past doesn't come cheap."

"What are the singers likely to want?" said Darcourt.

"Their figures are pretty well fixed, according to their reputations. For this job, you want second-rank singers —"

"Need we settle for that?" said Arthur.

"Don't misunderstand me. I mean second-rank, not second-rate. You don't want, and couldn't get, the biggest star names; they are booked up for three and four years ahead, and as they do a pretty restricted group of parts they wouldn't consent to learn a new role for a few performances. They aren't used to rehearsal, either. They just swoop in by plane, do their standard Violetta or Rigoletto or whatever it is without much reference to where they are or who they're with, and swoop out again, clutching their money. No, I'm talking about the intelligent singers who are also musicians, who can act and who keep their fat down. There are quite a lot of them now, and they're the opera of the future. But they're always busy, and they don't come cheap, so we shall have to hope luck is with us. I've already made a few inquiries, and I think we'll be all right. Chorus we can get in Toronto; lots of good people."

Admirable, thought Arthur. Just what he would have wanted. Lots of initiative in his friend Geraint. And yet — the business man in him would not be silent — money was being promised, and perhaps contracts offered, and who was authorizing all this? The would-be impresario and patron applauded, but the banker had nasty qualms. Powell was continuing.

"The singers aren't the only problems, let me tell you. Designer — where do you look for a designer now for an opera next summer? Far too late. But we've had a stroke of the greatest luck. There's a real comer who has been doing a lot of supervisory work for the Welsh National Opera, and she wants a chance to design something entirely her own. Dulcy Ringgold, her name is. I've talked to Dulcy on the phone, and she's keen as mustard. But there are conditions."

"Money?" said Darcourt.

"No. Dulcy isn't greedy. But she wants to do the whole thing as if it were being done under Hoffmann's supervision at one of his opera houses — Bamberg, for instance. And that means scene design in the early-nineteenth-century manner, with changes managed as if we had a staff of about fifty stagehands, when we'll probably have ten, and they'll have to learn old techniques that will astonish them. Because in those days stage-hands were really scene-shifters, and not button-pushers. It'll cost a mint."

"I suppose you've closed with her?" said Hollier. The more aquavit he drank, and the more beer he sent down to supervise the aquavit, the more dubious he became.

"I have her on hold," said Powell. "And I hope to God you agree with her plan."

"Does it mean monstrously heavy stuff, long intervals, mossy banks covered with artificial flowers, and a lot of rumbling behind the curtain?" said Arthur.

"Not a bit of it. This kind of stage dressing came before all that nonsense. Quite simply, it's a system where each scene consists of a painted back-drop, and five or six sets of wings on each side of the stage; but they are arranged on wheels so that the scenes change almost instantaneously — in out — in out — so that it's almost like movie dissolves. At the end of each scene the actors leave the stage and — whammo! — you're already in the next scene. But it takes some very nippy work backstage."

"Sounds wonderful," said Maria.

"It's magical! I don't know how we ever changed it for all this business of fixed settings and mood lighting that reflects nothing much but the mood of the lighting-designer. Pure magic!"

"Sounds to me like pantomime," said Hollier.

"It is a bit like pantomime. But what's wrong with that? It's magic, I tell you."

"You mean like the things one sees at Drottningholm?" said Darcourt.

"Just like that."

Nobody but Darcourt among the Foundation members had been to Drottningholm, and they were impressed.

"But why is it so expensive?" said Arthur. "It sounds to me like a few pieces of lath and a lot of canvas and paint."

"And that's what it is. It's the paint that costs money. Good scene-painters are rare nowadays, but Dulcy says she could do it with six good art-students and herself to supervise and do the tricky bits. But it takes time and it costs like the devil."

"If it's magic, we'll have it," said Arthur.

"That's the real Arthurian touch," said Maria, and kissed him.

"I declare for it, without reserve," said the Doctor. "It will mean that I — I mean Hulda — can have many scenes, and that is wonderful freedom for a composer. Indoor-outdoor; forests and gardens. Yes, yes, Mr. Cornish, you are man of fine imagination. I also salute you."

The Doctor kissed Arthur. On the cheek. Not one of her tongue-in-the-mouth kisses.

"With such a scheme of production, I suppose you see no obstacle to using The Questing Beast," said Hollier, cheering up visibly, if a little unsteadily.

"What in God's name is The Questing Beast?" said the Doctor.

"It was the monster whose pursuit was the lifelong occupation of Sir Pellinore," said Hollier. "I'm surprised you do not know. The Questing Beast had the head of a serpent, the body of a libbard, the rump of a lion, the hooves of a hart, and a great, swingeing tail; out of its belly came a sound like the baying of thirty couple of hounds. Just the thing for a magical opera."

"Oh Clem, you genius," said Penny Raven, and, not to be left out when kissing was toward, she kissed Hollier, to his great abashment.

"Well — I don't know," said Powell.

"Oh, you must," said Penny. "Hulda could make the Beast sing out of its belly! All those voices, in wonderful harmony. What a *coup de théâtre*! No, I suppose I mean a *coup d'oreille*. It would be the hit of the show."

"Just what I'm afraid of," said Powell. "You have a very minor character, Sir Pellinore, traipsing about the stage with a bloody great pantomime dragon, and taking all the attention. No! Nix on The Questing Beast."

"I thought you wanted imagination," said Hollier, with the hauteur of a man whose brilliant idea has been scorned.

"Imagination is not uncontrolled fantasy," said the Doctor.

"The Questing Beast is a vital part of the Arthurian Legend," said Hollier, raising his voice. "The Questing Beast is pure Malory. Are you throwing Malory overboard? I want to know. If I am to have any part in preparing this libretto — as you call it — I want to know the ground rules. What are your intentions toward Malory?"

"Good sense must prevail," said the Doctor, who had not been inattentive to the aquavit. "Myth must be transmuted into art, not slavishly reproduced. If Wagner had been ruled by myth, the Ring of the Nibelungs would have been trampled to death by monsters and giants and nobody would have understood the story. I have my responsibility here, and I remind you of it. Hulda's interests must come before everything. Besides, Hoffmann has not provided any music that could in any way be turned into a four-part chorus singing inside the belly of a monster, and probably not able to see the conductor. To hell with your Questing Beast!"

Arthur felt it was time to exert his skills as Chairman of the Board, and after five minutes, during which Hollier and Penny and Powell and the Doctor shouted and insulted each other, he was able to restore some sort of order, though the heat of passion in the room was still palpable.

"Let's come to a conclusion, and stick with it," he said. "We're talking about the nature of the libretto. We have to decide the ground on which it rests. Professor Hollier is determined on Malory."

"It's simple reason," said Hollier. "The libretto is to be

in English. Malory is the best English source."

"But the language, the language!" said Penny. "All that 'yea, forsooth', and 'full fain', and 'I woll welle'. Great to read but bloody to speak, let alone sing. Do you imagine you could write verse in that lingo?"

"I agree," said Darcourt. "We've got to have language that's clear, and permits rhyme, and has a romantic flavour. So what's it to be?"

"It's obvious," said Powell. "Obvious to anybody but a scholar, that's to say. Sir Walter's your man."

Nobody responded to the name of Sir Walter. There were looks of incomprehension on every face but Arthur's.

"Sir Walter Scott, he means," said he. "Haven't any of you read any Scott?"

"Nobody reads Scott nowadays," said Penny. "He's ceased to be a Figure and been demoted to an Influence. Too simple for scholarly consideration but can't be wholly overlooked."

"You mean in the universities," said Arthur. "Increasingly I thank God that I never went to one. As a reader I've just rambled at large on Parnassus, chewing the grass wherever it seemed rich. I read an awful lot of Scott when I was a boy, and loved it. I think Geraint is right. Scott's our man."

"Just about every big Scott novel was made into an opera. Not operas that are done much now, but big hits in their day. Rossini, Bellini, Donizetti, Bizet — all those guys. I've looked at them. Pretty neat, I'd say." It was Schnak who spoke. She had been almost unheard until this moment, and the others looked at her with wonder, as in one of those old tales where an animal is suddenly gifted with speech.

"We have forgotten that Hulda is fresh from her studies in musicology," said the Doctor. "We must listen to her. After all, she is to do the most important part of the work."

"Hoffmann read a lot of Scott," said Schnak. "Thought he was great. Sort of operatic."

"Schnak is right," said Arthur. "Operatic. *Lucia di Lammermoor* — still a great favourite."

"Hoffmann knew it. Probably was an influence on him, if you're hog-wild for influences," said Schnak. "Gimme some Scott, and let's see what can be done. It'd have to be a *pistache*, naturally."

"You must say *pastiche*, my dear," said the Doctor. "But you are right."

"Am I to understand that we are abandoning Malory?" said Hollier.

" 'Raus mit Malory," said Schnak. "Never heard of him."

"Hulda! You told me you did not know German!"

"That was two weeks ago, Nilla," said Schnak. "How do you suppose I got my musicology, without German? How do you suppose I read what Hoffmann wrote on his notes, without German? And I can even speak a little kitchen German. Honestly, you top people are dumb! You ask me questions like examiners, and you treat me like a kid. I'm supposed to be writing this thing, eh?"

"You're right, Schnak," said Powell. "We've been leaving you out. Sorry. You've hit the nail on the head. It must be Scott *pastiche*."

"If it's not to be Scott *pistache* I'll have to get down to reading *Marmion* and *The Lady of the Lake* right away," said Darcourt. "But how do we work?"

"Hulda will give you details about the music, and little plans that show you how the tunes go, so you can fit good words to them. And as quick as you can, please."

"I must ask to be excused," said Hollier. "If you need me for details of history, or costume, or behaviour, you know where to find me. Unless, of course, untrammelled, uninformed imagination is to determine everything. And so I bid you good-night."

(6)

"WHAT GOT INTO CLEM?" said Penny, as they drove away in Arthur's car. It was a fine car, but it was rather a squash in the back seat with Penny, Darcourt, and Powell, however politely they might try to restrain their bottoms.

"Just thwarted professorship," said Darcourt.

"Probably mid-life crisis," said Powell.

"What's that?" asked Arthur, who was driving.

"It's one of the new, fashionable ailments, like pre-menstrual bloat," said Powell. "Excuses anything."

"Really?" said Arthur. "Do you suppose I might have one of those? I've not been feeling quite the thing, lately."

"You're too young for it, my darling," said Maria. "Anyway, I wouldn't let you. It can make a man into a big baby. I thought Clem was being an awful baby."

"I've known he was a baby for years," said Darcourt. "A large, learned, very handsome baby, but still a baby. For me, the surprise of the evening was Schnak. She's coming out of her cell with a hell of a yell, isn't she? She's given us our orders."

"It's Old Sooty," said Penny. "I have my dark suspicions about Old Sooty. Do you know that kid has moved in with her? Now what does that mean?"

"You obviously want to tell us," said Maria.

"Do I have to tell you? She and Schnak are poofynooks. It's as plain as the nose on your face."

"It seems to be doing Schnak a power of good," said Arthur. "Clean, putting on a little flesh, finding her tongue, and she doesn't look at us any more as if she was just about to order up the tumbrils. If that's what lesbianism does, three cheers for lesbianism, I say."

"Yes, but haven't we some responsibility? I mean, are we delivering this kid gagged and bound into the hands of that old bull-dyke? Didn't you hear 'Nilla' and 'dear Hulda' all evening until you nearly threw up?"

"What about it?" said Maria. "She's probably the first person who has ever been nice to Schnak — really nice, I mean. Very likely the first person to talk to Schnak about music seriously and not just as an instructor. If it means a few rolls in the hay, the occasional bout of kindly kissing and clipping, what about it? Schnak's nineteen, for God's sake, and an exceedingly bright nineteen. The word genius has been whispered."

"What do you think, Simon?" said Penny. "You're the professional moralist."

"I think what Maria thinks. And as a professional moralist I think you have to take love where you find it."

"Even if it means being mauled and clapper-clawed by Dr. Gunilla Dahl-Soot? Thank you, Father Darcourt, for these advanced opinions."

"I'm in the dark about this business," said Arthur. "What do they *do*?"

"Oh, Arthur, that's what every man asks about lesbians," said Maria. "I suppose they do whatever comes into their heads. I'm sure I could think of lots of things."

"Could you really?" said Arthur. "You must show me. I'll be Schnak and you be Gunny, and we'll find out what happens in the gunny-sack. A new window on the wonders of the world."

"I think you're being frivolous and irresponsible," said Penny. "I am more and more convinced that this Snark of ours is going to turn out to be a Boojum."

"What *is* all this Snark and Boojum stuff?" said Arthur. "You've talked about it ever since you came in with us on this operatic venture. Some obscure literary reference, I suppose, designed to keep the uneducated in their proper place. Instruct me, Penny; I am just a humble, teachable money-man. Let me into your Druid Circle."

"Sorry, sorry Arthur; I suppose it *is* a private lingo but it says so much in a few words. You see, there's a very great poem by Lewis Carroll about the Hunting of the Snark; a lot of crazy creatures set off, they know not whither, in search of they know not what. The hunt is led by a Bellman — that's you, Arthur — full of zeal and umph, and his crew includes a Boots and a Banker, and a Billiard Marker and a Beaver who makes lace — probably you, Simon, because 'he often saved them from wreck, / Though none of the sailors knew how'. And there's a very peculiar creature who seems to be a Baker but turns out to be a Butcher, and he is omnicompetent —

> He would answer to 'Hi!' or to any loud cry,
>   Such as 'Fry me!' or 'Fritter-my-wig!'
> To 'What-you-may-call-um!' or 'What-was-his name!'
>   But especially 'Thing-um-a-jig!'
>
> While, for those who preferred a more forcible word,
>   He had different names for these:
> His intimate friends called him 'Candle-ends',
>   And his enemies, 'Toasted-cheese'.

— so that's obviously you, Geraint, you Cymric mystifier, because you have us all buffaloed about this opera business. It's just about a crazy voyage that somehow, in an unfathomable way, makes a kind of eerie sense. I mean, so many of us are professors — well, Clem and Simon and me, which is quite a few — and listen to this from the Bellman's definition of a Snark —

> The third is its slowness in taking a jest
>   Should you happen to venture on one,
> It will sigh like a thing that is deeply distressed:
>   And it always looks grave at a pun.

Isn't that what we've been doing all evening? Yammering about Malory and the scholarly approach to something that is utterly unscholarly in the marrow of its bones, because it's

Art. And Art is rum stuff — the very rummest. It may look like a nice, simple Snark, but it can suddenly prove to be a Boojum, and then, look out!

> 'For, although common Snarks do no manner of harm
>   Yet I feel it my duty to say,
> Some are Boojums —' The Bellman broke off in alarm,
>   For the Baker had fainted away.

Do you get what I mean, Arthur? Do you see how it fits in and haunts my mind?"

"I might see it if I had your mind, but I haven't," said Arthur. "Literary reference leaves me gaping."

"I bet it would have left King Arthur gaping," said Maria loyally, "if Merlin had got off a few quaint cracks from his Black Book."

"Yes, but I see how this whole thing could go very queer," said Penny. "And I had a hint of it tonight. That poor kid Schnak thinks she's tough, but she's just a battered baby, and she's being let in for something she certainly can't handle. It worries me. I don't want to be a busybody, or a soul-saver, or any of that, but surely we ought to *do* something!"

"I think you're jealous," said Powell.

"Jealous! Me! Geraint, I hate you! I've just decided. Ever since I met you I've wondered what I really think about you, you blathering, soapy Welsh goat, and now I know. You're in this for what you can get, and you don't give a maggoty shit for anybody else, and I hate you!"

"We're all in everything for what we can get, professor," said Powell. "And if not, why are we in it? What are you in it for? You don't know, but you hope to find out. Fame? Fun? Something to fill up the gaps in your life? What's your personal Snark? You really ought to find out."

"This is where I get out," said Penny. "Thank you for driving me home, Arthur. I can't get out unless you get out first, Geraint."

Powell stepped on to the pavement and bowed as he held the door for the furious Penny.

"You shouldn't have said that, Geraint," said Maria, when they drove away.

"Why not? I think it's true."

"All the more reason not to say it," said Maria.

"You could be right about Penny," said Darcourt. "Why is such an attractive woman unattached at her age? Why is she so flirtatious with men but it never leads to anything? Perhaps our Penny is looking asquint at something she doesn't want to see."

"A fight over Schnak is just what we need to relieve the dowdy simplicity of this opera venture," said Powell. "Art is so lacking in passion, don't you think? With the Doctor and Penny contesting like the Bright and the Dark Angel for the body and soul of Hulda Schnakenburg, we shall add a little salt to the dreary porridge of our lives."

(7)

ETAH IN LIMBO

WHAT DO THEY DO? *Arthur wants to know, and I, happy in my privileged position, may say that I do know.*

I must be careful about my privileged position. "Is there a cosier condition than being thoroughly pleased with oneself?" I must be careful not to become like Kater Murr. Even in Limbo, I suppose, one can sink into Philistinism.

But what Dr. Gunilla and Hulda Schnakenburg do is far from Philistine, and indeed far from the anti-Philistine world as I knew it when I was a part of what is now flatteringly called The Romantic Movement. Of course there were intense and intimate friendships between women then, but whatever physical amusement they generated was not known or seriously considered. Certainly some young ladies hung about each other's necks in public; they often dressed in identical

gowns; they swooned or had hysterics at the same time, for both swoon-
ing and hysterics were high among the feminine luxuries of the day, and
were thought to show great delicacy of feeling. But it was always
assumed that these sensitive creatures would marry at last, and after
marriage the intimacy with the female friend might become even more
precious. I suppose if, after the first raptures of marriage, your husband
was in the habit of coming to bed drunk, or smelling of the bawdy-house,
or in a mood to black an eye or give a few hard slaps to a critical wife, it
was delightful to have a friend who treated you with delicate respect and
who could perhaps rouse an ecstasy that your disappointing husband
thought was outside the emotional range of a well-bred woman. That
was how it was, you see: that special ecstasy was thought to be the
prerogative of whores, and whores became expert at faking it, and
thereby flattering their clients.

It was all quite different, in my day. Love was an emotion greatly
valued, but it was valued for its own sake, and an unhappy love or a
torturing love was perhaps even more valued than a love that was
fulfilled. After all, love is an ecstasy, but sex is an appetite, and one does
not always satisfy an appetite at the best restaurant in town. The bordel
where Devrient and I used to go in Berlin was quite a humble affair, and
the women there knew their trade and their place; they did not presume to
intimacy with the visitors, who were always called Mein Herr, unless
the visitors liked endearments and smutty talk, which was extra, and had
to be considered in the tip. It was in Russia and Poland that people who
liked that sort of thing became familiar with the whore and, in my
opinion, made fools of themselves. I cannot recall the face of a single
whore, though I employed many.

Why? Why did I go to the bordel, even when I was out of my mind
with love for the unattainable pupil, the lovely Julia Marc? Even in my
most love-stricken hours I did not cease to eat, or drink — or visit the
bordel. Love was not an appetite, but an ecstasy. Whores were not
women, but servants.

What about my wife? Do you suppose that when I was head over
ears in love with another woman I would insult my wife, my dearest
Michalina Rohrer, by seeking out her bed? Do you suppose I had no

respect for her, and all she meant to me? She was a fact, and an extremely important fact, of my life, and I would not have insulted her, even if she were unconscious of the insult — and I do not for a moment suppose she was ignorant of my passion for Julia. She had a close friend, by the way, and I never made inquiry or interfered in whatever may have passed between them. Nor, I suppose, did Dante, when he was sighing for his Beatrice. Dante was a very good family man, and so was I, in the manner of my time. Romantic love and a firm domestic life were not incompatible, but they were not expected to mingle. Marriage was a contract, to be taken seriously, and the fidelity it demanded was not to be trifled with. But the obsession of love might, and often did, lie elsewhere.

Is there love between Gunilla and Hulda? On Hulda's side I am sure it is so, and whether either of them expects it to last, as marriage is expected to last, I cannot say. It was Hulda's initiation into that sweet ecstasy; Gunilla is a woman of great experience. It was she, for instance, who introduced Hulda to what they called the Love Potion.

It was a sort of jam, really. Jam was the heart of it; the very best raspberry jam made by Crabtree and Evelyn. With the jam was mixed honey and a few chopped walnuts. Gunilla would spread a path of it on Hulda's tender belly, beginning at the navel and extending downward. Having licked the jam out of the navel, Gunilla would lick slowly and gently in a southward direction and in time — it all had to be done lentissimo e languidamente — to the pintle of ecstasy, and then there were sighs and sometimes cries. After a restful period of kissing, Hulda took her turn, anointing Gunilla's belly and performing the same slow ritual. With Gunilla it always ended in quite loud cries. It was she who most appreciated the walnuts, which gave, she said, a sort of traction that was very exciting.

All innocent and delightful, concluding with a bath together (enlivened with a couple of aquavits apiece) and a refreshing sleep. Who was harmed? Nobody. And there was no resorting to the bordel, simply as a convenience.

That is what I envy them. For it was in the bordel, somewhere — I cannot tell in what city of the many where I pursued my career — it came about that I acquired the disease that was one of the contributing elements in my early death. I underwent a cure, of course, but the cures in those days cured nothing except the debts of the physicians. I thought I had been cured, but later I knew better. That was in 1818, and when I became horribly ill and died in 1822 I knew that it was not simply the liver ailment that grew from all that champagne, or the mysterious paralysis that was at last diagnosed as tabes dorsalis — one of the many names given to the old, old disease — that carried me off. As it carried off poor Schubert, who, as I saw from the vantage of Limbo, was brought to wearing an absurd wig, to disguise the baldness that syphilis had brought upon him. And Schumann, who died of a self-inflicted starvation: but it sprang from the madness that had so long possessed him — madness that arose from the Morbus Gallicus.

It was my legs that first became useless to me, then the paralysis settled in my hands and I could not hold a pen. I was determined to complete **Arthur of Britain** if I could, and when writing was impossible I dictated my music to my wife, my dear faithful Michalina, who was a skilled amanuensis. But I could achieve nothing but sketches for the music I wanted — the sketches from which Schnak is so cleverly divining what was in my mind. The disease that made me unable to control the pen seemed to enlarge and enrich my musical imagination; I have long believed that certain poisons — tobacco and wine, to name two of the commonest — may do that in minds of fine quality, where the poisons do not induce the usual stupor. A truly Romantic notion, some would say. But the tortures and wrenchings that came with the inspirations were terrible, and it was to them that I at last succumbed.

It is the disease of genius, many people have said, because so many men of note, and many of them my contemporaries, died of it, or were hastened to the grave because syphilis underlay whatever it was the doctors said had killed them. Would I have sacrificed my genius to avoid the pain and degradation? Fortunately there is no necessity to answer that question.

V

I SIMPLY *adore* Canada! What I've seen, that's to say. Which isn't the whole thing, of course. Really only Toronto and the Royal Winter Fair. I'm going to try for a stop-over in Montreal on my way home — try out my French, you know — but I mayn't be able to spare the time. Must get back to my stud, you see. So much to be done at this time of year."

"I'm glad you approve of us," said Darcourt. "Now, about your father —"

"Oh, yes, Daddy. That's what we're here to talk about, isn't it? That's the reason for this lovely lunch in this absolutely super restaurant. Because you're writing about him, aren't you? I scribble a little myself, you know. Pony stories for children. They sell a few hundred thousand, to my surprise. But just before we get onto Daddy, there's one thing — rather hush-hush, but I know you're discreet — that I think isn't just the way it should be in Canada, and unless something is done before it goes too far it could let you down fearfully. I mean, it could bring about a drop in world prestige."

Ah, politics, thought Darcourt. Politics, which rages like the hectic in the veins of every Canadian, and quickly infects visitors — even Little Charlie, otherwise Miss Charlotte Cornish, who sat before him digging into the poached salmon.

"And what is that?" he asked, without wanting to know.

Little Charlie leaned forward conspiratorially, a loaded fork poised like a wand in her hand; there was a flake of salmon clinging to her lower lip.

"It's your farriery," she whispered. The flake was detached by the whisper and sped across the table toward Darcourt's plate. She was the sort of woman who combines acceptable table manners with obvious greed; the lapels of her excellent tweed jacket carried evidence of hasty, joyous gobbling.

"Farriery?" he said, puzzled. Had Canada's farriery gone to pot, and he had not noticed? Had the word some significance unknown to him?

"Don't imagine I'm faulting your vets," said Little Charlie. "First-class, so far as I can judge. But it's the degree below the vet; the farrier groom who is the real companion and confidant of the pony. The vet is there for the big stuff, of course: colic, and farcy, and strangles and all those dreadful things that can ruin a fine creature. But it's the farrier who gives the hot mash when the beastie is a wee bit sicky-pussy from a chill, or a tumble. It's the farrier who pets and comforts when things haven't gone just the way the beastie would like at a show. I call the farrier the pony's nurse. In fact, in my stud I have this most wonderful girl — well, she must be my age, but she's a girl to me — her name's Stella, but I always call her Nursie, and believe you me she lives up to her name. I'd trust Stella far beyond most vets, let me tell you."

"How lucky you are to have her," said Darcourt. "Now, about the late Francis Cornish, I suppose you have some memories of him?"

"Oh, yes," said Little Charlie. "But just a moment; I want to tell you something that happened yesterday. I was judging — head of the judges, really — and the most exquisite little Shetland stallion was brought in. A real winner! Eyes bright and well spaced; fine muzzle and big nostrils, deep chest and splendid withers, marvellous croup — a perfect picture! I tell you, I'd have bought him, if I could raise the cash. Won't tell you his name, because I don't want this to get around — though of course I trust you — and at his head was this groom, not a bit the kind of fellow you'd expect to see with such a little sweetie, and when the pony tossed his head — as they'll do, you know, because they know they're being judged, and they have pride — he jerked the bridle and said, 'Hold still, damn you,' under his breath! But I heard, and I tell you my heart went out to that little creature. 'Are you the farrier?' I said to him — not sharply, but firmly — and he said, 'Yeah, I look after him,' almost insolently. And I thought, well, I've seen quite a lot of that this last few days, and it sickens me. Then he jerked the bridle again and the pony nipped him! And he hit the pony on the nose! Well, of course that was that as far as judging goes. Show me a biter and I'll show you a potential bolter and probably a jibber. And all because of that brute of a groom!"

"Distressing, certainly," said Darcourt. They were moving on toward strawberry shortcake, made with tasteless imported strawberries, but that was what Little Charlie wanted, and Darcourt was trying to prime the pump of her memory. "Was your father fond of animals, do you recall?"

"Couldn't say," said Little Charlie, busy with her spoon. "It was pretty much all King and Country with him, as I was told it. But don't imagine that because I said I might have bought that stallion I'm really keen on Shetlands. Of course they sell well to people with children, because they look so sweet. But they're a deceiving kind of pony, you know. Such a short step. Keep a child too long on a Shetland and you may have spoiled her forever as a rider. What she needs as soon as she's big enough is a good Welsh, with a strain of Arab. They're the ones with style and action! They're my bread-and-butter. Not for polo, mind you. There it's Exmoor and Dartmoor, and I breed a lot of those. In fact — this is telling tales out of school but what the hell! — I sold an Exmoor stallion to His Royal Highness's stable a couple of years ago, and HRH said — I was told this very much in confidence — he'd never seen a finer little stallion."

"I won't tell a soul. Now, about your father —"

"He was a four-year-old and just coming into his best. For God's sake, I said to HRH's man, don't push him too hard. Give him time and he'll get you twenty-five to forty first-class foals every year until he's twenty. But if you push him now — ! Well, you'll never believe this, but I've seen a fine stallion forced to serve as many as three hundred mares a season, and after five years he's just plain knackered! Like people. Quality, not quantity, is the root of the whole thing. Of course they can soldier on. They're wonderfully willing, you know. But it's the sperm. The sperm count in an over-worked stallion goes down and down, and though he may look like Don Juan he's just Weary Willie. As Stella says — she's very broad-spoken, sometimes — his willy is willing but the trollybobs are weak. So that's it. Never, never be greedy with your stallion!"

"I promise you I never will. But now I really think we ought to talk about your father."

"Of course. Sorry, sorry, sorry. The ruling passion. I do rattle on. Stella says so. Well, as to Daddy, I never saw him."

"Never?"

"Not to remember. I suppose he saw me, when I was a tiny. But not after I'd begun to notice. But he cared for me. That's to say he sent money regularly to look after me, and all the farriery was left to my grandmother. Prudence Glasson, you know. The whole gang were related, in various distant degrees. You see, my mummy was Ismay Glasson, and her father was Roderick Glasson, who was kin to Daddy from another point of the compass. I wouldn't have bred them that way if it had been my stud, but that's all past and done with. My very first pony, when I was four — a sweet Shetland — had a ticket on his bridle, 'For Little Charlie from Daddy'."

"You remember your mother, of course?"

"No, not a bit. You see — this is the family skeleton — Mummy was a bolter. Not long after I was born she just took off, and left me to Daddy and my grandparents. Mind you, I think she was a sort of high-minded bolter; she went to Spain to fight in the war and I always assumed she was killed there, but nobody ever gave me any details. She was by way of being a beauty, but from pictures I'd say she was a bit over-bred; nervous and high-strung, and likely to bite, and bolt, and jib, and do all those things."

"Really? That's very helpful. I tried to see your uncle, Sir Roderick, in London at the Foreign Office, to ask a few questions about your mother, but it was impossible to make an appointment."

"Oh, Uncle Roddy would never see you, or tell you anything if he did. He's the original Stuffed Shirt. I've given up all hope of seeing him, not that I'm keen. But don't run away with the idea that I had a neglected or unhappy childhood. It was absolutely marvellous, even though St. Columb's was running down all the time I was growing up. I believe Daddy poured a lot of money into the family place — God knows why — but my grandfather was a hopeless estate manager. Our money from Daddy was watched rather carefully by a solicitor, so it didn't go down the drain, and it still doesn't, let me assure you. My little stud is built on that, and since I met Stella — you'd adore Stella, though she is a bit frank-spoken and you are a parson, after all — I've been as happy as a lark."

"So you really know nothing about your father? In your letter to the Cornishes here you rather suggested that he had some Secret Service connection."

"That was hinted at, but not much was said. Not much was known, I suppose. But you see Daddy's father, Sir Francis, was in that, and very deep, I believe, and how far Daddy followed in his footsteps I really don't know. It was the spy connection that kept Daddy from coming to see me, or so it was said."

"Spy? Do you think he was really a spy?"

"It's not a word Gran would ever hear used. If they're British intelligence agents they certainly aren't *spies*, she said. Only foreigners are *spies*. But you know how kids are. I used to joke about him being a spy, to raise the temperature a little. You know, the way kids do. They always told me to be very secret about it but I don't suppose it matters now."

"And did you know that your father was a painter, and a remarkable connoisseur, and had a reputation as an expert on pictures?"

"Never heard a word about that. Though I was knocked endways to find out he'd left a huge fortune! I did think of asking the Cornishes if they'd like to use some of it to finance some really super breeding — you know, the very best of the best. But then I thought, shut up, Charlie; that's greedy, and Daddy has treated you very well. So shut up! And I have. — Oh, crumbs, I must be off! Heavy afternoon ahead of me. Thanks for the super lunch. I shan't be seeing you again, shall I? Or Arthur and Maria, either. I fly on Friday. They're a super pair. Especially Maria. By the way, you're a great family friend, I believe; have you heard anything about her being in foal?"

"In foal? Oh, I see what you mean. No. Have you?"

"No. But I have the breeder's eye, you know. Right away there's something about a mare that tells the tale. If the stallion's clicked, I mean. — And now I must dash!"

As well as a stout woman may, she dashed.

(2)

ARTHUR WEPT. He had not done so since his parents died in a motor accident when he was fourteen; he was stricken by the grief that overcame him as he sat in Darcourt's study, a cluttered, booky room, into which a little watery November sun made its way cautiously, as if doubtful of its welcome. He wept. His shoulders shook. It seemed to him that he howled, although Darcourt, standing by the window, looking out into the college quadrangle, heard only deep-fetched sobs. Tears poured from his eyes, and salt downpourings of mucus streamed from his nose. One handkerchief was sodden and the second — Arthur always carried two — and the second was rapidly becoming useless. Darcourt was not the sort of man who has boxes of tissues in his study. It seemed to Arthur that his paroxysm would never end; new desolation heaved up into his heart as quickly as he wept out the old. But at last he sank back in his chair blear-eyed, red-nosed, and conscious that his fine tie had a smear of snot on it.

"Got a handkerchief?" he said.

Darcourt threw him one. "Feel better now, do you?"

"I feel like a cuckold."

"Ah, yes. A cuckold. Or as Dr. Dahl-Soot pronounces it, cookold. You'll have to get used to it."

"You're a bloody unsympathetic friend. And a bloody unresponsive priest, Simon."

"Not a bit of it. I am very sorry, both for you and Maria, but what good will it do if I join you in siren tears? My job is to keep a cool head and look at the thing from the outside. What about Powell?"

"I haven't seen him. What do I do? Beat him up?"

"And signal to the whole world what's wrong? No, you certainly do not beat him up. Anyhow, you're in this opera thing up to your neck, and Powell is indispensable."

"Damn it, he's my best friend."

"The cuckoo in the nest is often the best friend. Powell loves you, as a friend may very well love you. I love you, Arthur, though I don't make a song and dance about it."

"*That* kind of love. You have to because you're a priest. Like God, it's your métier."

"You don't know anything about priests. I know we are supposed to love mankind indiscriminately, but I don't. That's why I gave up practical priesthood and became a professor. My faith charges me to love my neighbour but I can't and I won't fake it, in the greasy way professional lovers-of-mankind do — the professionally charitable, the newspaper sob-sisters, the politicians. I'm not Christ, Arthur, and I can't love like Him, so I settle for courtesy, consideration, decent manners, and whatever I can do for the people I really do love. And you are one of those. I can't help you by weeping with you, though I respect your tears. The best I can do is to bring a clear head and an open eye to your trouble. I love Maria, too, you know."

"Indeed I do know. You wanted to marry her, didn't you?"

"I did, and in the kindest possible way she gave me the mitt. I love her even more for that, because Maria and I would have made a damned bad match."

"Okay, old Clear Head and Open Eye. Why did you ask her, then?"

"Because I was in the grip of passion. There were a thousand reasons for loving Maria, and I now see there were a million for not marrying her. I love her still, but don't worry that I want to play the role that Powell has played in your marriage."

"She told me she once had *le coeur tendre* for Hollier, and that you had proposed to her. And looked a fine ninny as you did it, what's more. Every woman has these boss-shots in her past. But she married me, and now she's wrecking it."

"Balls. You're the one who's wrecking it."

"Me! She's pregnant, damn it!"

"And you're sure it's not your child?"

"Yes."

"How? You use some contraceptive, I suppose. Condoms? They're very much in vogue at present."

"I hate the damned things. There they are, the morning after, leering wetly at you from the bedside table or the carpet, like the Ghost of Nooky Past."

"Maria uses something?"

"No. We wanted a child."

"So?"

"I had mumps, you remember. Badly. The doctors told me tactfully that henceforth I would be infertile. Not impotent. Just infertile. And it's irreversible."

"You told Maria, of course?"

"I hadn't got around to it."

"So the child must have been begotten by somebody else?"

"Yes, Sherlock Holmes."

"Must it have been Powell?"

"Who else is a possibility? You see — I hate telling you this — somebody came to me —"

"To tip you off?"

"Yes. A security man who works at night in our apartment building."

"One Wally Crottel?"

"Yes. And he said that Mr. Powell sometimes stayed late, and occasionally overnight when I was out of town, and as a convenience would it be a good idea if he gave Mr. Powell a key to the parking area?"

"And you said no."

"I said no. It was just a hint, you know. But it was enough."

"It was a mistake to underestimate Wally. So then —"

"Because of this opera business Powell comes and goes quite a lot, and if he stays late he uses our guest room. I didn't know he used it when I was away."

"Powell is a very using kind of man."

"So it seems."

"Have you told Maria now? About being infertile, I mean?"

"I told her after she told me she was pregnant. I didn't think she was as happy about a child as I would have expected, but I put it down to shyness. And I suppose I looked astonished — that's a poor word for it — and I couldn't say a word. She asked me what was wrong. I told her."

"Yes?"

"It took a few minutes, and all the time I was talking that hint from Crottel kept swelling in my mind, and at last I came out with it. Was it Powell? I said. She wouldn't say a word."

"Very unlike Maria to have nothing to say."

"She simply closed her mouth and looked as I've never seen her look before. Very big-eyed and tight-lipped. But smiling. It was enough to drive me mad."

"What did you expect? That she should fall at your feet and bathe them in her tears, and then wipe away the tears from your custom-made brogues with her hair? You don't know your own wife, my boy."

"You're damned right I don't. But it drove me crazy, and as I got hotter and hotter she just smiled that bloody smile and refused to say anything. So at last I said that her silence was answer enough. And she said, 'If that's what you think.' And that was all."

"And you haven't spoken a word to each other since?"

"We're not savages, Simon. Of course we speak. Very politely about commonplaces. But it's hell, and I don't know what to do."

"So you have come to me for advice. Sensibly, I may say."

"Oh don't be so bloody smug."

"Not smug. Don't forget I'm an old hand at this sort of thing. So shall we get down to it?"

"If you like."

"No, no; it's got to be if *you* like."

"All right."

"Well, for a starter, don't imagine I underestimate your hurt. It can't be any fun being told that you're not fully a man. But it's happened before. George Washington, for instance. Another mumps casualty, it seems. No children, though he was quite a man for the ladies. But he didn't do too badly. The Father of His Country, we are told."

"Don't be facetious."

"Wouldn't dream of it. But I refuse to take the great tragic line, either. This business of begetting children is important as one of the biological qualities of a man, but as civilization moves on, other qualities look at least equally important. You're not some wandering nomad or medieval peasant who has to have children because they are a primitive kind of insurance. This begetting business is terribly over-rated. All nature does it and Man is far from the champion. If you hadn't had mumps you would probably be able to squirt out a few million live sperm at a go, and one of them might make a lucky hit. Your cousin Little Charlie's favourite stallion has you backed right off the map; he probably averages ten billion possible little stallions every time Little Charlie collects her stud fee; that's what he's for. The boar is the real champ: eighty-five billions — and then he trots away looking for acorns, and never gives a thought to his sow, who turns again to her wallowing in the mire. But Man — proud Man — is something very different. Even the least of his kind has a soul — that's to say a lively consciousness of individuality and Self — and you are rather a superior man, Arthur. Unfortunately Man is the only creature to have made a hobby and a fetish of Sex, and the bed is the great play-pen of the world. Now you listen to me —"

"I'm listening."

"You come to me as a priest, don't you? You've made rather a joke of that, and call me the Abbé Darcourt — the tame cleric. The learned man on your staff. I'm an Anglican priest, and even the Church of Rome has at last had to admit that my priesthood is as valid as any. When I married you and Maria you had quite a strong fit of orthodoxy, and wanted the whole thing to be on the most orthodox lines. Well — be orthodox now. God may want you for something more important than begetting children. God has lots of sexual journeymen who can attend to that. So you'd better ask God what he wants of you."

"Don't preach at me, Simon. And I wish you wouldn't drag God into it."

"Booby! Do you suppose I have the power to drag Him out of it? Or out of anything? Very well, simpleton, don't call it God. That's only a shorthand term anyhow. Call it Fate or Destiny or Kismet or the Life Force or the It or any damned name you like but don't pretend it doesn't exist! And don't pretend that Whatever-You-Call-It doesn't live out a portion — a tiny portion — of its purpose through you, and that your pretensions to live your own life by the dictates of your intelligence are just so much nonsense, flattering to fools."

"No Free Will, then?"

"Oh yes. Freedom to do as you are told, by Whatever-You-Call-It, and freedom to make a good job of it or a mess, according to your inclination. Freedom to play the hand you're dealt, in fact."

"Preach, preach, preach!"

"I damned well will preach! And don't imagine you can escape. If you don't ask God, which is my word — my professional word — for what we are talking about, what He wants of you, God will certainly tell you, and in no unmistakable terms, and if you don't heed, you'll be so miserable your present grief will look like a child's tantrum. You liked orthodoxy when it seemed to be picturesque. It isn't picturesque now, and I advise you to think of yourself as a man, and a very fine man, and not as a competitor with Little Charlie's stallion, or some snuffling wild boar that will eventually end up in a Bavarian restaurant as the speciality of the day."

"So what do I do?"

"You make peace with your grief and take a long, thoughtful look at your luck."

"Swallow this insult, this infidelity? Maria, the person I love more than myself?"

"Bullshit! People say that, but it's bullshit. The person you love best is Arthur Cornish, because he's the one God has given you to make the best of. Unless you love him truly and deeply you are not fit to have Maria as your wife. She's a soul, too, you know, and not just a branch-soul of your own, like one of the branches of your Cornish Trust. Maybe she has a destiny that needs this fact that you call an infidelity. Ever thought of that? I mean it, Arthur. Your business is with Arthur Cornish, first and foremost, and your value to Maria and the rest of the world depends on how you treat Arthur."

"Maria has made Arthur Cornish a cuckold."

"Then you'd better make up your mind to one of two courses. One: You beat up Powell, or perhaps kill him, and create misery that will last for several generations. Two: you take a hint from this opera that has brought about the whole thing, and decide to be the Magnanimous Cuckold. And what that may lead to, God only knows, but in the tale of Great Arthur of Britain it has led to something that has fed the best of mankind for centuries."

Arthur was silent, and Darcourt went again to the window and looked out at weather that had turned to dismal autumn rain. Such silences seem long to those who keep them, but in reality it could have not been more than four or five minutes.

"Why did she smile in that peculiar way?" said Arthur at last.

"Take heed when women smile like that," said Darcourt. "It means they have sunk very deep into themselves, far below the mind of everyday, into Nature's ruthless mind, which sees the truth and may decide not to tell what it sees."

"And what does she see?"

"I imagine she sees that she is going to bear this child, whatever you may think about it, and care for the child, even if it means parting with you, because that's the job Whatever-It-Is has given her and she knows that there is no denying those orders. She knows that for the next five or six years it will be her child, as it can never be any man's. After that men may put some superficial stamp on it, but she will have made the wax that takes the seal. Maria smiles because she knows what she is going to do, and she smiles at you because you don't."

"So what do I do about her?" said Arthur.

"Behave as if you really loved her. What was she doing when last you saw her?"

"She didn't look much like an independent soul, to be frank. She was throwing up her breakfast in the john."

"Very right and proper, for a healthy young mother. Well, my advice is, love her and leave her alone."

"You don't think I should suggest she come to you?"

"Don't you dare! But Maria will either come to me, or she'll go to her mother, and my bet is she'll come to me. Her mother and I are roughly in the same line of work, but I look more civilized, and Maria still yearns powerfully for civilization."

(3)

DARCOURT WAS NOT ACCUSTOMED to being entertained by women; not, that is to say, entertained in restaurants by women who paid the bill. It was a ridiculous attitude, he knew, as certainly Dr. Gunilla Dahl-Soot would be charging this excellent dinner to the Cornish Trust. But, even though she was a fast, efficient gobbler, whereas he was a patient muncher, the Doctor was a different person as a hostess from the obstreperous guest at Maria's Arthurian dinner. She was considerate, kindly, charming, but not particularly feminine — in a word, thought Darcourt, she is very much man-to-man.

Her notion of conversation, however, was unconventional.

"What sins would you have liked to commit?" she asked.

"Why do you ask that?"

"It is a key to character, and I want to know you. Of course, you are a parson, so I suppose you press down very hard on any sinful ideas you have, but I am sure you have them. Everybody does. What sins? What about sex? You have no wife. Is it men?"

"No indeed. I am extremely fond of women, and I have many women friends; but I am not tormented by sexual desire, if that is what you mean. Or not often. Too busy. If Don Juan had been a professor, and Vice-Warden of his college, a secretary to a large philanthropic trust, and a biographer, we should never have heard of him as a great seducer. It calls for a lot of leisure, does seduction. And a one-track mind. I imagine Don Juan must have been rather a dull dog when he wasn't on the prowl."

"The Freudians think Don Juan really hated women."

"He had a funny way of showing it. I can't imagine sex with somebody I hated."

"You don't always know you hate them till push comes to shove. I speak idiomatically, you understand. I am not talking smuttily."

"Oh, quite."

"I was married once, you know. Less than a week. Ugh!"

"Sorry to hear that."

"Why? We all have to learn. I was a quick learner. It is not my destiny to be Fru Berggrav, I decided. So — divorce, and back to my own life and my own name. Of which I am very proud, let me tell you."

"I'm sure."

"A lot of people here laugh when they hear it."

"Not all names travel well."

"Soot is an honoured name in Norway, where my Soots came from. There was a very good painter in the last century who was a Soot."

"I didn't know."

"The people who laugh at my name have limited social experience."

"Yes, yes."

"Like Professor Raven. Is she a great friend of yours?"

"I know her well."

"A stupid woman. Do you know she has been on the telephone to me?"

"About the libretto?"

"No. About Hulda Schnakenburg. She made an awful muddle of it, but it was clear she thinks I am being very naughty with that child."

"I know. And are you?"

"Certainly not! But I am coaxing her into life. She has lived a life very much — how do I say it?"

"Very much denied?"

"Yes, that's the word. No kindness. No affection. I do not say love. Horrible parents."

"I've met them."

"True followers of Kater Murr."

"Hadn't thought of him as a religious teacher."

"Oh, you wouldn't have heard of him. He was a creation of our E. T. A. Hoffmann. A tom-cat. His philosophy was, 'Can anything be cosier than having a nice, secure place in the world?' It is the religion of millions."

"Indeed it is."

"Hulda is an artist. How good or how big, who can say? But an artist, certainly. Kater Murr is the enemy of all true art, religion, science — anything of any importance whatever. Kater Murr wants nothing but certainty, and whatever is great grows in the battleground between truth and error. 'Raus mit Kater Murr! That is what Hulda says now. If I play with her a little — you understand me? — it is all for the defeat of Kater Murr."

"All?"

"You are a sly one! No, not all. It is very agreeable to me, and to her as well."

"I am not accusing you."

"But you are being very clever. You have changed the conversation from what sins you would like to commit to what sins that silly, provincial woman accuses me of. Hulda will be all right. What is it she says? Okay. She will be okay."

"A little better than just okay, I hope?"

"Oh, but you understand. She is very bad at language. She says terrible things. She says she must 'maul over' these sketches of Hoffmann's. I look it up. She means 'mull'. And she says she will 'day-bew' with this opera. She means 'debut' and she uses it all wrong anyhow. But she is not a fool or a vulgarian. She just has no regard for language. It has no mystery, no overtones, for her."

"I know. Such people make you and me feel stuffy and pernickety."

"But she cannot be an artist in music and a hooligan in speech. You are careful about language."

"Yes."

"I know from what you have done on the libretto. It is really good."

"Thank you."

"That silly woman does not help you?"

"Certainly not so far."

"I suppose she thinks of me and it dries up the ink in her pen. And that beautiful fool Professor Hollier, who is too much a scholar to be even a very tiny poet. But what you give to Hulda is respectable poetry."

"No, no; you are too flattering."

"No I'm not. But what I want to know is — is it all yours?"

"What else could it be?"

"It could be pastiche. Which I am at last persuading Hulda not to call pistache. If so, it is first-class pastiche. But pastiche of what?"

"Now listen here, Dr. Dahl-Soot, you are being very pressing. You are accusing me of stealing something. What would you say if I accused you of stealing musical ideas?"

"I would deny it indignantly. But you are too clever to be deceived, and you know that many musicians borrow and adapt ideas, and usually they come out so that only a very subtle critic can see what has happened. Because what one borrows goes through one's own creative stomach and comes out something quite different. You know the old story about Handel? Somebody accused him of stealing an idea from another composer and he shrugged and said, 'Yes, but what did he do with it?' What is theft and what is influence, or homage? When Hoffmann suggests Mozart, as he does in some of his compositions, it is homage, not theft. So, do you have an influence?"

"If I'm going to talk to you in this way, I must insist on calling you Nilla."

"I shall be honoured. And I shall call you Simon."

"Well, Nilla, it is insulting to suggest that I am not a poet, but that I am presenting unquestionable poetry."

"Insulting, perhaps, but I think it is true."

"It suggests that I am a crook."

"All artists are children of Hermes, the Arch-Crook."

"Let me answer your earlier question: what sins would I like to commit? Very well; I have just the tiniest inclination toward imposture. I think it would be delightful to slip something not absolutely sincere and gilt-edged into a world where any sort of imposture is held in holy horror. The world of art is such a world. The critics, who themselves originate nothing, are so unforgiving if they catch an impostor! Indeed, the man whose life I am writing, and whose money is the engine behind the Cornish Foundation, once exposed an impostor — a painter — and that was the end of the poor wretch whose crime was to pretend that his masterly painting had been done by somebody long dead. Not the worst of crimes, surely?"

"So you are a crook, Simon? It makes you very interesting. And you are safe with me. Here: we drink to secrecy."

The Doctor took her wineglass in her hand and slipped her right arm through Darcourt's left. They lifted their arms, and drank — drained their glasses.

"To secrecy," said Darcourt.

"So — who are you robbing?"

"If you had to prepare this libretto, who would you rob? A poet, of course, but not a very well-known poet. And he would have to be a poet contemporaneous with Hoffmann, and a fellow-spirit, or the work would ring false. And amid the work of that poet you would have to interpose a lot of stuff in the same spirit, because nobody wrote a libretto about King Arthur that is lying around, waiting for such an occasion as this. And the result would be —"

"Pastiche!"

"Yes, and the craft of the thing would be sewing up the joins, so that nobody would notice and denounce the whole thing as —"

"Pistache! Oh, you are a clever one! Simon, I think you and I are going to be great friends!"

"Let's drink to that, Nilla," said Darcourt, and once again they linked arms and drank. Some people at a nearby table were staring, but the Doctor gave them a look of such Boreal hauteur that they hastily bent their heads over their plates.

"And now, Simon — who is it?"

"I won't tell you, Nilla. Not because I think you would

blab, but because it is very important to me to be the only one who knows, and if I lose that I may lose everything. Nor do I suppose the name would mean anything to you. Not at all a fashionable poet, at present."

"But a good one. When Modred is plotting Arthur's murder, you make him say:

> Let him lean
> Against his life, that glassy interval
> 'Twixt us and nothing:
> And upon the ground
> Of his own slippery breath, draw hueless dreams
> And gaze on frost-work hopes.

I felt cold when I read that."

"Good. And you saw how it fits Schnak's musical fragment? So genuine Hoffmann is mated with my genuine poet, and with luck we may get something truly fine."

"I wish very much I knew your poet."

"Then look for him. He's not totally obscure. Just a little off the beaten path."

"Is he this Walter Scott, about whom Powell spoke?"

"Anything good you can pinch from Scott is well known, and nothing but his best is of any use."

"Surely you will be found out when the opera is produced."

"Not for a while. Perhaps not for a long time. How much of a libretto do you actually hear? It slips by, as an excuse for the music, and to indicate a plot."

"You have changed the plot Powell told us about?"

"Not much. I've tightened it up. An opera has to have a good firm story."

"And the music ought to carry the story and make it vivid."

"Well — not in Hoffmann's day. In Hoffmann's operas and those he admired you get a chunk of plot, usually in pretty

simple recitative, and then the action stops while the singers
have a splendid rave-up about their feelings. It's the rave-up
that makes the opera; not the plot. Most of the plots, even
after Wagner, have been disgustingly simple."

"Simple — and few."

"Astonishingly few, Nilla, however you dress them up."

"Some critic said there were not more than nine plots in
all literature."

"He might as well have said, in all life. It's amazing, and
humbling, how we tread the old paths without recognizing
them. Mankind is wonderfully egotistical."

"Lucky for mankind, Simon. Don't grudge us our little
scrap of individuality. You talk like that woman Maria Cornish, with her wax-and-seal. What path is she treading, do
you think?"

"How can I tell till her full story is told? At which time I
shall probably not be around to have an opinion."

"She interests me very much. Oh, not what you are thinking. I don't want to break up her marriage, though she is a
lovely creature. But somebody will."

"You think so?"

"That husband of hers is all wrong for her."

"I'm not so sure."

"Yes. A cold fish. Not a scrap of feeling in him."

"Now Nilla, I see through you. You want me to contradict
you and tell you all I know about Arthur. All I'm going to tell
you is that you are wrong."

"What a man for secrets you are."

"Secrets are the priest's trade or he is no priest."

"All right. Don't tell. But that woman comes out of a very
different box from Arthur Cornish, who is all money and
careful plans, and Kater Murr."

"You're right about Maria. Wrong about Arthur. He is
scrambling upward from Kater Murr just as fast as he can."

"Oh? So he married Maria to get away from Kater Murr?

You let something slip, there. That woman is no Canadian."

"Yes she is. A Canadian can be anything. It is one of our very few gifts. Because, you see, we all bring something to Canada with us, and a few years won't wash it out. Not even a few generations. But if you are frying with curiosity, Nilla, I would be a rotten guest if I did not tell you a few things to appease you. Maria is half Pole and the other half is Hungarian Gypsy."

"What a strong soup! Gypsy, is she?"

"If you met her mother you would never doubt it. Maria doesn't hurry to admit it, but she is very like her mother. And Arthur is very fond of Maria's mother. No wise man marries a woman if he can't stand her mother."

"And this mother is still alive? Here? I want to meet her. I love Gypsies."

"I don't suppose there is any reason why you shouldn't meet her. But don't assume you are going to love her. Mamusia would smell patronage a mile away, and she would be rough with you, Nilla. She is what Schnak would call one rough old broad, and as wise as a serpent."

"Ah, now you are telling! That Maria is one rough young broad, for all her silly pretence of being a nice rich man's wife with scholarly hobbies. You have blabbed, you leaky priest!"

"It's this excellent wine, Nilla. But I have told you nothing that everybody doesn't know."

"So — come on, Simon — what about Arthur?"

"Arthur is a gifted financial man, chairman of the board of a great financial house, and a man with genuine artistic tastes. A generous man."

"And a wimp? A nerd? — You see how I learn from Hulda."

"Not a wimp, and not a nerd or anything that Hulda would know about. What he is you will have to find out for yourself."

"But what plot are he and his wife working out together? Which of the nine? Tell me, or I might hit you!"

"Don't brawl in a restaurant, it will get us thrown out. That would be deeply un-Canadian. I think I smell the plot, but if you think I am going to hint to you, you can think again. You're a clever woman; work it out for yourself."

"I will, and then probably I'll hit you. Or maybe kiss you. You don't smell bad, for a man. But you will take me to Maria's mother, at least?"

"If you like."

"I do like."

"You're a rough old broad yourself, Nilla."

"Not so old. But rough."

"I have a fancy for rough women."

"Good. And now what about cognac?"

"Armagnac, I think, if I may. More suitable to rough broads."

(4)

MARIA WAS UP TO MISCHIEF, and Darcourt knew it. Why else would she present herself in his study at half past four in the afternoon, pretending that she was passing by, and thought that he might give her a cup of tea? She knew perfectly well that he did not go in for elegant tea-drinking, and that it was a nuisance for him to find a pot, and some long-kept tea, and stew up something on his electric hot-plate. He knew perfectly well that if tea was what she wanted she would be welcome in the Common Room of her old college, where there was lots of tea. They both knew that she had come to talk about her adultery, but she was certainly not a repentant Magdalene. She was wearing a red pant-suit, and had a red scarf tied around her hair, and she smiled and tossed her head and rolled her eyes in a way that Darcourt had never seen before. Maria was not there to confess or repent, but to tease and defend.

"Arthur has been to see you," she said, after some small talk which neither of them pretended was anything but a conventional overture to real conversation.

"Did he tell you so?"

"No, but I guessed it. Poor Arthur is in a terrible state just now, and you're his refuge in terrible states."

"He was distressed."

"And you comforted him?"

"No. Comfort did not seem appropriate. Arthur is not a man to be given sugar-candy, and that's what an awful lot of comfort amounts to."

"So you know all about it?"

"I don't imagine so for a moment. I know what he told me."

"And you are going to scold me?"

"No."

"Just as well. I'm not in the mood to be scolded."

"Then why have you come to me?"

"Is it strange that I should look in on an old friend for a cup of tea?"

"Come on, Maria; don't play the fool. If you want to talk about this state of affairs, I'll certainly talk. I'm not the keeper of your conscience, you know."

"But you think I've behaved badly."

"Don't tell me what I think. Tell me what you think, if you want to."

"How was I to know that Arthur can't beget children? He never told me that."

"Would it have made a difference?"

"You simply don't understand what happened."

"In such a matter nobody understands what happened except the people directly involved, and they are not always clear about it."

"Oh, so you know that, do you?"

"I know a few things about life. Not many, but a few. I know that when a family friend plays the cuckoo in the nest it is an old, old story. And I know that when you toss your head and roll your eyes like one of Little Charlie's ponies you probably think that somebody has been using you badly. Was it Arthur?"

"Arthur wasn't frank."

"Arthur was distressed and ashamed, and you ought to know that. He would have told you, when a good time came. How frank have you been with him?"

"I haven't been frank yet. There hasn't been a good time."

"Maria, what kind of marriage have you and Arthur set up? You could have made a good time."

"A good time to crawl and weep and probably be forgiven. I absolutely refuse to be forgiven."

"You've done what you've done, and there is a price for that. Being forgiven may be a part of that price."

"Then I won't pay."

"Rather break up your marriage?"

"It wouldn't come to that."

"From what I know of Arthur, I don't suppose it would."

"It would come to being forgiven, and being one-down on the marriage score-board for the rest of my life. And I simply won't put up with that. I'm not going to spend years of saying, 'Yes, dear,' about anything important because I have a debt I can't discharge. There's going to be a child, as I suppose you know. And every time the child is troublesome or disappointing I'm not going to have Arthur sighing and rolling his eyes and being marvellously big about the whole damned thing."

"You think that's what he'd do?"

"I don't know what he'd do, but that's what I wouldn't endure."

"You have the Devil's own pride, haven't you?"

"I suppose so."

"You can never be wrong. Maria can never be at fault. Very well; live that way if you must. But I can tell you it's easier and more comfortable to be wrong now and then."

"Comfortable! You sound like Kater Murr. Do you know who Kater Murr is?"

"Why do people keep asking me that? You introduced me to Kater Murr yourself."

"So I did. Sorry. But since then I've got hold of Hoffmann's astonishing novel, and I feel as if Kater Murr had crept into my life and was making a mess of it. Kater Murr and his horrible, cosy philosophy says far too much about my marriage."

"Aha."

"Oh, for God's sake don't say Aha as if you understood everything. You don't understand anything about marriage. I thought I was happy. Then I found out what happiness could mean. For me it meant being less than myself and less than a woman. Do you know what the Feminist League says: 'A happy wife is a strike-breaker in the fight for female equality.'"

"Do they say that? But what kind of happiness are you talking about? It isn't a simple thing, Maria."

"It began to seem to me that happiness was what Kater Murr says it is — a cosy place where one is perfectly content with oneself."

"Well, for a lot of people Kater Murr is dead right. But not for you. And, as if you didn't know it, not right for Arthur. You underestimate your husband, Maria."

"Do I? Yes, and he underestimates me! It's all that bloody money! It cuts me off from everything I have been, and everything I want to be."

"Which is — ?"

"I want to be Maria, whoever Maria is! But I won't find out in this marriage I'm in now, because everywhere I turn

I'm not Maria; I'm Mrs. Arthur Cornish, the very rich blue-stocking whose stockings are getting to be a faded puce because all she does is be a slave to that bloody Cornish Foundation, and dish out money to people who want to do a thousand and one things that don't interest me at all. I've given up everything to that Foundation, and I've come to the end!"

"Oh, not quite the end, I hope. What about you and Arthur?"

"Arthur's getting very strange. He's so God-damned considerate about everything."

"And now you know why."

"The mumps thing? Why did it have to be mumps? Such a silly thing, and then it turns out to have a nasty side."

"Well, call it bilateral orchitis if you want a fancy label. Personally I prefer mumps, because it also means being melancholy, and out of sorts, and plagued by dissatisfaction. Which is what ails Arthur. He's thoroughly dissatisfied with himself, and being the man he is he thinks he ought to be especially nice to you because you're married to such a dud. He thinks he's a wimp and a nerd, and he's sorry for you. He knows that as he gets older his balls are going to shrivel up, and that won't be the least bit funny for him. He was afraid he'd lose you, and right now he thinks he's lost you indeed. Has he?"

"How can you ask?"

"How can I not ask? Obviously you've been sleeping with somebody who doesn't have Arthur's trouble, and you've been so indiscreet as to get pregnant."

"God, Simon, I think I hate you! You talk exactly like a man!"

"Well — I am a man. And as you obviously think there is some special feminine side to this business, you had better tell me about it."

"First of all, I haven't been *sleeping* with anybody. Not a succession of sneaky betrayals. Just once. And I swear to you it seemed to be somebody I didn't know; I have never had words with Powell that would have led to anything like that; I'm not really sure I like him. Only once, and it had to get me pregnant! Oh, what a joke! What an uproarious bit of mischief by the Rum Old Joker!"

"Tell me."

"Yes, yes — 'Tell me the old, old story,' as you like to sing. But it wasn't quite the old story you think. It was a much older story — a story that goes back through the centuries and probably through the aeons, from a time when women ceased to be sub-humans cringing at the back of the cave."

"A mythical tale?"

"By God, yes! A mythical tale. Like a god descending on a mortal woman. Do you remember one night when Powell was talking about the plot for this opera, and he was describing how Morgan Le Fay appears two or three times in disguise, and makes mischief?"

"Yes. We had a talk about stage disguise."

"Arthur said that it had always troubled him in the old plays when somebody puts on a cloak and hat and is accepted by the others as somebody he isn't. Disguise is impossible, he said. You recognize people by their walk, the way they hold their heads, by a thousand things that we aren't aware of. How do you disguise your back, he said; none of us can see our backs, but everybody else does, and when you see somebody from the back you may know them much more readily than if you see them face to face. Do you remember what Powell said?"

"Something about people wishing to be deceived?"

"Yes. That you will the deception, just as you will your own deception when you watch a conjuror. He said he had once taken part in a show put on in an asylum for the insane, where a very clever conjuror worked like a dog, and didn't get any applause whatever. Why? Because the insane were not his partners in his deceits. For them a rabbit might just as well come out of an empty hat as not. But the sane, the doctors and nurses, who were living and watching in the same world of assumptions as the conjuror, were delighted. And it was the same with disguise. On the stage, people accepted somebody in a very transparent disguise because the real deception was brought about by their own will. Show Lancelot and Guenevere a witch, and they accept her as a witch because their situation makes a witch much more acceptable than Morgan Le Fay in a ragged cloak."

"Yes, I remember. I thought it rather a thin argument at the time."

"But don't you remember what he said afterward? We are deceived because we will our own deception. It is somehow necessary to us. It is an aspect of fate."

"I think I remember. Powell talks a lot of fascinating Celtic moonshine, doesn't he?"

"You are cynical about Powell because you are jealous of his astonishing powers of persuasion. And if you are in that mood, there's no point in my going on."

"Yes, do go on. I'll promise to suspend my disbelief in Geraint Powell's ideas."

"You'd better. Now listen very carefully. About two months ago Powell came to see me about some business. You know he is making contracts with singers and stage people, and he is very scrupulous about showing them to Arthur, or me when Arthur's away, before he closes his arrangement with the artist. Arthur was away on this particular evening. In Montreal, as he often is, and I didn't know just when he might come back. That evening, late, or early the next morning. Powell and I worked late, and then we went to bed."

"Had nothing led up to that?"

"Oh, I don't mean we went to bed together. Powell often uses a room in our apartment when he is in town late, then he gets up early and drives off to Stratford before breakfast. It's an established thing, and very convenient for him."

"So Wally Crottel seemed to think."

"To hell with Wally Crottel. So — off I went to bed and to sleep, and about two o'clock Arthur came into the room and got into bed with me."

"Not unusual, I suppose."

"Not entirely usual, either. Since his illness, Arthur has a room of his own, where he usually sleeps, but of course he comes into my room when it's sex, you see. So I wasn't surprised."

"And it was Arthur?"

"Who else would it be? And it was wearing Arthur's dressing-gown. You know the one. I gave it to him soon after we were married, and I had it made in King Arthur's colours and with King Arthur's device: a green dragon, crowned in red, on a gold shield. You couldn't mistake it. I could feel the embroidered dragon on the back. He slipped into my bed, opened the dressing-gown, and there we were."

"All very much according to Hoyle."

"Yes."

"Maria, I don't believe a word of it."

"But I did. Or a very important part of me did. I took him as Arthur."

"And did he take you as Arthur?"

"That's what's so hard to explain. When a man comes into your very dark room, and you can feel your husband's dressing-gown that you know so well, and he takes you so wonderfully that all the doubt and dissatisfaction of weeks past melt away, do you ask him to identify himself?"

"He didn't speak?"

"Not a word. He didn't need to."

"Maria, it's awfully fishy. I'm no great expert but surely there are things you expect and are used to — caresses, sounds, and of course smells. Did he smell like Arthur?"

"I don't remember."

"Come on, Maria. That won't do."

"Well — yes and no."

"But you didn't protest."

"Does one protest at such a time?"

"No, I don't suppose one does. I do think I understand, you know."

"Thanks, Simon. I hoped you might. But one can't be sure. Men are so incalculable about things like that."

"You said it all yourself a few minutes ago. It's a story that roams back through the ages, and it's a story that doesn't grow old. It's the Demon Lover. Have you told Arthur?"

"How can I, when he's being so restrained and bloody saintly?"

"You'd better try. Arthur understands a lot of things you wouldn't suspect. And Arthur isn't perfectly in the clear in this affair. He didn't tell you what you had a right to know. You and Arthur had better have a *divano*. Nothing like a good Gypsy *divano* to clear the air."

(5)

THERE IS A SPECIAL FRUSTRATION that afflicts authors when they cannot claim enough time for their own work, and Darcourt was unwontedly irritable because he was not getting on with his life of the late Francis Cornish. The sudden illumination that had struck him in the drawing-room of Princess Amalie and Prince Max demanded to be explored and enlarged, and was he doing that? No, he was involved in the unhappiness of Arthur and Maria, and because he was truly a compassionate man — though he detested what the world thought was compassion — he spent a great deal of time thinking about them and indeed worrying about them. Like most dispensers of wisdom, Darcourt was bad at taking his own medicine. Worrying and fretting will do no good, he told his friends, and then when they had left him he fell into quicksands of worry and fretfulness on their behalf. He was supposed to be enjoying a sabbatical year from his university work, but the professor who does not leave his campus knows that no complete abandonment of responsibility is possible.

There was Penny Raven, for instance. Penny, who seemed to be the complete academic woman, scholarly, well-organized, and sensible, was in a dither about whatever was going on between Schnak and Gunilla Dahl-Soot. What was it? Do you know anything, Simon? Darcourt tried to be patient during her long telephone calls. I know that the Doctor and Schnak are getting on like a house afire with this opera, and are merciless in their demands on me that I should supply new material for the libretto, or change and tinker stuff I have already done: I am in and out of their house at least once a day, fussing over scraps of recitative; I never realized that a librettist lived such a dog's life. Verdi was an old softy compared with Gunilla. They are working, Penny, working! — Yes, yes, Simon, I realize that, but they can't work all the time. What is the atmosphere? I hate to think of that poor kid being dragged into something she can't handle. — The atmosphere is fine: master guiding but not dominating pupil, and pupil blossoming like the rose — well, perhaps not like the rose, but at least putting on a few shy flowers — clean and well-fed and now and then giving a sandy little laugh. — Yes, Simon, but *how*? What price is being paid? — I don't know, Penny, and frankly I don't care because it's none of my business. I am not a nursemaid. Why don't you go and see for yourself? You were supposed to be working with me on this libretto and so far you have done sweet-bugger-all. — Oh, but you're so good at that kind of thing, Simon, and I have this big paper to get ready for the next meeting of the Learned Societies and honestly I haven't a moment. But I'll come in at the end and touch up, I promise. — The hell you will, Penny. If I do it there'll be no touching up. I get all the touching up I need from Nilla, and in English verse she has a touch like a blacksmith. — All right, if you want to disclaim all responsibility for a young person who is supposed to be in your care, at least to some extent. — Not in my care, Penny; if she's in anybody's care it is Wintersen's care, and you won't get any outraged moral action out of him. And if you insist on sticking your nose in, you may get it punched by Schnak, so I warn you. — Oh, very well. Very well. But I'm worried and disappointed. — Good, Penny; you get right on with that. Meanwhile, do you know a two-syllable word meaning "regret" that isn't "regret"? Because "regret" isn't a word that sings well if it has to be matched up with a quarter-note followed by an eighth-note. That's the kind of thing I have to cope with. Listen — I think I've got it! How about "dolour"? Lovely word, right out of Malory, and the accent falls on the first syllable and pips off on the second. Singable! A nice big open vowel followed by a little one. — No, Simon. Won't do at all. Too olden-timesy and cutesy. — Oh, God, Penny! Get off my back, you — you *critic*!

Lots of conversations like that. Powell was right. Penny was jealous, mad as a wet hen because Gunilla had taken on Schnak as — what? As a pupil, of course, but also as a — what do you call it? When it's a man there are plenty of words. A minion, a pathic, a catamite, a bardash, a bumchum — but, when it was a woman? Darcourt knew no word for it. *Petite amie* might do. Did Penny want Schnak for herself? No, that wasn't Penny's style at all. In so far as she was anything of a sexual nature, Penny was a lesbian, but of the smothery-mothery variety, brooding possessively over the successes of her little darlings. Sexually a dog-in-the-manger, who would not eat herself, or suffer others to eat. Penny resented the buccaneering success of Dr. Gunilla, the easy command, the scorn of Kater Murr.

But every day, and all day, and sometimes in dreams, the biography of Francis Cornish nagged. Was it really fated to be such a worthy, dull, unremarkable book? The spy stuff was not bad but he wanted something bigger.

It was that picture, *The Marriage at Cana*. Where had he seen those faces? Not among the mass of drawings and rough sketches he had sent to the National Gallery. The picture was surely the lock that secured the real life of Francis Cornish, but where was the key? Nothing to do but search, and search, and search again. But where?

It was lucky that he was so very much *persona grata* at the University Library, where all the left-overs from Francis Cornish's crowded apartments were locked away, awaiting the attention of cataloguers. Certainly that material would not receive such attention quickly, because those packages were precisely what he had called them when he first transferred them to the Library. They were left-overs. Francis Cornish's splendid pictures, his enviable collection of modern art, Canadian modern art, Old Master drawings, rare books, and expensive art books, his musical manuscript accumulation (it was not sufficiently coherent to be thought of as a collection), and everything else of any value had gone to the galleries and library where they would be, in the glacier-like progress of cataloguing, put in order. But there was still the mass of left-overs, the stuff which had been glanced at, but under the pressure of time not thoroughly examined by him in his capacity as an executor with a job to do quickly.

Without any great hope in his heart, Darcourt decided that he must rummage through the left-overs. He told his friend at the Library what he wanted to do, and was promised every help. But help was exactly what he did not want. He wanted to snoop, and seek, and see if anything would crop up that would give him a hint about that astonishing picture.

The picture itself was known to the art world, though few people had seen it. But there was, of course, the definitive article that had been written about it by Aylwin Ross, and which had appeared in *Apollo* a few years ago. Before Francis

Cornish died, so he must have been acquainted with it. Must surely have approved it, or at least kept quiet about it. The article was well illustrated, and when Darcourt dug it out of the Library's files of *Apollo* it troubled him with new urgency. He read and reread Ross's elaborate, elegantly written explanation of the picture, its historical implications (something about the Augsburg Interim and the attempt to reconcile the Church of Rome with the Protestants of the Reformation), and Ross had concluded that the picture was the work of an unknown painter, but a master of fine attainment, whom he chose to identify simply as The Alchemical Master, because of some alchemical elements he identified in the triptych.

But those faces? Faces that seemed in some way familiar, when he saw the picture itself, in New York. They were not so compelling in the reproductions in *Apollo*, careful and excellent as those were. But there is a quality in an original canvas that no reproduction, however skilled, fully conveys. The people in the picture were alive in a way the people in the pages of *Apollo* were not. Those faces? He had seen at least some of them somewhere, and Darcourt was good at remembering faces. But where?

Nothing to do but go painstakingly through every scrap of unconsidered material that had been cleared out of Francis Cornish's Old Curiosity Shop of a dwelling when he, and Clement Hollier, and the late unlamented Professor Urquhart McVarish had worked as executors of the dead man's possessions. Could Urky McVarish have pinched anything vital? Probable enough, for Urky was a fine example of that rare but not unknown creature, the academic crook. (With a pang Darcourt recognized that he was already far advanced in that category himself, but, of course, being himself, it was rather different.) But it would not do, to assume that there was no clue to the great picture until he had sifted every possible portfolio and parcel, and the best thing would be to start at the bottom.

So, clad in slacks and a sweat-shirt in preparation for dirty work, Darcourt went to the Library, and with Archie's warm assent, began at the bottom.

The bottom was surely some stuff that neither he, nor Hollier, nor McVarish, had touched, because it did not seem to be directly related either to Cornish's collections or to Cornish himself. A secretary, who had been lent to the executors by Arthur Cornish, had been asked to do the dirty work — as secretaries usually are — and bundle up all this junk and — what? Oh, put it with the stuff for the Library. They can throw it out when they get to it, which may not be for years. We are in a hurry, hustled on to complete a heavy task by the impatient Arthur Cornish.

There it was, quite a heap of it, neatly bundled and wrapped, a proper secretarial job. Many hours of tedious search in those bundles. Darcourt had been an active parson for almost twenty years before he contrived to get himself appointed a professor of Greek, and left work he had come to dislike. But the parson years had made their mark, and as he tackled the mass, he found himself humming.

Hums can be important. Hums can tell of a state of mind of which the topmost layer of consciousness is unaware. Darcourt was humming an old favourite of his own:

> Guide me, O Thou great Jehovah,
> Pilgrim through this barren land;
> I am weak, but Thou art mighty;
> Hold me with Thy powerful hand;
> Bread of Heaven,
> Feed me till I want no more.

A great prayer, and because it came from the depths, and not from the busy, fussing top of the mind, it was answered. Oh, surely not answered? Are prayers ever answered? Can the thoroughly modern mind admit such nonsense?

The secretary had labelled every bundle in a neat, impersonal hand. There were no letters, and anyhow Darcourt had been all through whatever correspondence Francis Cornish had preserved. But there were bundles of newspapers, containing reports of artistic matters, all jumbled together but many of them about artistic forgeries, either suspected or detected. Francis had the horrible habit of keeping the whole newspaper, in which the relevant item was marked with a blue pencil, instead of cutting out what he wanted and filing it, as a man with any regard for his heirs would have done. There were several parcels of yellowing newspapers. Darcourt felt a biographer's guilt; he should have sifted this stuff, and he would do so, but not yet. Some of the marked articles were about the affairs, or the deaths, of people of whom Darcourt knew nothing. People suspected in Francis Cornish's Secret Service days? It could be. It was clear that as a spy Francis was sloppy and unmethodical. But here, right at the bottom, were six big packages, marked Photographs Not Personal. Surely nothing there? Darcourt had already ferreted out photographs of all the people that he needed to illustrate his book. Photographers keep very tidy files, and that had not been difficult; merely tedious. But he had determined to look at everything, and he untied the bundles, and found that they were old-fashioned family albums.

They were neat, and they were fussy, and every picture was identified underneath it in a tidy, old-fashioned hand. Ah, yes; the handwriting of Francis's grandfather, and the albums were the work, the beloved hobby, of the old Senator, Hamish McRory. He must have spent a good deal of money on them, for they had been specially made and every album was identified on its cover, in gold printing that had not tarnished (so it must have been true gold leaf), "Sun Pictures".

They were more personal than the secretary had suspected from a quick examination. The first three looked like a record of a turn-of-the-century Ontario town, streets deep in mud, or snow, or baked by summer sun, with lurching, drunken telephone poles and cobwebs of wires, and in the streets were horse-and-rig equipages, huge drays laden with immense, unmilled logs drawn by four horses apiece, and citizens in the dress of the day, some blurred because the Senator's lens had not been quick enough to stop them in action. There were scenes in a lumber-camp, where men struggled with chains and crude hoists to heave those immense logs onto the drays. There were loggers, strong men with huge beards, standing with their big woodsmen's axes beside trees they had felled, or sawn through. There were pictures of horses, giant Percherons, poorly groomed but well fed, and they too had their names carefully entered: Daisy, Old Nick, Lady Laurier, Tommy, Big Eustache, horses that dragged the logs from the forests, patient, reliable, and strong as elephants. This is where the first Cornish money came from, thought Darcourt. From lumbering, when lumbering was a very different matter from what it is today. Pictures of saw-pits, with the top-sawyer standing on the log above his monstrous saw, and the under-sawyer peeping from the bottom of the pit. Were they proud that the Senator had wanted to take their pictures? Their stiff faces betrayed nothing, but they had a look of pride in their bodies; they were men who knew their work. Fine stuff, this. A record of a Canada gone forever. Some social historian would love to get his hands on it. But there was nothing here of the faces Darcourt hoped to find.

On to the other three. This looked more promising. Priests, in soutanes and birettas, sitting in constrained postures beside a little table, on which a book lay open. A sharp-looking little man, obviously a doctor, for on his table lay an old-fashioned straight stethoscope and a skull. But this woman, in the little cap? This woman standing at her kitchen door, holding a basin and a ladle? These were the faces Darcourt wanted. Could they be — ?

Yes, indeed they were. Look, here in the fifth album! A lovely girl, and certainly Francis's mother in her youth. A stiff, soldierly man, wearing an eyeglass. Beyond a doubt these were the Lady and the one-eyed Knight from *The Marriage at Cana*. Underneath, the Senator had written, "Mary-Jim and Frank, their first week in Blairlogie". Francis's parents but not as he knew them from later pictures; these were Mary-Jim and Frank as the child Francis first knew them. And then — this was a treasure, this was the clincher! — a handsome, dark-browed young man, perhaps not more than eighteen; this was "My grandson Francis, on leaving Colborne College, 1929".

So there it was! He had the key to the lock in his hand at last! But was Darcourt excited, exultant? No, he was very calm, like a man from whom doubt and anxiety had all been swept away. Patience has been rewarded, he thought, and then put the thought from him as savouring of pride. There was one album left.

"Thou hast kept the best wine till the last". The inscribed banner that floated from the mouth of that strange angel in *The Marriage at Cana* was proven by what he now turned over, with a feeling of wonder. "My coachman, Zadok Hoyle"; the fine-looking, soldierly, but — to the observant eye — unlucky man who stood by a fine carriage and a pair of bays was unquestionably the *huissier*, the jolly man with the whip in *The Marriage*. And then — at last Darcourt lost his calm, phlegmatic acceptance of his great good luck — here, among pictures of bearded, ancient, youthful, hearty, and unstable citizens of Blairlogie at the turn of the century, was a picture of a dwarf, standing in front of a humble shop, squinting into the sun but grinning subserviently as the Senator — the local great man — took his Sun Picture. And underneath was written, "F. X. Bouchard, tailor". The dwarf who stood so confidently, so proudly, in *The Marriage* and — just possibly — the original of Drollig Hansel.

Was this — could it be — the awakening of the little man?

The kindly assistant librarian popped her head around the partition.

"Would you like a cup of coffee, Professor Darcourt?"

"By God, I would," said Simon, and the secretary, somewhat startled by the vehemence of his reply, set before him a waxed-paper cup of the liquid which the staff of the Library called, with scholarly generosity, coffee.

It was in this lukewarm, muddy draught that Darcourt drank to his good fortune. Here he sat, amid the evidence that settled a mystery of significance to the world of art. He, Simon Darcourt, had identified the figures in *The Marriage at Cana*, thereby showing it to be of our own time, telling in a finely contrived riddle the life experience of the painter. He had destroyed the fine-spun theory of Aylwin Ross and identified for all time The Alchemical Master.

It was the late Francis Cornish.

But it was not of the sensation in the art world Darcourt thought. It was of his book. His biography. It was not merely lifted out of the dullness he had feared; it had taken wings.

Like a good scholar he piled up the albums neatly on the big table in the alcove he was using. Never leave a mess. He blessed Francis Cornish and the primary precept of scholarship: never throw anything away. He would return tomorrow and make copious notes.

As he worked he was humming again. One of the metrical Psalms, this time.

> *That stone is made head corner-stone,*
> *Which builders did despise;*
> *This is the doing of the Lord,*
> *And wondrous in his eyes.*

(6)

OTTAWA IS NOT A PLACE to which anyone goes at the end of November simply for pleasure. Reputedly the coldest capital city in the world, in comparison with which Moscow is merely chilly, it is preparing at the end of the year for its annual ferocious assault on the endurance, good nature, and ingenuity of its inhabitants. Darcourt was glad that the National Gallery was luxuriously warm, and he scuttled between it and his hotel, his collar turned up against the sneaping winds from the river and the canal, cold in body but deliciously warm in spirit. Everything he found out from yet another and rigorous examination of what Francis Cornish had defined as his Old Master Drawings confirmed the great discovery he had made in the University Library.

Like everything else Francis had left behind him, the many portfolios and envelopes were a jumble, but a jumble of treasures, some substantial and some of less importance. The assemblages of Francis's own drawings were honestly labelled; student work, mostly; creditable in the detailed care they showed, and a little eccentric in the trouble the artist had taken in finding real old paper for his work, and preparing it for his silver-point studies. Why so much trouble for what was, after all, simply a student exercise? Each drawing was labelled, with detailed information about which original had been copied, and the date when the copy had been made. But there was about them a hint, which Darcourt took care not to allow to swell into a certainty, that the copy was almost as good as the original and in some cases was every bit as good — though it was identified as a copy. Francis, in another century and with a living to make, could have done well as one of those patient copyists who supplied wealthy tourists with copies of drawings they admired. The talent of the copyist may be very great — technically greater than that of many artists who would scorn such work and have no talent for it — but he remains a copyist.

There was one large brown envelope that Darcourt opened last, because he had a sense that it could contain what he was looking for. He wanted to tease himself, to work up an expectation that amounted almost to a fever, like a child that saves one parcel of its Christmas horde in vehement hope that it contains the gift most eagerly desired. Unlike the others, it was sealed; the gummed flap had been stuck down, instead of being merely tucked in, as was the case with all the others. It was labelled, not "Old Master Drawings", but "My Drawings in Old Master style, for the National Gallery". The Gallery authorities would probably not have allowed him to open it, or not without some Gallery representative being at his elbow as he did so, but Darcourt, who now regarded himself as a thorough-going crook, managed to sneak into the little kitchen where Gallery workers made their tea and coffee and secreted their biscuits, and quickly and efficiently steamed it open. And there it all was. If he had been a fainting man, he would have fainted.

Here were preliminary sketches for *The Marriage at Cana*; several plans for the groupings of the figures, and quick studies for heads, arms, clothes, and armour for the figures — and every head was a likeness, though not always a wholly faithful likeness, of somebody in the Sun Pictures taken by Grandfather James Ignatius McRory. No, not quite *every* head; the woman who stood in the centre panel was unknown to Grandfather, but she was very well known to Darcourt. She was Ismay Glasson, wife of Francis Cornish and mother of Little Charlie. Nor was there any source in the Sun Pictures for the figure of Judas; but he was Tancred Saraceni, caricatured in several of Francis's notebooks and plainly labelled. And the dwarf, so vaunting in *The Marriage*, so self-doubting in the photography; F. X. Bouchard, beyond a doubt. And the *huissier*; Zadok Hoyle, Grandfather's coachman. Why was he important enough to be included in the composition? Darcourt hoped that somehow he might find out, but it was not vital that he do so.

Most mysterious were the studies of that angel, who flew so confidently above the centre panel — so confidently that his influence extended over the whole three panels of the work. But here he was, and one of those drawings was identified as F. C., and although those were Cornish's own initials, this angel was certainly not Francis Cornish. — Was the drawing merely signed, in an idle moment? Or was this crazed, yet inexorably compelling and potent figure — this spook, this grotesque — some notion Francis cherished of his inner self? Had he thought so strangely of himself? Another puzzle, and Darcourt hoped he might solve it, but knew that he had no need to do so. Here were the originals of the people in *The Marriage*, and if not all of them could be equated with people Francis and Grandfather McRory had known, that did nothing to lessen the importance of his discovery. It was with a light heart that Darcourt carefully resealed the envelope, and left the Gallery, with much affability toward those who had permitted him to seek for material which they assumed, and quite rightly, was for information that would flesh out his biography of their dead benefactor.

Darcourt wanted time to come to terms with his discovery, surely the most extraordinary piece of luck that had ever come his way, so he travelled back to Toronto by train, and the journey, which would have taken just under an hour by air, filled the greater part of a day. It was just what he needed. The train was not crowded, and its alternation of simoom-like heat and bitter November draughts was vastly preferable to the "pressurized" atmosphere of a plane. What the train lacked in food — there were sandwiches of the usual railway variety — he made good with a large bar of chocolate and nuts. He had a book in his lap, for he was the kind of

man who must always have a book near as a protective talisman, but did not look at it. He thought about his find. He
gloated. He looked out at the sere, desolate landscape of
Eastern Ontario in November, and the bleak towns, so
charmless, so humble; to his gaze it might have been the
Garden of Eden and all the chilled passers-by so many Adams
and Eves. Sentences formed in his mind; he fastidiously chose
adjectives; he rejected tempting flights into literary extrava-
gance; he thought of several modest ways of presenting his
great discovery, which wholly changed the idea the world
was to receive of the late Francis Cornish. His journey passed
in something as near to bliss as he had ever known.

Bliss ended with the journey. When he arrived back at his
college the porter gave him a telephone message; he was to
call Arthur as soon as possible.

"Simon, I've rather an important favour to ask. I know
you're busy, but will you drop everything and go to Stratford
at once? To see Powell."

"What about?"

"Don't you know? Don't you read the. papers? He's in
hospital, rather badly banged up."

"What happened?"

"Car accident last night. Apparently he was driving reck-
lessly. In fact he was driving through the park, next to the
Festival Theatre, at great speed, and ran into a tree."

"Skidded off the road?"

"He wasn't on the road. He was in the park itself, zigzag-
ging among the trees and yelling like a wild man. Very drunk,
they say. He's all smashed up. We're terribly worried about
him."

"Naturally. But why don't you go yourself?"

"Bit delicate. Complications. Apparently he raved a lot
under anaesthetic, and the surgeon called me to explain —
and see if I had anything to say. He babbled a lot about Maria
and me, and if we rush down there to see him it lends colour

to a lot of speculation among the theatre people. You know what they are. But somebody must go. Indecent not to. Will you? Hire a car, of course, it's Foundation business as much as it's anything. Do go, Simon. Please."

"Of course I'll go if it's necessary. But do you mean he's spilled the beans?"

"Quite a few beans. The surgeon said that of course people fantasize under anaesthetic, and nobody takes it seriously."

"Except that he took it seriously enough to tip you off."

"There were assistants and nurses around when he was patching Geraint up — and you know how hospital people talk."

"I know how all people talk, when they think they've got hold of a juicy morsel."

"So you'll go? Simon, you *are* a good friend! And you'll call us as soon as you get back?"

"Is Maria worried?"

"We're both worried."

That was a good thing, thought Darcourt, as he sped toward Stratford in his hired limousine. If they were both worried about the same thing, and that thing was the mess they were in with Powell, it might bring them together, and put an end to all that polite conversation about nothing. Darcourt was in a somewhat cynical frame of mind, for he had gobbled a snack while waiting for the car, and it was not sitting well with all the chocolate he had eaten in the train. Indigestion is a great begetter of cynicism. In the back seat of the car, dashing through the November darkness, he had lost the happy mood of the daytime; here he was again, good old Simon, the abbé at the court of the Cornish Foundation, the reliable old fire-engine sent off to quench a blaze of gossip that Arthur and Maria took seriously.

We live in an age of sexual liberation, he thought, when people are not supposed to take marital fidelity seriously, and

when adultery, and fornication, and all uncleanness are perfectly okay — except when they come near home. When that
happens, there may be uproars that awaken the gossip colum-
nists, alert the divorce lawyers, and sometimes end in the
criminal courts. Especially so among prominent people, and
Arthur, and Maria, and Geraint Powell were all, in their
various ways, prominent, and just as touchy as everybody
else. Darcourt was of Old Ontario stock, descendant of
United Empire Loyalists, and from time to time an Old Ontario saw seemed to him to sum up a situation: "It all depends
whose ox is gored". The Cornish ox had been gored, and it
was probably impossible to conceal the wound. Still, he must
rush to stick a Band-Aid on the bleeding place.

Powell was in one of those hospital rooms which are
described as "semi-private"; this meant that he lay in the part
of the room nearest the door, and on the other side of the
white curtain that split the room down the middle lay somebody who had hired one of the hospital television sets; he was
listening to a hockey game, apparently of the first importance, with the volume turned well up. The commentators
were describing the play and discussing its significance, in a
high state of excitement.

"Oh, Sim *bach*, you darling man! How good of you to
come! Would you ask that bugger to turn down his bloody
machine?"

Geraint's head was heavily bandaged, though his face
could be seen; it was bruised, but no wounds were visible.
One arm was in plaster, and his left leg, swathed in some
medical wrapping, was hoisted upward in a sling that hung
from a metal brace attached to the bed.

"Would you please turn down the volume of your set? My
friend is very ill and we want to talk."

"Hey? What did you say? You'll have to speak up; I'm a
bit deaf. Great game, eh? The Hatters have got the Soviet
team on the run. My pet team. The Medicine Hatters. Best in

the League. If they win this one, we might get the Cup yet. Big night, eh?"

"Yes, but could you turn it down a bit? My friend is very ill."

"Is he? This'll cheer him up. Would you like to pull back the curtain so he can see?"

"Thank you, a very kind offer. But he really is suffering."

"This'll fix him. Hey — did you see that? Just missed it! Donniker is in great shape tonight. He's showing those Russkies what defence work is. Hey — look at that! Wowie!"

It appeared that nothing could be done. The man in the other bed was gripped by the ruling passion, and it was hopeless to talk to him.

"Well, old man, how are you?" said Darcourt.

"I am at the head of the Valley of Grief in the Uplands of Hell," Geraint replied.

He's had that one ready, thought Darcourt. This may be heavy going.

"I came as soon as I knew. What on earth has happened to you?"

"Retribution, Sim *bach*. I have made an utter balls of everything! My life is in tatters and I have nobody to blame but myself. This is punishment for sin, and I have nothing to do but accept it, swallow it, suffer it, take up my cross, prostrate myself before the Throne, and die! It runs in my family; my great-grandfather and my Uncle David both died of disgrace and despair. Turned their faces to the wall. I am trying to die. It's the least I can do under the circumstances. Oh God, my head!"

Darcourt sought out a nurse; she was down the hall at the nursing-station, where she and a clutch of nurses and interns were huddled around a tiny television screen, watching the great game. But she came long enough to go to the other side of the white curtain and turn down the set of the enthusiast who shared the semi-private, who protested that his deafness required greater volume. She also, at his urgent request, brought Darcourt a glass of Alka-Seltzer to assuage his raging stomach. In the somewhat less uproarious atmosphere, he tried to soothe Powell.

"Now Geraint, don't talk like that. They tell me you are doing nicely, considering everything. You are not going to die, so put that idea right out of your head. You will be up and around in about three weeks, they say, and must be quiet and help the medical people all you can."

"A positive attitude! That's what they keep telling me. 'You must take a positive attitude, because it helps greatly with the healing, and in a few weeks you'll be right as rain.' But I don't want to be right as rain! I don't deserve it. Let the tempest rage!"

"Oh, come on, Geraint! Don't carry on like that!"

"Carry on? *Carry on*? Sim *bach*, that is a bruising expression. Oh, how my head hurts!"

"Of course your head hurts when you shout like that. Just whisper. I can hear you if I come really close. Now tell me what happened."

"Malory, Sim *bach*. Malory is what happened. The night before last I was reading Malory; it quiets the mind, and it brings me very near to Arthur — King Arthur, I mean — and his court and his great schemes and his afflictions. My book fell open at the Madness of Lancelot. You know it? You must; everybody does."

"I remember it."

"Then you know what it says: 'he lepte oute at a baywyndow into a gardyne, and there wyth thornys he was all to-cracched of hys vysage and hys body, and so he ranne furth he knew not whothir, and was as wylde as ever man was. And so he ran two yere, and never man had grace to know him.' "

"And that is what you did?"

"In modern terms, that is what I did. I had been having a few, naturally, and reflecting on my outcast state, and the more I thought, the more of a miserable wretch I knew I was, and suddenly I couldn't hold in any longer. I leapt out of my window — not a bay — and on the ground floor by the mercy of God. I got into my car, and drove like hell, I don't remember where, but I ended up in that park and you know how spooky woods are at night, and as I drove the feeling became more and more Arthurian and Maloryesque, and there I was, roaring around among the trees, making sharp turns and narrow circles — all at incredible speed, boy; a great racing driver has been lost in me — and I became conscious that courtly pavilions were appearing out of the woods to the right and left —"

"The public conveniences, I understand. You very nearly smashed into them."

"That be damned! It was a great pavilion, a mighty tent, with flags floating."

"That must have been the Festival Theatre."

"Armed men and peasantry were skipping about among the trees, marvelling at me."

"The police certainly. I don't know about the peasantry, but there were plenty of witnesses. That's a very easily identified car you drive."

"Don't belittle my agony, Sim *bach*; don't reduce it to mere every-day. This was an Arthurian madness — the madness of Lancelot. Then everything went black."

"You hit a tree. You were crazy-drunk and driving very much to the public danger in a public park, and you hit a tree. I've been reading the papers on my way here. Now look, Geraint: I don't underestimate your temperament, or your involvement with Malory, but facts are facts."

"Yes, but what are the facts? I am not talking about police-court facts, or newspaper lies, but psychological facts. I was in the grip of a great archetypal experience, and what it looked like to outsiders doesn't count. Listen; listen to me."

"I'm listening, but you mustn't expect me to rush off into the moonshine with you, Geraint. Understand that."

"Sim — Sim, my dear old friend. Sim, who out of all mankind I look to for sympathetic understanding, hear me. You are very harsh, boy. Your tongue is so sharp it would draw blood from the wind. Sim, you don't know what I am. I am the son of a man of God. My father, now singing a rich bass in the Choir Invisible, was a very well known Calvinistic Methodist minister in Wales. He brought me up in the knowledge and fear of God. You know what that means. You are a man of God yourself, though of the episcopal, ritualist sort, for which I forgive you, but you must have the true knowledge in you someplace."

"I hope so."

"Sim — I have never forgotten or really forsaken my early doctrine, though my life has taken me into the world of art, which is God's world too, though horribly flawed in many of its aspects. I have sinned greatly, but never against art. You know what has been my downfall?"

"Yes. Booze."

"Oh, Sim, that is unworthy! A drop now and then to ease deep inner pain, but never my downfall. No, no; my downfall was the flesh."

"Woman, you mean?"

"Not woman, Sim. I have never been dissolute. No, not woman, but Woman, that highest embodiment of God's glory and goodness, with whom I have tried to enlarge myself and raise myself. But, wretch that I am, I took the wrong path. The flesh, Sim, the flesh!"

"Your best friend's wife?"

"The last — and undoubtedly the greatest — of many. You see, Sim, God tempts us. Oh yes, He does. Don't let us pretend otherwise. Why do we pray not to be led into temptation?"

"We pray not to be put to the test."

"All right, but we are put to the test, and for some of us the test is a right bugger, let me tell you, Sim *bach*. Look here: why did God endow me with a Byronic temperament, Byronic beauty of face, a Byronic irresistibility?"

"I have no idea."

"No, you haven't. You are a great soul, Sim; a great, calm soul, but nothing to speak of in the way of physical attraction, if I may be allowed the frankness of a friend. So you don't know what it's like to see some marvellous woman and think, 'That's mine, if I choose to put out my hand and take it.' You've never felt that?"

"No, I haven't, really."

"There you are, you see. But that has been my life. Oh, the flesh! the flesh!"

The man on the other side of the white curtain was pushing it as hard as he could with his hand. "Hey, knock it off, you guys, will you? How do you expect me to hear the game if you yell like that?"

"Shhh! Keep your voice down, Sim, like a good man. This is confidential. Call it a confession, if you like. Where was I? Yes, the flesh; that was it.

> *Love not as do the flesh-imprisoned men*
> *Whose dreams are of a bitter bought caress,*
> *Or even of a maiden's tenderness*
> *Whom they love only that she loves again,*
> *For it is but thyself thou lovest then —*

You know that? Santayana — and there are people who say he wasn't a fine poet! That was me; my love was all self-love and I have been a flesh-imprisoned man."

Geraint's face was wet with tears. Darcourt, who felt that this interview was going all wrong, but who had not a hard heart, wiped them away with his own handkerchief. But somehow he had to reduce this outpouring to order.

"Are you telling me that you seduced Maria just to test your power? Geraint, this two-bit Byronic act of yours has brought great unhappiness into the life of Arthur, whom you insist is your friend."

"It's this opera. Sim. You can't pretend a thing like that is just a stage-piece. It's a huge influence, if it's any good at all, and this thing is going to be good. I know it. This opera has brought me back to Malory, and Maria — whom I truly love as a friend and not as a man desires a woman — is none the less a real Malory-woman. So free, so direct, so simple, and yet so great in spirit and so enchanting. You must feel that?"

"I know what you are talking about."

"I knew it the first time I met her. What does Malory say? 'A fair lady and a passynge wise'. But I never said a word. I was true to Arthur."

"But you couldn't stay true."

"There came that night when we were talking about disguise, and I said that the beholder in very strong situations is a partner in the deception. He wills his own belief to agree with the desire of the deceiver. And Maria was scornful of that. Which surprised me, because she is so learned in medieval things, and surely has enough sense to understand that what underlay so much medieval belief is still alive in our minds today, and only waits for the word, or the situation, to wake it up and set it to work. That is often how we fall into these archetypal involvements, that don't seem to make any sense on the surface of things, but make irresistible, compelling sense in the world below the surface. Didn't Maria know that? I couldn't think otherwise for a minute."

"Well — you may have a point there."

"And so there came that night when Arthur was away, and I had dinner with Maria and we worked till midnight at business details; contracts and agreements and orders for materials and all the complexity of stuff that is involved in a job like getting this opera on the stage. Not a word did we say that Arthur could not have heard. But from time to time I felt her looking at me, and I knew that look. But I never looked back. Not once. If I had, I think that would have been the end of it, because Maria would have understood what was happening, and she would have checked it in herself, and in me, too, of course."

"Let's hope so."

"It was when I went to bed that I found I could not forget those looks, and I could not forget the laughing, rational Maria who had made fun of my theory of disguise. There I lay in bed, remembering those looks. So — I slipped into Arthur's room, and pinched his dressing-gown, which was that very Arthurian thing Maria had made for him, when they were newly married and were still joking about the Round Table, and the Platter of Plenty and all that, and I put it on over my nakedness, and stole barefoot into Maria's room, and there she was, asleep or almost asleep. A vision, Sim: a vision. And I demonstrated that my theory was true."

"Did you? Could you swear she thought you were Arthur?"

"How do I know what she thought? But she didn't resist. Was she under a delusion? I know I was. I was deep in such a tale as Malory might have told. It was an enchantment, a spell."

"Now, just a minute, Geraint. That wasn't Arthur's Queen, that was Elaine Lancelot visited in that way."

"Don't quibble. As a situation it was pure Malory."

"She must have known your voice."

"Oh, Sim, what an innocent you are! We did not speak a word. No words were wanted."

"Well, I'm damned."

"No, Sim, you are not damned. But I think I am damned. This was more than adultery. I was a thief in the night — a thief of honour. It was breaking faith with a friend."

"With two friends, surely?"

"I don't think so. With one friend. With Arthur."

"You put Arthur before Maria, whom you seduced?"

"I know that I deceived Arthur. I can't say if I deceived Maria."

"Well, whatever the fine points are, Maria is going to have a child, and it's certainly yours. Did you know that?"

"I know. Arthur told me. He wept, Sim, and every tear was like blood from my heart. That's something I can never forget. I wish I were dead."

"Geraint, that's self-indulgent rubbish! You're not going to die, and Maria is going to have your child, and Arthur will have to find some way of swallowing the pill."

"You see it from the outside."

"Of course. I am on the outside, but I was a friend of Arthur and Maria before you were, and I shall have to do anything I can to make things work."

"Don't you think of yourself as a friend of mine, Sim? Don't I need you at least as much as the other two? Me, the flesh-imprisoned man?"

"Stop blethering about the flesh as if it were the Devil himself!"

"What else is it? The Enemy of God, the Poison of Man, the livery of hell, the image of the animal, the Sinner's Beloved, the Hypocrite's refuge, the Spider's Web, the Merchant of Souls, the home of the lost, and the demon's dunghill."

"My God, is that what you think?"

"That is what my father thought. I remember him thundering those words from the pulpit. He was quoting one of our Welsh poet-divines, the great Morgan Llwyd. Isn't it lovely, Sim? Could you put it better?"

Powell, whose normal voice was impressive, had risen to a Miltonic resonance and grandeur, declaiming with bardic vehemence; the man in the neighbouring, concealed bed was cheering at the top of his voice. The Hatters had won! Won by a last-minute exploit of the redoubtable Donniker!

A small nurse, big with authority and anger, burst into the room.

"What's going on in here? Have you people gone crazy? Everybody on the corridor is complaining. We've got some very sick people on this floor, if you don't know it. You'll have to go."

She took Darcourt by the arm, as he was the only able-bodied rowdy, and pushed him firmly toward the door. In his astonishment and confusion at the goings-on of Geraint, he had no resistance, and allowed himself to be, in a moderate use of the term, thrown out.

(7)

DARCOURT WAS LOOKING FORWARD to his Christmas holiday. The doings of the autumn had worn him out, or so he thought. It was true that the mess of Arthur, Maria, and Powell drew heavily on his spiritual resources; although he was not at the centre of the affair, it seemed that he was expected to be confidant and adviser to all three, and that meant that he had to listen to them, give them advice — and then listen again while they rejected it. Of the three, Maria was the least troublesome. Her course was clear; she was going to have a baby, but for a woman of brains, highly educated and with a background sufficiently unusual to put her above bourgeois conventionalities, she was making heavy weather of it, and had decided that she had wronged Arthur irreparably. Arthur was being magnanimous; he had taken upon himself the role of The Magnanimous Cuckold and was acting it to the hilt. Magnanimity can be extremely vexatious to the bystanders, for it forces them into secondary roles that are not much fun to play. Powell was enjoying himself, finding new rhetorical ways of expressing his sense of guilt, and trying them out on his friend Simon whenever he visited the hospital.

It would all have been so much simpler if all three had not been utterly sincere. They were sure they meant everything they said — even Powell, who said so much, and said it so gaudily, and enjoyed saying it. If they had been fools, Darcourt could have told them so and called them to order. But they were not fools; they were people who found themselves in a tangle from which they could not escape and for which their superficial modernity of opinion offered no solace. Modern opinion stood no chance against the clamour of voices from — from where? From the past, it seemed. Darcourt did his best and poured out comfort as well as he could.

His chief difficulty was that he did not, himself, place much value on comfort. He regarded it as the sugar-teat stupid mothers pop into the mouth of the crying baby. He wished his friends would use their heads, but was well aware that their trouble was not one for which the head offers much relief; it insists on testing the aching tooth to see if it hurts as much as it did yesterday. Because he mistrusted comfort, he could only recommend endurance, and was told, in a variety of disagreeable ways, that it was easy to tell other people to endure. Ah, well, I'm their punching-bag, he thought. They are lucky to have a good, reliable punching-bag.

His own luck was that he was able to put aside his punching-bag character and rejoice in his role as triumphant artistic detective and potentially successful biographer. He wrote to Princess Amalie and her husband, and said that he had some new light to throw on their wonderful picture. Their reply was cautious. They wanted to know what he knew, and he wrote again, offering to explain everything when he had all his material in order. They were courteous but guarded, as people are likely to be when somebody offers to throw new light on a valuable family possession. Meanwhile he was marshalling his evidence, for, although he was sure what it meant, he had to make it convincing to people who might take it badly.

No wonder, then, he was looking forward to two weeks at Christmas when he thought he could put other people's troubles out of his head, and enjoy long walks, a mass of detective stories, and a great deal of good food and drink. He had made his reservation at an expensive hotel in the north woods, where there would certainly be other holiday-makers, but perhaps not of the heartiest, most athletic kind.

He had forgotten about his promise to take Dr. Gunilla Dahl-Soot to visit Maria's mother, the seeress, the *phuri dai*, the element in Maria's background that Maria was still anxious to put behind her.

"You really ought to talk to your mother," he said to Maria, during a *divano* when they were discussing the pressing problem for, it seemed to him, the twentieth time. It was really not more than the fourth. "She's an extremely wise old bird. You ought to trust her more than you do."

"What would she know about it?" said Maria.

"For that matter, what do I know about it? I tell you what I think, and you tell me I don't understand. Mamusia would at least see the thing from another point of view. And she knows you, Maria. Knows you better than you think."

"My mother lived a reasonably civilized, modern sort of life so long as she was married to my father. When he died, she reverted as fast as she could to all the old Gypsy stuff. Of course there is something to be said for that, but not when it comes to my marriage."

"You are more like your mother than you care to think. It seems to me you get more like her every day. You were very like her the first time you came to talk to me about this wretched business, all dolled up in red like the Bad Girl in a bad nineteenth-century play. But you have been getting stupider ever since."

"Thanks very much."

"Well, I have to be rough with you when you won't listen

to common sense. And I mean your common sense, not mine. And your common sense goes right back to Mamusia."

"Why not right back to my father?"

"That devout, ultra-conventional Catholic Pole? Is it because of him you've never considered doing the modern thing and having an abortion? Cut the knot, clear the slate, and begin again?"

"No, it's not. It's because of me. I am not going to do violence to what my body has undertaken without consulting my head."

"Good. But what you have just said sounds like your mother, though she would probably put it in much plainer terms. Listen, Maria: you're trying to bury your mother, and it won't work, because what you bury grows fat while you grow thin. Look at Arthur; he's buried his justifiable anger and jealousy and is giving a very respectable impersonation of a generous man who has no complaints. None whatever. But it isn't working, as I expect you know. Look at Powell; he's the lucky one of you three because he has the trick of turning everything that happens to him into art of some sort, and he is chanting away all his guilt in juicy Welsh rhetoric. He'll be off and away, one of these days, and as free as a bird. But you and Arthur will still be right here with Little What's-His-Name."

"Arthur and I call him Nemo. You know — Nobody."

"That's stupid. He is somebody, right now, and you will spend years finding out who that somebody is. Don't forget — *What's bred in the bone, etcetera* — What is bred in the bone of Nemo, as you call him? That gospel-roaring old father of Geraint's, among other things."

"Oh, don't be ridiculous!"

"Anything I say to you that makes sense to me you dismiss as ridiculous. So what's the good of threshing old straw?"

"Threshing old straw! One of your Old Ontario expressions, I suppose; one of your pithy old Loyalist sayings."

"That's what's bred in the bone with me, Maria, and if you don't like it, why do you keep coming back to me to hear it?"

(8)

DARCOURT AND DR. GUNILLA DAHL-SOOT arrived at the Gypsy camp in the basement of the Cornishes' apartment building well provided with food and drink. He had insisted on it, and the Doctor had agreed that they should, if possible, avoid the enormities of Gypsy cuisine. But they understood that if they were not to eat *soviako* and *sarmi* and kindred delights, they must take something tempting with them; they had a smoked turkey, and a large, rich Christmas cake as the foundation of their feast, and a basketful of kickshaws, as well as half a dozen bottles of champagne and some excellent cognac. Mamusia was delighted.

"This is kindness! I have been so busy these last days. My Christmas shop-lifting, you know," she confided to Gunilla, who did not blink an eye.

"It must take a lot of cleverness," said she.

"Yes. I must not be caught. Maria says that if I am caught and it gets out that she is my daughter, she will kill me."

"Because the Cornishes are so very Kater Murr?"

"I don't know what that is. But Arthur has a very respectable position."

"Yes, of course."

Mamusia went off into a fit of deep-throated laughter. "No, no, not to be disgraced by his mother-in-law." She looked inquiringly at Darcourt. "But you know all about this business, Father Darcourt."

"What business are you talking about, Madame Laoutaro?"

"Father, we are old friends, aren't we? Must we pretend?

Oh, you kiss my hand, very polite, and call me 'Madame' but we have a real understanding, don't we? We are old friends and old rogues, eh? Or do we have to keep quiet because of this very fine lady you have brought with you? Will she be shocked? She doesn't look to me as if she would be very much shocked."

"I assure you I have not been shocked in many years, Madame Laoutaro."

"Of course not! Shock is for stupids. You are a woman of the world, like me. So — you understand this joke? I must not disgrace the great Arthur because shop-lifting is a sin against money, and money is the Big God. But disgrace of the bed, and the heart, doesn't count. Isn't that a good joke? That is the *gadjo* world."

The door opened and Yerko came in. Unshaven, long-haired, unkempt, he was wearing a skin cap and some sort of rough skin coat. How he is reverting to his Gypsy world, thought Darcourt; who would believe that this fellow was once a business man, a gifted, inventive engineer.

"What is the *gadjo* world?" he said, shaking snow generously in all directions from the cap.

"We are talking of the little *raklo* upstairs. I will not call him the *biwuzo*."

"You'd better not, or I'll take my belt to you, sister. And you know that it is very rude to use Gypsy words when we are talking with our friends who are not Romany. You can never keep your mouth shut about the child upstairs."

"Only because it is such a good joke."

"I do not like your joke." Yerko turned to Gunilla and bowed deeply. "Madame, it is an honour to greet you." He kissed her hand. "I know you are a very great musician. I, too, am a musician. I honour greatness in our profession."

"I hear you are a noble player on the cimbalom, Mr. Laoutaro."

"Yerko. Call me Yerko. I am all through with Mister."

"They have brought a feast, brother."

"Good! I want a feast. I have at last beaten the insurance robbers."

"They are going to give us money?"

"No; but they are not going to sue us. That is victory enough. I went to them like this, and said, 'I am a poor Gypsy. I have nothing. Are you going to put me in jail? Are you going to put my sister in jail? We are old. We are sick. We do not understand your ways. Have mercy.' — Lots of that — At last they were tired of it, and of me, and told me to go away and never come into their grand building again. 'You are merciful,' I said, weeping. 'It is Christmas. You are moved by the spirit of Bebby Jesus, and He will reward you in Heaven.' I even tried to kiss the feet of the most important man but he jerked his foot away. Nearly kicked me on the nose. I said, 'You have forgiven us, before these witnesses, whose names I have. That is all I ask.' So now they can't sue us. That is *gadjo* law. We have won."

"Wonderful! We have beaten those crooks!" In her glee, Mamusia seized Darcourt by the hands and danced a few steps, in which he followed, as well as he could.

"But what about all those magnificent instruments that went up in flames?" he said, puffing.

"All gone. It is the will of God. The people who owned them must have insured them. But simple Gypsies know nothing of such things." Mamusia laughed again. "Now we feast. Sit on the floor, great lady. That is what our real friends do."

On the floor they sat, and immediately set about the turkey and the olives and the rye bread, using such implements as Yerko provided, some of them not very thoroughly washed. With plenty of champagne, Darcourt thought, it is not half bad. Gunilla, he saw, dug in with a good will, showing nothing of the refined manners he associated with her. Even so, he thought, the young Liszt might have feasted with Gypsies. She was especially attentive to the champagne, rivalling Yerko, and taking it straight from the neck of the bottle.

"You are a real fine lady!" said Yerko. "You do not hold away from our humble meal! That is high politeness. Only common people make a fuss about how they eat."

"Not when I brought it myself," said Gunilla, gnawing a drumstick.

"Yes, yes: I only meant that you are a guest in our house. No rudeness was intended."

"You will not get the best of her," said Mamusia. "I know who she is," she said to Darcourt. "She is the lady in the cards — you know, the one on the left of the spread? She is La Force. Very great strength, but used without any roughness. You are in this opera thing my son-in-law is so worried about?"

"So you know about that?" said Gunilla.

"What don't I know? You have heard about the spread? Father Simon here made me lay out the cards right at the beginning of that adventure, and there you were, though I didn't know you then. Do you know who any of the others in the spread are now, Father? All you could think of then was that my daughter Maria must be Empress. She, an Empress! I laugh!"

Mamusia laughed, and quite a lot of turkey and champagne flew about.

"Perhaps she is not the Empress, but she may be the Female Pope. She must be one of the women in the cards."

"I think she is the third in the oracle cards; that was Judgement, you remember? She is La Justice, who tries and weighs everything. But don't ask me how. That will be seen when the time comes."

"I see you have been thinking about the forecast," said Darcourt. "Have you identified any of the other figures?"

"They are not people, you know," said Mamusia. "They

are — *smoro*. Yerko, what is *smoro* in English?"

"Things," said Yerko, through a full mouth. "I don't know. Big, things."

"Might we say Platonic ideas?" said Darcourt.

"If you like. You are the wise man, Priest Simon."

"Is he the Hermit? I said so then but now I wonder," said Mamusia. "There is too much of the devil in our good Father for him to be the Hermit."

"You have left me behind," said Dr. Gunilla. "Is this a prediction about our opera? What did it say? Was it a good outlook for us?"

"Good enough," said Mamusia. "Not bad: not good. Hard to say. I was not at my best that night."

The Doctor frowned. "Are we heading toward a mediocrity?" she said. "Failure I can endure; success I like but not too much. Mediocrity turns my stomach."

"I know you are not a person who lives in the middle of the road," said Mamusia. "I do not need the cards to tell me that. Your clothes, your manners, the way you drink — all of it. Let me guess. You are funny about sex, too, eh?"

"Funny, maybe. Hilarious, not. I am myself." She turned to Darcourt. "That Raven woman has been calling me again. I had to be strong with her. 'You know Baudelaire?' I said. She said: 'You insult me. I am a professor of comparative literature. Of course I know Baudelaire.' 'Well then, chew on this,' I said: 'Baudelaire says that the unique and supreme pleasure of love lies in the certainty of doing evil; both men and women know from birth that in evil every pleasure can be found. Didn't you know that from birth? Or did you have a bad birth? A seven-months child, perhaps?' She put down her phone with a loud bang."

"Do you do evil in love?" said Mamusia.

"Good and evil are not my thing. I leave that to the professionals, like Simon here. I do what I do. I do not ask the world to judge it, or make it legal or give it a special place in the world or any of that. Listen, Madame; when I was quite a young girl I met the great Jean Cocteau and he said to me: 'Whatever the public blames you for, cultivate it, because it is yourself.' And that is what I have done. I am Gunilla Dahl-Soot, and that is all I can manage. It is enough."

"Only very great people can say that," said Yerko. "It is what I always say myself."

"Don't appeal to me as a moralist," said Darcourt. "I gave up moralizing years ago. It never worked twice in the same way." The champagne was getting to him, and also the cigar smoke. Good cigars are not accessible to shop-lifters, even those of Mamusia's talent. The cigars Yerko circulated were more than merely odious: they caught at the throat, like a bonfire of noxious weeds. Darcourt got rid of his as soon as he decently could, but the others were puffing happily.

"Madame," he said, for his biography was much on his mind. "You had some intuitions when you laid out the cards. 'You have awakened the Little Man,' you said, 'and you must be ready for what follows.' I think I know now who the Little Man is."

"And you are going to tell us?" said Mamusia.

"Not now. If I am right, the whole world will know in plenty of time."

"Good! Good, Father Simon. You bring me a mystery and that is a wonderful thing. People come to me for mysteries, but I need a few for myself. I am glad you remember the Little Man."

"Mysteries," said the Doctor, who had grown owlish and philosophical. "They are the blood of life. It is all one huge mystery. The champagne is all gone, I see. Where is the cognac? Simon, we brought cognac, didn't we? No, no, we don't need new glasses, Yerko. These tumblers will do very well." The Doctor poured hearty slops of cognac into all the glasses. "Here's to the mystery of life, eh? You'll drink with me?"

"To mystery," said Mamusia. "Everybody wants everything explained, and that is nonsense. The people that come to me with their mysteries! Mostly about love. You remember that stupid song —

> *Ah, sweet mystery of life*
> *At last I've found you!*

They think the mystery must be love, and they think love is snuggling up to something warm, and that's the end of everything. Bullshit! I say it again. Bullshit! Mystery is everywhere, and if it is explained, where's your mystery then? Better not to know the answer."

"The Kingdom of the Father is spread upon the earth and men do not see it," said Darcourt. "That's what mystery is."

"Mystery is the sugar in the cup," said the Doctor. She picked up the container of white crystals the delicatessen had included in the picnic basket and poured a large dollop into her cognac.

"I don't think I'd do that, Gunilla," said Darcourt.

"Nobody wants you to do it, Simon. I am doing it, and that's enough. That is the curse of life — when people want everybody to do the same wise, stupid thing. Listen: Do you want to know what life is? I'll tell you. Life is a drama."

"Shakespeare was ahead of you, Gunilla," said Darcourt. " 'All the world's a stage,' " he declaimed.

"Shakespeare had the mind of a grocer," said Gunilla. "A poet, yes, but the soul of a grocer. He wanted to please people."

"That was his trade," said Darcourt. "And it's yours, too. Don't you want this opera to please people?"

"Yes, I do. But that is not philosophy. Hoffmann was no philosopher. Now be quiet, everybody, and listen, because this is very important. Life is a drama. I know. I am a student of the divine Goethe, not that grocer Shakespeare. Life is a drama. But it is a drama we have never understood and most of us are very poor actors. That is why our lives seem to lack meaning and we look for meaning in toys — money, love, fame. Our lives seem to lack meaning but" — the Doctor raised a finger to emphasize her great revelation — "they don't, you know." She seemed to be having some difficulty in sitting upright, and her natural pallor had become ashen.

"You're off the track, Nilla," said Darcourt. "I think we all have a personal myth. Maybe not much of a myth, but anyhow a myth that has its shape and its pattern somewhere outside our daily world."

"This is all too deep for me," said Yerko. "I am glad I am a Gypsy and do not have to have a philosophy and an explanation for everything. Madame, are you not well?"

Too plainly the Doctor was not well. Yerko, an old hand at this kind of illness, lifted her to her feet and gently, but quickly, took her to the door — the door to the outside parking lot. There were terrible sounds of whooping, retching, gagging, and pitiful cries in a language which must have been Swedish. When at last he brought a greatly diminished Gunilla back to the feast, he thought it best to prop her, in a seated position, against the wall. At once she sank sideways to the floor.

"That sugar was really salt," said Darcourt. "I knew it, but she wouldn't listen. Her part in the great drama now seems to call for a long silence."

"When she comes back to life I shall give her a shot of my personal plum brandy," said Yerko. "Will you have one now, Priest Simon?"

"Thanks, Yerko, I don't think I will. I shall have to get the great philosopher back to her home and her pupil."

"Is that the girl who is doing the opera?" said Mamusia.

"The same. Present appearances to the contrary, I think the Doctor is doing her a lot of good."

"Now she is out of the way, what about this baby?" said Mamusia.

"Well, what about it? It's a fact."

"Yes, but a queer fact. It's not her husband's."

"If I may ask, how do you know that?"

"He can't make babies. I could see it as soon as he came home from the hospital. There is a look. This actor who haunts their house made the baby."

"How do you know?"

"Wally Crottel says so."

"Mamusia, Wally Crottel is an enemy to Maria, and to Arthur, and you mustn't trust him or listen to him. He wants to destroy them."

"Oh, you don't need to warn me against Wally. I have read his palm. A little good-for-nothing, but one can find out things from such people. Don't worry about Wally. I saw an accident in his palm. Yerko is maybe taking care of the accident."

"My God, Yerko! You're not going to rub him out?"

"Priest Simon, that would be criminal! But if he is to have an accident, it had better be the right one. Leave it to me."

"This baby," said Mamusia. "Maria wants a baby more than anything. Deep down she is a real Gypsy girl and she wants a baby at the breast. Now she has a baby and she would be happy if Arthur would be happy too."

"It's rather a lot to expect, wouldn't you say?"

"In these queer days people hire women to have babies when the wife can't do it. Why not hire a father? Doesn't this fellow Powell work for them?"

"I don't suppose they thought he would work for them in quite this way."

"That Powell is not an ordinary man. I think he is the Lover in the spread. You know how that card looks. A young man between two people and the one on the right is a woman, but who is that on the left? Some people say it is another woman, but is it? They say it is a woman because it has no beard, but what is a man without a beard? Not a man in every way, but still important enough to rule the beautiful woman. That figure wears a crown. A king, of course. Every spread is personal. Maybe in this spread that figure is King Arthur, and he looks as if he is pushing the young man toward the beautiful woman. And the beautiful woman is pointing to the lover as if she is saying, 'Is it this one?' And over their heads is the god of love and he is shooting an arrow right into the heart of the beautiful woman."

"You make it sound very plausible."

"Oh, the cards can be very wise. Also very tricky. So you know who the Little Man is? And you won't tell?"

"Not yet."

"Well, be careful. Maybe the Fool is tied up with the Little Man I had that hunch about. Father Simon, have you ever looked hard at that card of the Fool?"

"I think I remember it pretty clearly."

"What is the dog doing?"

"I don't remember the dog."

"Yerko, get the cards. And maybe just a thimbleful of your plum brandy."

While Yerko was busy, Darcourt looked at the prostrate Doctor. Her colour was better, and so far as a woman of her distinguished demeanour could do so, she was snoring.

"Look now. There he is. The Fool. You see he is going on a journey and he looks very happy. He is always going someplace, is the Fool. And he has a good fool's dress, but see, the pants are torn at the back. Part of his arse is showing. And that is very true, because when the Fool comes into our life, we always show our arses a little bit. And what does the little dog do with the bare arse? He is maybe nipping at it. What is the dog, anyway? He is a thing of nature, isn't he? Not learning, or thinking, but nature in a simple form, and the little dog is nipping at the Fool's arse to make him go in a path that the mind would not think of. A better path. A natural path that Fate chooses. Maybe a path the mind would not approve of, because the mind can be a fool too — but not the great, the very fine Fool that takes the special journey. The little dog is nipping, but maybe he is also sniffing. Because you cannot nip without you also sniff. You know how dogs sniff everybody? The crotch? The arse? They have to be trained not to do it, but they forget because they have the great gift of scent, which wise, thinking Man has almost murdered. The nose speaks when the eyes are blind. Man, when he thinks he is civilized, pretends he does not smell, and if he is afraid he stinks he puts on some stuff to kill his stink. But the little dog knows that the arse and the smell are part of the real life and part of the Fool's journey, and the natural things cannot be got rid of if you want to live with the real world and not in the half-world of stupid, contented people. The Fool is going just as fast as he can to something he thinks good. What do people say when somebody goes as hard as he can for something?"

"They say he goes for it bald-headed."

"People I know say he goes for it bare-arsed," said Yerko.

"You see, Father Simon? Somebody in all this destiny that is told in that spread of cards is going bare-arsed for something very important. Is it you?"

"You have amazed me, Mamusia, and in my amazement I shall speak the truth. Yes, I think it is me."

"Good. I thought you were the Hermit, but now I am sure you are the Fool. You are going far, and instinct is nipping at your arse, and you will have to understand that instinct knows you better than you know yourself. Instinct knows the smell of your arse — your backside that you can never see. — Listen, how much does my son-in-law pay you for what you do?"

"Pay me! Mamusia, I get some expenses now and again to put back in my own pocket what I have taken out of it to serve the Cornish Foundation, damn it, but not one red cent of pay have I ever had. I am always out of pocket. And I am getting sick of it. They think because I am a friend I love working my tail off for them, just to be one of the gang. And the trouble is they are right!"

"Father Simon, don't shout! You are a very lucky man and now I know you are the Fool. The great Fool who dominates the whole spread! Don't you take a penny! Not one penny! That is the Fool's way, because his fortune is not made like other men's. They pay everybody. This Powell, the baby-maker. This Doctor here, who is very good at her job, but is just La Force, you know, and sometimes puts her foot very wrong. And that girl, that child who is being given so much money for this opera job, and it may not be for her good. But you are free! You wear no golden chain! You are the Fool — Oh, I must kiss you!"

Which she did. And then Yerko insisted on kissing him too. A prickly, smelly embrace, but Darcourt recognized now that reality and truth can sometimes be very smelly.

Thus the party broke up, and Darcourt took Gunilla home in a taxi, and delivered her, still limp and silent, into the hands of Schnak.

"Oh, Nilla, you poor darling! What have they been doing to you?" she said as she supported her wilted teacher.

"I have been a fool, Hulda," said the Doctor, as the door closed.

Yes, but not the Fool! Exhilarated as he had not been in many years, Darcourt paid off the taxi and walked home, delighting in the chill air and his new character.

Searching for words to express this exultation, this state of unusual well-being, an Old Ontario phrase swam upward from the depths of his consciousness.

He felt as if he could cut a dead dog in two.

(9)

ETAH IN LIMBO

MY HEART GOES OUT TO DARCOURT. The life of a librettist is the life of a dog. Worse than the playwright, who may have to satisfy monsters of egotism with new scenes, new jokes, chances to do what they have done successfully before; but the playwright can, to some degree, choose the form of his scenes and his speeches. The librettist must obey the tyrant composer, whose literary taste may be that of a peasant, and who thinks of nothing but his music.

Rightly so, of course. Opera is music, and all else must bow to that. But what sacrifices are demanded of the literary man!

Psychology, for instance. The watered-silk elegances of feeling and the double-dealing of even the most honest mind; the gushes of hot emotion that rush up from the depths and destroy the reason. Can music encompass all that? Yes, it can in a way, but never with the exactitude of true poetry. Music is too strongly the voice of emotion and it is not a good impersonator. Can it make a character have a voice that is wholly his own? It can try, but as a usual thing the voice is always that of the composer. If the composer is a very great man, like the divine Mozart or, God help us all, the heaven-storming Beethoven, we love the voice and would not change it for even the masterly characterizations of Shakespeare.

You see, my trouble is that I am torn between Hoffmann the poet and fabulist, and Hoffmann the composer. I could argue with equal conviction on either side. I want the poet to be supreme, and the musician to be his accompanist. But I also want the musician to pour out his inspiration, and the poet must carpenter something with the right vowel sounds that obediently partner the music without pushing itself into prominence. What great line of poetry can anybody quote from an opera libretto? Even Shakespeare is reduced to a hack, after the libretto hack has hacked his lines to suit Maestro Qualcuno's demands. And then every simpleton says that Maestro Qualcuno has shown Shakespeare how it should be done.

If the musician is really sensitive to poetry, magic is the result, as in the songs of Schubert. But, alas, Schubert wrote truly terrible operas, and Weber had the fatal knack of choosing the worst possible people to write his libretti. Like that fellow Planché, who ruined **Oberon**. Oh, how lucky I am to have escaped the well-meaning drollery of Planché!

Now I have Darcourt, and what a task that poor wretch has been given! To prepare a libretto that will fit existing music, or rather the music that Schnak and the brilliant Doctor can make by enlarging on my notes.

*He is doing well. Of course he has to find some words that will carry the plot they have created for my **Arthur**. It is not precisely the plot I would have wished for. It smells a little of the present day — their present day. But it is not bad. It is more psychological than I would have dared to make it, and I am happy with that, for I was rather a fine psychologist, in the manner of my time. My uncanny tales were not just fantasies to amuse young girls on an idle afternoon.*

But Darcourt has had a really good idea. Whenever he can, he is drawing on the writings of a true poet. A poet not very well known, he says, but I would not know about that for I never read English with real understanding, and English poetry was an unknown country to me. But I like what he has fished up from his unknown. How right he is not to tell anybody who his unknown poet is! If they knew, they would want to stick a finger in the pie, and too many fingers in pies are the utter ruin of art and the curse of drama. No; let the secret remain a secret, and if anybody wants to ferret out the secret, good luck to them and probably bad luck to him.

*All artistic tinkering and monkeying is slave's work. I know. Once I undertook, as an act of friendship, to do something of the sort. I made a version of Shakespeare's **Richard III** for my dearest friend, Ludwig Devrient. It almost cost me that friendship, for Ludwig wanted all sorts of things that my artistic conscience revolted against. But Shakespeare wanted it thus, I would say, and he would shout To hell with Shakespeare! Give me a great effect here, so that I can take the audience by the throat and choke it with splendour! And then, in the next scene, you must arrange matters so that I can choke them again, and reduce them to an admiring pulp! My dear Louis, I would say, you must trust your poet and you must trust me. And then he would say what I could not bear: Shakespeare is dead, and as for you, you do not have to go on the stage with a hump on your back and a sword in your hand, and win the battle every night. So do what I say! After which, there was nothing for* *me to do but get drunk. Ludwig got what he wanted, but Richard III was never one of his greatest roles, and I know why. After it was over, the audience came unchoked, and the critics told them that Ludwig was a barn-stormer and a mountebank. Whom did he blame, then? Shakespeare, of course, and me along with Shakespeare.*

I like Darcourt, and not just because I pity him. The old Gypsy woman says he will be greatly rewarded, but old Gypsy women can be wrong. Who heeds a librettist? At the party after the performance, who wants to meet him? At whose feet do the pretty ladies fall? Whose lapel do the rich impresarios seize, clamouring for more, and greater, works? Not the librettist.

The old Gypsy is wrong. Or else I do not know as much about this affair as I hope I do.

Anyhow, I must bide the event, as Shakespeare says. Or does he? There are no reference libraries in Limbo.

VI

Darcourt's christmas holiday was a success beyond his hopes. His hotel in the north woods pretended to be a simple chalet, but was, in fact, luxurious, giving him a large room with broad windows looking down over a valley of pine forest; a proper room, with a desk and a good armchair in it, as well as the bed, and — rarest of hotel blessings — a good light for reading; a chest of drawers, a closet for his clothes, and a bathroom where there was provision for everything he could need, and in the form of a bidet and a frank notice warning him not to put his sanitary towels down the plumbing, for things he did not need. With a sense of deep content he unpacked and hung up clothes that gave no hint of his clerical character; he had invested in two or three shirts sufficiently gaudy for a country holiday, and some handsome scarves to tuck into his open collar. He had a fine pair of corduroy trousers, and, for long walks, boots that were, he had been assured, proof against cold and wet. He had two tweed jackets, one with leather patches on the elbows, sure signal that he was an academic, and not an academic of the sort that likes to ski, or slide downhill on a luge, or engage in casual conversations about nothing in particular. There were young people among the guests, who wanted to do these things, and older people who wanted to sit in the bar and pretend that they would prefer to ski, or luge; but the discreet lady whose job it was to see that everybody had a good time knew Darcourt at once for a man whose idea of a good time was to be alone. So he was civil to his fellow guests, and obedient to the convention that required him to make remarks about the weather, and smile at children, but on the whole he was left to himself and settled to two weeks of his own company with a deep sense of gratitude.

He walked after breakfast. He walked before dinner. He read, sometimes detective novels and sometimes fat, difficult books that primed the pump of his reflections. He made notes. But most of the time he brooded, and mused, and looked inward, and thought about being the Fool, and what that might mean.

The Fool; the cheerful rogue on a journey, with a rip in his pants, and a little dog that nipped at his exposed rump, urging him onward and sometimes nudging him in directions he had never intended to take. The Fool, who had no number but the potent zero which, when it was added to any other number, multiplied its significance by ten. He had spoken truly in Mamusia's cellar when he said that he believed that every-body had a personal myth, and that as a rule it was a myth of no great potency. He had been inclined to see his own myth as that of a servant, a drudge, not without value, but never an initiator or an important figure in anyone's life but his own. If he had been asked to choose a card in the Tarot that would signify himself, he would probably have named the Knave of Clubs, Le Valet de Baton, the faithful, loyal servitor. Was not that the character he had played all his life? As a clergyman, loyal to his faith and his bishop until he could stand it no more and outraged nature had driven him to become a teacher? As a teacher, generous and supportive to his students, the admin-istrative assistant to the head of his college, doing so much of the work for so little of the acclaim? As a friend, the patient helper of the Cornishes, and their crack-brained Cornish

Foundation, which had embarked on such a foolish exploit as giving form to an opera that existed in no more than a few ideas, scribbled in pain by a dying man? Oh, the Knave of Clubs to the life! But now Mamusia had declared as true what he had for some time felt in his bones. He was something better. He was the Fool. Not the servitor, napkin in hand, at the behest of his betters, but the footloose traveller, urged onward by something outside the confines of intellect and caution.

Had he not felt the truth of it? Had those promptings that had led him to the Sun Pictures, and the sealed portfolio in the National Gallery hoard, not come from somewhere not accountable to reason, deduction, scholarly craft? Was not his biography of his old friend Francis Cornish, which he had undertaken as an act of friendship, and chiefly to oblige Maria and Arthur, blossoming into something that none of Francis Cornish's heirs could have foreseen? If he could piece out the jigsaw that placed the figures in Grandfather McRory's photographed chronicle of Blairlogie (unlikely cradle for a work of art) in the great composition called *The Marriage at Cana* (dated as *circa* 1550 and attributed to the unknown Alchemical Master), would he not have established Francis as, at worst, a brilliant faker, and at best an artistic genius of a rare and eccentric breed? And how would he have done it? Not by being a crook, stealing from a library and a gallery, but by being a Fool and acting on a morality not to be judged by common rules. He was the Fool, the only one of the Tarot figures who was happily in motion — not falling as in the Tower, not endlessly revolving as in the Wheel of Fortune, not drawn ceremonially by horses as in the Chariot, but off on foot, bound for adventure.

This sort of self-recognition does not come to a man in his forties in a sudden flash. It offers itself tentatively, and is rejected as immodest. It asserts itself in sudden, unaccountable bursts of well-being. It comes as a joke, and is greeted with incredulous laughter. But in the end it will not be denied, and then it takes a good deal of getting used to. Without being self-deprecatory, Darcourt had the humility of a man who had, with his whole heart, embraced the calling of a priest. He was a priest in the tradition of Erasmus, or the ungovernable Sydney Smith, who was said to have jested away his chances of a mitre. He was a priest of the type of the mighty Rabelais. But was not Rabelais a true priest and also a Fool of God? Was he, Simon Darcourt, professor, Vice-Warden of his college, unpaid dogsbody of the Cornish Foundation, and (he sometimes thought) the only sane man in a congeries of charming lunatics, really a Fool of God? He was too modest a man to greet such a revelation with a whoop and a holler.

It was thus he mused while taking his long, solitary walks through the pine forests that surrounded his hotel. He was not one of those people — do they exist anywhere except in books? — who think in a straight line, with unescapable logic. Walking helped him to think, but that meant that walking allowed him to bob up and down in the warm bath of a mass of disjointed reflections. The warm bath had to be reheated every day, and every day the conclusion came a little nearer, until it became a happy certainty. His fellow guests, incorrigible gossips as people in a resort hotel always are, sometimes asked each other why the man with the leather patches on his elbows seemed so often to smile to himself, and not in answer to their smiles; and why, once or twice, he laughed softly but audibly while he was eating at his lonely table.

It was in the forest that he fared farthest in his astonishing recognition of what he was and how he must live. Canadians are thought of in the great world — whenever the great world thinks about them at all — as dwellers in a northern land. But most of them dwell in communities, large or small, where their lives are dominated by community concerns and accepted ideas. When they go into their forests, if they are not there to exploit the forests by chopping them down, they are there to rush downhill on skis, or bob-sleighs, to strain after accomplishment in winter sports, to make decorous whoopee at the bar or on the dance floor when the day's exertion is over. They do not go into the forests to seek what they are, but to forget what they suspect themselves to be. Sport numbs the concerns they have brought with them from the towns. They do not ask the forests to speak to them. But the forests will speak if they can find a listener, and Darcourt listened, as he trudged the solitary trails that had been ploughed out among the huge pines, and when — without an apparent breath of wind — powderings of snow fell from the trees onto his shoulders, he heeded the deeper suggestions which had nothing to do with the world of words.

He did not think only of himself, but of the people from whom he was taking a holiday. What a muddle of concerns had been set in action by Hulda Schnakenburg's apparently innocent desire to piece out some manuscript notes of music, in order that she might gain the doctorate in her studies that could lead to a place in the world of her art! Arthur's desire to escape his world of business and figure in the world of art as an intellectual and a patron; Geraint Powell's opportunist scheme to launch himself as a director of opera on an imaginative level; the seduction of Hulda Schnakenburg by the amoral but splendidly inspiring Dr. Gunilla Dahl-Soot; the recognition of Clement Hollier, fine scholar and renowned paleo-psychologist, as a man wholly at sea when faced with any imaginative notion that was not safely rooted in the dark and ambiguous past; the bitterness of Professor Penelope Raven, when confronted with an aspect of herself which she had disguised for half a lifetime; the uprooting of Maria, who was trying to balance her obligations as the wife of a very rich man, bound by the conventionalities of such a fate, against her inclination to become a scholar and get away from her Gypsy heritage; and of course that baby, still an unknown factor, though a living creature, who would never have come into being if Hulda, snooping through some musical manuscripts, had not come upon the skeleton of *Arthur of Britain, or The Magnanimous Cuckold*. They were driven by craving, of one sort or another, and if he were really the Knave of Clubs he was the servant of their craving. But suppose he were the Fool, driven by no craving but ready to follow his path, confident that his destiny and the mischievous little dog at his heels would guide him — was not that a vastly finer thing? The Myth of the Fool was a myth indeed, and he would live it as fully and as joyously as in him lay.

He had revulsions of feeling, as a man undergoing a great change must do. What on earth was he doing — he, a modern man, a trusted instructor of the young, a servant of the university as a temple of reason and intellectual progress — abandoning himself to an old Gypsy woman's blethers about the Tarot? If this was thinking at all, it was thinking of a superstitious, archaic nature. But then — it was so seductive, so firmly rooted in a past that it had served pretty well for millennia before the modern craze for logic. Logic, which meant not logic as a system applicable to whatever lay under the domination of inference and the scientific method, but debased logic, a means of straining out of every problem the whisperings of intuition, which was a way of seeing in the dark. Mamusia's hunches and her Tarot were only channels for her intuition, which, combined with his own, might open doors that were closed to logic. Let logic keep its honourable place, where it served man well, but it should not take absurd airs on itself as the only way of settling a problem or finding a path. Logic could be the weapon with which fear defies fate.

A word kept popping into his head which he had heard Gunilla use when she was introducing Schnak to the finer realms of musical composition. *Sprezzatura*. It meant, said Gunilla, a contempt for the obvious, for beaten paths, for what seemed to be obligatory to musical underlings; it was a noble negligence, a sudden leap in art toward a farther shore that could not be reached by the ferry-boats of custom.

Such leaps could, of course, land you in the soup. Had not Arthur's *sprezzatura*, arising probably from the first symptoms of mumps — the higher temperature, the irritable malaise — landed them all in this ridiculous opera venture? Was it a noble leap, or a plunge into the soup? Only time could show.

Was it part of the Arthurian myth, into which the Cornish Foundation seemed to have strayed, and which needed a great questing king, betrayed by his closest friend and his dearly beloved? Behind the time which was so imperiously signalled every noontide by the great observatory at Ottawa, and binding upon a million human activities, there lay the Time of Myth, the time of the mind, the habitation of all those nine plots of which he and Gunilla had spoken, and the landscape of quite another sort of life. Surely it is in the mind that we humans truly live, as animals do not; the mind, which is not the creature of the clock but of those moving planets and that vast universe whose mysteries are still, in the main, unknown to us?

Moonshine, thought Darcourt. Yes, perhaps it was moonshine, which the amateur logicians held in contempt because it threatened so much they held dear — their timorous certainty which was, when all was weighed up, certain of so very little. But they despised moonshine because they never looked at the moon. How many of the people he knew could, if asked to do so, say in which phase the moon was at the time they were questioned? Did the Fool travel by moonshine? If he did, he was in a happy state of confidence about where he was going, which very few of those who never looked at the moon seemed to be.

It was a fearful adventure to put off the servitor's livery of the Knave of Clubs, and put on the motley of the Fool. But had Darcourt, in all his eminently respectable life, ever had a real adventure? That was what the Time of Myth seemed to be urging him to do. When the time comes for truth to speak, it may choose an unfamiliar tongue; the task is to heed what is said.

When he left the forests to return to his life and its burdens, Simon Darcourt was a changed man. Not a wholly new man, not a man one jot less involved in the life of his duties and his friends, but a man with a stronger sense of who he was.

(2)

IF THE OPERA VENTURE seemed madness to Darcourt, it was more and more true and compelling to Schnak and the Doctor, who now had enough completed music to be nipped and tucked and patted and dowelled into an opera score. The final form had not been achieved but it was in sight. Not one of Hoffmann's themes and rough notes had been neglected, and the important part of the music rested upon them. But inevitably there were gaps, seams to be sewn and then concealed, bridges to be contrived to get from one piece of authentic Hoffmann to another. These were the tests that would show Schnak's quality. The Doctor suggested nothing, but she was quick to reject anything Schnak produced which seemed unworthy or unsuitable to the whole. Developing and orchestrating Hoffmann's notes was child's play to Schnak; finding Hoffmann's voice in which to devise her new material was a different matter.

The exactions of the Doctor and the exasperation of Schnak made life a hell for Darcourt. His job was to tinker scraps of language into appropriate lengths for the music which was written every day, and changed every day, until he lost all sense of a coherent narrative, or intelligible utterance. Sometimes the Doctor scolded him for the banality of what he prepared; sometimes she rejected it because it was too liter-

302   ROBERTSON DAVIES

ary, too hard to comprehend when sung, too obtrusively poetic. Of course the Doctor, who was an artist of considerable quality, was merely expressing her dissatisfaction with herself and what she could squeeze out of her pupil; Darcourt understood that, and was prepared to put up with it. But he was not ready to take snarling impudence from Schnak, who assumed she was privileged to be rudely capricious and exacting.

"This is shit!"

"How would you know, Schnak?"

"I'm the composer, I suppose?"

"You're an illiterate brat! What you call shit is the verse of a poet of great gifts, slightly adapted by me. It's utterly beyond your comprehension. You take it and be grateful for it!"

"No, no, Simon; Hulda is right. It won't work. We must have something else."

"What else?"

"I don't know what else. That's your job. What is wanted here is something that says the same thing, but says it with a good open vowel on the third beat of the second bar."

"That means reshaping the whole thing."

"Very well; reshape it. And do it now, so we can get on. We can't wait till tomorrow while you brood over a dictionary."

"Why can't you reshape your bloody music?"

"The shape of music is something you know nothing about, Simon."

"Very well. But I won't take any more lip from this stupid kid."

"Shit!"

"Hulda! I forbid you to use that word to the professor. Or to me. We must work without passion. Art is not born of passion, but of dedication."

"Shit!"

Then the Doctor might slap Schnak across the face, or, under other circumstances, kiss her and pet her. Darcourt never slapped Schnak, but sometimes it was a near thing.

Not all the work proceeded in this high-stomached mode, but it did so at least once a day, and sometimes the Doctor had to fetch champagne for everybody. The bill for champagne, thought Darcourt, must be mounting at a fearful rate.

He persisted. He swallowed insult, and in his new notion of himself as the Fool, he frequently gave insult, but he never gave up. He was determined to be a professional. If this was the way artists worked, he would be an artist in so far as a librettist was permitted such presumption.

It was not the way all artists worked. At least once a week Powell dashed up from Stratford in his snorting little red car, and his artistic method was all oil and balm.

"Lovely, lovely, lovely! Oh, this is very fine stuff, Simon. Do you know, when I am working on my other production — I'm getting up *Twelfth Night*, you know, for a May opening — I find words coming into my head that are not Shakespeare. They are unadulterated Darcourt. You've missed your calling, Sim *bach*. You are a poet. No doubt about it."

"No, Geraint, I am not a poet. I am exploiting a poet to produce this stuff. The arias, and the long bits, are all his — with some tinkering, I admit. Only the *recitativo* passages are mine, and because of the way Nilla wants things, they are absolute buggers, because they have to have all this loose accompaniment underneath, and stresses falling in places that defy any sort of poetic common sense. Why can't the singers just speak those parts, and sound like human beings and not crazed parrots?"

"Come on, Sim *bach*, you know why. Because Hoffmann wanted it otherwise, that's why. He was an adventurer, an innovator. Long before Wagner he wanted an opera that was sung clear through, not broken up with spoken passages or recitative that is simply gabble to bustle on the plot. We must be faithful to old Hoffmann, boy. We must never betray old Hoffmann."

"Very well. But it's killing me."

"No it isn't. I've never seen you looking better. But now I'm going to talk against everything I've just said. We must have one big number for Arthur in Act Three, where he says loud and clear what Love is, and why he's forgiving Guenevere and Lancelot. And there isn't a damned scrap of Hoffmann that does it."

"And so?"

"Well, it's obvious. Dear little Schnaky-Waky is going to have to write a tune all by her dear little self, and you're going to have to find words for it."

"No, no," said the Doctor. "That would indeed be untrue to Hoffmann."

"Listen, Nilla. More operas have been spoiled by too much artistic conscience than have ever been glorified by genius. Just for the moment, forget about Hoffmann. Or no, that's not what I mean. Think of what Hoffmann would do if he were still alive. I see him now, the wonderful bright-eyed little chap, chewing his quill and thinking, 'What we need in Act Three is a great big, smashing aria for Arthur that pulls the whole thing together, and knocks the audience out of their socks. It's got to be the one that everybody remembers, and that the barrel-organs play in the streets.' We don't have barrel-organs now, but he wouldn't know that. It's got to get the young, and the old, and if the critics despise it the critics of the next generation will hail it as genius."

"I will not agree to anything that has a cheap appeal," said the Doctor.

"Nilla — dear, uncompromising Nilla *fach* — there is the truly cheap art, and we all know what it is, but there is another kind of art, that goes far beyond what critics call good taste. Good taste is really just a kind of aesthetic vegetarianism, you know. You go beyond it at your peril, and you end up with schmalz like 'M'appari' in *Marta*. Or maybe you come up with 'Voi, che sapete', or 'Porgi amor', which is genius. Or you get the Evening Star aria out of *Tannhäuser* or the Habanera out of *Carmen* — and you can't say Wagner dealt in cheap goods, and Bizet wrote the one sure-fire opera. You artists really must stop kicking the public in the face. They're not all fools, you know. You've got to get something into this Hoffmann job that will lift it above a fancy academic exercise to earn Schnak a degree. We've got to wow 'em, Nilla! Can you resist that?"

"This is very dangerous talk, Powell. I'm not sure I should let Hulda listen. These are dirtier words than any even she knows."

"Come on, Nilla. I know this is the voice of the Tempter, but the Tempter has inspired some damned good stuff. Now listen carefully, Nilla. Have you ever heard this?

> *Though critics may bow to art,*
> > *And I am its own true lover,*
> *It is not art, but heart*
> > *Which wins the wide world over."*

Darcourt, who had been listening with delight to the spellbinder, roared with laughter. He lifted his voice in imitation of Powell's bardic chant, and continued:

> *"And it is not the poet's song,*
> > *Though sweeter than sweet bells chiming,*
> *Which thrills us through and through,*
> > *But the heart which beats under the rhyming."*

"Is that English poetry?" said the Doctor, her brows raised almost into her hair.

"Jesus, I think that's wonderful!" said Schnak. "Oh, Nilla, did you ever hear it said better?"

"I am not at home in English verse," said the Doctor, "but that sounds to me like — I will not use Hulda's word — but it sounds like crap. That is a new word I have learned and it is very useful. Crap!"

"The expression is unquestionably crap," said Darcourt. "But in the crap there is a precious jewel of truth. That is one of the problems of poetry. Even a terrible poet may hit on a truth. Even the blind pig sometimes finds an acorn."

"The professor sets us right, as he always does," said Powell. "Raw heart can't make art but woe to art when it snubs heart. By God — I ought to be a librettist! Now — will you do it?"

"I'll have a crack at it," said Schnak. "I've had about enough of writing music wrapped in Hoffmann's old bath-robe."

"I'll certainly have a crack at it," said Darcourt. "But on one condition. I find the verse before Schnak writes the music."

"Sim, *bach*, I see it in your eye! You have the verse already."

"As a matter of fact, I have," said Darcourt, and he recited it to them.

"Do that again, will you," said Schnak, looking at Darcourt without suspicion and resentment for the first time since they had met.

Darcourt recited it again.

"That's it!" said Powell. "Right on the pig's back, Sim *bach*."

"But is it good English verse?" said the Doctor.

"I'm not a man who awards marks to poets as if they were schoolboys," said Darcourt. "It is from the best of a very good man, and far beyond the level of an opera libretto."

"You're surely going to tell us who the very good man is?" said Powell.

"He's the man you spoke of as the base upon which we

should rest this opera, the first time we discussed it," said Darcourt. "It's Sir Walter Scott."

(3)

CAN IT BE TRUE, thought Darcourt, that I am sitting in this grand penthouse on a Sunday evening eating cold roast chicken and salad with three figures from Arthurian legend? Three people working out, in such terms as modernity dictates, the great myth of the betrayed king, the enchantress queen, and the brilliant adventurer?

Does the analogy hold? What did King Arthur attempt? He tried to extend the reach of civilization by demanding that his Knights, who belonged to an undoubted Elite of Birth, should embrace the concept of chivalry, thereby becoming an Elite of Achievement. Not just power, but the intelligent, unselfish use of power to make a better world; that was the idea.

What about Arthur Cornish, who is helping himself to currant jelly across the table? He belongs to a Birth Elite of a kind; of a Canadian kind, which thinks three generations of money are enough in themselves to make a man significant, do what he will. But Arthur wants to be an intellectual, and to advance civilization by the use of his power, which is his money; or rather, the money of the late Francis Cornish, the mysterious fortune which nobody can quite explain. Surely that is an attempt, and a very respectable attempt, to advance into an Elite of Achievement? Arthur Cornish probably commands more hard cash and more power than Arthur of Britain ever dreamed of.

Queen Guenevere lives in legend as a partner in an adulterous love that brought great grief to King Arthur. Not all the legends present her as a woman troubled by love alone; sometimes she is a discontented wife, an ambitious woman of a fretful spirit, a figure more solid and varied than Tennyson draws her.

Certainly Maria fills the bill. She had told Darcourt, not so very long ago, before she married Arthur, that she had fallen in love with him because of his frankness, his largeness of spirit, and also his attractive freedom from the academic world to which her own ambitions were confined. Arthur had offered her love, but also friendship, and she had found it irresistible. Yet a woman cannot live solely in the realm of her love; she must have a life of her own; she must shed light, as well as reflecting it. It looked as if Maria's light, since her marriage, had been somewhat under a cloud. She had tried too hard to be Arthur's wife, first, last, and all the time, and her spirit was in rebellion. How long had they been married? Twenty months, was it? Twenty months of forsaking all others and cleaving only unto him? It simply won't work. No woman worth marrying is nothing but a wife, if the man is something better than a roaring egotist, which Arthur certainly is not, for all his peremptory, rich man's ways in certain matters. Darcourt, himself unmarried, had seen many marriages, and united more couples, he thought in his Old Ontario way, than he could shake a stick at. The marriages that worked best were those in which the unity still permitted of some separateness — not a ranting independence, but a firm possession by both man and woman of their own souls.

Was it any use talking to Arthur and Maria about souls? Probably not. Souls are not fashionable, at present. People will listen with wondering acquiescence to scientific talk of such invisible entities as are said to be everywhere and very important, but they shy away from talk of souls. Souls have a bad name in the world of atomic energy.

Souls were a reality to Darcourt, however. Souls, not as gassy aspiration and unreal nobility, but as the force that divides the living human creature from the raw material for the mortician's craft. Souls as a totality of consciousness, what man knows of himself and also that hidden vast part of himself which knows and impels *him*, used and abused by everybody, called upon or rejected, but inescapable.

What about Powell? Now there was a man who would assert, with passionate eloquence, that he had a soul, but who was clearly driven by that portion of his soul that was not within the range of his direct knowledge, that part of the spirit that some people — Mamusia, for instance — would call his fate. But a man's fate is his own, more than he knows. We attract what we are. And it was Powell's fate that had drawn him to seduce his friend's wife, probably — no, Darcourt was sure, undoubtedly — with the complicity of Maria's fate, just as Lancelot had seduced, or been seduced by, Guenevere.

"Do you want more dressing on your salad, Simon?" said Maria. She and Arthur and Powell had been talking while Darcourt mused.

Yes, he would like more dressing on his salad. He really must not drift off into unheeding speculation while the others were talking. And what had they been talking about?

About the impending child, of course. They talked about it a good deal, and with a frankness Darcourt found astonishing. It was five months on its way, and Maria wore becoming gowns in which she did not look pregnant, like the women Darcourt saw in the streets who wore slacks in which their distended bellies were forced upon the world, but clever gowns that enhanced, without concealing, her increasing girth.

Arthur and Geraint were rivals in solicitude. Neither had been a father before, they said, sometimes as a joke but always with an undercurrent of concern. They fussed over Maria, urging her to sit when she was perfectly comfortable standing, and rushing to fetch her things that she did not greatly want. They urged her not to drive her car, to put her feet on a stool when she sat, to get plenty of rest, to drink milk (which her doctor told her not to do), to eat heartily, to eat wisely, to drink very little wine and no spirits, to put aside the more inflammatory parts of the newspapers. They were a little disappointed that she exhibited no irrational cravings for peculiar foods; they would have been overjoyed if she had made eerie demands for pickles drenched in ice cream. These were old wives' tales, said Maria, laughing at them. But, like prospective fathers from an earlier day, they were pestilent old wives, and they grew together in old-wifery. They were better friends than ever.

Had Arthur and Lancelot, in the mythical long ago, fretted and fussed so? Of course not; they had no ambiguous baby.

"The meeting with Schnak's parents went very well," said Powell.

"Who met them? Sorry, I haven't been attending," said Darcourt.

"Nilla insisted that Schnak ask them in. Nilla is very strict with Schnak and is teaching her manners. Won't listen to Schnak's fits of bad-mouthing her old folks. You must ask them here, Hulda dearest, she said, and we must be very, very sweet to them. And that's what they did."

"Were you there?" said Maria.

"Indeed I was. Wouldn't have missed it for the world. If I may say so, I was the star turn, the cherry on the cake. I got on with the elder Schnaks brilliantly."

"Tell all," said Maria.

"Well, they turned up, in answer to a telephone call from Schnak, which she made while Nilla stood over her with a whip, if I'm not mistaken. You've seen them. Not what I would call clubbable people, and they were all set to resent Nilla and lecture Schnak. But not a bit of it. Nilla was charming, and there was enough high-bred European atmosphere floating around for the elder Schnaks to recognize Nilla as a genuine grandee. Not just rich people, like you Cornishes, but a person of aristocratic quality. You'd be amazed how powerful that still is. She spoke to them quite a lot of the time in German, and that kept Schnak out of things, because although she understands pretty well, she can't say much in the old tongue. I don't know any more German than I need to follow a Wagner libretto, but I could tell that Nilla was being really gracious. Not patronizing, but speaking to them as equals, and as an older person like themselves, deeply concerned about Schnak. She talked about art, and music, and they softened up a bit under that and the rich cakes and the coffee with lots of whipped cream. They didn't soften much, although they were impressed by the huge heap of musical manuscript Schnak had piled up. Obviously the girl was working. What was sticking in their gullets was Schnak's rebellion against what they think of as religion. That was where I came in very strong."

"You, Geraint? You agreed with those bitter Puritans about religion?"

"Of course I did, Arthur, *bach*. Don't forget I grew up a Calvinistic Methodist, with a father who was a mighty shaman in the faith. I let them know that, of course. But, said I, look at me, deep into the world of art, and theatre and music, and the fatherhood and splendour of God is present to me every hour of my life, and infuses everything I do. Does God speak only with a single tongue? I asked them. Does His mighty love not reach out to those who have not yet come to the full belief, to the life of total faith? May He not speak even in the theatre, in the opera house, to those who have fled from Him into a world they think frivolous and abandoned to pleasure? Oh, my friends, you are blessed in knowing the fullness of God's revealed Word. You have not encountered, as I have, the God who knows how to speak to the fallen and the reprobate through the language of art; you have not met with the Cunning of God, by which He reaches out to His children who shut their ears to His true voice. Our God is stern with those like yourselves whom He has marked from birth as His own, but He is gentle and subtle with those who have strayed into worldly paths. He speaks with many voices, and one of the most winning is the voice of music. Your daughter has been greatly gifted in music and dare you say that she is not marked by God as one of His own, to be His instrument, His harp of Zion, to draw His erring children to Him? Do you, Elias Schnakenburg, say that your child may not be speaking — I say this with humility — through her music with the voice of God Himself? Do you? Can you presume so far? Oh, Elias Schnakenburg, I urge you, I beg you, to reflect deeply upon these mysteries, and then reject your daughter's vocation if you dare!"

"By God, Geraint, did you say that?"

"Indeed I did, Maria. That and a good deal more. I even gave them a touch of the old Welsh *hwyl*; I sang my peroration. Worked like a charm."

Maria was overcome. "Geraint, you bloody crook!" she said when she could speak.

"Maria, *fach*, you wound me profoundly. Sincere, every word of it. And true, what's more. Sim, *bach*, you know what preaching is. Did I say a word that you would not have spoken from a pulpit?"

"I liked that about the Cunning of God, Geraint *bach*. About the rest of it I can only say that I am sure you were sincere while you were speaking, and I am not surprised the elder Schnaks fell for it. Yes — on consideration I would say that what you told them was true. But I am not so sure about your intention in doing so."

"My intention was to make them like our opera, and to give them pleasure, and sew up the rent garment of the Schnakenburg family."

"And did you succeed?"

"Ma Schnakenburg was overjoyed to see her child clean and putting on some flesh; Pa Schnakenburg was, if I do not do the man injustice, glad to find Hulda in such classy company, because there is a snob in everybody, and Pa Schnak has not forgotten the elegant world of aristocratic Europe. I just put the cherry on the cake with some fancy theology."

"Not theology, Geraint. Rhetoric," said Darcourt.

"Sim, *bach*, I wish you would stop knocking rhetoric. What is it? It is what the poet calls upon when the Muse is sleeping. It is what the preacher calls on when he must reach ears that need tickling to get their attention. Those of us who live in the world of art would be flat on our arses most of the time if we had no rhetoric to hold us up. Rhetoric is only base when base men use it. With me, it is the way in which I arouse the ancient and permanent elements in the spiritual structure of man by measured, rhythmic speech. Your rejection of my rhetoric springs from a mean envy, and I am disappointed in you."

"Of course you're right, Geraint; those of us who lack the gift of the gab are suspicious of those who have it. But it's just spellbinding, you know."

"*Just* spellbinding, Sim *bach*! Oh, what a pitiable barrenness of spirit lurks in that pauper's adverb *just*! I weep for you!" Powell helped himself to another piece of chicken.

"You can't weep while you're stuffing your face," said Darcourt. "Didn't the Schnaks sniff anything peculiar about the bond between Nilla and their child?"

"Such enormities are unknown to them, I imagine. My recollection of the Bible includes no instance of naughtiness between women. That's why it has a Greek name. Those tough old Israelites thought deviance was entirely a masculine privilege. They think Schnak is putting on flesh because she has come under a Good Influence."

"Speaking as a woman, I don't see the attraction of Schnak," said Maria. "If I were of Nilla's inclination I could find prettier girls."

"Ah, but Schnak has the beauty of innocence," said Powell. "Oh, she's a foul-mouthed, cornaptious little slut, but underneath she is all untouched wonderment. I suppose she's been mauled by a few student morlocks, because it's the custom in the circle in which she moves, and kids fear to go against custom. But the real, deep-down Schnak is still flower-like, and Nilla's is just the delicate hand to pluck the flower. But you know what happens; or rather you don't, because none of you are gardeners; I slaved in my mam's garden all my boyhood. You pluck the first bloom, and other, stronger blooms hurry to replace it, and that is what is happening to Schnak."

"What blooms?" said Arthur. "God forbid that we should support a lesbian house of ill-fame. There are limits, even for the Cornish Foundation. Simon, hadn't you better look into this?"

"Quite right, Arthur. The bills I've been paying for champagne and pretty little cakes from the gourmet shops are horrendous. Can't these women sustain their passion on hamburger?"

"You're quite wrong," said Powell. "That's not the way things are going at all. Nilla has roused Schnak's dormant tenderness, and let me tell you, boyos, that's chancy work. Where will it strike next? I think she has her eye on you, Sim *bach*."

Darcourt was staggered, and not at all pleased that this suggestion was greeted with hoots of laughter from Arthur and Maria.

"I don't see the joke," said he. "The suggestion is grotesque."

"In love, nothing is grotesque," said Powell.

"Sorry, Simon. I don't suggest that you are a ridiculous love-object," said Arthur. "But Schnak —" he could not speak, and laughed himself into a coughing fit, and had to be slapped on the back.

"You'll have to dye your hair and go West," said Maria.

"Simon can look after himself, and he must stay here,"

said Powell. "We need him. If need be, he can take flight after the opera is safely launched. The opera is at the root of the whole thing. It was that poetry you quoted to her, Simon. Didn't you see her face change?"

"You were the one who quoted poetry," said Darcourt. "You Welsh mischief-maker, you quoted Ella Wheeler Wilcox to the girls, and Nilla very properly gagged, but Schnak ate it up.

> *It is not art, but heart*
> *Which wins the wide world over.*

You meant it as a joke, but Schnak swallowed it whole."

"Because it is true," said Powell. "Corny, but true. And I suppose it is the first bit of verse Schnak ever heard which went right to her heart, like the bolt of Cupid. But you were the one who trotted out some real poetry, and gave it to her for the culminating moment of our drama. — Simon has found the words for Arthur's great aria," he said to Arthur and Maria, "and it's just the very thing we want. Right period, decent verse, and a fine statement of a neglected truth."

"Let's have it, Simon," said Arthur.

Darcourt found himself embarrassed. The verses were so apt to the situation of the three people who sat at table with him; verses that spoke of chivalry, and constancy, and, he truly believed, of the essence of love itself. In a low voice — he could not bring himself to use Powell's full-throated bardic manner — he recited:

> *"True love's the gift which God has given*
> *To man alone beneath the heaven:*
> > *It is not fantasy's hot fire,*
> > > *Whose wishes, soon as granted, fly;*
> > *It liveth not in fierce desire,*
> > > *With dead desire it doth not die;*

> *It is the secret sympathy,*
> *The silver link, the silken tie,*
> *Which heart to heart, and mind to mind,*
> *In body and in soul can bind."*

The verses were received in silence. It was Maria who spoke first, and like a true university woman she set out on a criticism of the words which was rooted in what she had been taught; she had a critical system, unfailing in its power to reduce poetry to technicalities and to slide easily over its content. It was a system which, properly applied, could put Homer in his place and turn the Sonnets of Shakespeare into critic-fodder. Without intending to be so, it was a system which, once mastered, set the possessor free forever, should that be his wish, from anything a poet, however noble in spirit, might have felt and imparted to the world.

"Shit!" said Powell, when she had finished. And then began a very hot discussion in which Powell was strong for the verses, and Arthur quiet and considering, and Maria determined to declare all of Walter Scott second-rate, and his easy versifying the outcome of a profuse, trivial spirit.

She is fighting for her life, thought Darcourt, and she is perversely using weapons she has learned at the university. But did anybody learn much about love in a classroom?

He kept himself apart from the wrangle. It was easy, because only by determined shouting was it possible to come between Powell and Maria. Had there ever been such a scene at Camelot, he wondered. Did Arthur, and Guenevere and Lancelot, ever haggle about what had been done, and what lay at the root of it?

If these are really modern versions of the principals in that great chivalric tale, how did they appear in terms of chivalry? The Knights, and presumably the Knights' Ladies, were supposed to possess, or try to possess, twelve knightly virtues. There were many lists of those virtues, none wholly alike, but they all included Honour, Prowess, and Courtesy, and, all things considered, these three had those virtues in plenty. Hope, Justice, Fortitude? The men emerged from that test better than Maria. Faith and Loyalty it was perhaps not well to discuss, with Maria pregnant. And it would be tactless to speak of Chastity. Franchise, now — free and frank demeanour — they all had in their various ways. Largesse, that open-handedness which was one of the foremost attributes of a Knight, was the spirit of the Cornish Foundation. All that champagne and Viennese *gateaux* were largesse, as well as the great sums that were now beginning to appear on the horizon as necessary to get the opera on the stage. But Pity of Heart — that was an attribute which Arthur alone seemed to possess, and under all the ridiculous fussing about Maria's pregnancy it was plainly to be seen in him; Maria seemed to lack it utterly. Or did she? Was her rejection of Walter Scott just a fear of what she truly felt? *Débonnaireté* — now that was a good virtue for a Knight, and for anybody else that could achieve it; gaiety of heart, a noble indifference to trivial difficulties, a *sprezzatura*, in fact — Powell was the exemplar of that virtue, and, although he still had fits of eloquent remorse for what he had done, he was contriving to rise above it. He regarded himself as co-father with Arthur, and he played the role with style.

What is that all about, thought Darcourt. A deep Freudian would almost certainly declare that there was, between Arthur and Geraint, some dank homosexual tie, working itself out in possession of the same woman. But Darcourt was not disposed to Freudian interpretations. At best, they were glum half-truths, and they explained and healed extraordinarily little. They explored what Yeats called "the foul rag-and-bone shop of the heart", but they brought none of the Apollonian light that Yeats and many another poet cast upon the heart's dunghill. Sir Walter, so plainly writing of his darling Charlotte, knew something that had escaped the unhappily married Viennese wizard. The silver link. The silken tie.

Perhaps Arthur knew it, too. Maria was wearing out with argument, and seemed near to tears.

"Come on, darling. Time you were in bed," said Arthur. And that concluded the matter, for the moment, with Pity of Heart.

(4)

DARCOURT LONGED FOR SPRING with more than the ordinary Canadian yearning. His search for the people in *The Marriage at Cana* could not be completed until the snow was off the ground, and in Blairlogie the snow lingered and renewed itself until the middle of April.

Meanwhile he spent long hours at the Library, sifting the last scraps of what had been bundled up in Francis Cornish's apartment. It was three apartments, really, every one crammed with every sort of art object. Armed with what he already knew from his biographical burrowing and fossicking about the Cornish and O'Gorman and McRory families and their hangers-on and dependants, he was able to identify almost all of the figures in the great picture.

Some of them had been identified before. Darcourt knew almost by heart the article that had been published a quarter of a century before in *Apollo*, written by Aylwin Ross. It had put the cap on Ross's once-great reputation, and had established the beautiful young Canadian as an art historian to be taken seriously. How ingenious Ross had been, with his historical exposition about the Interim of Augsburg and the Catholic-Protestant row it had created in 1548. How convincing he was about his identification of Graf Meinhard of Düsterstein and his Lady, and Johann Agricola the scholar, and Paracelsus — this was a great coup, for portraits of Paracelsus are extremely rare — and even the jolly dwarf who was certainly, Ross knew, Drollig Hansel, who was, past question, the famous dwarf jester in the employ of the Fugger family of bankers. It was romance that might have rejoiced the heart of Sir Walter Scott. But it was all moonshine, and Darcourt knew it.

Graf Meinhard and his Lady were certainly portraits of the parents of Francis Cornish, and Johann Agricola was that schoolmaster at Colborne College who had put Francis's foot on the path of historical study, and of whom a snapshot had been tucked into a sketchbook of Francis's Blairlogie period. What was the man's name? Ramsay, was it? Yes, Dunstan Ramsay. As for Paracelsus, the shrewd little figure in a physician's gown who was holding a scalpel, there could be no doubt whatever that he was Dr. Joseph Ambrosius Jerome, of whom Darcourt knew little except that he had been the McRorys' family doctor, and had once been photographed by Grandfather McRory seated, with one hand on a skull, and the other holding just such a scalpel.

Sketches — there were scores of them, and many accorded with Grandfather's Sun Pictures. That dwarf was certainly François Xavier Bouchard, the little tailor of Blairlogie, seen by Grandfather fully clothed, but sketched by Francis lying on a table, stark naked and plainly dead. Was he being embalmed? Certainly there were several sketches among Francis's earliest drawings of nude figures in which there was a hint — only a few lines, but eloquent — of a figure who seemed to be the *huissier*, the man with a whip in the painting, and also the man photographed by Grandfather standing at the head of a splendid team of carriage horses; a man of ravaged good looks, always drawn with a gleam of pity in his eye; pity for the dead which was also a knightly pity of heart for the whole of mankind.

Given the sketches and the photographs that Darcourt had unearthed in the University Library and in the preliminary studies for the picture which had been, at Francis Cornish's express direction, sent to the National Gallery in Ottawa, the whole picture lay open. The two women disputing over the wine jars, between whom knelt the figure of Christ; beyond a doubt Francis's aunt, Miss Mary-Benedetta McRory, and her adversary was Grandfather's cook, Victoria Cameron. What could they have been quarrelling about? As they were at it, hammer and tongs, over the figure of Christ, perhaps Christ was at the root of their disagreement. But who was St. John, with pen and ink-horn? He eluded identification but might perhaps yield his secret later. There was no secret about the compelling portrait of Judas, holding firmly to his money-bag; there were enough sketches in the books Francis had filled at Düsterstein to mark him clearly as Tancred Saraceni, father in art to Francis, and an ambiguous *éminence grise* in the art world of forty years ago; a restorer of pictures of pre-eminent skill, who may perhaps have done a little more than restoration on some of his canvases.

There were other figures, not identifiable or not to be identified with utter certainty. That stout merchant and his wife; they could be Gerald Vincent O'Gorman, known after his Blairlogie beginnings as a very shrewd man in the Cornish Trust, and the woman must therefore be Mary-Teresa McRory, who had become Mrs. O'Gorman and, after a strong Catholic start, a shining light among Toronto Anglicans. But the woman with what appeared to be an astrological chart? No sign of her anywhere, either as a photograph or as a sketch. And those wretched children, in the background? They looked like Blairlogie children, but they had a vicious, depraved look that was dreadful to see on childish faces; they seemed to be saying something about childhood that is not often heard.

The central figures of the picture, who were plainly the wedding couple, offered no problem and admitted of no doubt. They suggested, but in no way imitated, Van Eyck's famous portrait of the Arnolfini couple; the suggestion lay in the intensity of their gaze, the gravity of their expression.

Beyond a doubt the bride was Ismay Glasson, of whom Darcourt had seen almost a hundred sketches, naked and clothed, and he knew her face — not quite beautiful but more compelling in its intensity than beauty usually is — as well as he knew any face in the world. This was the woman Francis had married, the mother of Little Charlie, the bolter and fanatic; although the figure of Francis extended its hand toward her, it did not quite touch the hand of Ismay, who seemed to hold back, and her gaze was not at her husband but at the handsome young man who figured as St. John.

The husband was Francis Cornish, a confession in the form of a self-portrait. Pictures of Francis were rare; apart from this picture, he had never painted himself, and none of his contemporaries had thought him sufficiently interesting for a sketch. Grandfather's photographs showed the dark, slight boy in the hideous costume of his childhood and youth: Francis in a sailor suit, standing on a giant tree trunk, above a group of muscular, bearded timber-workers; Francis in his Sunday best, sitting beside a small table on which lay his rosary beads and a prayer-book; Francis squinting into the sun on a Blairlogie street; Francis with his beautiful mother, uneasy in a starched Eton collar; a few group photographs from Colborne days, in which Francis figured as a prize-winner; one photograph of an amateur theatrical performance — some sort of student Follies — in which a lanky, thin Francis appeared in the back row, among the stage-managers and scene-painters, hardly noticeable behind all the girls in short skirts and the boys in blazers who had obviously danced and sung greatly to their own satisfaction. Nothing at all which said anything about Francis Cornish.

In *The Marriage at Cana*, however, his was the dominant figure to which all the rest of the composition related. Not that the placing or presentation of the figure was aggressive; there was no Look At Me about it. But this intently gazing man, dressed in blacks and browns, drew the viewer's eye back to himself, however intent it may have been on any of the other figures. Most self-portraits tend to glare at the onlooker. The painter, presumably looking into a mirror beside his easel, must glare, must have one eye looking straight into the eyes of the beholder, and the more self-conscious the painter, the more intent the glare becomes. Rembrandts, who dare to paint themselves full-face and objectively, are uncommon. Francis had painted himself looking not at his wife but straight out of the canvas. Yet his eyes did not meet and challenge those of the onlooker; they seemed to be looking over his head. The face was grave, almost sad, and among the faces of the others — the Bride elusive and somewhat sulky, St. John looking like an adventurer, the Knight and his Lady looking like important figures in their world, the two disputing women painted in obvious contention, and the old artisan (Grandfather McRory as St. Simon the Zealot, with his woodsman's tools) — this face, Francis's face, was looking out of their world into some other, private world. Darcourt had sometimes seen that look on the face of the old Francis whom he had known.

Finally — no, not quite finally — there was the woman who stood beside the bridal couple, the only figure in the pictured graced with a halo. The Mother of God? Yes, for the convention in which the picture was cast demanded that. But more probably the Mighty Mother of All. As the mother of everybody and everything, it was not necessary for her to look like anyone in particular. Her grave beauty was universal and her smile was of a serenity that rose beyond earthly considerations.

Was that serene smile intended to heal the hurt that was visible in the portraits of the bride and groom, in which the man extended a ring toward the fourth finger of his bride's left hand, and she seemed to be holding back, or perhaps withdrawing her hand from what he offered? To Darcourt, knowing what he knew, and immersed as he was in all the Sun

Pictures and the innumerable copies, sketches, and finished drawings that were all that remained of the truth of Francis Cornish's life, it seemed as if this extraordinary picture was an allegory of a man's ruin, of the destruction of his spirit. Had the wilful bolter Ismay really hurt him so deeply? After this picture, Francis had never painted seriously again.

> Shall I, wasting in despair,
> Die because a woman's fair?

The poet who wrote that, and all the easy philosophy of love that follows it, was a hardier soul than Francis. But not all men, or all lovers, are hardy souls. It seemed to Darcourt that Francis had not died because of Ismay's determination to follow her own star, but something within him had suffered mortal hurt, and the death that had overtaken him so many years afterward, when he died alone in his cluttered flat, was a second death, and it was not in Darcourt's power to say which had been the most significant cessation of being.

Darcourt would readily have admitted that he did not know much about love. He had had no youthful affairs, except in a superficial sense. His love for Maria, which he now knew to have been a folly from which he was lucky to escape, was all that he had known of passion. But he had the gift, not often given to deeply passionate men, to understand the joys and also the heart-stopping blows of fate that afflicted other people. The more he looked at the large reproduction, and also the detailed pictures of portions of *The Marriage at Cana* that accompanied Aylwin Ross's brilliant, wholly mistaken article in *Apollo*, the more he wondered if Maria, now great with Geraint Powell's child, had struck just such a blow to Arthur Cornish. Arthur was holding up very well, if that were true, but he had lost all *débonnaireté*. Arthur was certainly The Magnanimous Cuckold. But Arthur was not the clearly defined, generous, but ruthless spirit he had been when Darcourt first knew him. If it were so, who was to blame? The more Darcourt knew, the less he was inclined to blame or praise.

The final figure in the picture, however, had to await the spring before it could be identified, so far as possible, forever

That was the angel who floated in the air over the heads of the bridal pair and the Mighty Mother in the central panel of the triptych. Perhaps it was not quite an angel, but if not why was it suspended in air, without angelic wings? The first time one looked at the picture it seemed to throw the whole composition into confusion. Whereas the other figures were human, painted with love, and sometimes beautiful, sometimes noble, sometimes self-satisfied, sometimes — old St Simon was such a portrait — as wise beyond worldly wisdom this floating creature was a comic horror. Its pointed head, its almost idiotic expression, its suggestion of disorder of mind and deformity of body, were all out of key with the rest. And yet, the more one looked, the more it seemed to belong, to be almost necessary to whatever it was the whole composition was saying.

From its mouth came a scroll, suggesting one of the balloons that hold the words in a comic strip, and in the scroll were the words *Tu autem servasti bonum vinum usque adhuc*. Not very elegant as Latin, but the words spoken to the bridegroom by the governor of the feast at the Marriage at Cana: "Thou hast kept the good wine until now." Christ's first miracle; a puzzle, for nothing in the Gospel suggests that anyone but Christ and His Mother and a few servants knew the secret.

Was this picture, then, as well as an object of great beauty, a puzzle? A joke, a deeply serious joke, on future beholders?

April brought the answer, as Darcourt had hoped it would. He made the inconvenient train journey to Blairlogie and, armed with a shovel, a broom, and his camera, he went to the Catholic cemetery and there, high on the bleak hill, he visited once again the McRory family plot. It was dominated by large, tasteless stones commemorating the Senator and his wife, and Mary-Benedetta McRory. But there were a few humbler markers, one of them not a gravestone but a memorial to somebody called Zadok Hoyle, identified as a faithful servant of the family. And — here it was — in an obscure corner behind the biggest stone was a small marble marker, flat to the ground, and when Darcourt had cleared away the last lingering snow and ice, and an accumulation of lichen, it read, plainly, FRANCIS.

So: here it was. Among the sketches from Francis's boyhood years there were a number of an invalid figure, confined to a bed which was almost a cage; the figure in the bed was a pitiable deformity, of the sort that cruel people used to call a pinhead, blank of eye, sparse of hair, and wearing an expression, to use the word loosely, that would draw pity from the heart of an ogre. These sketches, rapid but vivid, were identified only by the letter F, except for one on which was laboriously written, in the hand of a boy who wished to be a calligrapher but did not yet know how, what seemed to have been copied from some royal signature, François Premier.

Francis the First? Now, thought Darcourt, I know all I need to know, and all I am ever likely to know. Truly the best wine has been kept until the last.

(5)

"THE CRONES ARE COMING," said Dean Wintersen's voice down the telephone. "They are expected today."

What crones? Was this some uncanny visitation of weird old women? What crones? Darcourt had been roused from his work on the biography of the late Francis Cornish, and his mind did not readily shift to the Dean's concern. The crones? Oh, yes! Of course! The Cranes. Had he not agreed that some people called Crane should come from an American West

Coast university to do something or other of a vaguely defined order about the production of the opera? That had been months ago and, having so agreed, and having it well understood that the Cranes were not to cost the Cornish Foundation anything, he had banished the Cranes from his mind, as a problem to be dealt with when it arose. Now, it appeared, the Cranes were coming.

"You remember them, of course," said the Dean.

"Remind me," said Darcourt.

"They're the assessors from Pomelo U.," said the Dean. "It was agreed they should sit in on the production of the opera. You remember the opera, don't you?"

Oh, yes; Darcourt remembered the opera. Had he not been slaving over the libretto for the past four months?

"But what are they going to assess?" said Darcourt.

"The whole affair. Everything connected with the opera from Schnak's work on the score to the last detail of getting the thing on the stage. And then the critical and public reaction."

"But why?"

"To get Al Crane his Ph.D., of course. He's an opera major in the theatre school at Pomelo, and when he has got his assessment together he will make a *Regiebuch* and present it as his thesis."

"His what?"

"His *Regiebuch*. A German expression. All the dope on the production of the opera will be in it."

"My God! He sounds like Divine Correction out of a medieval play. Does Dr. Dahl-Soot know? Does Geraint Powell know?"

"I suppose they do. You're the liaison man, or so I understood. Didn't you tell them?"

"I don't think I knew. Or fully realized."

"You'd better tell them, then. Al and Mabel will be seeing you right away. They're eager."

"Who's Mabel?"

"I'm not sure. I think she's not quite Mrs. Crane, but she's with him. Not to worry. Al has a big grant from the Pomelo Further Studies Fund to look after him. This is a courtesy schools of music frequently extend to one another. It'll be all right."

How lightly the Dean took such things! Doubtless that was the secret of being a dean. When, a couple of hours after his call, Darcourt gazed at Al and Mabel Crane, as they sat in his study, he wondered if it would really be all right.

Not that the Cranes looked menacing. Not at all. They had the look of expectancy Darcourt knew so well as an attribute of a certain kind of student. They wanted something to happen to them, and they wanted him to make it happen. They were probably in their middle twenties, but they had still the unfledged, student look. Apparently they travelled light and informally. It was cool in the Canadian spring, but Al Crane was dressed as if for a hot day. He wore chinos, a much crumpled seersucker coat, and a dirty shirt. The breast pocket of the coat hung heavily with a number of ball-point pens. His bare feet were thrust into sandals that would not last much longer. He had not shaved for two or three days, and his lantern jaws were dark. As for Mabel, the one arresting thing about her was that she was monstrously pregnant. The child she carried, though still unborn, was already sitting in her lap. Like Al, she was dressed for summer, the summer of Southern California, and she too was in a bad way for footwear. They both smiled, in a dog-like manner, as if hoping to be patted.

Al, however, knew what he wanted. He wanted several days with Hulda Schnakenburg, to go over the score of the opera and examine all the scraps of Hoffmann, which he called The Documentation, and then he wanted a few days with Dr. Dahl-Soot, whose presence in the matter was, he declared, awesome. Just to talk with Gunilla Dahl-Soot would be an enrichment. He wanted access to a Xerox machine, so that he could get facsimiles of everything, every inch of Hoffmann, every draft of Schnakenburg, every page of the completed score. He wanted to go over the libretto with whoever had prepared it, and he wanted to compare it with anything by Planché, from which it derived, or did not derive. He wanted to talk with the director, the designer, the designer of lighting, and the scenic artists. He wanted copies of every design, and every rejected design. He wanted to photograph the stage that would be used, and he wanted all its measurements.

"That'll do to be going on with," he said. "Then of course I'll sit in on all the rehearsals and all the musical preparation. I'll need a full C.V. from everybody involved. But right now, we're wondering where we are to live."

"I haven't any idea," said Darcourt. "You'd better talk to Dean Wintersen about that. There are lots of hotels."

"I'm afraid a hotel would be way beyond us," said Al. "We've got to watch the pennies."

"I understood the Dean to say that you had a generous grant from Pomelo."

"Generous for one," said Al. "Tight for two. For three, I should say. You can see how it is with Mabel."

"Oh, Al, do you think there's been a slip-up?" said Mabel. She was the kind of woman, Darcourt saw with alarm, who cries easily.

"Not to worry, Sweetness," said Al. "I'm sure the professor has everything lined up."

Don't be too sure, thought Darcourt. There had been a time, before he recognized himself as the Fool, when he would have been badgered into assuming full responsibility for these Babes in the Wood. But as the Fool he had other things to attend to. So he gave the Cranes the name of Dean Wintersen's secretary, and the telephone number at which the Doctor could be reached, and, by means of well-developed professorial will-power — the spiritual equivalent of the Chinese Chi-Kung — he shifted them off his chairs and out of his sight.

They went, thanking him profusely and assuring him that they looked forward to seeing him again. It had already been a terrific experience, they said, just meeting him.

(6)

DARCOURT WAS NOT SURE how he should approach Arthur and Maria about his discovery, now his certainty, of what *The Marriage at Cana* really was. Although the Cornish Foundation was in no way underwriting his biography of Francis Cornish, friendship and a sense of decency about a family with whom he was strongly involved made it obligatory that he should tell them what he had found, before he said anything to Princess Amalie and Prince Max. The picture belonged to the New York people, and who could guess what they might say to his information about their treasure? Was it a brilliant piece of detection in the world of art history, or was it the harsh unmasking of a fake? And if a fake, what did that mean in loss of money? That was trouble enough, but the touchiness of the Cornishes about anything that might reflect, however faintly, on the integrity of the great financial house was incalculable. So he dawdled, dotting i's and crossing t's in his documentation, and hoping that a favourable moment would declare itself.

The declaration came from an unexpected source. Wally Crottel was apprehended by the police selling marijuana to schoolchildren. In the playground of the Governor Simcoe Public School, Wally was plying a brisk trade in joints at the end of each school day, and some children, with that mixture of innocence and stupidity that marks a certain sort of childish mind, were walking home puffing proudly. Before the police could put the handcuffs on him Wally made an ill-advised break for freedom and was knocked down by a passing car; he was quite badly hurt, and was now in the General Hospital, with a policeman sitting outside his room, with nothing to do but read a paperback book which Mr. Carver told Darcourt was *Middlemarch*, an unexpected choice. Mr. Carver had tipped off the police about Wally's profitable sideline, and Mr. Carver could not conceal a deep satisfaction at Wally's fall.

"But you have to admit the guy was very well organized," he said. "He was growing the stuff in a corner of a parking lot behind the boarding-house building where he lived. It was quite a small job, but you don't need an awful lot of the old Mary-Jane to make a few joints, and Wally included a good deal of dried mint with it, to make it go as far as possible, and give a flavour kids liked. Wally was doing very well, for a small operator. Where the kids got the money to pay his price I don't know, but there are quite a few rich kids in that district, and I think some of them were retailing what they bought from Wally, adulterated with dried grass and God knows what. Little bastards! Imagine kiddy pushers! But we live in a very strange world, professor."

"We do, indeed. How did you get wise to Wally?"

"There's a guy lives in the basement of that building where Mr. and Mrs. Cornish have the penthouse that I've known for years. Looks like a slob, but he's not a real slob. I think he had it in for Wally, who was always snooping around that basement apartment, trying to find out how this man and his sister came to be living there. Now, the sister's a bit of a psychic, and sometimes the cops use her, when they want one. Oh, yes; we cops are not above tips from psychics, and sometimes they're very useful. You can't discount anything you hear, in the detective business."

"Will it go hard with Wally, when he comes to trial?"

"That crook Gwilt is hard at work, building up a case that

Wally comes from a broken home — you know what I mean? He'll do his best to keep Wally in the hospital as long as possible, so he can do whatever he can to get Wally tried before an easy judge. Fat chance! There aren't any easy judges when it comes to pushing drugs to kids. Wally is headed for a long, reflective retirement as a guest of the Crown."

"What could that mean?"

"Well, professor, it says on the books you can get life for pushing. Nobody does, but some of the sentences are tough. Let's look on the bright side and say Wally comes out of hospital with a short leg, or a hole in his head, or something showy like that. The judge might go easy on him. He'll still go to the pen, of course, but if he's a very good boy, and squeals on a few people he knows, and sucks up the governors and the chaplain, he might be on the street again in seven years, but not a minute less. I'd hope for nine or ten. Pushing to kids is very, very unpopular. Wally has lost face, as the Chinese say. Your friend with the book Wally was whimpering about can forget Wally. How is that nice lady?"

"At this moment, she's expecting a baby."

"Couldn't be better. If you see her, wish her luck from me."

The very night he heard of Wally's fall Darcourt hastened to the Cornishes' apartment, thinking that such news would create an atmosphere friendly to his real mission. He was not pleased to find Powell there before him, making himself very much at home. He could not possibly include Powell in any discussion about *The Marriage at Cana*. But he told Arthur and Maria about Wally, and about Carver's forecast of Wally's future.

"Poor old Wally," said Maria.

Arthur was dumbfounded. "Poor old — ! Maria, don't you see? This disposes of that business of Wally wanting his father's book. He wouldn't get anywhere with a court case about that."

"Aren't the courts supposed to forget past misdeeds, when somebody has been foully wronged?"

"They're supposed to, but they don't. From henceforth, Wally is null and void."

"I'm astonished at you men. Do you want to have your own way at the expense of a fellow creature's suffering?"

"I haven't the least objection to you getting your own way at the expense of anybody's suffering. Except mine, of course," said Arthur.

"Wally is suffering because he is stupid," said Darcourt. "Trying to break away from the cops! Ah, these amateurs! He is obviously a criminal of no real flair."

"Wouldn't you have tried to escape?"

"If I were hanging around schoolyards, peddling dope to kids, I would hope to have more grip on my job. If I were a criminal, I would try to use the brains God gave me."

"All right. Wally is a bad boy and Wally is stupid. But it ill becomes you, as a Christian priest, to be exulting and sniggering. Where's your pity?"

"Maria, stop playing the Many-Breasted Mother, gushing compassion like a burst waterpipe. You're kidding. You're just as glad as we are that Wally's out of the way."

"I shall indeed be a mother within quite a short time, and I think a show of compassion becomes me. I know my role." Maria smiled a farcical Madonna smile.

"Good! Then I'll play my role as a Christian priest. Arthur, will you get on the phone and send Wally your own lawyer? Meanwhile I'll phone the newspaper sob-sisters and shed a few tears about Wally's sad plight. Geraint, you lodge a complaint under the Charter of Rights. Wally was an employee of this building, and thus of the Cornish Trust, of which Arthur is the Big Cheese. So Arthur must rush to the aid of a victim of our social system. Maria, prepare to appear in court, heavy with child and wearing a veil, to say what a sweet little fellow Wally always was, and how Whistlecraft's denial of his name to Wally gave him an Anonymity Complex. Wally will have to go to jail, but we can float him in and out on a flood of tears. Of course we'll keep mum about how Wally tried to shake you down for a million. Come on, let's get to work. There must be more than one phone in this palace."

"Oh, I wasn't suggesting that we *do* anything," said Maria. "I was just suggesting that we *talk* a little more compassionately."

"You don't understand modern compassion, Sim *bach*. It's a passive virtue. I see what Maria means; let's pity Wally, and maybe send him a few grapes in the slammer. If anybody is going to be nasty to the criminal classes, it must be those horrible cops and the hard-faced men in the courts. That's what we pay them for. To make the world cosy for us. We smash Wally without having to harbour a hateful, revengeful thought; our servants do all that kind of thing for us."

"That's a new dimension of the Kater Murr philosophy," said Darcourt. "Thanks for explaining it to me, Geraint *bach*."

"After the baby is born, I think I shall write a whole volume, expanding Kater Murr," said Maria. "Hoffmann didn't begin to get all the good out of him. Kater Murr is really the foremost social philosopher of our time."

This was what Darcourt wanted. This was almost the old Maria, the woman infused with the spirit of François Rabelais, a spirit vowed to the highest reaches of scholarship and illuminated by a cleansing humour. Arthur, he thought, was looking decidedly better. Had some sort of new serenity descended on the Cornish household? Well — Powell was still there, and Powell was making himself very much at home.

"I must leave you shortly," said he, "but meanwhile I am enjoying the peaceful retirement of your dwelling. This is one place where I am sure I can't be got at by the abominable Al Crane."

"Oh, don't think you are safe here," said Arthur. "Last night Al and Sweetness turned up and he cross-examined me for two hours, taking a full five minutes to formulate each question. In the modern lingo, Al lacks verbal skills; lingually, Al is a stumblebum. He brought a tape-recorder, so that every precious Um and Ah would be preserved forever. He wanted to know what my Motivation was for putting the Fund behind the opera scheme. He doesn't believe anybody might do something for a variety of reasons; he wants one great, big, juicy Motivation which would be, he says, a significantly seminal thread in a complexity of artistic inspirations. He wants to identify all the threads that are woven into the complex tapestry of a work of art — I am quoting Al, you understand — but some threads are more seminal than others, and mine is wonderfully seminal; it could even be the warp, or maybe the woof, of the whole tapestry. I thought I would faint from boredom before I finally got him out of the house."

"Arthur did not suffer alone," said Maria. "All the time Al had him on the spot I was being bored rigid by Sweetness, who thanked me for receiving her in my Gracious Home, and then talked about what she called Our Condition. There are countless ways of making pregnancy nauseating, and I think Sweetness explored them all."

"Sweetness is delighted with you. She told me so," said Darcourt. "Because of your both being pregnant, of course. You and she, greatly in pod, are what she calls an Objective Correlative of the job of bringing this opera to birth. You, and she, and the opera all burst upon a waiting world at roughly the same time."

"Spare me Sweetness's scholarly insights," said Maria. "She is not an Objective Correlative of anything, and she disgusts me as parodies of oneself always do. She expects me to embrace her as a loving companion in gravidity, and if she gives me much more sisterly love I may miscarry. But she would be sure to interpret that as an ill omen for the opera, so

I don't think I'll oblige her. Never again does she cross the threshold of my Gracious Home."

"They didn't get a great welcome in Nilla's Gracious Home," said Powell. "Nilla doesn't know what an assessor is, and I can't tell her. I always thought the word meant a judge, or somebody who estimated something. What is an assessor, exactly, Sim *bach*?"

"It is something new in the academic world," said Darcourt. "Somebody who watches something happen, and gives an enormously detailed report on it; somebody who shares an experience, without having any real involvement with it. A sort of Licensed Snoop."

"But who issues the licence?" said Arthur.

"In this case, it seems to have been Wintersen. He says watching the production process will enrich Al immeasurably, and if Al develops his thesis into a book, it will give permanency to a deeply interesting and profoundly seminal experience."

"Nilla is not pleased," said Powell. "She knows only one meaning for seminal, and she thinks Al is being indecent in a male chauvinist way. She told him flatly there was nothing seminal in what she and Schnak were doing, and when he contradicted her she was very brusque. Said she had no time for such nonsense. Sweetness burst into tears, and Al said he fully understood the mercuriality of the artistic temperament, but the act of creation was seminal and it was his job to understand it so far as in him lay, which he seemed to think was pretty far. I just hope Al does not prove to be the condom in the act of creation." ·

"Not much fear of that," said Arthur.

"No fear at all, really. Nilla and Schnak have worked like Trojans. In fact, I wouldn't be surprised if Wintersen weren't encouraging a deputation of Trojans to come and measure the energy involved. How does Wintersen get into this act, anyhow?

"Dean of the Graduate School of Music," said Darcourt. "I think he sees himself as richly seminal in this whole project. Did you know that Al and Sweetness have been to see Penny Raven?"

"As a collaborator with you on the libretto?"

"A fat lot of collaboration Penny has done. Those Trojans had better have a word with me, when they are learning about work. But Penny is an old academic hand. She strung them along with some high-sounding nonsense, and when she phoned me about it she could hardly speak for laughing. Quoted from *The Hunting of the Snark*, as she always does."

"That Snark again," said Arthur. "I really must read it. What did she say?"

"It's an astonishing poem for descriptive quotes:

> *They sought it with thimbles, they sought it with care,*
> > *They pursued it with forks and hope;*
> *They threatened its life with a railway-share;*
> > *They charmed it with smiles and soap."*

"Sweetness provides the smiles and soap," said Maria. "I wonder if I shall manage not to kill Sweetness in some ingenious way. How does one get away with murder?"

"Exactly how does Sweetness come into this?" said Arthur. "Are they combining on this awful assessor game?"

"Hollier has the answer," said Darcourt. "They visited him, but they got nowhere. He examined them with great care, however, and he says that he sees Sweetness, in anthropological-psychological-historico terms as the External Image of Al's Soul."

"A terrible thought," said Maria. "Imagine looking into Sweetness's teary eyes and saying, 'My God, that's the best of me!' Al doesn't want to do anything important without her, she tells me. I'm not sure she didn't say she was his Muse. I wouldn't put it past her."

"I wish I didn't know *The Hunting of the Snark*," said

Powell. "I am up to my neck in producing this opera and I keep thinking —

> *The principal failing occurred in the sailing,*
> *And the Bellman, perplexed and distressed,*
> *Said he hoped, at least, when the wind blew due East,*
> *That the ship would not travel due West!*"

"You haven't got cold feet, have you, Geraint?" said Arthur.

"No colder than usual, at this stage in a big job," said Powell. "But I do see myself as the Bellman, when I wake up in the night, sweating. Everything is ready to go, you see. Got the score, got the cast, got the designs, got everything, and at last I must start on what Al would certainly call the seminal part. God grant that I am sufficiently seminal for the job. And now, with the greatest reluctance, I must leave this snug retreat, and go back to my desk. A million details await me."

He pulled himself out of his chair, with some effort. He still has a lame leg, thought Darcourt. It goes well with his generally Byronic personality. He has developed a sliding walk, to disguise his lameness, just like Byron. I wonder if it's conscious imitation — Byronic hero-worship — or if he can't help it?

With Powell out of the way, there was nothing for it but to plunge into his news about *The Marriage at Cana*. He told the tale as convincingly as he could; he wanted to open a new world to his friends, not frighten them with an explosion. For the first time, he spoke to them of his visit to Princess Amalie, to confirm that her Old Master drawing was, in fact, a portrait of herself, done in girlhood by a man on whom she had had a youthful crush. He did not think it necessary to speak of his thefts in the University Library and even in the National Gallery; these were, he now assured himself, not thefts in the ordinary sense, but adventures on the journey of the Fool, guided by intuition and governed by a morality that was not to everybody's taste. If everything worked out as he hoped, what he had done justified itself, and if he were not lucky, he might find himself in jail. With gentleness, but determination, he told of his astonishment when, in the Princess's drawing-room, displayed among a number of convincing Old Masters, and in itself convincing to any eye but his own, he saw *The Marriage*, and with shocked astonishment recognized the faces as belonging to Grandfather McRory's Sun Pictures, and to Francis Cornish's numerous, neglected sketchbooks. There could be no doubt about it, he insisted: Francis was The Alchemical Master, and the great picture was not yet fifty years old.

Arthur and Maria heard all this more or less in silence, though now and then Arthur whistled. It was necessary to come to the real point.

"You understand what this will mean to my biography of Francis," he said. "It is the justification of the book. The climax. It establishes Francis as a very great painter. Working in the mode of a bygone day, but a great painter none the less."

"But in the mode of a bygone day," said Arthur. "He may be a great painter, but that makes him unmistakably a faker."

"Not at all," said Darcourt. "There is not a shred of evidence that Francis meant to deceive anybody. The picture was never offered for sale, and if it hadn't been for the war, he would undoubtedly have taken it with him when he left Düsterstein, and nobody will convince me that he would have tried to palm it off as a sixteenth-century work. The Princess knows about it. The picture was stashed away in a store-room of the castle, and when the castle was taken over during the occupation of Germany it disappeared with a lot of other stuff. It was restored to the Düsterstein family after the war, by the Commission that dealt with such matters, of which Francis was a member. That's a bit fishy, but we don't know the details. And the family — that's to say Princess Amalie — has it still."

"That doesn't answer my question," said Arthur. "Why did he paint it in this sixteenth-century manner? And look at this article in *Apollo*, that explains it all. If it wasn't meant to deceive, why paint it like that?"

"That's where we come to the point that is going to be the making of my book," said Darcourt. "You don't remember Francis in any detail. But I do. He was the most inward-looking man I have ever known. He turned things over and over in his mind, and he reached conclusions. That picture is the most important of his conclusions. It represents what he thought most important in his life, the influences, the cross-currents, the tapestry, as Al Crane would say if he had a chance. In that picture Francis was making up his soul, as surely as if he had been some reflective hermit, or cloistered monk. What you see in the picture is the whole matter of Francis, as he saw it himself."

"Yes, but why in this mock sixteenth-century style?"

"Because it is the last style in which a painter could do what Francis was doing. After the Renaissance do you see any pictures that reveal all that a man knows about himself? The great self-portraits, of course. But even when Rembrandt painted himself in old age, he could only show what life had done to him, not how life had done it. With the Renaissance, painting took a new turn, and threw away all that allegorical-metaphysical stuff, all that symbolic communication. You probably don't know that Francis was an expert on iconography — the way you discover what a painter meant, instead of just what anybody can see. In *The Marriage* he means to tell his own truth, as clearly as he can. And he wasn't telling it to someone else. The picture was a confession, a summing-up, intended simply for himself. It's a magnificent thing in several different ways."

"Who's the peculiar angel?" said Maria. "You left him out when you told us who all the characters were. He's obviously somebody of the greatest importance."

"I am virtually certain he was Francis's elder brother. Only one of the sketches is labelled, but it is identified as Francis the First, and I can only guess that he was a very deep influence on Francis the Second's whole life."

"How? It looks like an idiot," said Arthur.

"Presumably it was an idiot. You didn't know your uncle. He was a deeply compassionate man. Oh, he had the reputation for being a curmudgeon, and he didn't suffer fools gladly, and often he seemed to have no tolerance for people at all. But I knew him, and he was far beyond what people mean when they say tender-hearted — which can mean cabbage-headed. He had a sense of the profoundly tragic fragility of human life that I have never known in anyone else, and I am as sure as I can be of anything that it was the knowledge of this grotesque creature, this parody of what he was himself, that made him so. He was a romantic in his youth; look at the way he has painted the girl who became his wife, and let him down so painfully. Look at the dwarf; Francis knew that poor wretch, alive and dead, and he did what he could to balance the scales of Fate when he painted him. All the portraits in *The Marriage* are judgements on people Francis knew, and they are the judgements of a man who had been rudely booted out of a youthful romanticism into a finely compassionate realism. Now Arthur, for God's sake don't ask me again why he painted this summing-up of his life in this bygone style. It was the only style that would contain what he had to say. The Old Masters were deeply religious men, and this is a deeply religious picture."

"I never heard anyone suggest that Uncle Frank was religious."

"The word is greatly misunderstood in the turmoil of our day," said Darcourt, "but in so far as it means seeking to know, and to live, beneath the surfaces of life, and to be aware of the realities beneath the superficialities, you may take it from me that Francis was truly religious."

"Uncle Frank a great painter!" said Arthur. "I don't know just how to cope with it."

"But it's bloody marvellous!" said Maria. "A genius in the family! Aren't you thrilled, Arthur?"

"There have been some rather bright people in the family, but if they were geniuses, or near it, they were financial geniuses. And don't let anybody tell you that financial genius is just low cunning. It's the real intuitive goods. But this sort of genius — For a financial family a painter is rather a skeleton in the cupboard."

"There is something about a cupboard that makes a skeleton very restless," said Darcourt. "Francis Cornish is loudly demanding to be let out."

"Your problem is going to be these people in New York. How will they like it when you reveal that their treasured Old Master — the only known work of The Alchemical Master — is a phoney?"

"It isn't a phoney, Arthur," said Maria. "Simon has been telling us what it is, and phoney is the last word to use. It is an astonishing personal confession in the form of a picture."

"Arthur is right, though," said Darcourt. "They will have to be approached with the greatest tact. I can't go to them and say, Listen, I have news for you: they must want me to come, to hear what I have to tell them. It's the difference between 'Come in, Barney,' and 'Barney, come in.'"

"I suppose that's one of your Old Ontario gobbets of folk wisdom," said Maria.

"Yes, and a very wise one, when you think about it. I can't just tell them what I know, and stop short. I must give them an idea about where this discovery might lead."

"And where would that be?" said Arthur.

"It certainly can't be the devaluation and destruction of

the picture as a work of art. It must point a new way."

"Simon, I know you. I see it in your eye. I see it wriggling up your sleeve. You have a scheme. Come on — tell."

"Well, Maria, I wouldn't say I had a scheme. Just a vague idea, and I feel rather embarrassed about bringing it out, because it is sure to sound stupid."

"This modesty is just camouflage for some real Darcourt craftiness. Out with it."

So, diffidently, but not artlessly — because he had been rehearsing what he would say for several days — Darcourt told them what he had in mind.

There was a long silence. After a while Maria fetched drinks; whisky for the men and for herself a glass that looked like milk, but was of a rich, golden colour. They sipped, amid further silence. At last Arthur spoke.

"Ingenious," he said, "but I mistrust ingenuity. It's too damned clever."

"A little better than just clever," said Darcourt.

"Too many intangibles. Too many things that cannot be controlled. I'm afraid the answer must be no, Simon."

"I'm not ready to take that as your final word, Arthur," said Darcourt. "Please think about it for a while. Forget it and then think about it again. Maria, what do you think?"

"I think it's very foxy."

"Oh, please! Foxy is a nasty word."

"I didn't mean it nastily, Simon. But you must admit that it's a poopnoddy scheme, if ever there was one."

"Poopnoddy?" said Arthur. "Is that one of your Rabelaisian words?"

"Go to the head of the class, Arthur," said Maria. "Rabelaisian in spirit, though I don't know quite what he would have said in French. *Avalleur de frimarts*, or something like that. Intending to deceive the unwary, anyhow. I must have a few Rabelaisian words to counteract Simon's cataract of Old Ontario folk-sayings, about Barney and all the gang."

"If you think those people in New York are unwary, you are out of your mind," said Darcourt.

"But I think you think Arthur and I are unwary."

"If you had been wary, would you ever have got yourselves into this opera thing?"

"That's beside the point."

"I think it's the very finest end of the point. What has it brought you?"

"We don't know, yet," said Arthur. "We shall have to wait and see."

"While you're waiting, will you give some thought to my idea?"

"Now that you've brought it up, I don't see how we can help it."

"Good. That's all I ask. But I must talk to the New York people, you know. After all, I am going to explode their picture. From one point of view, that is."

"Look, Simon, can't you somehow soft-pedal the whole business of the picture?"

"No, Arthur, I can't and I won't. It isn't just the heart of my book. It's the truth, and you can't suppress truth forever. That skeleton is banging very loudly on the doors of the cupboard, and if you don't want to let it out my way, you may be sure somebody else will eventually let it out by smashing the cupboard. Don't forget all those sketches Francis bequeathed to the National Gallery."

"Will that concern us? We don't own the picture."

"No, but I shall have written the book and if I soft-pedal this material it will be shown up as a stupid, know-nothing book. I don't see why I should put up with that, just to satisfy your Kater Murr notions."

"You make a lot of fuss about your damned book."

"My damned book will be on the shelves when all of us are dust, and I want it to be the best book I can leave behind me. And I ask you, Arthur, as a friend, to think of that.

Because I am going to write it, and write it my way, whatever you choose to do, and if it costs me your friendship, that will be part of the price of authorship."

"Simon, don't be pompous. Maria and I value your friendship highly, but we could live without it if we had to."

"Oh shut up, both of you!" said Maria. "Why can't men ever disagree without all this high-stomached huffing and puffing? No friendships are going to be broken, and if you and Simon part brass rags, Arthur, I'll leave you and live in sin with him. So shut up! Have another drink, Simon."

"Thank you, no. I have to be going. But do you mind telling me what that stuff is you are drinking? It looks delicious."

"It is delicious. It's milk with a good slug of rum in it. My doctor recommends it at bedtime. I haven't been sleeping well, and he says this is better than sleeping-pills, even if the milk is a bit fattening for a lady in an interesting condition."

"Marvellous! Do you think I could have a small one of those? After all, I am great with book, and I need all the little comforts of one who is about to give birth."

"Will you get it for him, Arthur? Or are you too much on your dignity to help poor Simon in his delicate state? I was drinking this last night when Al and Sweetness were here, and Sweetness was shocked."

"Shocked by rum and milk? — Oh, thanks, Arthur. — What shocked her?"

"She gave me a long, confused talk about what she called the foetal alcohol syndrome; booze in pregnancy can lead to pixie-faced, pin-headed, mentally retarded children. I knew something about that; you have to drink rather a lot to be in danger. But Sweetness is a zealot, and she's deep into the squalor of pregnancy, poor wretch. I heard all about her agonizing little balls of gas, which won't come up or go down; and how she can't do a thing with her hair — not even wash it, I thought, looking at her; and she has to be dashing off every half-hour to what she delicately calls the tinkle-pantry, because her bladder capacity is now minimal. She is paying the full price nasty old Mother Nature can exact for Al's baby. I just hope it's a nice baby."

"Did she say why they don't get married, if they are so devoted?"

"Indeed she did. Sweetness has a cliché for everything. They do not admit that their union would be hallowed more than it is, if some parson mumbled a few words over them."

"I wonder why people like that always talk about parsons mumbling a few words. I've married lots of people and I never mumble. I would scorn to mumble."

"You have no proper respect for cliché. Performing your ignominious, outdated office, you ought to mumble for very shame."

"I see. I'll remember that. Am I to mumble at the christening, by the way? I'd very much like to."

"Of course, Simon dear. Mumble, mumble, mumble."

"Have you chosen any names, yet? Always wise to be ready with names."

"Arthur and I haven't made up our minds, but Geraint keeps putting forward Welsh names that are crammed with ancient chivalry and bardic evocation, but are rather demanding for the Canadian thick tongue."

Darcourt had finished his rum and milk, and took his leave. Maria was loving and kind, and Arthur was friendly, with a hint of reserve. On the whole, Darcourt thought he had achieved about as much as he expected.

As he walked home he thought about pixie-faced, pin-headed, mentally retarded children. That was what Francis the First had been. But had Francis the First's mother been a heavy drinker? Nothing he had found in his investigations suggested it. But a biographical researcher must reconcile himself to the fact that there are many things he will never know.

(7)

"IT CERTAINLY SEEMS AS THOUGH *le beau ténébreux* had been much more shadowy than any of us suspected," said Princess Amalie.

"Frankly, I am astounded! Astounded!" said Prince Max, who liked to multiply his verbal effects. "I remember Cornish well. Charming, reserved fellow; spoke little but was a splendid listener; handsome, but didn't seem aware of it. I thought Tancred Saraceni lucky to have found such a gifted assistant; his picture of the Fugger dwarf was a little gem. I wish I had it now. And certainly the Fugger dwarf looked very much like the dwarf in *The Marriage*."

"I remember that curious man Aylwin Ross saying precisely that when the Allied Commission on Art had a chance to look at both pictures. Ross was no fool, though he came to grief in a rather foolish way."

The speaker was Addison Thresher. He is the man to watch and the man to convince, thought Darcourt. The Prince and Princess Amalie know a lot about pictures, and a very great deal about business, but this man knows the art world, and his Yes or No is decisive. Until now he has given no hint that he had known *The Marriage at Cana* in Europe. Watch your step, Darcourt.

"Did you know Francis Cornish well?" he asked.

"I did. That's to say, I met him in The Hague when he made that astonishing judgement on a fake Van Eyck. He played with his cards very close to his vest. But I had a few chats with him later in Munich, during the meetings of the Art Commission. He told me something then that clicks with your surprising explanation of this picture, that we have all loved for so many years. Do you know how he learned to draw?"

"I have seen the beautiful copies of Old Master drawings he made when he was at Oxford," said Darcourt. He saw no reason to say more.

"Yes, but before that? It was one of the most extraordinary confessions I ever heard from an artist. As a boy he learned a lot about technique from a book written by a nineteenth-century caricaturist and illustrator called Harry Furniss. Cornish told me he used to do drawings of corpses in an undertaking parlour. The embalmer was his grandfather's coachman. Furniss was an extraordinary parodist of other men's styles; he once showed a gigantic hoax exhibition in which he parodied all the great painters of the late Victorian era. Of course they hated him for it, but I wish I knew where those pictures are now. Drawing lies at the root of great painting, of course — but imagine a child learning to draw like that from a book! An eccentric genius. Not that all genius isn't eccentric."

"Do you really think our picture was the work of *le beau ténébreux*?" said the Princess.

"When I look at these photographs Professor Darcourt has been showing us, I don't see how I can think anything else."

"Then that smashes the favourite in our collection. Smashes it to smithereens," said Prince Max.

"Perhaps," said Thresher.

"Why perhaps? Isn't it shown to be a fake?"

"Please — not a fake," said Darcourt. "That is what I am anxious to prove. It was never intended to deceive. There is not a scrap of evidence that Francis Cornish ever attempted to sell it, or show it, or gain any sort of worldly advantage from it. It was a picture of wholly personal importance, in which he was setting down and balancing off the most significant elements in his own life, and doing it in the only way he knew, which was by painting. By organizing what he wanted to look at in the form and style that was most personal to him. That is not faking."

"Try telling that to the art world," said the Prince.

"That is precisely what I shall try to do in my life of

Francis. And I hope I'm not immodest in saying that I shall do it. Not to unveil a fake, or smash your picture, but to show what an astonishing man Francis Cornish was."

"Yes, but my dear professor, you can't do one without the other. We shall suffer. We shall be made to look like fools, or collaborators in a deception. Think of that article in *Apollo* that Aylwin Ross wrote, explaining the sixteenth-century importance of this picture. It's well known in the world of art history. A very clever piece of detective work. People will think we kept our mouths shut to save our picture, or else that we were victims of Francis Cornish's little joke. No — his big joke. His Harry Furniss joke, as Addison has told us."

"Incidentally, that figure of the fat artist who is drawing on a little ivory tablet is Furniss to the life, now that I know what we know," said Thresher.

"Francis was not wanting in humour. I admit it. He loved a joke and particularly a dark joke that not everybody else understood," said Darcourt. "But that again is an argument on my side. Would a man who intended to deceive put such a portrait of a known artist — and an artist at work — in such a picture as this? I repeat: this is not a picture for anyone but the painter himself. It is a confession, a deeply personal confession."

"Addison, what would you say was the market value of this picture, if we didn't know what Professor Darcourt has told us?" said Princess Amalie.

"Only Christie's or Sotheby's could answer that question. They know what they can get. A good many millions, certainly."

"We were ready to sell it to the National Gallery of Canada a few years ago for three millions," said Prince Max. "That was when we wanted to raise some capital to expand Amalie's business. Aylwin Ross was the Director then, but at the last minute he couldn't raise the money, and not long after he died."

"That would have been cheap," said Thresher.

"We were rather under the spell of Ross," said the Princess. "He was a most beautiful man. We offered him several pieces, at an inclusive price. This was by far the cheapest. But in the end they went to other buyers. We decided to keep this one. We like it so much."

"And you have so many others," said Thresher, not altogether kindly. "But three million was certainly a bargain. Now, if it weren't for what we have heard this evening, you could treble or quadruple that money."

This was Darcourt's moment. "Would you sell now, if you could get a price that pleased you?"

"Sell it as a distinguished fake?"

"Sell it as the greatest work of The Alchemical Master, now known to be the late Francis Cornish? Let me tell you what I have in mind."

With all the persuasive skill he could summon up, Darcourt told them what he had in mind.

"Of course, it's extremely conditional," he said when he had finished, and the Prince and the Princess and Thresher were deep in consideration.

"Very iffy indeed," said Thresher. "But it's a hell of a good idea. I don't know when I've heard of a better in forty years in the art world."

"There is no hurry," said Darcourt. "Are you willing to leave it with me?"

And that was where the matter rested when Darcourt flew back to Canada.

(8)

"I REALLY THINK one of the names must be Arthur. After all, it was my father's name, and it's my name, and it's a good name. Not unfamiliar; not peculiar; easy to pronounce; has good associations, not the least of them being this opera."

"I entirely agree," said Hollier. "As a godfather, with a right to give the boy a name of my choice, I declare for Arthur."

"No regrets about Clement?" said Arthur.

"It's not a name I've ever liked much."

"Well, thank heaven one name is settled. Now, Nilla, you're the godmother. What name have you chosen?"

"I have a weakness for Haakon, because it was my father's name, and it is a name of great honour in Norway. But it might embarrass a Canadian child. So also with Olaf, which is another favourite of mine. So — what about Nikolas? He need not even spell it with a 'k' if he doesn't want to. A fine saint's name, and I think every child should have a saint's name, even if it isn't used."

"Brilliant, Nilla. And eminently reasonable. Nikolas let it be, and I'll undertake that he uses the 'k' to keep him in mind of you."

"Oh, I'll keep him in mind of me. I intend to take my work as godmother very seriously."

"Well then — Geraint?"

This, thought Darcourt, is where the trouble lies. To be melodramatic, this is where the canker gnaws. Geraint has all the Welsh passion for genealogy, and names, and he wants to keep signalling that he is this child's true father. This is going to call heavily on Arthur's skill as a Chairman.

"Of course, I think at once of my own name," said Powell. "A beautiful, poetic, sweetly-sounding name which I bear with pleasure. But Sim *bach* advises strongly against it. Of course I wish to confer a Welsh name on the boy, but you all keep nattering about how hard they are to pronounce. Hard for whom? Not for me. To me, you see, a name has great significance; it colours a child's whole outlook on itself and gives it a role to play. Aneurin, for instance; a great bardic name. He of the Flowing Muse —"

"Yes, but bound to be pronounced 'An Urine' by the unregenerate Saxons," said Arthur. "Remember poor Nye Bevan and what he went through. The Sitwells always called him Aneurism."

"The Sitwells had a very vulgar streak," said Powell.

"Unfortunately, so have lots of people."

"There are other splendid names. Aidan, for instance; now there's a saint for you, Nilla! And Selwyn, which means great ardour and zeal; that would spur him on, wouldn't it? Or Owain, the Well Born; suggesting a distinguished descent, particularly on the father's side. Or Hugo, a name very popular in Wales; I propose it rather than the Welsh Huw, which might look odd to an uninstructed eye; it is the Latin form. But the one I propose with pride is Gilfaethwy, not one of the greatest heroes of the *Mabinogion* but especially appropriate to this child, for reasons that need not be chattered about now. Gilfaethwy! Nobly wild, wouldn't you say?"

"Pronounce it again, will you?" said Arthur.

"It is simplicity itself. Geel-va-ith-ooee, with the accent lightly on the 'va'. Isn't it splendid, boyos? Doesn't it smack of the great days of legend, before Arthur, when demigods trod the earth, dragons lurked in caves, and mighty magicians like Math Mathonwy dealt out reward and punishment? Powerful stuff, let me tell you."

"How do you spell that?" said Hollier, ready with pencil and paper. Geraint spelled it.

"Looks barbarous on the page," said Hollier.

Powell took this very badly. "Barbarous, you say? Barbarous, in a country where every name from every part of the earth, and ridiculous invented names, are seen in the birth announcements every day? Barbarous! By God, Hollier, let me tell you that the Welsh had enjoyed five centuries of Roman civilization when your ancestors were still eating goat with the skin on and wiping their arses with bunches of thistles! Barbarous! Am I to hear that from a pack of morlocks who can think of nothing except what is easy for them to pronounce or has some sentimental association? I pity your ignorance and despise you."

"That, by the way, is a Dickensian quotation," said Hollier. "I'm sure you could find something more bardic to express your contempt."

"Now, now, let's not come to harsh words," said Darcourt. "Let's make a decision, because I have things to say to you, parents and godparents, and we must make up our minds."

But Powell was in a black sulk, and it took a lot of cajoling to make him speak.

"Let the child have the commonest of Welsh names, if you must have it so," he said at last. "Let his name be David. Not even Dafydd, mark you, but bloody English David."

"Now that's a good name," said Gunilla.

"And another saint's name," said Darcourt. "David let it be. Now — what order? Arthur Nikolas David?"

"No. It would spell AND on his luggage," said Hollier, who seemed to be suffering an unexpected bout of practicality.

"His luggage! What a consideration," said Powell. "If you insist on this damned reductive nonsense, why don't you call the child SIN?"

Arthur and Darcourt looked at each other bleakly. Was Geraint going to let the cat out of the bag? This was what nobody wanted, except Powell, whose Welsh dander was up.

"Sin?" said Hollier. "You're joking. Why sin?"

"Because that is what he will be called by his bloody country," shouted Powell. "Social Insurance Number 123 dash 456789, and when he gets his pension in old age he will be SOAP 123 dash 456789. By the time he is SOAP nobody will have any other name except the one the God-damned civil servants have given him! So why don't we steal a march on them and call him SOAP from the start? This is a land dead to poetry, and I say the hell with it!" In his indignation he drained a large whisky at a gulp, and filled his glass again, to the brim.

It was a time to rise above passing furies and disdains, so Darcourt said, in his most honeyed tones, "Then it's to be Arthur David Nikolas, is it? An excellent name. I congratulate you. I shall pronounce the names with my warmest approval. Now, about the other matters."

"Let me remind you right away that I am a convinced unbeliever," said Hollier. "I know too much about religions to be humbugged by them. So you don't get around me with your priestcraft, Simon. I am simply doing this out of friendship for Arthur and Maria."

Yes, and because you were the first to have carnal knowledge of the child's mother, thought Darcourt. You don't fool me, Clem. But what he said was, "Oh yes, I have long experience of unbelieving godparents, and I know how to respect your reservations. All I ask is assurance of your willingness to cherish the child, and help him when you can, and advise him when he needs it, and do the decent thing if his parents should not see him into manhood. Which God forbid."

"Obviously I'll agree to that. I'll take part in the ceremony as an ancient observance. But don't ask for acceptance as a spiritual force."

"No, none of that. But if there is to be a ceremony, it must have a form, and I know the form which is appropriate. Now, Nilla, what about you?"

"No doubts and no reservations," said Gunilla. "I was brought up as what the grocer Shakespeare calls 'a spleeny Lutheran', and I am very fond of children, especially boys. I am delighted to have a godson. You can rely on me."

"I'm sure we can," said Darcourt. "And you, Geraint?"

"You know what I am, Sim *bach*. A Calvinist to the soles of my boots. I am not sure that I trust you. What are you going to ask me to promise?"

"I shall ask you, in the child's name, to renounce the devil and all his works, the vain pomp and glory of this world, with all covetous desires of the same, and the carnal desires of the flesh."

"By God, Sim, that's very fine. Did you write that?"

"No, Geraint, Archbishop Cranmer wrote it."

"A good hand with the pen, that Archbishop. And I renounce these things for the child, not for myself?"

"That's the idea."

"You see how it is. As a man of the theatre — as an artist — I couldn't really set aside pomp and glory, because that's what I live by. As for covetousness, my whole life and work is hedged with contracts, drawn up by covetous agents and the monsters who regulate the economics of the theatre. But for the boy — for young Dafydd, whom I shall call Dai when we get to know each other — I'll renounce away like billy-o."

"Do we really promise that?" said Hollier. "I like that about the devil. That's getting down to realities. I hadn't realized the baptismal service delved quite so deep into the ancient world. You must lend me the book, Simon. There's good stuff in it."

"What trivial minds you men have," said Gunilla. "When you talk about artists living for pomp and glory, Powell, speak for yourself. What you say, Simon, seems to me to mean keeping the boy up to high principles. Making a man of him. You need have no doubts about me."

"Good," said Darcourt. "May I see you all at the chapel on Sunday, then, at three o'clock? Sober and decently dressed?"

When they were leaving, Powell going off to his accustomed bedroom, Darcourt took his opportunity to speak to Maria alone.

"You said nothing about names, Maria. Have you no preference as to what the child should be named?"

"I haven't forgotten my Gypsy ways, Simon dear. When the child came out of me and gave a cry, they laid it on my breast, and I named him. Gave him his real name. Whispered it into his tiny ear. And whatever you do on Sunday, that will be his name forever."

"Are you going to tell me what the name is?"

"Certainly not! He will never hear it again until he reaches puberty, when I shall whisper it to him again. He has a proper Gypsy name, and it will go with him and protect him as long as he lives. But it is a secret between him and me."

"You have been ahead of me, then?"

"Of course. I didn't think I'd do it, but just before he left my body forever, I knew I would. What's bred in the bone, you know."

(9)

EXCEPT FOR ONE MINOR MISHAP, the christening went smoothly. Only the parents, the godparents, and the baby were present; the Cranes had to be told plainly that they might not come. Al murmured incoherently about objective correlatives and the link between the birth of the child and the birth of the opera. It would, he said, make a terrific and unexpected footnote to the *Regiebuch*. Mabel begged to be allowed to come simply on the ground that she wanted to see what a christening was like. But when Darcourt suggested that she could manage that by having her own impending child christened, she and Al were quick to say that they did not believe that a few words mumbled by a parson over their child could make any difference to his future life.

Darcourt forbore to tell them that he thought they were wrong, and silly in their wrongness. He had reservations about many of the things which he, as a clergyman, was expected to believe and endorse publicly, but about the virtues of baptism he had no doubt. Its solely Christian implications apart, it was the acceptance of a new life into a society that thereby declared that it had a place for that new life; it was an assertion of an attitude toward life that was expressed in the Creed which was a part of the service in a form archaic and compressed but full of noble implication. The parents and godparents might think they did not believe that Creed, as they recited it, but it was plain to Darcourt that they were living in a society which had its roots in that Creed; if there had been no Creed, and no cause for the formulation of that Creed, vast portions of civilization would never have come into being, and those who smiled at the Creed or disregarded it altogether nevertheless stood firmly on its foundation. The Creed was one of the great signposts in the journey of mankind from a primitive society toward whatever was to come, and though the signpost might be falling behind in the march of civilization, it had marked a great advance from which there could be no permanent retreat.

Hollier had decided to accept the baptismal ceremony as a rite of passage, an acceptance of a new member into the tribe. Good enough, thought Darcourt, but such rites had a resonance not heard by the tin ear of the rationalist. Rationalism, thought Darcourt, was a handsomely intellectual way of sweeping a lot of significant, troublesome things under the rug. But the implications of the rite were not banished because some very clever people did not feel them.

Powell wanted to be a godfather with his fingers crossed. He wanted to make promises he had no intention of keeping — and indeed who can hope to keep the promises of a godfather in all their ramifications? Very well. But Powell wanted to be a godfather because it was as near as he was likely to come to being acknowledged as the real father of the child. Powell could not resist a solemn ceremony of any kind. He was one of the many, who should not therefore be despised, who wanted serious inner matters given a serious outer form, and this was what made him a true and devout child of the drama, which at its best is precisely such an objectification of what is important in life. Darcourt thought he knew what Powell meant better than Powell did himself.

He had no misgivings about Gunilla. There was a woman who could see beyond the language of a creed to the essence of a creed. Gunilla was sound as a bell.

As for Arthur and Maria, the birth of the child seemed to have drawn them nearer than they had ever been before. The blessing that children bring is a cliché. It is as corny as the rhymes of Ella Wheeler Wilcox about art. But one of the most difficult tasks for the educated and sophisticated mind is to recognize that some clichés are also important truths.

It is a cliché that the birth of a child is a symbol of hope, however disappointed and distressed that hope may at last prove to be. The baptism is a ceremony in which that hope is announced, and Hope is one of the knightly virtues in a sense that the Cranes, for instance, had not understood, and might perhaps never understand. The hope embodied in the small body of Arthur David Nikolas as Darcourt took him in his arms and sained him, was, in part, the hope of the marriage of Arthur and Maria. The silver link, the silken tie.

It was after the blessing of the child, and the saining with water, that the slight accident occurred. Following an old custom, now revived by ritualists like Darcourt, he lighted three candles from the great candle that stood beside the font, and handed them to the godparents, saying, "Receive the light of Christ, to show that you have passed from darkness to light."

Hollier and Gunilla, understanding that they did this on behalf of the child, took their candles with dignity, and Gunilla bowed her head in reverence.

Powell, startled, dropped his candle, spilling wax down his clothes, and scrambled for it on the floor, murmuring, unsuitably, "Oh, my God!" Maria giggled and the child, which had been an angel of propriety even when its head was wetted, gave a loud wail.

Darcourt took the candle from Powell, relighted it, and said, "Receive the light of Christ, in your astonishment of heart, to show that you have passed from darkness to light."

"That was a bloody good ad lib of yours, Sim bach," said Powell, at the party afterward. "I've never heard a better on the stage."

"I think yours was even better, Geraint bach," said Darcourt.

(10)

THE ARTISTS AND ARTIFICERS who are assembled to put an opera on the stage make up a closed society, and no one who is not of the elect may hope to penetrate it. There is no ill-will in this; it is simply that people deep in an act of creation take their whole lives with them into that act, and the world outside becomes shadowy until the act is completed, the regular schedule of performances established, and the strength of association somewhat relaxed.

Those who are on the outside feel this keenly. As the last weeks of work on *Arthur of Britain* progressed, Arthur and Maria sensed the chill. Of course they were welcome everywhere — which is to say that nobody quite liked to ask them to go away. They were known to be the "angels". They paid the bills, the salaries, all the multifarious costs of a complicated project, and therefore they had to be treated with courtesy; but it was cold courtesy. Even their intimate friend Powell whispered to their other intimate friend Darcourt, "I wish Arthur and Maria weren't always bumming around while we're working."

Darcourt had his place in the adventure; he was the librettist, and however unlikely it was that any words would be changed at so late a point in the proceedings, he was free to come and go, and if Powell suddenly wanted him to explain a difficult passage to a singer, it was a nuisance if he were not at the rehearsal. Because of her shadowy association with the libretto, even Penny Raven appeared at rehearsals without any questioning looks. But not the angels.

"I feel as conspicuous and out of place as tan shoes on a pallbearer," said Arthur, who was not given to simile in the ordinary way.

"But I want to see what they're doing," said Maria. "After all, we must have some rights. Have you looked at the bills lately?"

Perhaps they had expected lively doings, with Powell standing in front of a stage filled with singers, shouting and waving his arms like a policeman at a riot. Nothing of the sort. The rehearsals were quiet and orderly. The unpunctual Powell was always present half an hour before a rehearsal began, and he was stern with latecomers, though these were few, and always had reasonable excuses. The ebullient Powell was quiet and restrained; he never shouted, was never discourteous. He had absolute command and used it with easy authority. Was this artistic creation? Apparently it was, and Arthur and Maria were astonished at how quickly and surely the opera began to take shape.

Not that it seemed like an opera, as they conceived of an opera, in the first two weeks of rehearsal. These took place in Toronto in large, dirty rooms belonging to the Conservatory, and the Graduate School of Music, which had been hired for the work. In charge of these was Waldo Harris, the first assistant to Powell; he was a bland, large young man who never lost his calm in the midst of complexity, and he seemed to know everything. He had an assistant, Gwen Larking, who was called Stage Manager; she had two other girls to do her lightest bidding. Miss Larking occasionally and excusably showed some emotion, and the assistants, who were beginners, did run and fuss, and brandish their clip-boards until Miss Larking frowned at them, and even hissed at them to shut up. But these young women were serenity itself compared with the three students called gofers (because they were always being told to go for coffee, or go for sandwiches, or go for somebody who was wanted in a hurry). The gofers were the lowest, most inconsiderable form of theatrical life. At rehearsals these seven clustered around Powell like iron filings around a magnet, and talked in whispers. They all dealt very largely in paper, and took notes without cease. The provision of new, sharp pencils was part of the gofers' job.

But these were all less than Mr. Watkin Bourke, who was called the *répétiteur*, or coach.

It was Watty's job to see that the singers knew their music, and this meant everything from long hours at the piano with the principals who knew their music but wanted advice about phrasing, to principals who read music with difficulty (though they never admitted this) and had to be taught their parts almost by rote. It was Watty's job to train the Chorus, and this meant the ten gentlemen, apart from Giles Shippen, the tenor lead, and Gaetano Panisi, who played Modred, who made up King Arthur's Knights, and the Ladies who were their vocal counterparts. The Chorus were all good musicians, but twenty-two good singers do not make a chorus, and they had to be gently persuaded to sing together, and not merely to sing in tune, but to sing in tune as a unity, and to vary their intonation subtly to agree with leading singers who might become the teeniest bit flat or sharp under dramatic stress. In all of this Watty, a small, hatchet-faced, intense man, and a brilliant pianist, was masterly.

Watty, like Powell, never shouted or lost his temper, though from time to time a great weariness might be seen to pass over his small, intelligent face. Such weariness, for instance, as was brought about by his encounter with Mr. Nutcombe Puckler, a bass baritone entrusted with the role of Sir Dagonet.

"I quite understand that Mr. Powell wants us to have individuality, as Knights of the Round Table," he said. "Now, the other chaps are all pretty straightforward, aren't they? Knights, you see. Just brave chaps. But Sir Dagonet is described as Arthur's Fool, and of course that's why I have been cast for it. Because I'm not a chorus singer or a small-parts man — not at all; I'm a *comprimario* with quite a big reputation as a comic. My Frosch, in *Die Fledermaus*, is known all over the operatic world. So presumably I'm cast as Sir Dagonet to get some comedy into the opera. But how? I haven't a single comic bit to sing. So something has to be introduced, you see, Watty? Some comic relief? I've been thinking a lot about it, and I've found just the place. Finale of Act One, when Arthur is haranguing the Knights about the wonders of Knighthood. It's heavy. Lovely music, of course, but heavy. So — that's surely where we bring in the comic relief. Now what's it to be — my Blurt or my Sneeze?"

"I don't follow," said Watty.

"Haven't you seen me? They're my two best laugh-getters. When Arthur's going on about Knighthood, couldn't I have a cup of wine? Then, just at the right moment, I give 'em my Blurt. I choke on the wine and spew a lot of it over the people near by. Never fails. Or, if that's a bit too strong, there's my Sneeze — just a simple, loud sneeze, you see — to relieve the atmosphere. My Blurt is really a comic extension of my Sneeze, and of course I don't want to obtrude, so the Sneeze might be best. But you ought to hear my Blurt before you make a decision. I'd like to know now, you see, before we go into rehearsal on the floor, so I can be thinking about it and tailor my Blurt — or my Sneeze — to come in just at the right moment. Because timing is everything in comedy, as I'm sure you know."

"You must talk to Mr. Powell," said Watty. "I have nothing to do with the staging."

"But you see my point?"

"Yes, indeed."

"I don't want to be obtrusive, you understand; I just want to bring what I can to the ensemble."

"It's Mr. Powell's department."

"But may I say which you think best? The Blurt or the Sneeze?"

"I have no opinion. It's not my department."

It was an astonishment to Arthur and Maria, and to Darcourt as well, that Watty played from a full orchestral score, instructing the singers what they might expect to hear as they sang, and when they were momentarily silent; the singers worked from sketchy music, giving their vocal line and a hint or two of orchestration; the preparation of all this music, which was in Schnak's wondrous hand, had cost a small fortune.

At the musical rehearsals Dr. Dahl-Soot was present, but not a voice. She spoke to no one but Watty, and very quietly. She whispered now and then to Schnak, who was her shadow, learning her craft — learning eagerly and rapidly.

The first general rehearsal took place in a dirty, ill-lit basement room in the Conservatory. It smelled of the economical lunches that had been consumed there for years by students; there was a pervasive atmosphere of bananas in their last stages of edibility, mingled with peanut butter. There was not much space, for there were three sets of timpani stored there, and in a corner an assembly of double-bass cases with nothing in them, like a conference of senators.

"How are we going to work here?" said Nutcombe Puckler. "There isn't room to swing a cat."

"Will you all please sit down," said Gwen Larking. "There are chairs for everybody."

"As this is a new work," said Powell to the group, "and because the libretto offers some complexities, I want to begin today by reading through all three acts."

"No piano," said Nutcombe Puckler, who had a fine grasp of the obvious, as became an opera comic.

"Not a musical reading," said Powell. "You all know your music — or you should — and we won't sing for a day or two. No; I want you simply to read the words, as if this were a play. The librettist is with us, and he will be glad to clear up any difficulties about meanings."

The company was in the main an intelligent one, perhaps because it was not what conventional critics would call a company of the first order. The singers were, upon the whole, young and North American; though they had all had plenty of opera experience they were not accustomed to the usages of the greatest opera theatres of the world. Reading held no terrors for them. There were one or two, of whom Nutcombe Puckler was the leader, who could not see any reason to speak anything that could possibly be sung, but they were willing to give it a try, to humor Powell, in whom they sensed a man of ideas who knew what he was doing. Some, like Hans Holzknecht, who was to sing the role of Arthur, did not read English with ease, and Miss Clara Intrepidi, who was to be Morgan Le Fay, stumbled over words that she had sung with no difficulty in her rehearsals with Watty. The one who read like an actor — an intelligent actor — was Oliver Twentyman, and the best of the group found that by Act Two they were trying, with varying success, to read like Oliver Twentyman.

If the company was youthful in the main, Oliver Twentyman balanced matters by being old. Not astronomically old, as some people insisted; not in his nineties. But he was said to be over eighty, and he was one of the wonders of the operatic world. His exquisitely produced, silvery tenor was always described by critics as small, but it had been heard with perfect clarity in all the great opera theatres of the world, and he was a favourite at Glyndebourne and several of the more distinguished, smaller American festivals. His particular line of work was characters of fantasy — Sellem in *The Rake's Progress*, the Astrologer in *Le Coq d'Or*, and Oberon in *A Midsummer Night's Dream*. It had been a great coup to get him for Merlin. His reading of his part in the libretto was a delight.

"Marvellous!" said Powell. "Ladies and gentlemen, I beg you to take heed of Mr. Twentyman's pronunciation of English; it is in the highest tradition."

"Yes, but are not the vowels very distorted?" said Clara Intrepidi. "I mean, impure for singing. We have our vowels, right? The five? Ah, Ay, Ee, Oh, Oo. Those we can sing. You would not ask us to sing these impure sounds?"

"There are twelve vowel sounds in English," said Powell; "and as it is a language which I myself had to acquire, not being born to it, you must not think me prejudiced. What are those vowels? They are all in this advice:

> Who knows ought of art must learn
> And then take his ease.

Every one of the twelve sings beautifully, and none gives such delicacy as the Indeterminate Vowel which is often a 'y' at the end of a word. 'Very' must be pronounced as a long and a short syllable, and not as two longs. I am going to nag you about pronunciation, I promise you."

Miss Intrepidi pouted slightly, as though to suggest that the barbarities of English speech would have no effect on *her* singing. But Miss Donalda Roche, an American who was to sing Guenevere, was making careful notes.

"What was that about knowing art, Mr. Powell?" she said, and Geraint sang the vowel sequence for her, joined by Oliver Twentyman, who seemed, with the greatest politeness, to wish to show Miss Intrepidi that there were really twelve differentiated sounds, and that none of them were describable as impure.

On the whole, the singers enjoyed reading the libretto, and the day's work showed clearly which were actors who could sing, and which singers who had learned to act. Marta Ullmann, the tiny creature who was to sing the small but impressive role of Elaine, came out very well with

> *"No tears, no sighing, no despair*
> *No trembling, dewy smile of care*
>> *No mourning weeds*
>> *Nought that discloses*
>> *A heart that bleeds;*
> *But looks contented I will bear*
> *And o'er my cheeks strew roses.*
>
> *Unto the world I may not weep,*
> *But save my Sorrow all, and keep*
>> *A secret heart, sweet soul, for thee,*
>> *As the great earth and swelling sea."*

But it was not quite such a good moment when Donalda Roche and Giles Shippen tried to read, in unison,

> *"O Love!*
> *Time flies on restless pinions*
>> *Constant never:*
>> *Be constant*
> *And thou chainest time forever."*

Nor was Miss Intrepidi the celebrated audience-tamer she was reputed to be when faced with her words to the villain Modred:

> *"I know there is some maddening secret*
> *Hid in your words (and at each turn of thought*
> *Comes up a skull) like an anatomy*
> *Found in a weedy hole, 'mongst stones and roots*
> *And straggling reptiles, with his tongueless mouth*
> *That tells of Arthur's murder."*

But Miss Intrepidi was a real pro, and having made a mess of her words she cried, "I'll get it; don't worry — I'll get it!" and Powell assured her that nobody had the least doubt she would.

When the reading was completed, late in the afternoon, Gunilla spoke to the company for the first time.

"You see what our Director is doing?" she said. "He wants you to sing words, not tones. Anybody can sing the music; it takes an artist to sing the words. That's what I want, too. Simon Darcourt has found us a brilliant libretto; Hulda Schnakenburg has realized a fine score from Hoffmann's notes, and we must think of this opera as, among other things, an entirely new look at Hoffmann as a composer; this is music-drama before Wagner had put pen to paper. So — sing it like early Wagner."

"Ah — Wagner!" said Miss Intrepidi. "So now I know."

All of this, and the careful rehearsals which followed — on the floor, as Powell said, meaning that he was planning the moves and when necessary the gestures of the singers — was victuals and drink to the Cranes. (They were always referred to as the Cranes, though Mabel took pains to explain that she was still Mabel Muller, and had sacrificed nothing of her individuality — though she had obviously sacrificed her figure — in their spiritual union.) Al cornered and buttonholed everybody, and made himself conspicuous in his desire not to be obtrusive. He was on the prowl to capture and note down every motivation, and the notes for the great *Regiebuch* swelled to huge proportions. Oliver Twentyman was a Golconda to Al.

Here was tradition! Twentyman had, in his young days, sung with many famous conductors, and his training had become legendary in his lifetime. He had worked, when not much more than a boy, with the great David ffrangcon-Davies, and repeated to Al many of that master's precepts. More wonderful still, he had worked for three years with the redoubtable William Shakespeare — not, he explained to the gaping Al, the playwright, but the singing-teacher, who had been born in 1849 and had worked with many of the great ones until his death in 1931 — who had always insisted that singing, even at its most elaborate, was based upon words, upon words, upon words.

"It's like a dream!" said Al.

"It's a craft, my boy," said Nutcombe Puckler, who was still waiting for a decisive word about the Blurt, or possibly just the Sneeze. "And never forget the funny stuff. Wagner hadn't much use for it; he thought *Meistersinger* was a comic opera, of course, and you should have seen my Beckmesser in St. Louis a few years ago! I stopped the show twice!"

Al was a special nuisance to Darcourt. "This libretto — some of it gets close to poetry," he said.

"That was the idea," said Simon.

"Nobody would take you for a poet," said Al.

"Probably not," said Darcourt; "when are you expecting the baby?"

"That's a worry," said Al. "Sweetness is getting pretty tired. And worried, too. We're both worried. We're lucky to be sharing this great experience, to take our minds off it."

Mabel nodded, hot, heavy, and dispirited. She longed for the move to Stratford, out of the terrible, humid heat of a Toronto summer. As she lay on the bed in their cheap lodgings at night, while Al read aloud to her from the macabre tales of Hoffmann, she sometimes wondered if Al knew how much she was sacrificing to his career. As women have wondered, no doubt, since first mankind was troubled by glimmerings of what we now call art, and scholarship.

"Will you give my feet a rub, Al? My ankles are killing me."

"Sure, Sweetness, just as soon as we finish this story."

Why, he wondered, was Sweetness crying when, twenty minutes later, he got around to rubbing her feet?

(11)

ETAH IN LIMBO

WHAT AN AMUSING DRAMA life is when one is not obliged to be one of the characters! No, no; that sounds like Kater Murr! But I have enjoyed myself more in the past few weeks than at any time since my death. Homer was quite wrong about the gloomy half-life of the dead. The remoteness, the removal, of my afterlife is vastly agreeable. I see all the people who are preparing my opera; I comprehend their feelings without needing to share them painfully; I applaud their ambitions and I pity their follies. But as I am wholly unable to do anything about them, I am not torn by guilt or responsibility. It is thus, I suppose, that the gods view humankind. (I apologize if, by speaking of "the gods" in the plural, I am being offensive to whatever awaits me when I move into the next phase of my afterlife.) Of course, the gods could intervene, and frequently did so, but not always happily from a human standpoint.

The trials of Powell and Watkin Bourke are very familiar to me. How often have I wrangled with singers who thought Italian was the only language of song, and who cried down our noble German as barbarous. Of course they made exquisite sounds, some of them, but they had a limited range of meanings for their sounds; Italian is a dear language and we owe much to it, but our northern tongues are richer in poetic subtlety, in shadows, and shadows were the essence of my work both as composer and as author. How I have struggled with singers whose one desire was to "vocalize" — a word that had just come into fashion and seemed to them the height of elegance and musical refinement. How deliciously they yelled when one wished that they should utter some meaning! How pressingly they would urge me to change German words to others with which they could make a prettier sound! And how incomprehensible was the word that lay ravaged at the bottom of any sound they made, as they roared, or cooed, or squalled, or sobbed with such richness of inane musicality! "Gracious lady and supreme artist," I would say to some fat bully of a soprano, "if you pronounce the word on the tone no louder than you could speak it, it will be sound *enough, and replete with significance that will ravish your hearers."* But they never believed me. Nothing encourages self-esteem like success as a singer.

And why not? If you can stir an audience to its depths with your A altissimo, what need you care for anything else?

Or if you can make an audience laugh, is it surprising if you cease to care how? This man who wants to sneeze, or blurt his wine in somebody's face, is different only in kind from the Jack Puddings of my time. With them all comedy was rooted in sausage; give them a sausage to eat and they would undertake to keep a sufficient part of the audience in roars of mirth for five minutes; allow them to add an onion to the sausage and it was eight minutes. How sad such merriment is! How divorced from the Comic Spirit!

I am becoming devoted to Schnak. Devoted, that is to say, only as a spirit may be; she is cleaner since the Swedish woman seduced her, but she is without charm. It is her musical genius that enslaves me. Yes, genius is the word I shall use. By that word I mean that she will have enough individual quality to impose herself upon the music of her time as a truly serious artist, and she may achieve fame, even if it follows her death. After all, Schubert is now known as a genius of the first order, yet when I became aware of his work very few people in my part of Germany had heard of him, and he did not survive me by more than five years. Of all the music I know, Schnak's, working on the foundations I laid down, most resembles that of Schubert. When she has done it best, our work together has that melancholy serenity, that acceptance of the pathos of human life, that speaks of Schubert. Dr. Dahl-Soot knows it, but the others say the music is like Weber, because they know that Weber was my friend.

That strange ass Crane is tracing all the music to Weber. He is one of those scholars who is certain that everything in art is laboriously derived from something that came before it. Much as I admired Weber, I never saw a Weber score to which I would willingly have signed my own name.

Poor Schubert, dying slowly, as I did, and of what was essentially the same disease. Nobody, so far as I know, has found out why that *disease causes one man to die a driveller and a horror, and another to compose, in his last year, three of the supreme pianoforte sonatas in all the realm of music.*

I should not be hard on Crane. Perhaps he is worrying about that baby, or his swollen woman, Mabel Muller. There is an erotic unction about Al that must not be ignored. Mabel, poor wretch, must be ranked low on the list of the victims of art.

There are other victims, of course, and, from my point of view, greater ones. I am sad for the Cornishes, Arthur and Maria. They long so humbly to be counted among the artists, but they are not given even the artistic status accorded to Nutcombe Puckler. Without meaning to be cruel, the artists, and even those novices in art, the gofer girls, reject them because they do not appear to be doing anything, although it is their money that is the underpinning of the whole affair. Not doing anything, when every day they write fat cheques for this, that, and the other? Writing those cheques because they truly love art and wish it to prosper! Writing those cheques because they would sing if they could, or paint their faces and join the crowd on the stage!

I sometimes saw people like them in the theatres where I worked as Powell works now. Wealthy merchants, or minor nobility, who footed the bills, and not always to gain a place in the ranks of society but because they so greatly loved those things that they could not do. A patron has one of two courses: he may domineer and spoil the broth by insisting on too much salt or pepper; or he may simply do what God has enabled him to do, and that is to pay, pay, pay! I was as bad as anyone in my time. I kissed hands, bowed low, and paid compliments, but I eagerly wished them all in hell, because they were underfoot when my work was being done. Seeing myself as my own creation, the master-musician Johannes Kreisler, I scorned my patrons and saw in them nothing but the disciples of the odious Kater Murr! As if there were no self-seeking among artists! I wish I could comfort Arthur and Maria, who feel the subtle cold of the artists' scorn, but placed as I am, I cannot do it.

I can see, however, that their fate is different, and who may hope to escape his fate? They are living out, in a comic mimesis, the fate of

Arthur and Guenevere, but to be ruled by a comic fate is not to feel oneself as a figure of comedy. It is their fate to be rich, and to seem powerful, in a world of art where riches are not of first importance, and their power is unavailing.

Like all the others, I long for the move to Stratford.

VII

WHEN THE COMPANY MOVED to Stratford and, in Powell's phrase, went into high gear on the production, it would have been easy to miss the fact that Schnak was deeply in love with Geraint. She tagged after him; but the Stage Manager, her assistants, and the gofer girls also tagged after him. She hung upon his words; but Waldo Harris, the Stage Director, and Dulcy Ringgold, the Designer, also hung upon his words. Nobody took any notice of Schnak's infatuation but Darcourt; nobody else saw the special quality in her tagging and hanging. Nobody else saw the lovelight in her eyes.

They were not eyes in which one would look for the lovelight. They were small, pebbly, squinty little eyes. Nor was Schnak a figure upon whom love sat like an accustomed garment; her motion was not graceful, because, in one of Darcourt's Old Ontario phrases, she was as bow-legged as a hog going to war; her voice was as snarly as ever, though under Gunilla's guidance her vocabulary was larger and not so dirty; she had no graces, and the least of the gofers could have wiped the floor with her in a contest of charm. But Schnak was in love, and this was not a matter of bodily awakening and bodily satisfaction as it had been with Gunilla, but beglamoured and yearning passion. This is the romanticism in which her work has drenched and soused her; I am sure she tosses on her bed and murmurs his name to her pillow, thought Darcourt.

He took his chance to ask Gunilla if she were aware of this. "Oh, yes," said the Doctor; "it was bound to happen. She must try everything, and Powell is an obvious mark for a young girl's love."

"But you don't mind?"

"Why should I mind? The child is not my property. Oh, we have had merry hours, to the great scandal of that fat busybody Professor Raven, but that was a teacher-and-pupil thing. Not love. I have known love, Simon, and with men also, let me assure you, and I know what it is. I am not such a romantic as to think of it as the great educational force — broadening her experience, enlarging her vision, and all that nonsense — but it is something everybody feels who is not a complete cabbage. I must see that it doesn't spoil her work; people seem to have forgotten that all this elaborate contrivance boils down to an examination exercise, and Hulda must get her degree, if there is not to be a great waste of money."

Elaborate contrivance indeed it was. The company was lucky in having the theatre for the last three weeks of rehearsal. Not the stage; not yet. There was still a week of performances of a play which called for only one small set, but all the workrooms and both rehearsal rooms were now devoted to _Arthur_, and during the last two weeks the stage would be available to the singers when it was not wanted by the technicians.

The technicians bulked very large. It seemed to Darcourt that they almost swamped the opera. On huge paint-frames in one of the workrooms the scenery was being painted, for Powell wanted proper scenes, and not the usual wrinkled cyclorama, suggesting a sky that had shrunk and faded in the wash.

"In Hoffmann's day there was no stage light, in our sense," he said, "and anything like a lighting effect had to be painted on the scenery. And that's how Dulcy is doing it."

Dulcy Ringgold was not what Darcourt would have thought of as a theatrical character. She was small, she was shy, she laughed a great deal, and she seemed to regard her responsibilities as the best joke in the world.

"I'm really just a glorified dressmaker," she said, through a mouthful of pins, as she draped something on Clara Intrepidi. "Just that nice little woman Miss Dulcy, who is so clever with her fingers." She did something that made Miss Intrepidi look taller and slimmer. "There dear; if you can suck up your gut the teeniest bit that will do very nicely."

"The gut is what I breathe with," said Miss Intrepidi.

"Then we'll drape this a little more freely," said Dulcy, "and maybe put a wee thingy just here."

At other times, Dulcy was to be seen with a filthy bandana wrapped around her head, on the bridge that swayed before the paint-frame, putting special touches on huge drop-scenes that were being painted from her carefully squared-off watercolour designs. Sometimes she was in the basement, where the armour was made, not with the ring of the sword-smith's hammer, but with the chemical whiff of Plexiglas being moulded. It was here, too, that all the swords, and Arthur's sceptre, and the crowns for Arthur and his Queen were made, and studded with foil-backed glass jewels that gave a splendidly Celtic richness to post-Roman Britain. Dulcy was everywhere, and Dulcy's taste and imagination touched everything.

"I hate theatre where the audience is told to use its imagination," she said. "That's cheap. The audience lays down its good money to rent imagination from somebody who has more than they ever dreamed of. Somebody like me. Imagination's my only stock-in-trade." She said this as she whisked off a brilliant little sketch for a fool's head which was to be made in pretended metal and attached to the hilt of Sir Dagonet's sword. But it was not all of her stock-in-trade.

Darcourt picked up a large book from her workbench.

"What's this?" he said.

"Oh, that's my darling and my deario, James Robinson Planché; his *Encyclopaedia of Costume*, a revolutionary book in stage design. He was the first man, believe it or not, who really cared if stage dress had any roots in the realities of the past. He designed the first *King John* that really looked like King John's time. I don't copy his pictures, of course. Strictly accurate historical costume looks absurd, as a usual thing, but dear Planché is a springboard for one's imagination."

"I don't suppose even Planché knew what King Arthur wore," said Darcourt.

"No, but he would have given a jolly well-informed guess," said Dulcy, patting the two large books tenderly. "So I load up on dear Planché, and then I guess too. Lots of dragons; that's the stuff for Arthur. I'm putting Morgan Le Fay in a dragon head-dress. Sounds corny, but it won't be when I've finished with it."

So: the omnicompetent Planché is going to have a finger in the pie, even if we don't use his horrible libretto, thought Darcourt. He was — just a little — losing his heart to Dulcy, but so was every other man who came near her. It appeared, however, that Dulcy was somewhat of Gunilla's way of thinking about sex, and although she flirted outrageously with the men, it was with Gunilla she went to dinner.

Here is a world where sex is not of first, second, or perhaps even third importance, thought Darcourt. How refreshing.

Sex was, however, rearing its wistfully domestic head with the unhappy Mabel Muller. The weather in Stratford proved to be just as hot as it was in Toronto, and Mabel's legs swelled, and her hair drooped, and she bore her burden of posterity with visible effort. She tagged everywhere after Al, who was like a man possessed, making notes here, and taking photographs with an instant camera there, and getting in everyone's way while making obstructive efforts to avoid doing precisely that. Not that Al forgot her or excluded her; he gave her his heavy briefcase to carry, and they always ate the sandwiches Mabel brought from a fast-food shop together, while he harangued — "extrapolated" was the fine word he used — on all that he had noted, or photographed.

"This is pure gold, Sweetness," he would say from time to time. To Sweetness it was fairy gold, no sooner touched than lost.

It would be unjust to say that Al grudged the time needed to rush Mabel to the hospital when at last her pains became too much to be ignored. "They're coming every twenty minutes now," she whispered, tearfully, and Al made just one more essential note before seizing her by the arm and leading her out of the rehearsal room. It was Darcourt who found them a taxi and urged the driver to lose no time in getting them to the hospital. They had made no arrangements, had not even seen a doctor, and Mabel was admitted in Emergency.

"Something is not quite right with Mabel," said Maria, later in the day, to Darcourt. "Her pains have stopped."

"Al was back for the end of the rehearsal," said Darcourt. "I thought everything must be going smoothly."

"I'd like to brain Al," said Maria. "That's the trouble with these irregular unions. No guts when the going is rough. I'd hang around the hospital if I could, but Arthur has to get back to his office for a couple of days and I am going with him. New developments in the Wally Crottel affair. I'll tell you later. There's really nothing for us to do here. Geraint seems to feel that we're underfoot."

"I'm sure not."

"I'm sure yes. But Simon, will you be a darling and keep an eye on Mabel? She's no concern of ours, but I'm concerned just the same. Will you get in touch if we should do anything?"

That was why Darcourt found himself in the comfortless waiting-room of the hospital's maternity ward at four o'clock in the morning. Al had left at half past ten, promising to phone early next day. Darcourt was not alone. Dr. Dahl-Soot had also turned up, after Al's departure.

"Nothing could be less in my line than this," she said. "But that poor wretch is a stranger in a strange land, and so am I, so here I am."

Darcourt knew better than to say it was very good of her.

"Arthur and Maria asked me to keep an eye on things," he said.

"I like those two," said the Doctor. "I didn't greatly like them when we first met, but they grow better on acquaintance. They are a very solid pair. Do you think it's the baby?"

"Partly the baby. A very fine baby. Maria is suckling it."

"She is? That's old style. But I believe very good."

"I don't know," said Darcourt. "As we academics say, it's not my field. But it's a very pretty sight."

"You are a softy, Simon. And that's as it should be. I wouldn't give a damn for a man who was not a softy in some ways."

"Gunilla, do you think we single people are apt to be sentimental about love and babies and all that?"

"I am not sentimental about anything. But I have sentiment about many things. That's an English-language difference that is very useful. Not to have sentiment is to be almost dead."

"But you have taken — pardon me for saying so — a decidedly anti-baby road."

"Simon, you are too intelligent a man to be as provincial as you sometimes pretend. You know there is room in the world for everything and every kind of life. What do you think marriage is? Just babies and eating off the same fork?"

"God forbid! Because it's either very early in the morning or very late at night, I'll tell you what I really think.

Marriage isn't just domesticity, or the continuance of the race, or institutionalized sex, or a form of property right. And it damned well isn't happiness, as that word is generally used. I think it's a way of finding your soul."

"In a man or a woman?"

"With a man or a woman. In company, but still, essentially, alone — as all life is."

"Then why haven't you found your own soul?"

"Oh, it isn't the only way. But it's one way."

"So you think I might find my soul, some day?"

"I'd bet very heavily on it, Gunilla. People find their souls in all sorts of ways. I'm writing a book — the life of a very good friend of mine, who certainly found his soul. Found it in painting. He tried to find it in marriage, and it was the most awful mess, because he was a soppy romantic at the time, and she was one of those Sirens who inevitably leave the man with a cup of Siren tears. Rather a crook, judged by the usual standards. But in that mess Francis Cornish found his soul. I know it. I have evidence of it. I'm writing my book about it."

"Francis Cornish? One of these Cornishes?"

"Arthur's uncle. And it's Francis's money that is supporting this fantastic circus we are engaged in now."

"But you think this Arthur will find his soul in his marriage?"

"And Maria, too. And if you want to know, I think King Arthur found his soul, or a big piece of it, in his marriage to Guenevere — who was rather a crook, if you read Malory — and that is what a lot of this opera is about. *Arthur of Britain, or The Magnanimous Cuckold*. He found his soul."

"But is this Arthur a magnanimous cuckold?"

Darcourt did not need to answer, for at this moment a doctor, in his white garment and cap, came into the room.

"Are you with Mrs. Muller?"

"Yes. What's the news?"

"I'm very sorry. Are you the father?"

"No. Just a friend."

"Well — it's bad. The child is stillborn."

"What was the trouble?"

"She seems not to have had any pre-natal advice whatever. Otherwise we'd have done a Caesarian. But when we found out the foetus had a disproportionately large head for the birth canal, it was already dead. Death from foetal distress, it's called. We're very sorry, but these things do happen. And as I say, she hadn't had any previous medical attention."

"May we see her?"

"I wouldn't advise it."

"Does she know?"

"She's very groggy. It was a long labour. Somebody will have to tell her in the morning. Would you do that?"

"I'll do that," said Dr. Gunilla, and Darcourt was grateful to her.

(2)

WHEN DR. DAHL-SOOT VISITED THE HOSPITAL the next morning she did not need to give the bad news. Al was with Mabel, who was hysterical.

"There was what the English call A Scene," she told Darcourt. "You see Al, that odious pedant, had not even troubled to find out whether the child was a boy or a girl, and when Mabel demanded to see the child the head nurse explained that it was impossible. Why? Mabel wanted to know. Because the body was no longer available, said the nurse. Why not? said Mabel, very fierce. Because nobody had asked for the body to be reserved for burial by the parents, said the nurse. Mabel understood that. 'You mean they've put my baby in the garbage?' she said, and the nurse said that was not the way the hospital thought of what it had done, which was what was most often done with stillborns. But she wouldn't give details, except that it was a boy and perfect except for an unusually big head. Not abnormal. Apparently it's Mabel who is slightly abnormal. You know Mabel. A fool, and weak as water, but those people can make an awful hullabaloo when they are outraged, and she was ready to kill Al. And Al — really, Al ought to have been put in the garbage at birth — kept saying, 'Calm down, Sweetness, you'll see it all differently tomorrow.' Not a tender word, not a hug, not a thing to suggest that he was involved in the affair at all. I kicked Al out, and talked to Mabel for a while, but she's in a very bad way. What are you going to do?"

"Me?"

"You seem to be the one who is expected to do something when real trouble comes up. Are you going to see Mabel?"

"I think I'd better see Al first."

Al thought Mabel was being utterly unreasonable. She knew what a load of work he had, and how important it was to his career — which meant their joint career, if they stuck together. Hadn't he gone to the hospital with her? And returned after dinner, as Darcourt well knew? Hadn't the doctor said the baby might be held up for several hours because first babies were unaccountable? Was he supposed to sit there all night, and then do a day's work that he had all planned, and that would need every ounce of energy and intellect he could muster? If there hadn't been this accident — this stillbirth business — everything would have been absolutely okay. As it was, Mabel was raising hell.

The trouble, he assured Darcourt, was that Mabel had never really freed herself from her background. Very conventional, middle-brow people, with whom Al had never hit it off. They kept asking why he and Mabel didn't get married, as if having somebody mumble a few words, etc. Al thought he had pretty well lifted Mabel above all that crap, but under stress — and Al admitted that the loss of the child amounted to stress — it all came flooding back, and Mabel was once again the insurance salesman's child from Fresno. Wanted the baby given what she called "decent burial". As if having somebody mumble a few words, etc., over a thing that had never lived could change anything. Al would be frank. He wondered if the arrangement with Mabel would weather this storm. He guessed he had to face it. People on two such different levels of education — though Mabel was majoring in sociology — would never really see eye to eye.

Al wanted to do the right thing, of course. Mabel wanted to go home. Wanted her mother. Can you figure that, in a woman of twenty-two? Wanting her mother? Of course the Mullers were what is called a very close family. But Al couldn't swing it. His grant from Pomelo was enough for one, and damned tight for two, and the fare back to Fresno would screw him up. Could Darcourt persuade Mabel to take it easy for a few days, and probably see things differently?

Darcourt said he would look into the matter and do what seemed best.

That meant that he phoned Maria, in Toronto, and put the matter to her. "I'll come at once," said Maria.

It was Maria who fetched Mabel from the hospital, paid all the bills, set her up in a room near her own in a hotel, and gave Al a piece of her mind that astonished them both, so conventional was it in tone and content. It was Maria who sent Al to a druggist for a breast-pump, of which Mabel had dire need, and this was Al's lowest moment. A breast-pump! He would willingly go into a drugstore and ask for condoms. That was dashing. But a breast-pump! The squalor of domesticity engulfed him. It was Maria who drove Mabel to the airport, when she was fit to travel, and bought her ticket to Fresno and mother. Coping with Mabel, who was sentimentally grateful and woman-to-woman, and bereft-mother-to-happy-mother, tried Maria very high, but she endured all, and never uttered a word of complaint or irony, even to Darcourt. Not even Mabel's frequent, tearful hints that fate was certainly good to the rich, and tough on the poor, provoked her to any speaking of her mind. But to herself she said it was enough to turn her milk.

"You've behaved beautifully," said Darcourt. "You deserve a reward."

"Oh, but I've had a reward," said Maria. "You remember I was hinting about Wally Crottel? The most wonderful luck — the book's turned up!"

"But you said you had thrown it away."

"So I did. But that was the original — you know, that crumpled, stained, interlined, grubby mess that Parlabane left. When I sent it to the publishers, one of them thought a ghost might be able to wrench a book out of it, so he had a Xerox made — quite indefensibly, but you know what publishers are — and sent it to his favourite ghost, who reported that it was pretty hopeless. But recently the ghost sent back the Xerox, which he had unearthed on his desk — obviously a ghost of the uttermost degree of literary messiness — and the publisher, belatedly, but honourably, sent it to me. And I've sent it to Wally."

"But Wally's in jail, awaiting trial."

"I know. I sent it to Mervyn Gwilt, with a teasing, palavering letter, full of nifty bits of Latin. Told him to get it published if he could."

"Maria! You may have committed yourself to some appalling legal claim!"

"Well — no. Not really. I showed the letter to Arthur, and he laughed a lot, but then he got one of his lawyers to rewrite it, and a fine juiceless job he made of it. Not a word of Latin. Lawyers are only half the fun they used to be when they knew Latin. But apparently it's a watertight letter, admitting nothing, relinquishing nothing, but letting Wally have what he wanted, which was a peep at m'dad's book."

"And so that's that."

"As Wally seems likely to get seven years at least, that's probably that."

"Maria, you do have the Devil's own luck!"

Al said no word of thanks to Maria about her part in his crisis. It did not occur to him, so engrossed was he in his *Regiebuch*, and if it had occurred to him, he would not have dared, for a woman who could talk to him as Maria had done was somebody best avoided. The musicologist in Al came uppermost; hadn't there been an opera called *All's Well That Ends Well*? He looked it up. Yes, there it was, by Edmond Audran, whose best opera was *La Poupée*, which meant The Baby, didn't it? Remarkable how fate, and music, and life were all mixed up. It made you think.

(3)

DURING THIS INCIDENT, which did not impinge at all on the preoccupation of the company, preparations for the opera were going ahead rapidly. The play which had commanded the stage had finished its run of performances, and Powell and his forces had the full run of the theatre. Scenes were hung from the flies and all the forty-five sets of ropes that controlled them were adjusted and balanced for use. A splendid set of curtains was brought in from a rental warehouse and hung behind the proscenium, so that they could be swept aside and upward from the centre in the gloriously theatrical manner of the nineteenth century. Powell demanded, and got, a set of footlights installed. In vain did Waldo Harris demur that nobody used such things any more.

"Hoffmann's theatre used 'em, and they are very becoming to the ladies," said Powell. "We won't make all the women look like skulls, with nothing but overhead light. And get that bloody rack of lamps taken down from in front of the proscenium; it's totally out of character and we can do without 'em; the light from the front of the balcony will be quite enough."

Powell was busy, so far as was possible, transforming the small opera theatre that belonged to the Stratford Festival into a charming early-nineteenth-century house.

"We're going to use those pretty little doors that give onto the forestage," he told Darcourt, "and we'll just dim the house lights to half, because in Hoffmann's day the audience sat in full light, and everybody could see their neighbours, and chat and flirt if they didn't like the show. Flirtation's a good old sport and due for a revival."

He had worked with Dulcy Ringgold to prepare pretty cartouches which decorated the little boxes beside the stage; one bore the arms of the town, and the other the arms of the province, but so treated that they had a playful, rather than an official, air. They looked like fine plaster-work, but they were pressed in the same light material as the armour worn by Arthur's Knights.

All of this activity caused a good deal of noise, but nevertheless the singers stepped onstage from time to time and bellowed or neighed into the auditorium, and agreed that it was a nice resonant house. They were still working in rehearsal rooms under the guidance of Watkin Bourke, who appeared to put in a twelve-hour day.

The company took on new vitality when they were able to claim the theatre as their own, and friendships were struck up, enmities sharpened, and jokes whispered behind hands.

One of these originated with Albert Greenlaw, one of the black singers, who played the role of Sir Pellinore. He had found a great toy in Nutcombe Puckler, who was a comedian by profession, but never thought of himself as comic.

"Do you realize," said Greenlaw to Vincent LeMoyne, the other black Knight, "that Nutty gets letters from his dog? Yes, I'm not kidding, *from his dog*! The dog's in England, of course, but the dog writes twice a week. And in Cockney, what's more! 'Dear Marster, I miss you terrible, but Missus says we has to be brave and go walkies every day just as if you was 'ere. My roomatism is chronic but I takes me pills reglar, and don't have to get up in the night more than a few times, which is an improvement, Missus says. Hurry back, covered with laurels and bring lots of lovely green bones. Love from your Woofy in which Missus joins.' Can you beat it! I've known dog-nuts, but I never met a dog-nut as nutty as Nutty. Why do you suppose the dog talks Cockney?"

"It's a class thing," said Wilson Tinney, who played Gareth Beaumains. "Dog must be loving and beloved, but *not* a social equal. Certainly not a superior. Can you imagine Nutty with a titled dog? 'Dear Puckler, your wife is looking after me splendidly in your absence, and I look forward eagerly to August 12, when the grousing begins. Accept my assurance that I look upon you not as a master, but as a humble friend.' That wouldn't do at all."

"Do you know what I think?" said Vincent LeMoyne; "I think Nutty's wife writes those letters. I suspect the dog's illiterate."

"You astonish me!" said Greenlaw. "Do you suppose Nutty knows?"

There was a coolness between Miss Virginia Poole, who, as the Lady Clarissant, was the only member of the female chorus to have a named role, and Gwen Larking, the Stage Manager; Miss Poole thought she should have a dressing-room apart from the Chorus, but she had been put — "thrown" was the word she used — with them in a large basement room. She appeared in all three acts and had two costumes, and yet Marta Ullmann, who appeared in only one scene as Elaine, had a dressing-room of her own on the stage level. If this was an intentional slight, what lay behind it? If it was an oversight, should it not be put right as fast as possible?

There was a row, lasting for a day, between Powell and Waldo Harris, because a trapdoor that Powell had ordered had not been cut in the stage. But if it were cut, said Waldo, it would go down into the orchestra pit, rather than the undercroft of the stage proper. Why had he not been told earlier? demanded Powell. He wanted Merlin to appear as if by magic at that particular spot, downstage right, and Mr. Twentyman had been rehearsing for four weeks with that in mind. All right, said Waldo, he would have it cut, and it would mean reducing the size of the orchestra by five members. Here Dr. Dahl-Soot intervened, and the question was somehow resolved without bloodshed, and without the trap-door.

"Perhaps I could come down from the flies on a wire," suggested Mr. Twentyman. "I've done it before, you know."

Oliver Twentyman had made himself popular with every-body in the theatre, without particularly exerting himself to do so. But his great age, and his charm, and above all his assumption that everyone wanted to please him, made slaves of the gofers (to whom he brought charming Belgian choco-lates in pretty little packages), and convinced Gwen Larking that she was his champion and must shield him from all harm, and caused Waldo Harris to put a special reclining-chair in his dressing-room, as well as a little heater, in case there might be early autumn chill. In return Mr. Twentyman gave advice about how to pronounce English when singing, with Hans Holzknecht as an eager pupil, and even Clara Intrepidi as an overhearer, rather than a committed listener. She was still dubious about a language with so many vowels.

Thus matters moved toward the final rehearsals, and a controlled, highly professional excitement rose.

The stage was still pretty much in the grip of the techni-cians, but time was found to accustom the actors to singing in the theatre. Not always at full strength, Darcourt found; sometimes they "marked", which meant that they sang quietly, skipped their high notes or sang them an octave below pitch, and were altogether so intimate that they seemed determined to keep the music a secret. Watkin Bourke performed prodigies on an ancient upright piano that stood on the forestage; he was still playing from a full orchestral score, and showed great firmness in keeping Al Crane from snatching this for his own information. Gunilla, who had taken a powerful scunner to Al, was determined that he should not see the music at close range if she could avoid it, and Al whined to Powell that this was a hardship, but Powell was not to be moved. Al had as yet not succeeded in getting the copies he wanted, and was not happy when he was told that he might get something for himself once the opera was in performance.

There was great activity, too, on the part of the public relations people, who wanted tasty bits of gossip to send out to the press, which had not shown much interest in *Arthur*. The report from the box-office was discouraging; even the first night had not been sold out, and would have to be papered with passes. A few of the more learned critics, who had asked for scores to study, had not been pleased when told that none were available, as Dean Wintersen had forbade any public examination of the music until Schnak's examiners had gone over it thoroughly. As the opening drew near, the report was that less than thirty-three per cent of the tickets for all performances had been sold. If Dr. Dahl-Soot was not concerned about this, the management of the Festival was disgruntled. Darcourt, the eager amateur, wished heartily for a public success, and fretted that it appeared unlikely.

He was sitting in the balcony of the theatre, during one of the mysterious marking rehearsals, when he became aware of a presence behind him, and of a smell that he thought he recognized. It was not really a bad smell, but it was a heavy, furry smell, rather like the bears' cage in a zoo. A soft, velvety bass voice rumbled in his ear.

"Priest Simon — a word, if you please."

Turning, he found Yerko leaning forward over his shoulder.

"Priest Simon, I have been taking note. Watching with great care. Everything seems to be going well, but a vital element of opera success is still missing. You know what I mean?"

Darcourt had no idea what this large, overwhelming Gypsy could possibly mean.

"The Claque, Priest Simon. Where is your Claque? Nobody says a word about it. I have inquired. The P.Or. people do not seem to know when I speak of a Claque. But you do, surely?"

Darcourt had heard of a claque, but knew nothing about it.

"Without the Claque — nothing. How can you expect anything else? Nobody knows this opera. An opera audience must contain people who know the work intimately. Nobody will dare to applaud if they don't know where, and when, and why. They might make an embarrassing mistake — look foolish. Now listen very carefully. I know the whole business of the Claque from top to bottom. Did I not work for years at the Vienna Opera under the great Bonci — related, but not so you could talk about it, to the noble tenor of that name? I was Bonci's right-hand man."

"You mean hired applause? Oh Yerko, I don't think that would do at all."

"Certainly it would not do if you talk of hired applause. That is not a Claque; that is a noisy, untrained rabble. No, look: a Claque is a small body of experts; applause, certainly, but not unorganized row; you must have your *bisseurs* who call out loud for encores; your *rieurs* who laugh at the right places — but just appreciative chuckles to encourage the others, not from the belly; your *pleureurs* who sob when sobs are needed; and, of course, the kind of clapping that encourages the uninformed to join, which is not vulgar hand-smacking that makes the clapper look like a drunk. Good clapping must sound intelligent, and that calls for skill; you must know what part

of the palm to smack. And all of this must be carefully organized — yes, orchestrated — by the *capo di claque*. That's me.
We won't talk money; this is a gift from my sister and me to
our dear Arthur. We give him a success! But get me twelve
seats — four balcony, two on each side of the ground floor
well toward the front, and four in the last two rows, centre —
and we can't fail. Of course two seats for me and my sister —
because we shall appear in evening dress and sit in the middle
of the house — and the thing's done."

"But Yerko — it's very kind, but isn't it a sort of lie?"

"Is P.Or. a lie? Would I lie to you, my friend?"

"No, no, certainly not; but it's lying to somebody, I feel
sure."

"Priest Simon, listen; remember the old Gypsy saying —
Lies keep the teeth white."

"I must say it's very tempting."

"You fix it up."

"I'll talk to Powell."

"But not a word to Arthur. This is a present. A surprise."

Darcourt did talk to Powell, and Powell was delighted.
"Just in the real early-nineteenth-century style!" he said.
"He's right, you know. Unless the audience is led, most of it
won't know when to clap or what to like. A claque's just
what we need."

So Darcourt gave Yerko the approving word. This is following the path of the Fool, he thought, and, all things considered, it's good sport.

(4)

WHAT NOBODY COULD POSSIBLY HAVE CONSIDERED good sport was
Schnak's examination. It affected everybody in the company,
from the stage crew, who thought it a pompous nuisance, to
Albert Greenlaw, who said it gave him the heebie-jeebies,

and to Hans Holzknecht and Clara Intrepidi, who were told by Dr. Gunilla that they must give their best in the performance involved, and that no "marking" or saving the voice was permitted.

The form of the examination was unusual. After some haggling it was agreed that it could not take place in the School of Music, and that the examiners must journey to Stratford to do their work. They were to examine the candidate orally in the morning, in the upstairs crush-bar of the theatre, and after luncheon they were to see a performance of the opera. It made a long day for them, said Dean Wintersen. He said nothing about what sort of day it made for Schnak.

There were to be three dress rehearsals before the first night of the production, which was scheduled for a Saturday. It was on the Wednesday, therefore, that a special small bus left the Music School in Toronto at a quarter to eight in the morning, with seven academics aboard.

"I must say I find this exceedingly irregular," said Professor Andreas Pfeiffer, who was the External Examiner, a great panjandrum of musicology imported for the occasion from an important school of music in Pennsylvania.

"You mean seeing a performance of the opera?" said Dean Wintersen, who had entertained Pfeiffer at dinner the night before and had already had enough of him.

"Of that I say nothing," said Professor Pfeiffer. "I mean this business of being haled across the countryside at an early hour. Last night I slept very poorly, thinking about what lay ahead. It is difficult to compose oneself under such circumstances."

"You must admit the circumstances are unusual," said the Dean, lighting his first cigarette of the day.

"Perhaps too unusual," said Pfeiffer. "May I politely request you not to smoke? Very disagreeable in an enclosed vehicle."

The Dean threw his cigarette out of the window.

"Ah, ah! You didn't douse it!" said Professor Adelaide O'Sullivan. "That is how forest fires are started. Can we stop? I'll get out and stamp on it."

This was done, and Professor O'Sullivan, having dodged and darted a hundred yards to the rear, amid heavy traffic, found the cigarette, which had gone out of itself on the city street, and which she trampled to bits, as a matter of principle.

This put the journey off to a start marked by underground feeling. Professor George Cooper, a stout Englishman, had already gone to sleep, but Professor John Diddear was covertly pro-Dean, as he himself liked to smoke during examinations, as a way of passing the time, and he knew that it would be impossible with Pfeiffer and O'Sullivan so strongly against it. Professor Francesco Berger, who was the examiner from the University's own department of music, and a man of peace, tried to improve the atmosphere by telling a joke, but as he was not a man with much narrative sense, he spoiled it, and made matters worse. Professor Penelope Raven, who was the seventh of the group, laughed too loudly, all alone, at the non-climax, and was stared into silence by Pfeiffer.

It took the bus a little under two hours to reach Stratford, and the driver had to put up with a good deal of cautionary exclamation from Professor Pfeiffer, who was a nervous passenger. But at last the examiners found themselves in the crush-bar of the theatre, accommodated with a large table, and lots of pencils and pads, and several jugs of coffee. Professor Pfeiffer, who never drank coffee, was given a bottle of Perrier by Gwen Larking, the Stage Manager, who had appointed herself beadle of the occasion; she left an awed gofer on the spot, to fetch, carry, and do the bidding of the academics.

The protocol of an oral examination for a doctorate in music is not extreme, but it can be severe. Schnak, who was hanging about, dressed in a skirt at Gunilla's bidding, shook hands with all of the examiners, and shaking hands was not a courtesy that came easily to her. Gunilla introduced her to Professor Pfeiffer, who made it clear that this was an honour for Schnak; he put out his hand, which she barely touched. It was like ceremonially forgiving the headsman, before he does his work.

Then Wintersen asked Schnak to go downstairs and wait until she was called; she marched off, in the charge of the jailer-gofer, who looked as solemn as eighteen can. Dr. Gunilla, the director of the thesis project, was present as an examiner, and also in the character, familiar in courts-martial, of Prisoner's Friend. She was greeted with cordiality by the Canadians, but Professor Pfeiffer, who had his own opinions about the Doctor's international reputation, managed to put a chill on her reception.

The Dean, who was an old hand at such affairs, groaned in spirit. He had been warned that Pfeiffer was a bastard but his reputation as a musicologist was great, and so he must be endured.

The Dean, by virtue of his office, was the chairman of the examination, and he began according to Hoyle, by asking the examiners if they were all acquainted. They were, and in some cases too well. He drew their attention to three copies of the full score of *Arthur* which lay on the table for ready reference.

The Dean next called upon Professor Andreas Pfeiffer, as external examiner-in-chief, to place his report before the committee.

Professor Pfeiffer did so, taking just under an hour. It was a fine late August day outside, but by the time Pfeiffer had unpacked his budget of doubt and distaste it was February in the examination room. Professor Berger, who was a genial man and liked Schnak, managed, as internal examiner-in-chief, in twenty minutes to shove the calendar back to approximately late December, but a post-Christmas gloom was still to be felt.

The other examiners, called upon to say their say, were brief. Not more than ten minutes was taken by Penny Raven, who managed to establish that she had evolved a libretto for the opera, with some unspecified outside help from a literary man.

"I hear nothing of Planché," said Professor Pfeiffer. Both Penny and Gunilla looked at him with deadly menace, but he was impervious to any outside influence.

Now, the processions, the parades of the picadors, the recognition of the President, the preening by the matador, and all the ceremonial of the ring having been performed, it was time to bring in the bull. Dean Wintersen nodded to the gofer (by this time a thorough Shakespearean jailer), and Schnak was brought back to the table, wilted with almost two hours of solitary anxiety. She was seated next to the Dean, and asked to explain her choice of the thesis project, and her method of work in realizing it. Which she did, very badly.

Professor Pfeiffer was first let loose upon her. He was a matador of immense skill, and for thirty-five minutes he nagged and harassed the wretched Schnak, who had no verbal ease, no rhetoric of any kind, and made long, unpromising pauses before most of her answers.

Professor Pfeiffer showed disappointment. The bull had no style, no pride of the ring, seemed really unworthy of a matador of his repute.

But as the torture proceeded, Schnak took refuge more and more often in a single answer: "I did it like that because it came to me like that," she said. And although Professor Pfeiffer greeted this with doubtful looks, and once or twice with disdainful snorts, one or two of the other examiners, notably Cooper and Diddear, smiled and nodded, for they were themselves, in a modest way, composers.

Now and again Dr. Dahl-Soot interposed. But Pfeiffer shut her up, saying, "I must not allow myself to think that the candidate's supervisor carried undue weight in the actual work of composition; that would be wholly inadmissible." Dr. Gunilla, fuming, but tactful, remained silent after that.

When at last, by repeatedly looking at his watch, the Dean made it clear that Professor Pfeiffer must close his interrogation, Dr. Francesco Berger took over, and was so genial, so anxious to put Schnak at her ease, suggested so often that he approved of what had been done, that he almost upset the applecart. His colleagues wished Berger would not overdo it. When their time came to ask questions, they were brief and merciful.

It was George Cooper, who had dozed through much of the examination, who asked: "I notice that you have used some keys at important moments in the opera that would not perhaps have suggested themselves first to most composers. A flat major, and C flat major, and E flat major — why those? Any special reason?"

"They were ETAH's favourites," said Schnak. "He had a theory about keys and their special characters, and what they suggested."

"ETAH? Who is ETAH?" said Professor Pfeiffer.

"Sorry. E. T. A. Hoffmann; I've got into the way of thinking of him as ETAH," said Schnak.

"You mean you identify yourself with him?"

"Well, working from his notes and trying to get into his mind —"

Professor Pfeiffer said nothing but made a derisive noise in his nose. But then — "These theories of key characterization were very much a thing of Hoffmann's time," he said. "Romantic nonsense, of course."

"Nonsense or not, I think we ought to hear a little more about it," said Cooper. "What did he think about those keys?"

"Well — he wrote about A flat major: 'Those chords carry me into the country of eternal longing.' And about C flat major: 'It grasps my heart with glowing claws'; he called it 'the bleak ghost with red, sparkling eyes'. And he used E flat major a lot with horns; he called it 'longing and sweet sounds'."

"Hoffmann was a drug-taker, wasn't he?" said Professor Pfeiffer.

"I don't think so. He boozed a lot and sometimes he came near to having the horrors."

"I'm not surprised, if he could talk that sort of rubbish about the character of keys," said Pfeiffer, and was ready to drop the subject. But not Schnak.

"But if that's the way he thought, oughtn't I to respect it? If I'm to finish his opera, I mean?" she said, and Professor Diddear made a noise in *his* nose, as if to suggest that Professor Pfeiffer had been caught napping.

"I suppose you explain your excessive use of extraneous modulation as coming from Hoffmann's adulation of Beethoven?"

"Hoffmann adored Beethoven and Beethoven thought a lot of Hoffmann."

"I suppose that is so," said the great musicologist. "You should remember, young lady, what Berlioz thought about Hoffmann: a writer who imagined himself to be a composer. But you have chosen to devote a great deal of work to this minor figure, and that is why we are here."

"Perhaps to suggest that Berlioz could have been wrong," said Dr. Gunilla; "he made a fool of himself often enough, as critics always do."

She knew that Dr. Pfeiffer had written an essay about Berlioz which accorded Berlioz about seventy marks out of a hundred, which was as far as the Professor was inclined to go. If she could use Berlioz as a stick with which to beat Pfeiffer, so be it.

It was one o'clock.

"Ladies and gentlemen, I remind you that our work this morning is only a part of this unusual examination," said the Dean. "We assemble again at two in the theatre, for a private performance of this opera, conducted by Miss Schnakenburg, on which a portion of your decision must necessarily rest. Proof of the pudding, you know. Meanwhile the Cornish Foundation has invited us to lunch, and we are already late."

Professor Pfeiffer did not like lunching as a guest of the Cornish Foundation. "Are they not involved?" he asked the Dean. "Is the candidate not their protégée? I do not like to use such a term, but is this an attempt to buy us?"

"I think it's just decent hospitality," said the Dean, "and, as you know, hospitality is a co-operative thing. The Romans very wisely used the same word for 'host' and 'guest'." Pfeiffer did not understand, and shook his head.

The luncheon took place at the best restaurant in Stratford — the small one down by the river — and Arthur and Maria did everything they could to make the examiners happy. Easy work with Berger, Cooper, Diddear, and Penny Raven. Easy work with the Dean, and even with Professor Adelaide O'Sullivan, who was only a bigot about tobacco. Professor Pfeiffer, however, and Dr. Dahl-Soot had thrown aside the decorum of the examination room and were going at it, hammer and tongs.

"I totally disagree with this procedure of witnessing a performance of this work," said the Professor. "It brings in elements extraneous to what we are to decide."

"You don't care if it can be seen as effective on the stage?"

"I care only if it is effective on the page. I agree with the late Ernest Newman: a great score is more finely realized when one reads it in the tranquillity of one's study than when one sits in a crowd and endures the ineptitudes of orchestra and singers."

"You mean you can do it better in your head than a hundred accomplished artists can do it for you?"

"I can read a score."

"Better than, say von Karajan? Than Haitink? Than Colin Davis?"

"I do not follow the purpose of your line of questioning."

"I am just trying to find out how great a man you are so that I can treat you with appropriate reverence. I can read a score, too. Am pretty well known for it, in fact. But it's still better when I raise the baton and a hundred and twenty artists set about their work. I am not an opera company in myself."

"So? Well — make of it what you will, but I rather think I am. No, I never drink wine. A glass of Perrier, if you please."

What Professor Pfeiffer did not drink was certainly compensated for by what the others drank. It had been a thirsty morning. Before lunch was over, all but Pfeiffer were jovial, and Professor George Cooper showed a tendency to bump into tables, and laugh at himself for doing so. They were, after all, musicians under the professorial gown, and a well-set table was one of the elements in which they lived. They all thanked Arthur and Maria with a heartiness that made Professor Pfeiffer suspect the worst. But he could not be bought. Oh no, not he.

(5)

FIRST IN THE LINE OF DRESSING-ROOMS on the stage level was a small kennel reserved for the use of the conductor, when there was one, and a quick-change room if that should be needed. Here sat Schnak, desolate and alone. She had known rejection before this: had there not been the boy who said that sex with her was like sleeping with a bicycle? She had known the loneliness of leaving home and parents. She had known the bitterness of being a loner, of not fitting into any group, while being still too young and insignificant to wear loneliness like a badge of honour. But never had she known wretchedness like this, when she was about to take a great step forward in her life as an artist.

She knew that she would not fail. Francesco Berger had made it clear to her, a few weeks ago, that the examination was a rite of passage, a ceremonial and scholarly necessity; the School of Music would not permit the examination to take place if it were not ninety-five per cent certain to be a success. The examination was either the last and most demanding of the torments of student life, or the first and simplest of the torments of professional life. She had nothing to fear.

Nevertheless, she feared. Her experience as a conductor had been confined to a few bouts with a student orchestra, which was fractious enough, because inexperienced. A professional orchestra was something very different. These old pros were like livery-stable horses: they were used to all sorts of riders, and they were determined to do, so far as possible, what they chose. Oh, they wouldn't wreck the performance; they were musicians, through and through. But they would be sticky about tempi, sluggish about entrances, perfunctory in phrasing; they wouldn't be bossed by a raw kid. Gunilla would conduct at all the public performances, unless Gunilla was kind and let her do one or two mid-week shows. Gunilla knew how to get what she wanted out of an orchestra, and she had the kind of sharp tongue musicians respect — professionally severe, but not personal. What had she said to the harpist yesterday? "The *arpeggi* must be deliberate, like pearls dropping in wine, not slithering like a fat woman slipping on a banana skin." Not Oscar Wilde, but good enough for a rehearsal. Gunilla had coached her, had allowed her to conduct a full orchestra rehearsal, and had given her an hour of notes afterward. But once she lifted her baton this afternoon, she was alone. And that old hellion Pfeiffer would be watching every minute.

The dressing-room was unbearable. She wandered out to the stage, which was set for the Prologue, and as it was lighted only by one harsh lamp high up in the flies it was as charmless as an unlit stage always is. Below her, under the device of rollers, like corkscrews, that produced the effect of gently heaving waves, she heard voices: Waldo Harris, Dulcy, and Gwen Larking, arguing with Geraint.

"They work perfectly well, but they make too much noise," said Waldo. "I don't suppose you'd agree to leaving them out altogether? We could probably rig up something that would look like moving water."

"Oh, no!" said Dulcy. "These are the darlings of my heart — and absolutely authentic for the way they did things in 1820."

"They've cost a fortune to make," said Waldo. "I guess it would be a shame to scrap them."

"But what can you do?" said Geraint.

"We'd have to dismantle the three rollers and put rubber on the parts that engage. That'd do it, I think."

"How long will it take?" said Geraint.

"An hour, at least."

"Then take an hour, and do it," said Geraint. "I want to see it this afternoon."

"Can't," said Gwen Larking. "The curtain must go up sharp at two. It's Schnak's examination, remember?"

"What of it? An hour won't kill them, surely?"

"From what I hear about this morning, an hour's delay would put them in a very bad temper. Especially that old fellow who makes all the trouble. We mustn't make things difficult for Schnak."

"Oh, damn Schnak! That miserable little runt is more bother than she's worth!"

"Come on, Geraint, be a sport. Give the kid her chance."

"You mean Schnak's chance is more important than my production?"

"Yes, Geraint, from now till half past four Schnak's chance is more important than anything else. You said so yourself, to the whole cast, yesterday," said Dulcy.

"I say whatever is best at the moment, and you know it."

"What's best at the moment is that we leave this piece of machinery till later."

"This is just the trade-unionism of women. God, how I hate women."

"All right, Geraint; hate me," said Gwen. "But give Schnak her chance, even if you hate her later."

"Gwen's right," said Waldo. "I said an hour, but it could be two. Let's leave it for the moment."

"O Jesu mawr! O anwyl Crist! Have it your way then!" Geraint could be heard going off in a huff.

"Don't fuss! We'll manage the appearance of the sword! It'll do for today," said Waldo, but there was no sound of an appeased director.

Schnak threw up her lunch-time sandwich and cup of coffee into the toilet. It had turned to gall within her. When she had wiped her face and doused it with cold water, she went back to her dressing-room and looked at herself in the mirror. Damned Schnak. Miserable little runt. Yes, Geraint was right.

He'd never love me. Why would anybody love me? I love Geraint even better than I love Nilla, and he hates me. Look at me! Short. Scrawny. Awful hair. Face like a rat. Those legs! Why did Nilla say I had to wear a black jacket and this white blouse? Of course he hates me. I look just bloody awful. Why can't I look like Nilla? Or that Maria Cornish? Why is God so mean to me?

A tap at the door, and a gofer (the prettiest gofer) put her head inside.

"Fifteen minutes, Schnak," she said. "And the best of luck. All the girls have their fingers crossed for you."

Schnak snarled, and the gofer withdrew quickly.

After fifteen minutes more of repetitious self-hate the last call came — from outside the door — and Schnak made her way downstairs, through the undercroft to the stage, and into the orchestra pit. There they sat, the thirty-two villains who meant to destroy her. Some of them nodded to her pleasantly; the concert-master, and Watkin Bourke at the harpsichord, whispered, "Good luck."

If there is any applause when you step onto the podium, turn and bow to the house, Nilla had said. There was no applause, but from the tail of her eye she could see that the seven examiners had placed themselves here and there in the auditorium, and in the front row, right behind her, a full score on his knees and a flashlight in his hand, sat the ominous Professor Pfeiffer. What a seat to choose, she thought.

The little red light-signal from the Stage Manager flashed on, and at the same time the oyster eye of the closed-circuit television camera directly in front of the conductor's desk, which would carry Schnak's every movement to backstage monitors, for Stage Management, Chorus, and offstage sound of every kind, gave a gloomy blink, like an undersea monster.

She tapped the music desk, raised her baton — one of Gunilla's own, specially made and perhaps intended as a talisman — and when she gave the down beat, the first mysterious chord of the Prologue rose at her.

The orchestra, aware of her nerves, but oblivious of her hatred, played well, and after fifteen slow bars of the Prologue the curtain swept upward to show the Enchanted Mere. In front of it stood Oliver Twentyman, splendid as Merlin, and Hans Holzknecht, armoured and cloaked as King Arthur. Merlin apostrophized the waves, and not quite on cue the great sword Caliburn rose above the unmoving waters.

Arthur seized it, and invoked all the magic of the sword. Everything seemed to be going well, until Schnak felt herself being tapped — almost punched — in the back, and when she ignored this, there was a loud whistle, and Professor Pfeiffer's voice crying, "Hold it! Hold it! Repeat from Letter D, please!" Schnak dropped her baton and the music stopped.

"What's the matter?" It was Dean Wintersen's voice.

"I want to hear it again from Letter D," said Pfeiffer. "They are not playing what is written in the score."

"A minor change in rehearsal." said Gunilla's voice. "Some addition to the wood-winds."

"I am speaking to the conductor," said Pfeiffer. "If there has been a change, why is it not in the score as it was presented to us? Repeat from Letter D, if you please."

So the music was repeated from Letter D. Holzknecht, who had been pleased with his performance, was not pleased by this unexpected encore; Oliver Twentyman flashed a charming smile at Professor Pfeiffer across the footlights like someone humouring a child, and the Professor did not like it.

Nevertheless, the repeat was performed, and all went well until the end of the Prologue. It had been seen through a scrim, a transparent curtain which lent mystery to the stage, and as this was whisked up into the flies, it did not whisk obligingly, but caught on the first wing on the right side of the stage, and there was a terrible ripping. The scrim was halted in its progress, and Gwen Larking appeared at the side of the stage accompanied by a large man with a pole who fished the scrim away from what was catching it. This did not dismay the stage crew, or the singers, who were used to such mishaps, but it struck coldly into the heart of Schnak, who was sure this would be counted against her by her merciless foe.

What happened during the long afternoon was not, as Geraint wildly cried, like the Marx Brothers in *A Night at the Opera*, but it included more than the usual number of technical troubles. What really put the rehearsal to the bad was the frequent interruption of Professor Pfeiffer, who demanded, in all, seven repeats of music which he said — quite rightly — was not entirely as it appeared in the score he had been sent three weeks earlier. When he did not stop proceedings by whistling loudly through his teeth, like a policeman, he could be heard muttering, and demanding more light to help him in making notes. The opera, which should have taken two and a half hours, without the single fifteen-minute interval, took rather more than four, and the singers became demoralized, and were far below their best. Only the orchestra, firmly professional, sawed and tooted and strummed imperturbably, and did, under the circumstances, pretty well.

Six of the seven examiners had given up the struggle before the rehearsal finished. They had heard enough, had liked what they heard, had enjoyed lunch, and were ready to wrap the affair up and get back to their homes. Professor Pfeiffer, whose eyes were fixed on his score, never seemed to look at the stage and was impatient when technical problems brought the performance to a halt. Nobody, therefore, noticed that it was not Schnak who conducted the last scene, but Watkin Bourke, who did so from the harpsichord. Schnak had disappeared, and the orchestra had assumed that she was ill and were not, all things considered, surprised.

Even they were surprised, however, when a loud siren was heard outside the fire exit on the right-hand side of the auditorium, and Gwen Larking, appearing from one of the proscenium doors, jumped from the stage to open it and admit four men with a stretcher, who hurried across the front of the theatre, trampling Professor Pfeiffer's feet as they did so, and disappeared through the pass-door on the stage left. But the music went on, somewhat rockily, until, moments later, the four men reappeared, carrying a stretcher upon which lay the body of Schnak, under a blanket. The stage had filled, meanwhile, with actors in costume, several stage-hands, the gofers, and Arthur and Maria, who stood at the footlights with Geraint Powell. The body of Schnak was carried before them, thought Darcourt, who had been in the darkness at the back of the theatre, very much as if they were looking down at it from Arthurian battlements, and their astonishment and dismay were not in the least theatrical, but real and stamped with terror. The little procession reached the door, the stretcher disappeared, and the siren grew fainter as the ambulance sped away.

There was excitement, of course, the kind of excitement over an unexpected happening that only a theatrical company can generate. What was it? Why was it? What had happened? What should be done?

It was Waldo Harris who called for order and explained. When Schnak had not appeared on the podium for the last scene, one of the gofers had gone to see what was amiss, and, not finding her in her dressing-room, had looked in the ladies' lav. And there she was, very ill and unconscious.

Had she tried to kill herself? Nobody knew, and they must not think like that until there was more news from the hospital. Miss Intrepidi let it be known that if it was an attempt at suicide, she, for one, was not surprised, after the way the poor child had been treated during the rehearsal. An Intrepidi party formed immediately, and murmured against Professor Pfeiffer, who was unaware of it and took no notice. He was anxious to continue with the examination.

"This is unfortunate," he said, "but not perhaps crucial. We can meet now, and make our decisions. I have a great many questions to ask, particularly about the libretto. Where can we be private?"

"But we can't have an examination without the candidate," said Penelope Raven.

"We've had an examination till I'm bloody sick of it," said George Cooper. "Let's give her the degree and be done with it."

"Give her the degree when there are still vital questions to be asked?" Professor Pfeiffer was scandalized. "I am far from satisfied."

"You must admit these are unusual circumstances," said Dean Wintersen. "It can hardly be said we've cut corners. We've been at it all day. Surely we can come to an agreement now?"

"Agreed! I move acceptance of the thesis and the obligatory performance as completion of the work for the doctoral degree," said Francesco Berger.

"Excuse me! As the External Examiner that is my privilege," said Professor Pfeiffer.

"Well then, for Christ's sake use your privilege," said George Cooper. "This is ridiculous! That girl may be dead, or dying."

"I fully understand the compassionate grounds for a hasty decision," said Pfeiffer; "but in my experience compassionate grounds are rarely sound grounds, and I should like to feel that this examination has been completed in proper form. Frankly, I should like to defer a decision for a week, during which we should attend at least two more performances."

"Sorry to sound like a dean," said Wintersen, "but I really must overrule you, Professor. I shall call for a vote, naming the examiners in alphabetical order. Professor Berger?"

The vote was six for acceptance of the degree, Professor Pfeiffer abstaining, and the Dean forgoing his privilege of casting a vote. The examination was over, and Schnak, dead or alive, was therewith a Doctor of Music.

The Cornishes took over. Darcourt was asked to take the examiners to dinner, as they had been detained so long. Gunilla announced her determination to go to the hospital at once, with Arthur and Maria. Professor Pfeiffer said he didn't want any dinner, but this deceived no one. The singers were shooed off to their dressing-rooms, big with the drama of the afternoon.

Geraint called Waldo and Gwen to him, and set about a long budget of notes he had taken during what was, to him, a disappointing and tediously delayed rehearsal. He would show proper emotion, he said, when everything was ship-shape and Bristol fashion.

(6)

WHAT WOULD A STRANGER MAKE of this room, if he should happen in here by mistake, thought Darcourt. A beautiful young mother sits in the dim light of the only lamp, suckling her child; the long dressing-robe she wears might belong to any time during the past two thousand years. There are two very large beds in the room and in one of them, under the heavy coverlet, lie two women; one in early middle age and of distinguished, hawk-like face and the other softly pretty, her dark eyes full of mischief. The older woman's arm is around the neck of her companion, and caresses it. In the second bed I lie myself, fully dressed except for my shoes, and beside me lies a man of great beauty and palpable energy; his open shirt-collar and longish curly dark hair might belong to any time during the last two hundred and fifty years. We too are partly covered, for the August night is chilly, but there is no affec-tionate link between us. The only other figure in the room is the man whose back is turned to us; he stands at the dressing-table, which has been turned into a pretty well-stocked bar.

The room itself? It looks as if one of those half-timbered houses, perhaps from Stratford-on-Avon or Gloucestershire, had been turned inside out. Dark beams appear to support a structure of lumpy white plaster. This style of interior finish is intended, undoubtedly, as a compliment to the Shakespeare Festival which is the chief glory of this town.

This is Maria and Arthur's room in the motel where they

have been staying, intermittently, for the past three weeks observing — so far as they have been made welcome to observe — the completion of all the preparations for the presentation of *Arthur of Britain*, and they are entertaining Gunilla, and Dulcy Ringgold, and Geraint and myself. It is ten o'clock at night. We are gathered to talk about the strange behaviour of Hulda — henceforth and forever Doctor Hulda — Schnakenburg, who was borne from her doctoral examination on a stretcher a few hours earlier.

All things considered, the intruding stranger might think it an odd scene, a mixture of the domestic and the reposeful. Or was it some muddle of group sex, arranged for observers of peculiar tastes?

"She's going to be all right," said Arthur, turning to give Gunilla another strong Scotch. "But it's bound to be a little bit embarrassing when she rejoins us. The hospital people want her for a couple of days at least. Her digestive tract has suffered what they call serious insult. They've been swilling her out."

"Little fool," said Gunilla. "Nearly a hundred Aspirin and half a bottle of gin. Where would she have got the idea that it would kill her?"

"She didn't mean to kill herself," said Arthur. "It was what it is now fashionable to call a gesture of despair."

"No, no, don't patronize her," said Gunilla. "She meant to kill herself, undoubtedly. She was just badly informed, as many suicides are."

"You must admit she made a very effective scene out of it," said Dulcy. "I was moved. Blubbed quite a lot, I confess it without shame."

"She saw herself as Elaine, the Lily Maid of Astolat," said Maria. "Dying of love for the faithless Lancelot. Hulda has learned a great deal from this opera, quite apart from the music. She did it to make you feel cheap, Geraint, just as

Elaine made Lancelot feel cheap. Now, Davy my pet, time to change sides." She shifted the feeding child to her other breast.

"Do all babies make that slurping noise when they are feeding?" said Geraint.

"It's a very nice noise, and no impertinent questions from you, my lad. You're in the doghouse."

"I'm damned if I'm in the doghouse," said Geraint. "You can't blame me. I won't put up with it."

"You'll have to put up with it," said Dulcy. "Of course it's unjust, but who are you to escape all of the world's injustice? This is one of those cases where the female side in the great struggle undoubtedly wins. You scorned her love, which God knows was obvious enough, and she tried to kill herself. Doghouse for you. Bitter shame upon you, Geraint Powell, you heart-breaker, for not less than two weeks."

"Bullshit!"

"Coarseness ill becomes a man in your position. You are cast as the haughty, gallant, gay Lothario, and if you have any dramatic sense at all — which is what you're paid to have — you will play the part to the hilt."

"Is nobody on my side? Sim bach, say a few eloquent words in my defence. How am I to blame?"

"Well, to be totally fair and even-handed, Geraint, I have seen you, now and then, casting inflammatory smiles in her direction."

"I smile at everybody, particularly when I don't mean anything by it. Perhaps I smiled — a meaningless grimace of courtesy — at Schnak now and then when she kept getting under my feet. I swear upon the soul of my dear mother, now adding a fine mezzo to the heavenly choir, that I meant nothing, nothing whatever, by it. I smile at you Nilla, and at you, Dulcy, and God knows I don't expect it to get me anywhere, you horrible old dikes."

"Dikes!" said Gunilla indignantly. "How dare you use

such a word to me — to us. You are a boor, Geraint."

"Isn't he a boor, Nilla? That's precisely what he is. A boor.

> *She loved thee, boor; she loved thee, cruel boor;*

Shakespeare, freely adapted for the occasion." Dulcy was enjoying herself greatly. Indignation and Scotch were working strongly inside her.

"She didn't love me, even if she thought she did."

"It comes to the same thing."

"Yes, I fear it does," said Darcourt. "Poor old Schnak was in the grip of one of the great errors of the frenzied lover. She thought because she loved, she could provoke love in return. Everybody does it, at some time. I speak as the voice of calm reason."

"And you ignored her cruelly," said Arthur. "Doghouse for you, Geraint."

"I suppose I must make a statement," said Geraint. "What I am about to say does not spring from vanity, but from bitter experience. Listen to me, all of you. Since I was but a winsome lad, women have insisted on falling for me. It has something to do with chemistry, I suppose. Chemistry and the fact (which I state without any vanity whatever) that I am absurdly good-looking. Result, a lot of trouble for me. But am I to blame? I refuse to accept blame. Are beautiful women to blame because men fall for them? Is Maria to blame because just about everybody who sees her falls in love with her, or at least looks upon her to lust after her? I'll bet that even Sim *bach*, bloodless old turnip though he is, loves Maria. Can Maria help it? The idea is too ridiculous for discussion. So why am I to blame because Schnak, who is emotionally warped and retarded, gets silly notions about me? My beauty has been a large part of my success as an actor, and I tell you I'm bloody sick of it. That's why I want to get out of acting and into directing. I will not be sighed at and lallygagged over by audiences of hungry females. I have too keen an intelligence to value such admiration, which is simply aroused by the Livery of Hell — my physical appearance. I am close to middle age, and my beauty is giving way to a ravaged distinction. I have a gammy leg. So perhaps I can look forward to the remainder of my life in peace."

"I wouldn't count on that, Geraint," said Arthur. "You must bear your cross. Even if your looks are going, the chemistry is bubbling away as merrily as ever. But we're wandering from the point. The point is Schnak. What are you going to do about Schnak?"

"Why must I do anything about her? I'm not going to encourage her, if that's what you have in mind. I can't abide the shrimp. It isn't just that she's ugly to look at. Her voice goes through me like a rusty saw, and her impoverished vocabulary grates on me unbearably. Even if I were willing to forgo beauty, I simply must have the luxury of language. It isn't just that she looks ugly. She sounds ugly, and I want none of her."

"You make a terrible fuss about voices, Geraint," said Maria.

"Because they are terribly important, and usually neglected. Listen to you, Maria; music every time you open your lips. But most women don't even know that's possible. It is one of the three great marks of beauty. It totally changes the face. If Medusa speaks like a goddess, you can't tell her from Minerva."

"Very Welsh, Geraint," said Dulcy.

"And none the worse for that, I suppose?" said Geraint.

"There, my dumpling, that's enough," said Maria, and putting little David over her shoulder she patted his back gently. The child gave a mighty belch, extraordinary for his age.

"That boy is obviously going to grow up to be a sailor," said Arthur.

"Or a great lord of finance, like his daddy," said Maria. "Will you call Nanny, darling?"

When Nanny came she was not the stout, red-faced figure of stereotype, but a girl in her early twenties, smart in a blue uniform; David was her first charge.

"Come on, my lambie," she said, in a Scottish voice that made Geraint glance at her approvingly. "Time for bed."

She took the child over her shoulder, and this time David gave a long, reflective fart. "That's the boy," said Nanny.

"David has more sense than the lot of you," said Geraint. "He has summed up this whole argument in a masterly blast. Let's hear no more of it."

"Oh, but we must," said Maria. "You can't get out of it. Even if you didn't encourage Schnak, you must comfort her. The logic is clear, but it would take too long to spell it out."

"I'll throw up the show, first," said Geraint, and, dragging himself from under the heavy cover, he stamped out of the room. He avoided the cliché of slamming the door.

The others chewed over the rights and wrongs of the situation for quite a long time, until Darcourt fell asleep. It was midnight when they went to their own quarters. The big motel was full of people associated with *Arthur* in one way or another, and Albert Greenlaw insisted on calling it Camelot. Was there a lot of gossip at Camelot about Lancelot and Elaine? Malory doesn't say.

(7)

GERAINT WAS AT THE HOSPITAL the next day, as soon as rules permitted. Schnak was in a room for two, but by good luck the other bed was empty. She sat up in bed, wan and bedraggled, in a hospital gown that had once been blue and was now a poor grey, eating a bowl of orange Jell-O, washed down with an eggnog.

"You see how it is, old girl," said Geraint. "Just one of those unlucky things. Neither of us to blame. The working of Fate."

"I've been a selfish shit and embarrassed everybody," said Schnak. Tears did nothing to improve her looks.

"No, you haven't and you aren't. And I wish you'd take a vow to stop saying 'shit' all the time; talk shit and your life will be shit."

"My life is shit. Everything goes contrary with me."

"Mrs. Gummidge!"

"Who's Mrs. Gummidge?"

"If you're a good girl and get well soon I'll lend you the book."

"Oh, somebody in a book! All you people like Nilla and the Cornishes and that man Darcourt seem to live out of books. As if everything was in books!"

"Well, Schnak, just about everything *is* in books. No, that's wrong. We recognize in books what we've met in life. But if you'd read a few books you wouldn't have to meet everything as if it had never happened before, and take every blow right on the chin. You'd see a few things coming. About love, for instance. You thought you loved me."

Schnak gave a painful howl.

"All right then, you think you love me now. Come on, Schnak, say it. Say, 'I love you, Geraint.'"

Another howl.

"Come on. Out with it! Say it, Schnak."

"I'd die first."

"Look, Schnak, that's what comes of building your vocabulary on words like 'shit'. Great words choke you. If you can't say love, you can't feel love."

"Yes I can!"

"Then say so!"

"I'm going to be sick."

"Good. Here's a basin. I'll hold your head. Up she comes!

Hmm — doesn't look too bad, for what you've been doing to yourself. Almost as good as new. I'll just put this down the john, then you have a sip of water and we'll go on."

"Leave me alone!"

"I will not leave you alone! You've got to whoop up more than that eggnog if you're to be really well. Let me wipe your mouth. Now we'll try again: say, 'I love you, Geraint.' "

The defeated Schnak buried her face in her pillow, but among the sobs she managed to whisper, "I love you."

"That's my brave girl! Now look at me, and I'll sponge your eyes. I'm your friend, you know, but I don't love you — not the way you think you love me. Oh, my dear old Schnak, don't think I don't understand! We've all had these awful hopeless passions, and they hurt like hell. But if we were romantic lovers, the kind you're thinking of, do you suppose I'd hold your head while you puked, and mop your face, and try to make you see reason? The kind of love you're dreaming about takes place on mossy banks, amid the scent of flowers and the song of birds. Or else in luxurious chambers, where you loll on a *chaise longue*, and I take off your clothes very slowly until we melt into a union of intolerable sweetness, and not a giggle or a really kind word spoken the whole time. It's the giggles and the kind words that you need for the long voyage."

"I feel like a fool!"

"Then you're quite wrong. You're not a fool, and only a fool would think you were. You're an artist, Schnak. Maybe a very good one. Romantic Art — which is what's kept you busy since last autumn — is feeling, shaped by technique. You've got bags of technique. It's feeling that kills you."

"If you grew up like I grew up, you'd hate the word feeling."

"I grew up in a boiling tank of feeling. All tied up, somehow, with religion. When I said I was going to be an actor my parents raved as if they'd seen me in Hell already. But my dad was a fine actor — a pulpit actor. And my mam was Sarah Bernhardt twenty-four hours a day. They poured it all into the chapel, of course. But I wanted a bigger stage than that, because I had an idea of God, you see, and my God showed himself in art. I couldn't trap God in the chapel. An artist doesn't want to trap God; he wants to live and breathe God, and damned hard work it is, stumbling and falling."

"I hate God."

"Good for you! You don't say, 'There is no God,' like a fool; you say you hate Him. But Schnak — you won't like this, but you have to know — God doesn't hate you. He's made you special. When Nilla is being confidential she hints that you may be really special. So think of it this way: give God His chance. Of course He'll take it anyway, but it's easier for you if you don't kick and scream."

"How can anybody live God?"

"By living as well as they can with themselves. It doesn't always look very well to the bystanders. Truth to yourself, I suppose you'd call it. Following your nose. But don't expect me to explain. My dad was the explainer. He could go on about living in God's light till your head swam. Duw, he was a fine preacher! A true God-intoxicated man. But he thought God had one, single, unwinking light for everybody, and that was where he and I fell out."

"Now that I've said what you made me say — don't you say anything?"

"Yes. I say it won't do. Suppose I took you up on it, and we had an affair, you loving and me using you as long as it lasted — which wouldn't be long. It would be a cheat. I haven't time or inclination for that, and when it finished you would be bitter, and you're quite bitter enough already. What about Gunilla? Did you love her?"

"It wasn't the same."

"No love ever is the same as any other. The lucky ones get the big thing. You know — 'The silver link, the silken tie' —

but it's not common. That's one of the big mistakes, you know — that everybody loves in the same way and that everybody may have a great love. You might as well say that everybody can compose a great symphony. A lot of love is misery; bad weather punctuated by occasional flashes of sunlight. Look at this opera we're busy with; the love in it is pretty rough. It's not the best of Arthur's life, or Lancelot's, or Guenevere's."

"It's the best of Elaine's."

"Elaine wasn't a gifted musician, so don't try that on. She had your trouble, though. 'Fantasy's hot fire, / Whose wishes, soon as granted, fly.' You set those words to some very good music. Didn't you learn anything from them? Schnak, if you and I set out on a love affair, you'd have had enough of it in two weeks."

"Because I'm ugly! Because my looks make everybody sick! It isn't fair! It's a curse! That Cornish bitch, and Nilla and Dulcy all look great and they can do anything with you, or any man! I'll kill myself!"

"No, you won't. You've got other fish to fry. But truth's truth, Schnak; you're no beauty queen and that's just something you have to put up with, and it isn't the worst affliction, let me tell you. What do you suppose Nilla looked like at your age? A big gawk, I'll bet. Now she's marvellous. When you're her age, you'll be totally different. Success will have given you a new look. You'll be a kind of distinguished goblin, I expect."

Schnak howled again, and hid her face in the pillows.

"I'm sorry if that hurt your feelings, but you see, Schnak old girl, I'm under considerable stress myself. Everybody says I have to talk to you, and be nice to you, though I protest I hadn't an inkling of the way you felt about me, and I won't take any responsibility. I can't run the risk of feeding your flame, and making things worse. So I'm talking entirely against my inclination. You know how I am; I love to talk and talk as gaudily as I can, just for the pleasure it gives me. But with you, I'm trying to speak on oath, you see. Not a word I don't truly mean. If I let myself go, I could rave on about the Livery of Hell, and the demon's dunghill, and all the rest of it. Welsh rhetoric is part of me, and my curse is that the world is full of literal-minded morlocks who don't understand, and think I'm a crook because their tongues are wrapped in burlap and mine is hinged with gold. I've been as honest as I know how. You see, don't you?"

"I guess so."

"Good. Now I must go. A million things to attend to. Get well as fast as you can; we want you on the first night, and that's the day after tomorrow. And — Schnak, here's a kiss. Not a romantic one, or a brotherly one, God forbid! but a friendly one. Fellow artists — isn't that it?"

He was gone. Schnak dozed and thought, and dozed and thought, and when Gunilla came to see her late in the afternoon, she was decidedly better.

"It must have cost him a good deal to talk like that," said Gunilla, when Schnak had given a version of what Geraint had said. "Lots of so-called lovers wouldn't have been as direct with you, Hulda. It isn't easy to be like Geraint."

(8)

IT WAS THE FINAL DRESS PARADE, on the Friday afternoon preceding the final dress rehearsal, which was to take place the same night. In Row G of the theatre sat a little group: Geraint Powell the dominant figure, with Dulcy Ringgold as his first lieutenant and Waldo Harris on his other side; in front of them sat Gwen Larking, with both her assistants, and a gofer poised to run with messages too delicate to be shouted toward the stage. One by one the actors, dressed and made up for their roles, walked to centre stage, did little excursions to right and left, bowed, curtsied, drew weapons. Now and then

Geraint shouted some request to them; when they replied they shaded their eyes against the stage light, to see him if they could. Geraint whispered comments to Dulcy, who made notes, or explained, and occasionally expostulated if he wanted something that could not be managed in the time that was left before the opening.

A queer moment, thought Darcourt, who sat further back, by himself. The moment when all that is important is how the singer looks, not how he sings; the moment when everything that can be done to make the singers look like the people they represent has been done, and whatever has not been achieved must be accepted. A moment when inexplicable transformations take place.

The two black Knights, for instance, Greenlaw and LeMoyne, who looked superb in armour and the turbans Dulcy had given them to mark them as men of the East. But Wilson Tinney, as Gareth Beaumains, simply looked dumpy, although he was not an ill-looking man in his ordinary dress. His legs were too short. When he appeared without his armour he looked like a kewpie doll in his short robe. He had made himself up with very red cheeks, doubtless to suggest a life of adventure on horseback, but the effect was merely doll-like. In his robes as Merlin, Oliver Twentyman was convincingly magical, because his legs were long; he loved dressing up, and was enjoying himself. Giles Shippen, the Lancelot, looked less like a heart-breaker in costume than out of it; he was a reasonable figure, but he had Tenor written all over him, and his big chest made him look shorter than he really was.

"Did you put lifts in his shoes?" hissed Geraint to Dulcy.

"As much as I dared, without putting him in surgical boots," said she; "he just doesn't look like much whatever you do."

"Nobody will believe a woman would leave Holzknecht for him. Hans looks magnificent."

"Every inch a ruler," said Dulcy; "but everybody knows women have funny tastes. Nothing to be done, I'm afraid, Geraint."

As was to be expected, Nutcombe Puckler had a great deal to say, and was full of complaint. "Geraint, I simply can't hear in this thing," he said. He was referring to his camail, a headpiece of chain armour that hung down from his fool's bonnet to his shoulders, over his ears. "If I can't hear, I may make a false entrance and screw up. Can't something be done?"

"The effect is splendid, Nutty. You look the perfection of a merry warrior. Dulcy will put some pads under it, just over your ears, and you'll be all right."

"It fidgets me," said Nutty. "I can't bear to have my ears covered on the stage."

"Nutty, you're far too much of a pro to let a little thing bother you," said Geraint. "Give it a try tonight and if it really doesn't work, we'll find another way."

"Like hell we will," murmured Dulcy, making a note.

Among the women the assumption of costume brought about similar changes in emphasis. As Queen Guenevere, Donalda Roche looked handsome, but very much a woman of the present day, whereas Marta Ullman, as the Lady Elaine, looked so much a creature of the Middle Ages, and so infinitely desirable, that none of the men could take their eyes off her. Clara Intrepidi, as Morgan Le Fay, looked an undoubted sorceress in her gown of changing colours and her dragon head-dress — but a sorceress who was a fugitive from some unidentified opera by Wagner. She was taller than any of the men except Holzknecht, and her appearance suggested that when she was at home she had a full suit of armour in her closet.

"Can't be helped," whispered Dulcy, "unless she consents to act on her knees, or sitting down all the time. Luckily she's

Arthur's sister; great height runs in the family. Look at it that way."

"Yes, but look at Panisi," said Geraint. "He's supposed to be her son, and Arthur's son as well. Surely a child of those two would be a giant?"

"Incest makes for funny-looking children," said Dulcy. "Use your imagination, Geraint. You did the casting, you know."

The ladies of the court were, upon the whole, a splendid group, except for Virginia Poole who, as the Lady Clarissant, looked like a woman with a grievance, as indeed she was, onstage and off. Dulcy had put some of the younger women in the *cotehardie*, a tight-fitting medieval bodice that showed off a fine bust to the utmost advantage.

"You've let your natural inclinations run away with you, haven't you, dear?" said Geraint.

"You bet I have. Look at Polly Graves; it would be a black sin to muffle up such a splendid pair of jugs. And Esther Moss; an evocation of the mystic East? A whiff of Baghdad in Camelot?"

"They didn't look quite that way in the designs."

"Don't fight your luck, Geraint. These girls are for the tired business man."

"And woman, dear. I'm not complaining. Just surprised. You never know what's under rehearsal clothes, do you?"

"Primrose Maybon looks good enough to eat with a silver spoon," said Waldo.

"Too bad the women look so much better than the men," said Gwen Larking. "But our sex does have its compensations, when we can show 'em off."

"Let's see you with your trains over the arm, girls," said Dulcy. "Left arm, Etain. That's the girl."

To Darcourt they all looked wonderful, even the nuisance Puckler. Dulcy had drawn heavily on Planché's *Encyclopaedia*, and she had obviously studied the work of Burne-Jones, but the result was all her own. If not all the singers looked as well as they should in their costumes, the total effect was superb, because of the way in which colours called to one another, not obviously but subtly, in every grouping. This was an element in the opera of which Darcourt, the greenhorn in the theatre, could have had no idea.

When every costume had been seen in its final form, and all the notes made and all the complaints heard, Geraint called: "Before we break, I want to rehearse the curtain calls. Stand by, will you." And when at last these tableaux had been arranged to his satisfaction — "And of course when that's over, you, Hans, go to stage right and bring on Nilla, who takes her bow, and then, Nilla, you beckon into the wings for Schnak. And Schnak, you must come on in full fig — the fullest fig you possess — and Nilla takes your hand and you curtsy."

"I what?"

"You curtsy. You mayn't bow; not old enough. If you don't know what a curtsy is, get somebody to show you. Thank you. That's all for now. I want to see all the animal-handlers backstage right away, please."

"But why me?" said Darcourt to an unwontedly pleading Schnak, who had sidled up to him with her request when the rehearsal was over, and the singers had gone to their dressing-rooms.

"You know what a curtsy is, don't you?"

"I think so. But get one of the women to show you. It's their kind of thing."

"I don't want to. They hate me. They'd triumph over me."

"Nonsense, Schnak. They don't hate you. The younger ones are probably afraid of you, because you're so clever."

"Please, Simon. Be a good guy, eh?"

It was the first time she had ever called him Simon, and Darcourt, whose heart was not of stone, could not say no.

"All right. Here's a nice quiet place. So far as I can remember from my dancing-school days, it goes like this."

They had found a dark nook backstage, near the scene-painters' dock.

"First of all, you must stand up straight. You tend to slump, Schnak, and it won't do if you're going to curtsy. Then, slowly and with dignity, you sweep your right leg behind your left, and fit the knee lightly into the left leg joint. Then you descend, gently and slowly as if you were going down in an elevator, and when you get to the bottom, bend your head forward, from the neck. Keep your back straight all the time. It's not a cringe; it's an acknowledgement of an obligation. Now watch me."

Rather stiffly, and with perhaps too much of the dowager in his manner, Darcourt curtsied. Schnak had a try and fell over sideways.

"It isn't easy. And it's very characteristic, you know. Don't be pert, but don't be grandiose, either. You are a great artist, acknowledging the applause of your audience. You know you are their superior in art, but they are your patrons, and they expect the high courtesy of an artist. Try again."

Schnak tried again. This time she did not topple.

"What the hell do I do with my hands?"

"Keep them where your lap would be if you were sitting down. Some people wave the right hand to the side in a sweeping gesture, but that's a bit stagy and too advanced for your age. You're getting it. Try again. And again. Keep your head straight and look at the audience; only bow when you're all the way down. Again. Come on. You're getting it."

Darcourt curtsied repeatedly to Schnak, and Schnak curtsied to Darcourt. They bobbed up and down, facing one another, somewhat like a pair of heraldic animals on either side of a coat of arms; Darcourt's knees were beginning to whimper, but Schnak was learning one of the minor accomplishments of a public performer.

From above them came a sharp burst of applause, and a cry of Bravo. They looked up; suspended well above them, on the painting-bridge, were three or four stage-hands and Dulcy Ringgold, watching with undisguised delight.

Darcourt was too old and too wily to be disconcerted. He kissed his hand to the unexpected audience. But Schnak had fled to her dressing-room, hot with shame. She had much to learn.

(9)

"WE HEAR MARVELLOUS REPORTS about you, Simon," said Maria as she and Arthur sat with Darcourt in the favourite restaurant. "Dulcy says it was heart-lifting to see you teaching Schnak to curtsy. She says you were *très grande dame.*"

"Somebody had to do it," said Simon, "and so few women these days are up to their job as females. I think of starting a small school to teach girls the arts of enchantment. They certainly won't learn anything from their liberated sisters."

"We live in the age of the sweat-shirt and the jeans," said Arthur. "Charm and manners are out. But they'll come back. They always do. Look at the French Revolution: in a generation or two the French were all hopping around like fleas, bowing and scraping to Napoleon. People love manners, really. They admit you to one or another of a dozen secret societies."

"Schnak must look as well as possible when she takes her bow," said Darcourt. "Did I tell you I had a phone call from Clem Hollier? He's going to be here tomorrow night, and he wanted to know whether he should wear dinner clothes or tails. For taking his bow, you understand."

"Is Clem taking a bow?" said Maria. "Whatever for?"

"You may well ask. But his name appears on the program as one of the concocters of the libretto, and he seems to think that a clamorous audience will demand his appearance."

"But did he do anything?"

"Not a damned thing. Not even as much as Penny, who simply bitched and found fault and was cross because I wouldn't tell her where the best lines came from. But Penny is coming, in full fig, and I shouldn't be surprised if she expects to take a bow, too."

"Are you taking a bow, Simon?"

"I haven't been asked, and upon the whole I think not. Nobody loves a librettist. The audience wouldn't know who I was."

"You can lurk in the shadows with us."

"Oh, don't be bitter, Arthur," said Maria. And to Darcourt, "He's rather touchy because we've been cold-shouldered so much during the last few weeks."

"During the last year," said Arthur. "We've done everything we were asked, and rather more. We've certainly footed all the bills, and they aren't trivial. But if we turn up at a rehearsal and cling to the walls, Geraint looks at us as if we were intruders, and the cast glare, or smile sweetly like old Twentyman, who seems to think it's his job to spread sweetness and light even in the humblest places."

"Don't be hurt, darling. Or at least, don't show it. I expect we're on the program, somewhere."

This was a moment Darcourt had been dreading. "There was a slip-up," he said; "quite by accident the acknowledgement of the help of the Cornish Foundation was left off the program. Easily explained. The Festival generally arranges those things through its own administration, you see, and as this was a sort of special production, not quite of the Festival, though under its umbrella, there was an oversight. I didn't see a proof till this afternoon. But don't worry. Slips are being stuffed into every program at this moment, with the proper acknowledgement on it."

"Typewritten, I suppose?"

"No, no; one of those wonderful modern multilith processes."

"Same thing."

"An understandable error."

"Completely understandable, in the light of everything else that connects the Cornish Foundation with this opera. I don't know why they bother. Who gives a damn, so long as the show goes on?"

"Oh, please, Arthur, the Festival is very much aware of its benefactors."

"I suppose the benefactors take care, in the most unmistakable way, that it is so. We haven't been aggressive enough, that's the answer. Next time we must take care to push a little harder. We must learn the art of benefaction, though I must say I'm not looking forward to it."

"You thought of yourself as a patron in the old sense, the nineteenth-century sense. Not surprising, when one thinks of the nature of this opera. But better times will come. More was lost at Mohacs Field."

Arthur was somewhat appeased, but not entirely.

"I'm sorry you feel slighted, Arthur, but I assure you — no slight was intended."

"Simon, let me explain. You mustn't think Arthur is soreheaded, or pouty. That simply isn't in his nature. But he — I should say we — thought of ourselves as impresarios, encouraging and fostering and doing all that sort of thing. Like Diaghilev, you know. Well, not really like Diaghilev. He was one of a kind. But something along those lines. You've seen how it was. Nary a foster or an encourage have we been permitted. Nobody wants to talk to us. So we've played it Geraint's way, and everybody else's way. But we've been surprised and a little bit wistful."

"You've been as good as gold," said Darcourt.

"Exactly!" said Arthur. "That's precisely what we've been. As good as gold. We've been the gold at the bottom of the whole thing."

"Gold isn't really a bad part to play," said Darcourt. "You've always had it, Arthur, so you don't know how other people see it. It's no use talking about Diaghilev; he never had a red cent. Always cadging for money from people like you. You and Maria are just gold — pure gold. You are a very rich couple, and you have genius with money, but there are things about gold you don't know. Haven't you any notion of the jealousy and envy mixed with downright, barefaced, reluctant worship gold creates? You've put your soul into gold, Arthur, and you have to take the bitter with the sweet."

"Simon, that is positively the nastiest, ugliest thing you've ever said! My soul into gold! I didn't ask to be born rich, and if I have a talent for money it doesn't mean I put money above everything! Have you missed the fact that Maria and I have a real, gigantic, and mostly unselfish passion for the arts and we want to create something with our money? I'll go further — no, shut up, Maria, I'm going to speak my mind — we want to be artists so far as we can, and furthermore we want to do something with Uncle Frank's money that he would really have thought worthy. And we're treated like money-bags. Bloody, insensitive, know-nothing money-bags! Not fit to mix on equal terms with shit-bags like Nutty Puckler and that self-delighted sorehead Virginia Poole! At the first dress rehearsal I was standing in the wings, keeping my mouth shut, and I was shushed — shushed, I tell you — by one of those damned gofers when Albert Greenlaw was snickering and whispering, as he always is! I asked the kid what ailed her, and she hissed, 'There's an examination going on, you know!' As if I hadn't known about the examination for months!"

"Yes, Arthur. Yes, yes, yes. But let me explain. When art is in the air, everybody has to eat a lot of dirt, and forget about it: When I said you have put your soul into gold I was simply talking about the nature of reality."

"And my reality is gold? Is that it?"

"Yes, that's it. But not the way you think. Do please listen and don't flare up all the time. It's the soul, you see. The soul can't just exist as a sort of gas that makes us noble when we let it. The soul is something else: we have to lodge our souls somewhere and people project their souls, their energy, their best hopes — call it what you like — onto something. The two great carriers of the soul are money and sex. There are lots of others: power, or security (that's a bad one), and of course art — and that's a good one. Look at poor old Geraint. He wants to project his soul on art, and because he's a very good man it murders him when all kinds of people think he must project it on sex, because he's handsome and has indefinable attraction for both men and women. If he simply went in for sex he could be an absolute bastard, with his advantages. But art can't live without gold. Romantics pretend it can, but they're wrong. They snub gold, as they've snubbed you, but in their hearts they know what's what. Gold is one of the great realities, and like all reality it isn't all wine and roses. It's the stuff of life, and life can be a bugger. Look at your Uncle Frank; his reality was art, but art gave him more misery than joy. Why do you suppose he became such a grubby old miser in his last years? He was trying to change his soul from a thing of art to a thing of money, and it didn't work. And you and Maria are sitting on the heap he piled up in that attempt. You're doing a fine thing, trying to change the heap back into art again, but you mustn't be surprised if sometimes it brings you heartbreak."

"What have you projected your soul on, Simon?" said Maria. Arthur needed time to think.

"I used to think it was religion. That was why I became a priest. But the religion the world wanted from me didn't work, and it was killing me. Not physically, but spiritually.

The world is full of priests who have been killed by religion, and can't, or won't, escape. So I tried scholarship, and that worked pretty well."

"You used to tell us in class, 'The striving for wisdom is the second paradise of the world,'" said Maria. "And I believed you. I believe it still. Paracelsus said that."

"Indeed he did, the good, misunderstood man. So I took to scholarship. Or returned to it, I suppose I should say."

"And it has served you well? Perhaps I should say you have served it well?"

"The funny thing is, the deeper I got into it, the more it began to resemble religion. The real religion, I mean. The intense yielding to what is most significant, but not always most apparent, in life. Some people find it in the Church, but I didn't. I found it in some damned queer places."

"So have I, Simon. I'm still trying. Will go on trying. It's the only way for people like us. But —

> *The flesche is brukle, the Fiend is slee*
> *Timor mortis conturbat me*

That's how it is, isn't it?"

"Not for you, Maria. You're far too young to talk about the fear of death. But you're right about the Flesh and the Fiend, even if it makes you sound like Geraint."

"I think of that sometimes, when I look at little David."

"No, no," said Arthur. "That's all over. Forget about it. The child wipes all that out."

"There speaks the real Arthur," said Darcourt, and raised his glass. "Here's to David!"

"I'm sorry I whined," said Arthur.

"You didn't whine — not really whine. You just let loose some wholly understandable indignation. Anyway, we all have a right to a good whine, now and then. Clears the mind. Cleanses the stuffed bosom of that perilous stuff that weighs upon the heart — and all that."

"Shakespeare," said Arthur. "For once I recognize one of your quotations, Simon."

"How one comes to depend on Shakespeare," said Maria. " '*What potions have I drunk of Siren tears* —' Remember that one?"

" '*So I return rebuked to my content,*
And gain by ill thrice more than I have spent,' "

said Darcourt. "Yes; that's a good one. Puts it very concisely."

"Thrice more than I have spent. Or rather, thrice more than Uncle Frank has spent," said Arthur. "I suppose you're right, Simon. I do think a lot about gold. Somebody must. But that doesn't mean I'm Kater Murr. Simon, we've been turning over in our minds that scheme you were talking about a while ago. That would be more in Uncle Frank's line, don't you think?"

"I wouldn't have mentioned it, otherwise," said Darcourt.

"You said you thought the New York people would listen to an offer."

"If it were put the right way. I think they would appeal to you, Arthur. Collectors, connoisseurs, but of course they don't want to be made to look foolish. Not like people who have been in any way associated with a fake. They're not Kater Murr, either. If it came out that they had been cherishing a picture which was just a simple, barefaced fake it wouldn't do them any good, either in the art world, or in the world of business."

"What is their business?"

"Prince Max is the head of an importing company that brings vast quantities of wine to this continent. Good wine. No cheap schlock, adulterated with Algerian piss. No fakes, in fact. I've seen some of his things on your table. Probably you didn't notice the motto on the coat of arms on the bottles: 'Thou shalt perish ere I perish'."

"Good motto for wine."

"Yes, but the motto is a family motto, and it means Don't try to get the better of me, or you'll wish you hadn't."

"I've met some of those in business."

"But you must bear in mind that the Princess is a business woman, too. Cosmetics, in the most distinguished possible way."

"What's that to do with it?"

"Dear Arthur, it means simply putting the best face on things. That's what they'll want to do."

"So you think they'll want a whopping price?"

"This is an age of whopping prices for pictures."

"Even fakes?"

"Arthur, I may be brought to crowning you with this bottle — which isn't one of Prince Max's, by the way. How often do I have to tell you that the picture isn't a fake, was never meant to be a fake, and is in fact a picture of the most extraordinary and unique significance?"

"I know. I've heard all you've said about it. But who will convince the world of it?"

"I will, of course. You're forgetting my book."

"Simon, I don't want to be a brute, but how many people will read your book?"

"If you follow my suggestion, hundreds of thousands of people will read it, because it will explain Francis Cornish's life as a great artistic adventure. And a very Canadian sort of adventure, what's more."

"I don't see this country as a land hotching with artistic adventure, or deep concern about the soul, and if you do, I think you're off your head."

"I do, and I'm not off my head. I sometimes think I'm ahead of my time. You haven't read my book. It isn't finished, of course, and how it ends hangs entirely on the decision you make. The ending can be fantastic, in both the literal and the colloquial meanings of the word. You don't know what a good long look at your uncle's life brings to the surface, in a mind like mine. You've got to trust me, and in this sort of thing you don't trust me, Arthur, because you're afraid to trust yourself."

"I trusted myself in this opera venture. I hustled the Foundation into doing something that hasn't worked out."

"You don't know if it has worked out, and you won't, until long after tomorrow night. You have the amateur's notion that a first performance tells the whole story about a stage piece. Did you know the St. Louis people are already interested in *Arthur of Britain*? If the opera doesn't cause a stir here, it may very well do so there. And in other places. Of course, you hustled us into this job. And now you think it was just the beginning of your mumps. But great achievements have sprung from stranger things than a dose of mumps."

"All right. Let us proceed. With caution. I suppose I'd better take over, and see these New York people."

"And I suppose you'd better do nothing of the sort," said Maria. "You leave it to Simon. He's a downy old bird."

"Maria, you are beginning to sound like a wife."

"The best wife you'll ever have," said Maria.

"True. Very true, my darling. By the way, I'm thinking of calling you Sweetness, in future."

Maria put out her tongue at him.

"Before you degenerate into embarrassing public connubiality," said Darcourt, "let me call your attention to the fact that the dress rehearsal must now have almost completed the first act of this opera Arthur has decided to hate. We'd better get over to the theatre, and be slighted and neglected, if that's the way it goes. As for this other thing, shall I go ahead?"

"Yes, Simon, you go ahead," said Maria.

Arthur, characteristically, was calling for the bill.

(10)

IT IS THE FIRST NIGHT of *Arthur of Britain*.

Gwen Larking speaks through the intercom to all dressing-rooms and the Green Room: "Ladies and gentlemen, this is your half-hour call. Half an hour till curtain, please."

The early birds have been ready long since. In his dressing-room Oliver Twentyman lies in his reclining-chair. He is made up and dressed, except for his magician's gown, which hangs ready to put on. His dresser has tactfully left him alone, to compose himself. Will this be his last appearance? Who can say? Certainly not Oliver Twentyman, who will go on appearing in operas as long as directors and conductors want him — and they still want him. But this will probably be his last creation of a new role; nobody has ever sung Merlin in *Arthur of Britain* before, and he intends to give the audience something to remember. The critics, too, those chroniclers of operatic history, upon the whole so much more reliable than their brethren who deal with the theatre. When Oliver Twentyman is no more, they will say that Merlin, undertaken when he was already over eighty, was the best thing he had done since he sang Oberon in Britten's *Dream*. He liked being old — and still a great artist. Age, linked with achievement, was a splendid crown to life, and took the sting from death.

> . . . an old age, serene and bright,
> And lovely as a Lapland night,
> Shall lead thee to thy grave.

Wordsworth knew what he was talking about. Oliver Twentyman murmured the words two or three times, like a prayer. He was a praying sort of man, and often his prayers took the form of quotations.

Onstage Waldo Harris was having the last, he hoped, of

many sessions with Hans Holzknecht about Hair on the Floor. Many years ago — Holzknecht would not say how many, nor would he identify the opera house (though it was a great one) — he had found, during the last act of *Boris Godunov*, that he was choking. Choking so that he could scarcely utter. Something had invaded his throat and was strangling him. Instead of singing he was on the verge of throwing up. It was a situation in which the best of the artist must unite with the best of the man to overcome a difficulty all the greater because it could not be identified. Somehow — there were times when he thought it must have been Divine intervention — he had sung his way — sung well and truly, though in agony — to the end of the act and then, when the curtain was down, he had rushed to his dressing-room, and called for the theatre doctor, who, with a forceps, had removed from his throat a twenty-inch human hair! From a wig? From some shedding soprano in the chorus in an earlier scene? Whatever the source, there it was, a hair of great length which had, in its situation, behaved with the malignance of an animate thing! In one of his great intakes of breath while lying, as the distraught Tsar, on the floor, he had sucked up that hair, and he had it yet, preserved in a plastic bag, which he showed to every stage management in every theatre where he appeared, as a warning of what could happen if the stage were not properly swept, not once, but at every possible time, during a performance. He did not want to be a nuisance, nor did he wish to appear neurotic, but a singer meets perils of which the public knows nothing, and he begged — begged with all the authority of his place in the company — that he might have the assurance of Waldo Harris that the stage would be properly swept whenever the curtain was down. Which assurance Waldo gave, sympathetic, but also wishing that Holzknecht would accept one positive answer, and shut up about hairs on the stage.

In the Prompt Corner, Gwen Larking was fussing. She would not have thought of it as fussing, but as she was redoing and perfecting things that had already been done, and done to perfection, there is no other word for it. Gwen was, in herself, the perfection of a Stage Manager, which meant that she was impeccable in her attention to detail, alert for any mishap and capable of meeting it, and a monument of assurance to nervous artists. And the greatest fusser of them all, beneath an impassive exterior.

She was dressed for her work in an expensive pant-suit, and a blouse of deceptive simplicity. She had made her two assistants and the three gofers dress themselves similarly, as near as it was in their destiny to come to her own stripped-down elegance. Art deserves respect, and respect is mirrored in proper dress. Let those members of the audience who so wished appear in the theatre looking as if they had just come from mucking out the cowshed; it was up to the stage crew to dress as if they were about important work. The gofers had to be warned about bangles and chains that jingled; of course such things could not be heard on the stage but they might be distracting in the wings.

The Prompt Corner was called so because of tradition; nobody could possibly have prompted anyone onstage from it. Indeed, the stage could not be seen from it, except fleetingly. But over Gwen Larking's desk, which looked like the conductor's own, lay a full score of the opera, in which every detail of the production was recorded, for instant reference. This was what Al Crane would have given an ear to get his hands on, but Gwen guarded it jealously, just as she guarded the conductor's full score, which lived in the safe in Waldo Harris's office.

Gwen Larking twisted the lucky ring on the fourth finger of her left hand. Nothing would have persuaded her to admit that it was a lucky ring. She was a Stage Manager, devoted to certainty, not luck. But it was in truth a lucky ring, a Renaissance cameo, a gift from a former lover, and all the gofers knew it, and had somewhere found lucky rings of their own, for Gwen was their ideal.

Darcourt did not hear the half-hour call, because he was in the favourite restaurant, entertaining two eminent critics. Arthur and Maria had refused to do anything of the sort, but the line between eminent critic from New York and distinguished guest is so fine that Darcourt had decided he had better give them dinner. Very, very eminent critics can eat and drink any amount, without in the least compromising their impartiality of opinion, and have indeed been known to bite the hand that has fed them, without noticing. Darcourt was aware of this, but thought a modest dinner would give him a chance to provide the critics with some information.

In the case of Claude Applegarth, who was undoubtedly the most popular and widely read of New York critics, information was cast on stony ground, for Mr. Applegarth had been a critic of the theatre arts too long to be concerned with the background of anything. The wisecrack was his speciality; that was what his readers expected of him and was he not, after all, himself a popular entertainer? He would not have attended *Arthur* if it had not been that his annual visit to the Shakespearean portion of the Festival coincided with this opening so closely that it could not decently be neglected. Not that opera was his thing, at all; it was in the criticism of musicals that he was felt as a great and usually blighting influence.

It was a different matter with Robin Adair, whose word on opera was — well, not law, but rather the judgement of the Recording Angel. A notable musicologist, a translator of libretti, a man of formidable culture, and — rarest attribute of all — a real lover of opera, he was avid for any information Darcourt could give him, and questioned like a cross-examiner.

"The details I have received are just vague enough to provoke a thousand questions," he said. "The libretto, for instance. If Hoffmann had gone no further than sketching the work, how much of a libretto existed? Had Planché any hand in it? I hope not. He ruined *Oberon* with his jokey nonsense. Is there a coherent libretto?"

"I gather from Dr. Dahl-Soot that the word 'sketch' is somewhat too dismissive for what Hoffmann left in the way of music. There was a good deal of it, all of which is in the score. The basis of it, in fact."

"Yes, but the libretto. It can't have been finished. Who has done it?"

"As you will see from the program, I have."

"Ah? And on what basis? Original work of your own? You see, of course, that if this is to be considered as the completion of a work by Hoffmann — dead in, when was it, 1822? — the libretto is of greatest importance. There must be a congruity of style not at all easy to achieve. Do you think you have managed that?"

"Not really for me to say," said Darcourt. "But I may tell you this: by far the greatest part of the libretto is either drawn exactly from, or slightly adapted from, the work of a poet of undoubted genius who was Hoffmann's contemporary and devout co-religionist in romanticism."

"And his name is — ?"

"I am sure that a man of your reputation for out-of-the-way scholarship will recognize his hand at once."

"A puzzle? How delightful! I love a puzzle. I shall see you afterward and give you my guess, and you must say if I am right."

"Do you think we might have just a little more champagne?" said Mr. Applegarth. "Now listen: whoever wrote the bloody words, there has never been a good play or musical about King Arthur. Look at *Camelot*. A turkey."

"A fairly tough old bird by now," said Mr. Adair.

"Nevertheless, a turkey. I said it then and I say it now. A turkey."

"Tell me something about this Cornish Foundation," said Mr. Adair. "I understand it's a man and a woman with a dummy board. They have ambitious ideas about patronage."

"They can't have enough money for anything really big," said Mr. Applegarth, who now had a second bottle of champagne and was somewhat less morose. "The modern Medici! That's what they all want. Won't work in the modern world."

"Oh, surely fine things have been done by patrons even during this year," said Mr. Adair.

"Listen," said Mr. Applegarth. "Patronage only worked when artists were humble. Some of 'em wore livery. An art patron today is a victim. The artists will crucify him and mock him and caricature him and strip him naked, if he hasn't got the drop on them from the start. Only when the Medici or the Esterhazys had their heel on the artist's neck did it work. Admit artists to equality and the jig's up, because they don't believe in equality. Only in their own superiority. Sons of bitches!" he said, gloomily filling his glass.

"The Cornishes have tried very much to leave the artists to their own devices in this affair," said Darcourt. "I must admit they feel that they have been somewhat shouldered aside by the artists."

"You don't surprise me at all," said Mr. Applegarth.

"Ah, well — the artistic temperament. Not all sweetness and light," said Mr. Adair, rather as though he felt he had a foot in the artist's world.

"I see that it's half past six," said Darcourt. "Perhaps we should be getting to the theatre. Seven-o'clock curtain, you know."

"I hate these early curtains," said Mr. Applegarth. "They ruin dinner."

"Oh come along, Claude," said Mr. Adair. "It's for our

benefit you know. Early curtain so the critics can make their deadline."

"Not on a Saturday night," said Mr. Applegarth, who had passed from the morose, through the sardonic, to the combative stage of critical preparation. "Bloody *Arthur*. Why can't they leave him in his grave?"

"Nobody knows where his grave is," said Mr. Adair, Scottish fount of information as he was.

"It'll be on this stage, tonight," said Mr. Applegarth, obviously ready to assure that it should be so.

Gwen had called the quarter-hour. From the dressing-rooms could be heard the humming, the buzzing, now and then the full-throated vocalization, of singers getting their voices under command. In front of the curtain early birds among the audience — the kind of people who like lots of time to study their programs — could be heard arriving. Up and down the corridors among the dressing-rooms walked Hans Holzknecht, wishing the company good luck. "Hals und beinbruch!" he shouted, and if it was a man, he gave him a sharp knee in the rump.

In the wings, out of earshot of Gwen Larking, Albert Greenlaw was about his favourite sport of instructing the gofers in the lore and tradition of the theatre. They stood about him, devouring the fine Belgian chocolates they had been given earlier by Oliver Twentyman, who believed in first-night presents, especially to the humbler members of the company.

"I don't know if I ought to tell you," he said, "because it is not the thing little girls ought to know. But if you're *really* set on a stage career —"

"Oh yes, Albert. Be a sport. Tell us."

"Well then, honey-child, you ought to know about critics. There are some in the audience tonight who are of the cream of that very creamy cream. And you can tell those real ones from the fellows who are just from local papers by one infallible sign, and it is this." His voice sank to a whisper. "They never go to the john."

"Not during the show?" said the prettiest gofer.

"Not *ever*. From womb to tomb — not *ever*. Nobody has ever met a critic in the Men's, anywhere on this earth."

"Albert, that can't be," said a dubious gofer, but in a tone that betrayed that she very much wished it to be so, and thirsted for marvels.

"Would I kid you? Have you ever known me to kid you? I'll tell you something that will be invaluable to you when you are all happy wives and mothers — or maybe just mothers, in these carefree days. When your child is born, take a look right away at where its teeny-weeny exit ought to be. If it isn't there, honey, you've borne a critic."

"Albert, I don't believe it!"

"Fact. Medical fact. Imperforate anus, it's called, in medical circles. And it's the mark of the critic. The real, top-flight critic. They have two or three of them, pickled, in the medical museum at Johns Hopkins and there you can observe the phenomenon as plain as if it were labelled No Exit. The little fellows, they're like you and me; they have the normal disposal facilities. But not the biggies. No, no, no. Remember your Uncle Albert told you."

"They say Claude Applegarth is here tonight," said Schnak. She and Dr. Gunilla were in the small dressing-room reserved for the conductors. It was very close, for the Doctor was smoking one of her black cigars.

"Who is Claude Applegarth?" she asked.

"He's supposed to be the most influential critic in New York. And I suppose that means the world," said Schnak, who had all the Canadian awe of New York.

"I do not know his name," said the Doctor. "And I blow

my nose in his hair," she added. This was to encourage Schnak, who was trying to dissemble her terror. Gunilla would conduct in the pit tonight, of course, but Schnak was to be offstage conductor; when the Chorus sang in the wings, it was she who must direct them, taking her time from a monitor on which appeared a ghostly, grey Gunilla. She must do this with an unwieldy baton that was, in fact, a small red lamp on the end of a metal stick, and her beat, never elegant, became ridiculous when she waved what the Chorus called her fairy wand.

Conducting! Oh, conducting! Would she ever master it? Conduct the libretto, not just the score, Gunilla was always saying. Easy for Gunilla, tall, elegant, romantic figure. In the evening dress that Dulcy had rigged up for her, Schnak felt like a scarecrow. With a razor she had painfully hoicked the hair from her armpits, and now, in Dulcy's creation, they did not show. But they hurt. At this moment, Schnak would gladly have forgone any future as a public performer.

"Five minutes, please, ladies and gentlemen. Overture and beginners in five minutes." Gwen's voice, low and clear, came from the speaker on the wall.

"Perhaps you should go to your post," said the Doctor.

"I haven't anything until after the Overture."

"But I have," said the Doctor. "And I should like to be by myself."

Darcourt, standing in the foyer, saw that at the five-minute call, which he could not hear but which he knew was being given, a special group of people arrived, and quickly dispersed themselves into twos and threes. There was nothing positively disturbing about them, but they seemed somewhat overdressed for the occasion. Of course, many of the people who had already entered the theatre were in evening clothes — dinner suits and dinner frocks — but several of these men wore full dress and white ties that spoke of antiquity. The ladies tended to be dressed in plushy materials, well worn and somewhat sprung in the seat. One had a plume in her hair, and another sported a metal headpiece studded with impressive, but not totally convincing, gems. It was the Yerko Claque, and in the midst of them Yerko rose like a mountain in shirt and tie that had grown yellow with time, and a coat, the tails of which hung to his calves; beside him was Mamusia, and it was she who wore the paste jewels and kid gloves that had once been white; they reached well above her elbows. The group comported itself with a stateliness rarely seen on the North American continent, and certainly never in Stratford.

Yerko's eye met Darcourt's, without a spark of recognition.

Well, God help us, here we go, thought Darcourt, and went inside to claim his seat.

ARTHUR OF BRITAIN

AN OPERA IN THREE ACTS planned and sketched by E. T. A. HOFFMANN and completed from his notes by Hulda Schnakenburg under the direction of Dr. Gunilla Dahl-Soot.

CHARACTERS

King Arthur of Britain	Hans Holzknecht
Modred, the King's nephew	Gaetano Panisi
Sir Lancelot	Giles Shippen
Merlin	Oliver Twentyman
Sir Kay the Seneschal	George Sudlow
Sir Gawaine	Jean Morant
Sir Bedevere	Yuri Vollmer
Sir Gareth Beaumains	Wilson Tinney
Sir Lucas, Butler	Mark Horrebow
Sir Ulphius, Chamberlain	Charles Bland
Sir Dynadan	Mark Luppino
Sir Dagonet, the Fool	Nutcombe Puckler
Sir Pellinore	Albert Greenlaw
Sir Palomides	Vincent LeMoyne

Queen Guenevere	Donalda Roche
Morgan Le Fay, sister to the King	Clara Intrepidi
The Lady Elaine	Marta Ullmann
The Lady Clarissant	Virginia Poole

Ladies of the Court: Ada Boscawen, Lucia Pozzi, Margaret Calnan, Lucy-Ellen Osler, Appoline Graves, Etain O'Hara, Esther Moss, Miriam Downey, Hosanna Marks, Karen Edey, Minnie Sainsbury

Heralds: James Mitchell, Ulick Carman

Attendants: Bessie Louth, Jane Holland, Primrose Maybon, Noble Grandy, Ellis Cronyn, Eden Wigglesworth

ff   ff   ff   ff   ff   ff

Costumes and settings designed by Dulcy Ringgold, and executed in the Festival workshops.
Scenic Artist: Willy Grieve
Head Carpenter: Dicky Plaunt

ff   ff   ff   ff   ff   ff

Lighting Director: Waldo Harris
Stage Manager: Gwenllian Larking
Concert-Master: Otto Klafsky
Répétiteur and Harpsichordist: Watkin Bourke
Director: Geraint Powell
Conductor: Gunilla Dahl-Soot

ff   ff   ff   ff   ff   ff

The Libretto realized by Simon Darcourt, assisted by Penelope Raven and Clement Hollier.

The public relations people had done their job efficiently. The house was decently full and not with an audience of despair, recruited from nurses' residences and old folks' homes. Darcourt found himself sitting next to Clement Hollier; he reflected that he had never seen Hollier in evening dress before, and the learned man stank pungently of some spicy toilet water or after-shave. This may be hard to endure, thought Darcourt. But he could not ponder long on this, for the house lights dimmed, and Dr. Gunilla Dahl-Soot strode into the orchestra pit, shook hands with the concert-master, and bowed elegantly to the audience.

The audience responded eagerly. They had never seen anything like Gunilla, with her masculine good looks, her magnificent green tailcoat, and her ample white stock, and their expectations for the evening rose. The show, they felt, had begun.

Gunilla raised her baton, and the first heavy chords, stating the theme of Caliburn, were heard, and gave way to a firm but melancholy theme, the theme of Chivalry, which was developed for perhaps three minutes, until the point in the score marked by Letter D was reached; then the splendid red curtains swept upward and back, to disclose King Arthur and Merlin standing on the brink of the Enchanted Mere.

This was something for which the audience was wholly unprepared. Geraint, Waldo Harris, and Dulcy Ringgold had laboured faithfully to reproduce the stage dressing of the early years of the nineteenth century — the stage as Hoffmann would have known it. From the footlights — for there were footlights — the stage rose in a gentle rake which reached backward to the full forty feet of stage space, and on each side were six sets of wings, painted to represent a British forest in springtime as perhaps Fuseli might have imagined it; at the back, in front of a splendidly painted backcloth, the rollers which had been so much trouble a few days before were revolving silently, giving an impression of gently heaving water. It was a perspective scene in the nineteenth-century manner, designed to be beautiful and to complement the stage action, rather than to persuade anyone that it mimicked some natural reality.

An "objective correlative" to the music, thought Al Crane, and scribbled a note in the darkness. He was not entirely sure what the phrase meant, but he thought it meant something that helped you to understand something else and that was good enough.

The audience, which had never seen anything like it, burst

into loud applause. Canadians are great applauders of stage settings. But Gunilla, who was not aware of this national custom, turned upon them with the face of a Gorgon. She gave a hiss of menace and waved a hand as if to quell the sound. Assistance came from an unforeseen quarter; there were gentle shushings, not angry but politely rebuking, from all over the house. Yerko's Claque had moved into action and from then onward it directed the applause with fine certainty of taste. The clappers were quieted, and the voice of Oliver Twentyman, high and pure as a silver trumpet, was heard invoking the power of Caliburn to elevate and refine the life of Arthur's Court, and to give a new meaning to Chivalry.

Darcourt breathed with relief. A very tricky corner had been turned. He gave himself up to the music, and in time the curtains closed, and the Overture — for it was a true Hoffmann overture, employing the voices of singers — moved to its completion.

When the curtains rose immediately on Act One, the scene was a hall in the Court of Arthur, and a fine sight, but not one that suggested chivalry, particularly; the Knights and their Ladies had not that look of stricken consecration which is associated with chivalry on the stage. Nutcombe Puckler was, as Geraint had directed him, "horsing around and playing the goat" with a cup-and-ball, but not too distractingly. The Knights paid him little heed. The Ladies — Polly Graves' splendid jugs well downstage and Primrose Maybon equally prominent — declared themselves, and their situation, in the best operatic manner. Darcourt was well pleased with the old ballad he had adapted to a theme of Hoffmann's and which put the opera off to a somewhat folkloric start.

> Arthur our King lives in merry Caerleon
>   And seemly is to see:
> And there he hath with him Queen Guenevere
>   That bride so bright of blee.

Thus sang the Knights. "So bright of *what*?" hissed Hollier in his ear.

"Blee! You know — *blee*! Complexion. Shut up!"

The Ladies took up the ballad strain:

> *And there he hath with him Queen Guenevere*
> *That is so bright in bower:*
> *And all his brave knights around him stand*
> *Of chivalry the flower.*

The Knights, pleased with this handsome compliment, make what might be called a statement of policy, joined by the Ladies:

> *O Jesu, Lord of mickle might,*
> *That died for us on rood,*
> *So maintain us in all our right,*
> *For we come of a noble blood.*

But they are not permitted to take their ease in this Kater Murr conception of their society. Preceded by four pages holding in check four very large Irish wolfhounds, King Arthur and his Queen appear, and Arthur tells them of the revelation at the Enchanted Mere:

> *Leaf after leaf, like a magician's book*
> *Turned in a dragon-guarded hermitage*
> *By trees — dishevelling spirits of the air —*
> *My plan unfolds.*

And he charges them with his chivalric code, in which noble blood must be partnered by noble deeds. Let them henceforth be *bons*, *sages et cortois*, *preux et vaillans*. And as an act of good faith, he pledges himself to the service of the Christ of Chivalry, and in only slightly less degree to the service of his Queen, as the Vessel of his Honour, the scabbard of Caliburn. The scene ends when the Knights bind themselves in the same terms to their Ladies.

This was received with warm approval by the audience, and Darcourt began to feel somewhat more at ease. But — what is this? Darcourt knew, but the audience did not, and Darcourt could not have foreseen their astonishment when, with no interfering curtain, and the barest minimum of mechanical sound, the scene changed visibly from Arthur's Court to a nearby chapel, where Morgan Le Fay and her son Modred were plotting the theft of the scabbard of Caliburn. What happened, if you knew, was that the twelve wings that flanked the court scene were drawn silently back out of sight, and wings suited to the ruin were left in view; at the same moment a drop scene was lowered at the back of the stage, and the great hall seemed to have melted imperceptibly into its successor.

"Those nineteenth-century people knew a trick or two," whispered Hollier.

Indeed they did, thought Darcourt, but he said nothing, for the scenery-applauders were hard at it, and Yerko's Claque were quietly reducing them to silence.

Morgan Le Fay and her son plotted. Good stuff, thought Darcourt, as Modred — Gaetano Panisi, a splendid bass, though a stumpy figure — gave velvety utterance to his scorn for Arthur and the chivalric ideal:

> . . . Let him lean
> Against his life, that glassy interval
> 'Twixt us and nothing: and upon the ground
> Of his own slippery breath, draw hueless dreams,
> And gaze on frost-work hopes.

Back to the hall in the Court — another swift transformation. Back to Arthur, charging his Knights to undertake the Holy Quest for the Grail, which shall be the heart and splendour of his new chivalry. He lifts the great sword to ask a blessing on it, and while he does so Morgan Le Fay steals the scabbard. Splendid scene of mounting vigour culminating in a great Chorale of the Grail, almost Wagnerian in conception.

"Going well," said Hollier, as he and Darcourt made their way up the aisle. But when Darcourt went into the little room behind the manager's office he found Geraint, drinking whisky in huge swigs, and furious.

"What in the name of God do those morlocks think they're up to?" he said. "Applauding the scenery!"

"It's very fine scenery," said Darcourt. "Most of them have never seen such scenery. It was outlawed sixty years ago when there was all that blethers about letting the audience use its imagination. A fat lot of good that was!"

"I think it's the acting they like," said Hollier. "Do you remember what Byron said? 'I am acquainted with no immaterial sensuality so delightful as good acting.' You must remember, Powell; you're a great Byron enthusiast. That little chap Panisi is marvellous. And Holzknecht, too, of course, but one always admires villains more than heroes."

It was plain that Hollier had something on his mind, and after he had accepted a drink he overcame his diffidence. "Geraint, about curtain calls — I suppose it will be expected that those of us who have provided the libretto for the opera should make some appearance? Not that I am anxious to do so. I really hate all this sort of public nonsense. But if it's expected — ?"

"Just go around through the pass-door when the final curtain comes down," said Geraint. "Gwen will show you what to do, and you'll have lots of time, because there will be plenty of applause — that's guaranteed. When Gwen shoves you on, you'll be blinded by the lights, so don't fall into the orchestra. Try not to look any more of a mutt than literary people usually do on a stage full of actors. Just bow. Don't do anything fancy. And don't leave the stage till all the hullabaloo is over."

"You'll be there, yourself, of course?"

"I may, or I may not."

"But you're the director!"

"Indeed I am, and since this afternoon at four o'clock I have been the most unnecessary creature involved in this opera. Nobody needs me. My work is done. I am wholly superfluous."

"Surely not!"

"Surely yes! If I cut my throat at this minute the opera would progress through its appointed number of performances not a whit the worse."

"But you've made it."

"I have not made it. Hoffmann, and Gunilla and Schnak, and all those singers and musicians have made it. And even you fellows have made it. I have supplied the trickery and whoredom of the show. The stuff that appeals to people who don't care much for music."

"Rubbish, Geraint," said Darcourt, who saw a fine Powell tantrum coming. "You've been the energy and encouragement of the whole affair. We've all warmed ourselves at your fire. Don't think we don't know it. You're indispensable. So cheer up."

"I know you, Sim *bach*. In a minute you'll be rebuking me for self-pity."

"Perhaps so."

"You don't know what an artist is, you nice, controlled, reasonable man. You don't know the shadow of the artist — the sieve of vanity, the bile of bitterness, the bond of untruth that is bound with icy chains to all the sunlight and encouraging and he's-a-jolly-good-fellow of being an opera director. I am exhausted and I am not needed. I am sinking into such a slough of despond as only an artist whose job is finished must endure. Go on, both of you! Go back to your seats. Float in the warm waters of assured success. Leave me! Leave me!" By this time he was drinking straight from the bottle.

"I really think we'd better go," said Darcourt. "I couldn't bear to miss what's coming next. But do try to pull yourself together, Geraint *bach*. We all love you, you know."

What was coming next, to begin Act Two, was the scene of the Queen's Maying, over which Powell, and Waldo, and Dulcy had toiled and contrived for months. As the curtains drew back, after a brief and lovely prelude, it seemed to the audience that they could see immeasurably deep into a grove of hawthorn trees in snowy bloom. Far in the blossom-misted distance appeared Queen Guenevere, mounted on a black horse, riding at ease in her side-saddle, as a page led the horse forward. One by one, wearing white mantles, the Ladies of the Court made their way into the front of the scene, but never so far as to obscure the figure of the distant Queen. They did not sing; they seemed enchanted, as the whole scene was one of enchantment, and while the music rose and fell, they grouped themselves in a tableau of expectation. They carried garlands of May blossom. Something truly wonderful was happening.

Darcourt knew how the effect was achieved. He had attended most of the rehearsals and heard many of the arguments during which the notable scene had been planned. Nevertheless, he was caught in its magic and he understood, what he had not known before, that much of the magic of a great theatrical moment is created by the audience itself, a magic impalpable but vividly present, and that what begins as trickery of lights and paint is enlarged and made fine by the response of the beholders. There are no great performances without great audiences, and this is the barrier that film and television, by their utmost efforts, cannot cross, for there can be no interaction between what is done, and those to whom it is done. Great theatre, great music-drama, is created again and again on both sides of the footlights.

He enjoyed the extra pleasure of the man who knows how it has been done. It had been the suggestion of Waldo Harris, not to the casual eye an imaginative man, that for this scene the forty-foot depth of the stage should be increased by opening the huge sliding doors to the storage rooms, and beyond them into the workshops, so that in the end a vista of a hundred feet could be attained. Not a great depth, surely, but with the aid of perspective painting it could be made to seem limitless. And — this had tickled Waldo and Dulcy so that they giggled for days — when first Queen Guenevere was seen, at the farthest distance, on her black steed, it was not Donalda Roche, a woman of operatic sturdiness of figure, but a child of six, mounted on a pony no bigger than a St. Bernard. At a point perhaps sixty feet from the footlights the midget Guenevere rounded a grove of trees to be replaced by a larger child, mounted on a larger pony, led by a larger page. This Guenevere, forty feet from the footlights, disappeared for a moment in May blossom and it was Donalda Roche from then onward, on a black horse of normal stature. Behind her, pages led two magnificent white goats with gilded horns. Waldo and Dulcy had played with this illusion, and refined it, until it changed from a simple trick of perspective into a thing of beauty.

Of course, it would not have been possible without the finest pages in Schnak's score. There had been three related themes, obviously meant as the foundation for an extended piece of music in Hoffmann's notes, and Schnak and Gunilla had decided that these should be developed into a prelude to Act Two, a preparation for the scenes of love and betrayal in which Guenevere and Lancelot, under the malign influence of Morgan Le Fay, would consummate their passion and suffer a double remorse, for Lancelot had also been tricked into a union with the maiden Elaine. But when Geraint heard the first developments of the prelude, he demanded that it should be the music for The Queen's Maying, and overbore the musicians, who of course wanted it as pure music. This was the passage which, at her examination, had persuaded Schnak's examiners (all but the difficult Dr. Pfeiffer) that Schnak was certainly a doctor of music, and probably a good deal more than that.

So here it was, not as a symphonic piece, but as an accompaniment to an act of lovely trickery, or, if you prefer, a masterwork of stage magic.

When it was being rehearsed, some of the singers were not pleased that what was probably the finest part of the score made no use of their voices. Nutcombe Puckler, indeed, referred to it as "this *silent* music", and Hans Holzknecht had some hard words about pantomime. But it proved itself masterly in performance.

The audience, partly quelled by Yerko's Claque, which had been stealthily teaching them to wait for their cues, and partly because they were enthralled by what they saw and heard, were still as mice until the end, when the Queen, joined by her special Knights, bearing white shields, moved gently off the stage to the place where Gwen had cleared space for what was — Queen, horse, Knights and Ladies — rather a crowd which must on no account be halted in its progress. Then they broke into three minutes of sustained applause. Three minutes is a long time for furious clapping, and when the first minute had passed Yerko let loose his forces in every part of the house, and their cries of Bravo were so heart-lifting that several non-claquers joined in. But as they were not trained mid-European bawlers, they had little chance against the professionals in approbation.

Was a voice heard to cry, "Bravo, Hoffmann"? There was, and it was the voice of Simon Darcourt.

Gunilla, though not by inclination apt to recognize an audience except with frosty courtesy, bowed again and again. Gunilla was, after all, a great artist, and such approbation is very sweet to the performer's ear.

"That's fetched 'em," shouted Hollier in Darcourt's ear. "I think we've got 'em now!"

We? thought Darcourt, applauding till his hands smarted. Who's we? What had you to do with this? What had I to do with it? The music, of course, is Hoffmann-cum-Schnak, and very fine, too. But this magic belongs to Geraint Powell, and to Dulcy and Waldo, whom he fired and inspired with his own sense of theatre.

And to Hoffmann. He had raised his voice for Hoffmann. Not solely Hoffmann the composer, who might not have been as good a musician as Schnak, but Hoffmann who lived and died when Romance was blossoming in all the arts. To the spirit of Hoffmann, indeed. This was certainly the Little Man who had been aroused by the Cornish Foundation and all the people it had touched.

The Second Act moved rapidly. The scene outside Merlin's cave, where the enchantress Morgan tricks the good old man into the revelation: Arthur can only be destroyed by one born in the month of May. The exultation of Morgan, for it is her son — also, by incest, the son of Arthur, though Arthur does not know it — who is the May-born. The fateful words of Morgan:

> *The trembling ray*
> *Of some approaching thought, I know not what*
> *Gleams on my darkened mind. . . .*

And Modred's response:

> *I feel it growing, growing*
> *Like a man's shadow when the moon floats slowly*
> *Through the white border of a baffled cloud:*
> *And now the pale conception furls and thickens —*

The temptation of Guenevere by Lancelot. His declaration of love and her sad cry:

> *Oh no! I'll not believe you; when I do*
> *My heart will crack to powder.*

The revelation to the lovers Guenevere and Lancelot that the Maid Elaine, whom Lancelot deflowered when under

Morgan's evil spell, must die of her love, but die gladly:

> *Oh, that sweet influence of thoughts and looks!*
> *That change of being, which to one who lives*
> *Is nothing less divine than divine life*
> *To the unmade! Love? Do I love? I walk*
> *Within the brilliance of another's thought*
> *As in a glory.*

And Lancelot's recognition of the treachery of his love, and his bitter acceptance of implacable destiny:

> *I never felt my nature so divine*
> *As at this saddest hour.*

The audience — not, one would have supposed, greatly susceptible to Arthurian romance — were now wholly in the grip of the opera, and the buzz of enthusiasm at the interval was heartening.

Darcourt had something very much on his mind.

"Penny," he said, cornering her in the foyer, "will you let Clem have your seat for the third act? I'd like you to be with me for at least a part of this."

"Nicely said, Simon, but I know what you mean. I've been talking with Clem, and whatever he has been dousing himself with, he's overdone it. I was almost asphyxiated, and I know what you must have been going through. 'A bundle of myrrh is my well beloved to me: he lieth all night between my breasts'. But not if I can help it. I'll be delighted to relieve you. We've pulled it off nicely, don't you think?"

We, again. What have you done? thought Darcourt. A few sessions of bitchy criticism of my work.

"My guess, for what it's worth, is that our Snark is really a Snark, and not a speck of a Boojum. Did you ever hear such enthusiasm? In Canada, I mean, the Home of Modified Rapture."

"It is certainly going well," said Darcourt, who had sighted Yerko leaning, with pachydermatous elegance, over a very small but excitable lady with orange hair. "Let's go in. Third Act any minute now."

The Third Act was very much as Geraint had outlined it, so long ago as it now seemed, when they had dined unhappily on Maria's Arthurian feast. Perhaps inevitably the emphasis was different. The music for Merlin, when he denounced the villain Modred, was arresting:

> *Thy gloomy features, like a midnight dial,*
> *Scowl the dark index of a fearful hour. . . .*

And later:

> *Transparent art thou as a poisoned glass*
> *Through which the drinker sees his murderer smiling.*

Then Modred's unrepentant, properly villainous death:

> *Why, what's the world and time? A fleeting thought*
> *In the great meditating universe;*
> *A brief parenthesis in chaos.*

But it was Hans Holzknecht, as the King, who had the best of it. Fine actor, fine singer, he drew the most from the shattered Arthur's recognition of his unrecognized incest, the bitterness of his son Modred's hate, and — heaviest of all — the betrayal by his beloved wife and his beloved friend. But his invocation to Love, as a charity beyond even the poetry of fleshly possession, was his best moment, and his conclusion —

> *It is the secret sympathy,*
> > *The silver link, the silken tie,*
> *Which heart to heart, and mind to mind,*
> > *In body and in soul can bind.*

— moved many of the audience, somewhat to their embarrassment, to tears.

Walter Scott is very good, but Schnak has raised him to

another level, thought Darcourt. I wonder if she really understood what she was setting to music? If so, there's hope for
her, tormented child as she is. But with musicians you can
never be quite sure.

At the death of Arthur, the scene melted magically again
to the shores of the Enchanted Mere, which had not been seen
since the Overture. But it was not quite the same scene, for
this was deeply autumnal; leaves, and a few snowflakes,
scudded across the stage where the Knights stood, leaning on
their swords. They sang:

> *The wind, dead leaves and snow,*
> *Doth hurry to and fro,*
> *And once, a day shall break*
> *O'er the wave,*
> *When a storm of ghosts shall shake*
> *The dead, till our King wake*
> *From the grave.*

The body of Arthur — but not the living Holzknecht — was
placed in a shallow craft in which it sailed across the water,
and as it disappeared Merlin flung after it Caliburn, now
safely in its scabbard, and an armoured hand rose from the
waves and seized it. The great chords that had introduced the
opera were heard again, and the curtain fell.

Marshalled by Gwen Larking, Penny Raven, Clement
Hollier, and Simon Darcourt appeared during the final cur-
tain-call. Nobody knew who they were or why they were
there, but at the end of every operatic first night a few people
make inexplicable appearances, and the charity of the
audience includes them.

Geraint, surprisingly steady on his feet, was thunderously
applauded. He appeared to be in excellent spirits and looked
wondrously romantic in full evening dress. He and Gunilla
were, indeed, the commanding figures in the rather untidy
tableau at the final curtain.

Schnak, Darcourt observed with satisfaction, managed a number of curtsies without a stagger.

(11)

ETAH IN LIMBO

CHAMPAGNE! *So much of it, and not a drop for me. It is one of the inconveniences of Limbo that one retains all one's carnal appetites but is utterly debarred from satisfying them. So, as I move unseen through the party that follows the first public performance of my* **Arthur**, *I am aware of brimming glasses and full bottles everywhere, and because of my spiritual condition — we are very chaste in Limbo, oh yes, very chaste — I am denied even the elfin satisfaction of tipping a few glasses down shirt-fronts and into the crannies of bosoms. I, who once drank champagne from pint pots! But I gather that the wine has gone up in the world and this crowd sips it reverently.*

I suppose this is my night of triumph. My opera, projected but never finished, has now been finished indeed, and on the whole to my satisfaction. Am I a little jealous of the Schnakenburg child? Certainly she has a deft hand with orchestration, and what I sense to be a developing gift for melody, but I do not feel the true Romantic fervour in her, not yet. Perhaps it will never come again, as we knew it who first felt its pain and beauty; we, of whom it was my luck to be among the foremost.

Did I like the performance? Ah, there we move into a realm where I cannot be sure of my answer. The music was played and sung vastly better than it would have been in my Dresden days. The orchestra far outshone the assemblage of villains I had to put up with, and the Dahl-Soot woman had much of the daemonic spirit of my own Kapellmeister Kreisler. The stage pictures were thrilling. The singers, marvellous in the telling, could act, and did so, even when they were not singing. What would the Eunike family — three of whom I had to use in my production of **Undine** *— have said to that? This was indeed a music drama, performed with a unity of style and intent quite impossible in my time.*

But — one is a creature of one's time. I missed elements in this production that were familiar, rather than good.

The prompter, for one. Oh, those prompters of my time, who all seemed to have been born old, all born with a cold in the head, all addicted to snuff and brandy, all foul-tempered and all soured from the nape to the chine with their personal failure as composers, or singers, or conductors! They crouched in the little hutch among the footlights, which was shielded from the audience, as a usual thing, by an ornamental shell, bent forward into a hood. Only their heads showed above the stage level, and their heads were heated to roasting-point by the oil lamps in the footlights. Below stage level they were frozen by the draughts of the undercroft of the stage, and every time the stage-hands set a trap in action there was a rush of air as some god or demon was whisked upward onto the stage, and the prompter was choked with the dust of years. In this living hell the prompter hissed his directions to the singers and flung them their cues just before they were to sing, often giving them the note in the cracked voice of a man dying of phthisic, complicated by snuff and the scenery dust — which some of the more spiteful singers took care to kick in his face.

Why would I miss the prompter? Believe me, one often misses the afflictions and inadequacies of the past as truly as its splendours. I knew many prompters, and attended the funerals of several, and these singers who are such good musicians that they can manage without him seem to me to be, somehow, unnatural.

I miss the backstage life. The Green Room, where the singers congregated when they were not wanted onstage, and where one's consequence in the troupe determined with mathematical exactitude how near one might sit, or stand, to the stove. But even more I miss the dressing-rooms, so tiny, so characteristically redolent of the scent preferred by the singer, beneath which might often be discerned the reek from the chamber-pot, which lived in a little cupboard by itself, on top of which was the basin and ewer so the singer might wash his hands, when he could persuade his servant to bring him some hot water from its only source — the carpenter's room under the stage. The stove in the Green Room was very precious to the poorer folk of the theatre, for the dressing-

rooms, if they were heated at all, had only a little iron box in which some charcoal could be burnt, and charcoal cost money and had to be fetched by servants who had to be tipped.

What complexity of romance and delicious intrigue took place in those dressing-rooms, the best of which contained a couch or even, sometimes, a bed for one, which could, with some contrivance, become a bed for two!

This handsome theatre is so much better than any I ever knew. This audience is so much more polite — yes, polite and well-bred, as audiences in my day never were — and I swear this audience was more musically receptive than any I could count upon. They hardly needed a claque, though the one they had was efficient. The spirit of Kater Murr was present — indeed, when is that ultra-respectable Philistine ever absent from public performance — but Kater Murr has learned much with the passing of time. His fur has a new gloss. Yes, yes; times change, and in some things times even grow better.

But — one is a creature of one's time. Does the divine Mozart, I wonder, ever look in at the countless presentations of his operas, so psychologized and philosophized? Could it be that he feels as strange, as wistful, as I have done at the realization and presentation of my **Arthur**?

Shall I hear it again?

I suppose I could hang about, but I do not think I shall do anything of the kind. I have watched **Arthur** brought into being, I have watched the complexities it has introduced into so many lives, and, as an artist, it becomes me to know when enough, even of one's own art, is enough.

Besides, I have had intimations from — I do not know who whispered, and am too tactful to inquire — that my time in Limbo is completed. After all, it was a piece of unfinished work that brought me here, and that work is now done. **Arthur** is done, and sufficiently well done, and I'm off and away.

Farewell, whoever you are. Remember Hoffmann.

VIII

THE COMPLETION of Darcourt's poopnoddy scheme took almost three years from the fall of the final curtain on *Arthur of Britain*. Government bodies, great galleries, connoisseurs of art, publishers of books, and great sums of money all move with the uttermost deliberation, and to persuade them all to fit into a coherent plan calls for the extreme of diplomacy and tact. But Darcourt did it, and did it furthermore without ulcers or heart palpitations or too many private bouts of hysteria. He did it, he told himself, by pursuing the path of the Fool, marching merrily on his way, trusting to his intelligent nose and the little dog of intuition nipping at his rump to show him the path, overgrown and tortuous as it was.

So, on a December afternoon, in the presence of a distinguished assembly, the Francis Cornish Memorial Gallery was officially opened by the Governor General, and was agreed by everyone — or almost everyone — to be a notable addition to the National Gallery of Canada, to reflect the greatest credit on everyone concerned, and especially upon Arthur and Maria Cornish, whose names, as the prime movers in the plan, were never allowed to escape the notice of the public. If the contribution of the Cornishes to the opera production had been under-prized, and if their understandably hurt feelings had not been adequately salved, they were thanked to the point of embarrassment in the establishment of the Francis Cornish Memorial Gallery.

Of course they protested; of course their modesty was outraged, and they were entirely sincere in their protests and their sense of outrage. Nevertheless, it is very sweet to be recognized as public benefactors, and to be compelled to protest and feel outrage. Sweeter by far than to feel over-looked, under-prized, and intrusive when one is sincerely try-ing to do something for the furtherance of culture — for the hateful word, so much licked and pawed by Kater Murr, cannot conveniently be avoided. Arthur and Maria were modest, and were not displeased that the world should see that they were modest.

Darcourt, too, was modest, and for the first time in his life he had something of substantial public interest to be modest about. His book, the long-projected life of the late Francis Cornish, had been published a year earlier, and had received attention not only in Canada but throughout the English-speaking world, and indeed everywhere that books about extraordinary painters are read. Not all of the attention was flattering, but his publishers assured him that the attacks and the disparagement also had their value. Critics do not lash themselves into a high aesthetic tizzy about things that are insignificant. Nor were these critics all concerned with paint-ing; many of them were critics of culture in a more general sense, and several of these were tarred with the recently fashionable Jungian brush, and had even read some of the writings of Jung. What delighted these, and enraged many of the art critics, was the Introduction to the book that had been contributed by Clement Hollier, whose reputation in such matters where art, time, and the enduring and many-layered human psyche kissed and commingled, was very great indeed. Clem, so hopelessly out of his depth in the creation of an opera libretto, was a very big gun in the world where Dar-court's biography took its place. Paleo-psychology and the history of human culture was what the knowing ones called it, and it was not everybody who could follow Clem in its overgrown paths. Thus Darcourt found himself a significant explainer in a number of important worlds, and invitations to lecture — which were in some cases demands that he appear to defend himself — were piling up on his desk.

Such invitations had to wait until the Francis Cornish Memorial Gallery had been shaped, and assembled, and formally opened to the world. After that, his Old Ontario folk wisdom told him, it would be time enough to cut a dead dog in two.

The work was not easy. First of all, Prince Max and the Princess Amalie had to be persuaded to sell *The Marriage at Cana* to the National Gallery. There had to be assurance that they would not, under any circumstances, be accused of having harboured a fake, and shown it to the world as a genuine painting dating from the sixteenth century. They had never offered the picture for sale under false pretences; but on the other hand they had never denied the interesting explanation of the picture that had been contained in that persuasive article by Aylwin Ross, and which was there to be consulted in the authoritative pages of *Apollo*. It was in the light of this splendid piece of art detection that they had allowed it to be exhibited in a great American gallery, which had for a time considered buying it. They must not seem guileful, only reserved, and it must be apparent to everybody that their hands were clean. This could be managed, and it was managed, by the brilliant critic Addison Thresher, who washed their hands and laundered the picture — though the hateful word "laundered" was never, never used — and set the price the Cornish Foundation paid for it. If a percentage of that awesome sum later passed into the hands of Addison Thresher, surely it was to be expected that he would be recompensed for his work, and his great reputation which set at rest all, or nearly all, doubts.

This involved delicate negotiation, but it was as nothing to the work of persuading the National Gallery of Canada that it should accept a picture of such curious provenance, and show it with pride in a room specially devoted to it, even if it did not cost the Gallery a cent.

People who control important galleries are very far from being stupid, but they are not accustomed to thinking of pictures psychologically. If the picture, whose beauty they readily acknowledged, were the work of a Canadian who had painted it less than fifty years ago, why had he painted it in a sixteenth-century style, on an authentic old triptych, with paints that defied any of the tests that had been used? Yes, yes; the picture was a masterpiece, in the old sense of being a work undertaken by a painter who wished to prove himself a master. But what kind of a master? Francis had been a pupil, certainly the best pupil, of Tancred Saraceni, who was himself a supreme master of picture restoration, and so much a master that it was suspected that he had revised, or even re-created, some old pictures into forms that were vastly superior to what they had originally been. People whose lives and reputations are devoted to pictures have fits at any suggestion of faking. Faking is the syphilis of art, and the horrid truth is that syphilis has sometimes lain at the root of very fine art. But connoisseurs and great galleries shrink from saying to the world: Here's a fine, poxy piece of painting, beautiful, uplifting, sincerely describable as great — though of course, because of its ambiguity, not precisely the sort of thing you can safely recommend to Kater Murr. For him and his kind, everything must be Simon Pure — or, if you prefer the term, kosher. Kater Murr is very active among the connoisseurs and the galleries.

It was here that the testimony of Clement Hollier was invaluable. If a man wants to paint a picture that is intended primarily as an exercise in a special area of expertise, he will do so in a style with which he is most familiar. If he wants to paint a picture which has a particular relevance to his own life-experience, which explores the myth of his life as he understands it, and which, in the old phrase, "makes up his soul", he is compelled to do it in a mode that permits such allegorical revelation. Painters after the Renaissance, and certainly after the Protestant Reformation, have not painted such pictures with the frankness that was natural to pre-Renaissance artists. The vocabulary of faith, and of myth, has been taken from them by the passing of time. But Francis Cornish, when he wanted to make up his soul, turned to the style of painting and the concept of visual art which came most naturally to him. He did not feel himself bound to be "contemporary". Indeed, he had many times laughed at the notion of contemporaneity in conversation with both Hollier and Darcourt, mocking it as a foolish chain on a painter's inspiration and intention.

It must be remembered, added Darcourt, that Francis had been brought up a Catholic — or almost a Catholic — and he had taken his catholicity seriously enough to make it a foundation of his art. If God is one and eternal, and if Christ is not dead, but living, are not fashions in art mere follies for those who are the slaves of Time?

All of this had been thoroughly explored by Darcourt in his life of Francis Cornish, but he had to go over it many times in person, before many committees of solemn doubters.

The bigwigs of the National Gallery, who regarded themselves quite reasonably as the guardians of Canada's official artistic taste, hummed and hawed. They heard; they understood; they admitted the adroitness of the argument; but they were not convinced. A man who painted in a bygone style, and who had the effrontery to do it with an accomplishment and imagination notably absent among the best modern Canadian artists, was not someone they could readily embrace. He had played the fool with one of the most sacred ideas still left to a world where the notion of sacrosanctity had become abhorrent — the idea of Time. He had dared to be of a time not his own. Surely such a person was either touched in his wits or else — this was a grave fear — a joker? Government bodies, the worlds of connoisseurship and art, dread jokes as the Devil dreads holy water. And when a joke also involves great sums of money — money, the very seed and foundation of modern art and modern culture — the dread quickly mounts to panic, and Kater Murr has catfits.

Nevertheless, Darcourt, staunchly aided by Hollier, and supported at every turn by Arthur and Maria, prevailed at last, and on that December day the Francis Cornish Memorial Gallery was opened.

It was a gallery in the sense that it was a large room devoted solely to the triptych of *The Marriage at Cana* and, on the other walls, a display of supportive material that showed what the Canadian origins of the picture were. Grandfather McRory's Sun Pictures, enlarged so that they could be studied in detail, and the people of Blairlogie, the people of Grandfather's household, and the medieval isolation of that backwoods town could be made apparent to anyone who chose to look. On another wall were Francis's careful studies in Old Master style, as evidence of how the extraordinary technical skill of the great picture had been acquired. And on the third wall the most intimate of all Francis's drawings — hasty sketches done in the undertaker's workroom, quick impressions of Tancred Saraceni and Grandfather's coachman which linked them with Judas and the *huissier* in the great picture, and the arresting studies — drawn with so much adoration — of Ismay Glasson, clothed and naked and, plain for all to see, the Bride in *The Marriage*. Not all the figures in the great picture were represented in the sketches and drawings, but most of them were, and perhaps the most arresting were the photograph of F. X. Bouchard, the dwarf tailor, by Grandfather, and the pitiful figure of the dwarf naked on the embalmer's table, drawn by Francis; the most casual looker could not fail to see that this was the proud dwarf in parade armour who looked out at the spectator from the triptych.

It had been agreed by Arthur and Maria and Darcourt that the sketches which identified the grotesque angel as Francis the First should not be shown. Some mystery must be left unexplained.

With these exhibitions were explanatory notes, written by Darcourt, for what Hollier wrote was not plain enough for the widest possible public. But what could be plain only to visitors who had understood what the whole room said were the words painted in handsome calligraphy on the wall above the great picture:

> *A Man's life of any worth is a continual allegory —*
> *and very few eyes can see the Mystery of his life — a*
> *life like the scriptures, figurative.   JOHN KEATS.*

(2)

"ARE YOU HAPPY WITH IT, Simon," said Maria; "I do hope you are. You've worked so hard to make it happen."

She and Arthur and Darcourt sat at dinner after the grand opening. The Governor General and his entourage had been thanked and bowed into their cars; Prince Max and Princess Amalie and the ever-attentive Addison Thresher had been escorted to the airport and seen off with many expressions of goodwill, as well as some whispered words to Darcourt from the Princess in which she thanked him yet again for the tact with which any connection between her own Old Master drawing from Francis's hand (now so widely seen in her cosmetic advertisements) had been avoided; Clement Hollier and Penny Raven had been watched as they disappeared down the chute toward another plane to Toronto. The captains and the kings and the scholars had all departed, and the three friends were happily alone at their table.

"As happy as it's in my nature to be," said Darcourt. "A kind of golden glow. And I hope you're happy, too."

"Why wouldn't we be?" said Arthur. "We've been lauded and complimented and petted beyond our deserts. I feel rather a fake."

"It was all the money," said Maria. "I suppose it's silly to underestimate money."

"Uncle Frank's money, almost every penny," said Arthur. "The cupboard is nearly bare. It'll take a few years before the cistern has refilled to the point where the Foundation can do anything else."

"Oh, it won't be forever," said Maria. "The bankers think about three years. Then we shall be able to do something else."

"What's going to be your attitude?" said Darcourt. "Are you going to be the Sword of Discretion or the Gushing Breast of Compassion?"

"The Sword every time," said Arthur. "Offer the breast and somebody will bite it. Until you've tried it, you can have no idea of how hard it is to give away money. Intelligently, that's to say. Look at this Gallery. What a fight we had to get it."

"Oh, but a very genteel, high-minded fight," said Darcourt. "What a tricky balancing of egotisms of various weights, and varying interests, some of which you're not supposed to know about. What a lot of jockeying so that nobody has to say thank-you in such a way that they lose face. I'll bet old Frank is laughing his head off, if he knows anything about it. He was an ironic old devil. And his big secret — that loony angel who was his parents' first attempt at a Francis — is still a secret, though it's almost certain that some toilsome snoop will root it out sooner or later. Not everything is on those apparently explanatory walls."

"It's been an adventure, and I've always hankered for adventures," said Arthur. "And the opera was an adventure, too. That was Frank's doing, and we shouldn't forget it."

"How can we?" said Maria. "Isn't it still going on? Schnak is doing well, in a quiet way."

"Not so quiet," said Darcourt. "The opera hasn't been done again; not yet, but there are nibbles. But that big central passage — The Queen's Maying — has been played several times by very good orchestras, and always with a note that it comes from the opera. Schnak is on her way, and there is even some renewed interest in Hoffmann as a composer, Nilla tells me."

"You know I hated Nilla when I first met her," said Maria. "She was so awful at that Arthurian dinner. But she's the perfection of a fairy — or I suppose I should say lesbian — godmother. She sends Davy the most wonderful wooden toys, trains and farm carts and things, and she's determined we must take him to Paris for her to see. Not like that stinker Powell. He writes now and again but he never mentions the boy. Just his own dear little self. Mind you, he's doing marvellously well. A terrific *Orfeo* in Milan, when last heard of. Even Clem is a better godfather. He's given Davy a wonderfully illustrated book of the Arthurian legend, which he will be able to read when he's about ten. And Penny has given him a first edition of *The Hunting of the Snark*. Have these professors no understanding of what a child of three is?"

"Perhaps it was really meant for you," said Darcourt. "The Snark was a pretty fair comment on that opera job, and in the end the Snark was only half a Boojum."

"I've never got around to reading that poem," said Arthur. "Simon — lighten my darkness, I beseech you. What the hell *is* a Snark? And a Boojum? I suppose I ought to know."

"You won't ever know if you don't read it," said Darcourt. "But just for the moment, a Snark is a highly desirable object of search which, when found, can be unexpected and dangerous — a Boojum, in fact. All Snarks are likely to be Boojums to the unresting, questing Romantic spirit. It's a splendid allegory of all artistic adventures."

"Allegory. Allegory — I know what an allegory is. Simon, you've put that quotation from Keats right over Uncle Frank's picture. 'A Man's life of any worth is a continual allegory'. Do you really believe that?"

"Haven't I convinced you?" said Darcourt. "It's one of those magnificent flashes that Keats popped into letters. That comes from a gossipy letter to his brother and sister. Just a piece of a letter, but what an insight!"

"You've convinced me several times, but I keep coming unconvinced. It's such a terrifying thought."

"Such an enlarging thought," said Maria. " 'A Man's life of any worth' — it forces you to wonder whether your life is of no particular worth, or if it has a mystery you can't see."

"I think I'd rather say my life was of no particular worth than face the idea of a pattern in it that I don't know, and probably never will know," said Arthur.

"You mustn't dream of saying that your life is of no particular worth, my darling," said Maria. "Because I know better."

"But an allegory seems such an extraordinary thing to claim for oneself," said Arthur. "It's like commissioning a statue of yourself, stark naked, holding a scroll."

"Keats wrote at the gallop," said Darcourt. "He might equally well have said that a man's life has a buried myth."

"I don't see that making it any easier."

"Arthur, you are sometimes remarkably obtuse — not to say dumb," said Darcourt. "Now — I think I've had enough of this excellent Burgundy to ask you a very personal question. Haven't you seen your own myth in all that opera business? Your myth, and Maria's myth, and Powell's myth? A fine myth, and as an observer I must say you all carried it through with style."

"Well, if you want to cast me as Arthur — though how do you know it isn't just a trick of the name? — Maria has to be Guenevere, and I suppose Powell is Lancelot. But we weren't very Arthurian, were we? Where's your myth?"

Darcourt was about to speak, but Maria hushed him. "Of course you don't see it. It's not the nature of heroes of myth to think of themselves as heroes of myth. They don't swan around, declaiming, 'I'm a hero of myth.' It's observers like Simon and me who spot the myths and the heroes. The heroes see themselves simply as chaps doing the best they can in a special situation."

"I flatly decline to be a hero," said Arthur. "Who could live with that?"

"You haven't any choice," said Darcourt. "Fish up a myth from the depths and it takes you over. Maybe it's had its eye on you for a long time. Think — an opera. What was it Hoffmann said? — you dug it up, Maria."

" 'The lyre of Orpheus opens the door of the Under-world'."

"He must have been a wonderful little chap," said Arthur. "I've always thought that, though of course I couldn't have put it like that. But I still don't see the myth."

"It is the myth of the Magnanimous Cuckold," said Darcourt. "And the only way to meet it is with charity and love."

After a long silence, and reflective sipping of wine, Arthur spoke.

"I choose not to think of myself as magnanimous."

"But I do," said Maria.

The Lyre of Orpheus is the third novel in a trilogy that includes *The Rebel Angels* and *What's Bred in the Bone*.

THE REBEL ANGELS

A cast of unforgettable characters is featured in this rich and vivid novel of passion and murder, smouldering beneath the surface of a sophisticated Canadian university. Maria Theotoky, a ravishingly beautiful graduate student is pursuing a hopeless affair with her professor; Simon Darcourt, a professor of Greek is pursuing a hopeless affair of a different sort; Clement Hollier, a renowned scholar and professor nurtures a passion for the darker side of medieval psychology; John Parlabane, an unstable and defrocked monk whose miserable existence ends tragically; Arthur Cornish, a wealthy young businessman who inherits a troublesome bequest of priceless works of art. The reader is drawn spellbound into a mystical plot where he is effortlessly entertained and instructed, puzzled and amused . . . an enchantingly mysterious novel by Canada's preeminent man of letters.

WHAT'S BRED IN THE BONE

Francis Cornish was always good at keeping secrets. From the well-hidden family secret of his childhood to his mysterious encounters with a small-town embalmer, a master art restorer, a Bavarian countess, and various masters of espionage, the events in Francis's life were not always what they seemed.

In this wonderfully ingenious portrait of an art expert and collector of international renown, Robertson Davies has created a spellbinding tale of artistic triumph and heroic deceit. It is a tale told in stylish, elegant prose, endowed with lavish portions of Davies's wit and wisdom.